CW01064664

Stitches of Time and Heartstrings

Skylar Logan

Published by Skylar Logan, 2024.

This is a work of fiction. Similarities to real people, places, or events are entirely coincidental.

STITCHES OF TIME AND HEARTSTRINGS

First edition. October 1, 2024.

Written by Skylar Logan.

Chapter 1: Fraying Threads

The air inside "Stitch & Thread" is infused with a comforting blend of fabric softener and the faint scent of jasmine from the potpourri my mother insisted on placing near the register. As I push open the creaking door, the familiar jingle of the tiny bell above announces my arrival, a sound that used to bring warmth and joy but now echoes like a ghost of my past. Dust motes dance lazily in the slanted rays of sunlight that filter through the large front windows, illuminating the shelves stacked high with vibrant rolls of fabric—cotton florals, silks in every shade of the sunset, and rich wool blends. Each bolt tells a story, from the whimsical patchwork that reminds me of childhood summer days spent stitching tiny skirts for my dolls to the luxurious velvets my mother always favored for her evening wear.

Montgomery Springs, with its quaint, tree-lined streets and friendly locals, feels both familiar and foreign. The town hasn't changed much since I left, but I can't shake the feeling that I have. Time has a way of shifting perspectives, and what once felt cozy now seems stifling, as if the walls are closing in with each breath I take. I set my purse down on the counter, the same oak surface that has held countless cups of coffee and the weight of dreams. There's a faded photo of my mother pinned to the wall—a snapshot from a summer fashion show decades ago, where she stood proudly among models, her vibrant smile radiating an unyielding passion for fabric and design.

I glance toward the back of the store, where the sewing room beckons like an old friend. The walls are plastered with swatches and sketches, remnants of my mother's brilliance. My heart tightens as I remember the late nights spent huddled over sketches, my mother guiding my hand with a steady patience, teaching me the nuances of creating something beautiful from mere threads. But those memories are tainted now by the shadows of her illness, a reality that looms like a storm cloud over my return. I wonder if she'll remember our late-night sewing sessions or if the disease will have unraveled that part of her as it has slowly unraveled our family.

"Is that you, Emma?" My father's voice pulls me from my reverie. He appears from the back room, his hair a patchy gray that betrays the stress of managing a failing business and a wife in decline. There's a weariness in his eyes, the kind that comes from years of fighting against the current. Yet, when he sees me, a flicker of hope ignites—a small spark in an otherwise dim room.

"Hi, Dad." I offer a tentative smile, but it feels like a fragile thread ready to snap under the weight of unspoken words.

He steps closer, enveloping me in a hug that feels both comforting and foreign. "It's good to have you back," he says, though the underlying tension in his voice tells a different story.

I nod, biting my lip to suppress the swell of emotions. "I didn't have anywhere else to go." The admission hangs in the air, heavy and unyielding, like the drapery fabric that weighs down the window treatments in the display room. My father steps back, his expression softening, but the moment is fleeting.

"Let's get you settled. You know where everything is." He gestures toward the workroom, and I follow his lead, my heart racing as I step into the familiar chaos. The cutting table is cluttered with half-finished projects, remnants of a life once bursting with creativity.

I pick up a frayed piece of fabric—a floral cotton print that once felt cheerful and inviting. Now it feels like a relic, a reminder of brighter days. I can't help but wonder if I've come back to revive this place or to bury it. As I sift through the projects my mother left behind, I notice a stack of papers—designs for a collection she never had the chance to finish. Each sketch is meticulously crafted, a testament to her talent and dedication. I feel a pang of guilt. What if I had been here? What if I could have helped?

"What's the plan for the store?" I ask, breaking the silence that has settled around us like dust. My father shrugs, his shoulders heavy with unspoken burdens.

"We keep hoping for a miracle. Business hasn't been good since... well, you know."

The unspoken word—"illness"—lingers in the air. I swallow hard, my throat tightening as I look away, focusing instead on the various tools scattered across the table: scissors, threads, and a dusty sewing machine that has seen better days.

"Maybe I could help with the designs?" I venture, trying to bring light to the gloomy atmosphere.

His gaze sharpens, but there's a glimmer of something—perhaps hope or resignation. "You think you can? After everything?"

"Why not? I used to be pretty good at it." I offer a wry smile, though I'm not entirely sure I believe my own words. My fashion dreams crumbled in New York, leaving me feeling like a discarded pattern piece, cut out but never sewn together.

"Your mother would love that," he says softly, his voice barely above a whisper. "She always believed in your talent."

The thought makes my heart swell and ache simultaneously, a contradictory mix of pride and sorrow. I take a deep breath, resolving to find a way to honor her legacy and maybe, just maybe, rediscover a part of myself in the process.

As I delve into the sketches, a sense of purpose washes over me. Each design represents a memory, a dream not yet extinguished. Perhaps Montgomery Springs could become more than just a backdrop for my failures; maybe it could serve as a canvas for new beginnings.

The morning light spills through the shop's windows, casting playful shadows across the wooden floor, and I feel a rush of memories flood back—my mother guiding my small hands as I learned the delicate art of sewing, her laughter ringing out like a song as I struggled to follow her precise stitching. It was in this very room that my dreams first took shape, alongside the clinking of needles and the soothing hum of the sewing machine. Now, standing here, I feel like an intruder in my own past, a jigsaw piece that has lost its original picture.

I gather a few scattered sketches from the cutting table, tracing the lines with my fingers as if I could somehow awaken the dormant creativity within me. There's a grace to my mother's designs—a fluidity that speaks of her elegance and expertise. I take a deep breath, inhaling the scent of paper and ink mingled with the fabric. This place, once a sanctuary, feels charged with an energy I can't quite place. It's as if the walls are whispering stories, secrets of resilience and love woven into the very fabric of the shop.

As I shift my gaze around the room, my heart flutters at the sight of the sewing machine, its metallic body gleaming like an old friend. I can't resist the pull it has on me, and I make my way over, brushing off the dust that has gathered like a veil over its intricate workings. I lift the presser foot and run my fingers along the smooth surface, recalling how my mother would encourage me to let the machine guide my hands, to trust in the rhythm of creativity. I can almost hear her voice, a soothing balm for my frayed nerves.

Determined to reclaim a piece of that forgotten passion, I set the machine up, the clatter of the needle piercing through the fabric rekindling a fire I thought had extinguished. Each stitch feels like a heartbeat, pulsing with new life. I select a bright turquoise fabric, one that evokes a sense of joy, and begin cutting out patterns, allowing my intuition to guide me. The rhythm of the machine soon drowns out my anxieties, and I lose myself in the art of creation, feeling as if I've slipped into a time warp where the past and present dance together harmoniously.

As the afternoon sun drifts lazily across the sky, my father's voice interrupts my reverie. "Emma, you're really getting into it, aren't you?" He stands at the doorway, arms crossed, a hint of admiration in his tone. The weariness in his eyes softens, revealing a glimmer of hope.

"I forgot how much I loved this," I reply, my hands still moving deftly. "I think I might be able to bring some new life to the shop."

His expression shifts, a mixture of pride and uncertainty. "Your mother would be so proud." The sentiment is a gentle reminder of my mother's unwavering belief in me, a beacon that has guided me through the fog of my doubts.

In that moment, a realization settles in—the boutique is not just a business; it's a canvas where I can paint my identity anew, a chance to weave my narrative into the tapestry of Montgomery Springs. The thought fills me with warmth and trepidation, as if standing at the precipice of a grand adventure.

I set down the fabric, a smile tugging at my lips. "Maybe we can host a fashion show, Dad. Showcase some new designs, attract a crowd. I can use my contacts from New York—"

He cuts me off, his expression shifting from hopeful to guarded. "Emma, you've just returned. It's a big step."

"Dad, I know what you're thinking. I failed in New York, but that doesn't mean I can't succeed here. This is different." The fervor in my voice surprises even me, a spark igniting within my chest.

"I just don't want you to feel pressured. Montgomery Springs is... well, it's not New York."

"I don't need New York to define my success," I assert, grounding myself in the moment. "Maybe all I need is this place to find out who I really am."

He studies me, the lines on his forehead deepening as he contemplates my words. "If you think you can manage it..." His voice trails off, a mixture of uncertainty and reluctant acceptance.

"Let's take it one step at a time. We can work together." I feel the warmth of my conviction infusing the air between us. It's a promise wrapped in vulnerability, a commitment to reclaiming not only the shop but also the family bond that has frayed over the years.

In the days that follow, I transform the store, my fingers dancing across the bolts of fabric like a musician crafting a symphony. I throw open the windows, letting the fresh air sweep away the dust of neglect, breathing new life into the space that has felt so stagnant. With each stroke of my fabric scissors, I reshape not just the aesthetic of the shop but also my own narrative, reclaiming the vibrancy of my youth while layering it with the wisdom of my experiences.

I dive into the logistics of planning a fashion show, enlisting the help of a few childhood friends who still live in town. There's Sarah, who runs the local bakery and has a flair for event planning, and Mia, a talented photographer who captures life through her lens with an artist's eye. Together, we brainstorm ideas, scribbling notes on coffee-stained napkins and laughing over shared memories, the bonds of friendship rekindling with each passing day.

Montgomery Springs becomes a tapestry of preparation and excitement, the small-town charm wrapped in an aura of anticipation. The community buzzes with whispers of the upcoming event, a mix of skepticism and curiosity as I work to reignite the spark of creativity that once thrived in this quaint corner of the world.

One evening, as we gather in the back room of the boutique, the air thick with the scent of freshly baked pastries and the sound of fabric rustling, Sarah leans in, her eyes sparkling with mischief. "You know, Emma, this could be the comeback story we didn't know we needed. You, a fashion guru returning to save the day!"

Mia snickers, "Or the small-town girl trying to make it big. Either way, it sounds like the plot of a movie."

I chuckle, the warmth of their camaraderie wrapping around me like a cozy quilt. "I just hope I don't trip on the runway."

"You'll be fine," Sarah reassures, patting my shoulder. "You're going to be amazing. We're all rooting for you."

And in that moment, surrounded by laughter and the gentle chaos of creation, I feel the threads of my past intertwining with the fabric of my present, weaving a new narrative filled with potential and hope.

The weeks pass in a whirlwind of activity, each day a flurry of fabric swatches, design sketches, and laughter echoing through the newly revived boutique. The once-quiet streets of Montgomery Springs begin to buzz with life as word spreads about the upcoming fashion show. I find myself immersed in a rhythm that feels both exhilarating and terrifying. With each passing day, the weight of my mother's legacy settles on my shoulders, a gentle reminder that this is not just about me—it's about honoring her spirit and the love she poured into this place.

Mornings are spent drafting designs, the sunlight filtering through the windows casting a golden hue on my workspace. I drape fabrics over dress forms, letting my imagination soar as I envision the vibrant collection taking shape. The fabrics are alive, their textures inviting exploration and experimentation. I think of my mother, who had a gift for pairing colors and patterns with a keen eye that seemed almost supernatural. I long to channel that same intuition, to breathe life into my creations as she did.

In the afternoons, Sarah and Mia drop by, and together we dive into logistics, piecing together the various elements of the show. The community center, a charming brick building with ivy creeping up its sides, becomes our venue of choice, the perfect setting to showcase not only my designs but also the spirit of our town. Sarah's enthusiasm is infectious as she crafts flyers, her excitement turning mundane tasks into a joyful scavenger hunt for the best way to promote our event. Meanwhile, Mia captures the preparations with her camera, immortalizing moments of chaos and laughter that bind us closer together.

One afternoon, as we set up the makeshift runway in the community center, a flutter of nerves ripples through me. "What if nobody comes?" I blurt out, the words escaping before I can catch them.

"Don't be ridiculous," Sarah replies, tossing her hair over her shoulder. "Everyone in this town will want to see what you've created. This is Montgomery Springs! We support our own."

Her confidence is like a buoy, lifting my spirits, and I cling to it as we continue to arrange chairs and position lights. Just as I start to relax, a voice calls out from the entrance, breaking through the clamor of our preparations.

"Is this where the magic is happening?"

I turn to see a familiar figure standing in the doorway, a playful smile spreading across his face. It's Derek, my childhood friend and the town's most charming handyman. He's wearing a tool belt slung low on his hips, his brown hair tousled and a hint of mischief in his eyes.

"Derek!" I exclaim, a rush of warmth flooding through me. "What are you doing here?"

"I heard there was a fashion show, and I thought I'd come lend a hand. Plus, I wanted to see how my favorite fashionista is doing." His teasing tone brings a grin to my face, and my heart does a little dance at the familiarity of it all.

"I could definitely use some help with the setup," I say, waving him over. "We're almost done, but I wouldn't mind an extra set of hands."

As we work together, our banter flows effortlessly, weaving a comfortable rhythm into the day. Derek has always had a knack for making me laugh, and as we position the chairs and test the lighting, I find myself remembering why I enjoyed his company so much.

"You know," he says, smirking as he adjusts a spotlight, "the last time I was at a fashion show was when my mom dragged me to one of those frilly dress things. I think I walked out wearing a turtleneck and shorts."

I laugh, imagining young Derek parading around in a disheveled outfit while the audience gawked. "You should wear that to my show. It'll be a hit."

The camaraderie is refreshing, a reminder of the simplicity of our childhood friendships. As the afternoon wanes, Derek's presence feels like a grounding force amidst the whirlwind of preparations.

"Do you ever miss the big city?" he asks, a hint of curiosity lacing his voice.

"Sometimes," I admit, the weight of that question hanging in the air. "But honestly, I think I needed this—needed to reconnect with home and my roots."

He nods, his expression thoughtful. "Montgomery Springs has a way of pulling you back in, doesn't it? There's something special about this place."

As the sun begins to set, casting an orange glow over the town, the excitement of the fashion show envelops me. The event unfolds like a delicate fabric, each layer contributing to a larger design. The anticipation of unveiling my collection intertwines with my desire to prove to myself and the community that I can forge my own path, separate from the shadow of my past failures.

The night of the fashion show arrives, and the community center is buzzing with life. Local families, friends, and curious townsfolk fill the seats, their chatter a comforting hum that soothes my nerves. The runway is adorned with twinkling lights, illuminating the space with a warm glow that echoes the heart of Montgomery Springs.

As I stand backstage, surrounded by my creations, I catch glimpses of the audience through the curtain. Faces filled with warmth and encouragement bolster my confidence, reminding me of the support that has always existed in this town, even when I felt alone in the hustle of New York.

Finally, the moment arrives. The soft music swells, and the first model steps onto the runway, wearing a flowing gown in rich emerald, its fabric catching the light like a cascading waterfall. I feel a rush of exhilaration and pride as each model showcases my designs, a tapestry of creativity woven together with threads of love and resilience.

The audience's applause is thunderous, reverberating through my heart as I step onto the stage for the final bow. In that moment, I realize that this is not just a fashion show; it's a celebration of community, a reminder that even amidst struggles, we can rise together. My heart swells with gratitude as I look out at the smiling faces, and for the first time in a long while, I feel like I belong.

As the applause fades, I step backstage, overwhelmed with emotion. Derek rushes over, his smile wide. "You did it, Emma! That was incredible!"

"I can't believe it," I say, still processing the whirlwind of the evening. "Thank you for being here."

He gives me a quick hug, and in that moment, I feel a connection deepen—a spark that had always flickered between us, now igniting into something more profound.

As the night winds down, laughter and conversation fill the air, and I feel an overwhelming sense of purpose. Montgomery Springs is not just my hometown; it's a canvas where I can continue to create, to grow, and to heal. Each thread, each fabric, each laugh shared with friends strengthens the tapestry of my life, reminding me that every moment—both joyous and challenging—can be woven together into a beautiful narrative, a story waiting to unfold.

Chapter 2: The Reluctant Reunion

The aroma of freshly brewed coffee mingled with the faint scent of cinnamon rolls wafting from the local bakery, creating an inviting atmosphere that both comforted and unsettled me. Montgomery Springs was a town frozen in time, where the quaint streets still echoed with laughter and secrets. I stepped into the café, my heart pounding as if each beat were a countdown to some unknown fate. The walls were adorned with art from local creators, colorful splashes of life against the backdrop of wood paneling that had likely witnessed countless reunions and farewells.

As I scanned the familiar faces, a swell of nostalgia washed over me. There was Mia, my childhood best friend, standing behind the counter, her hair pulled back into a sleek ponytail, eyes sparkling with determination. She had always been the firecracker of our duo, her ambition now apparent in the way she commanded the room. Mayor Mia—those two words felt foreign yet perfectly fitting. She caught sight of me, her expression shifting from surprise to delight in an instant. "You made it back!" she exclaimed, her voice melodic, cutting through my inner turmoil like a warm knife through butter.

I smiled, trying to quell the trepidation bubbling within me. "Yeah, just for a bit," I replied, my words tentative, as if any certainty might shatter in this intimate space. She stepped out from behind the counter, wrapping me in a hug that felt like a lifeline thrown into turbulent waters. I inhaled the familiar scent of her shampoo, a sweet mix of flowers and something distinctly her.

"Tell me everything," she urged, her enthusiasm contagious as she poured us each a cup of coffee. I noticed the way she leaned against the counter, a confident posture that hinted at the myriad responsibilities she now balanced as mayor. As we settled into a cozy booth by the window, the sunlight poured in, illuminating the small imperfections in the table—a scratch here, a water stain there—a reminder of how time etched its mark on all things, including our friendship.

I found myself hesitating, the words lodged in my throat like stubborn marbles. My past loomed large, a shadow I couldn't quite shake off, and I didn't want Mia to see how deeply it affected me. Instead, I feigned nonchalance, recounting mundane updates about life in the city, while internally wrestling with the weight of my choices. The whispers around town about how I "fled" Montgomery Springs felt palpable, swirling in the air between us. Yet, as Mia shared her own tales of local politics and community events, I was momentarily swept away, forgetting my past failures.

But just as I began to relax, the bell above the café door jingled, heralding the arrival of another familiar face. My breath caught in my throat as I turned to see Carter walk in, his presence like a magnet pulling at the forgotten parts of my heart. He hadn't changed, not really—his dark hair tousled just so, a confident stride that spoke of years of exploring art and life, a hint of mischief in his deep-set eyes that seemed to dance with unspoken stories.

"Wow, look who it is," Mia said with a teasing grin, clearly enjoying the moment far too much.

Carter's gaze landed on me, and for a brief second, the world outside the café faded away. My stomach flipped as he approached our table, an easy smile breaking across his face. "Hey, I didn't know you were back," he said, his voice smooth like the coffee I clutched tightly.

"Just visiting," I managed, feeling the flush creep up my cheeks. The past bubbled to the surface, memories of stolen glances and shy smiles in high school. Our conversation was a jigsaw puzzle of fragmented sentences, both of us fumbling around the edges, trying to fit together pieces of a shared history that had never really left us.

As we spoke, the tension in the air sparked, electrifying the space around us. My mind danced back to afternoons spent in his art studio, the scent of paint and the chaos of half-finished canvases surrounding us. I remembered the way he had looked at me then, his eyes alight with creativity and dreams, igniting something in me that I hadn't fully understood.

Yet as quickly as the chemistry surged, a wave of reality crashed down. The complications of my family's business loomed large, the weight of responsibilities pulling at my shoulders like an anchor. I could almost hear the echoes of my mother's words, a reminder of the life I was expected to lead, one far removed from the whims of youthful romance.

Our conversation was punctuated by laughter and comfortable silences, but every smile I shared with Carter felt like a betrayal to the duties that awaited me. The shadow of my family's legacy loomed large, a constant reminder that I wasn't just an individual—I was part of a lineage that demanded my attention. Yet, in that moment, surrounded by the warmth of the café and the familiarity of Carter's presence, I longed to escape those obligations, even if just for a fleeting instant.

As the afternoon sun dipped lower in the sky, casting golden rays that seemed to wrap around us like a comforting blanket, I could feel the walls of Montgomery Springs shifting around me. I was no longer just the girl who left; I was returning, intertwined in the fabric of a town that had shaped me, for better or worse. And standing there with Carter, the warmth of old feelings reignited within me, I found myself torn between the past I longed to revisit and the future I was expected to embrace.

The sun dipped lower in the sky, casting a warm, golden glow that illuminated the café's worn wooden floors, each scuff and scratch telling its own story. As I sipped my coffee, I felt the liquid warmth seep into my bones, but it couldn't quite chase away the chill of anxiety that clung to me. My heart raced as I attempted to navigate the small talk with Mia and Carter, the light banter drifting like autumn leaves in the wind. I had hoped for a reprieve from the inevitable scrutiny that accompanied my return to Montgomery Springs, yet here I was, caught in the undertow of nostalgia and unspoken expectations.

Mia leaned forward, her gaze sharp and inquisitive. "So, what brings you back to our little slice of heaven?" she asked, a teasing lilt in her voice, but her eyes held an intensity that suggested she saw right through my façade. I fiddled with the edge of the table, the rough grain of the wood grounding me in reality.

"I just needed a break," I replied, choosing my words carefully, as if they were fragile glass ornaments I didn't want to shatter. "Things got a bit overwhelming back in the city."

Carter leaned back in his chair, arms crossed, an amused smile playing at the corners of his mouth. "Overwhelmed? Or just running away?" he prodded gently, his tone playful yet probing. I felt the heat rush to my cheeks, the reminder of my past igniting an uncomfortable mix of shame and indignation.

"Let's not psychoanalyze her just yet," Mia interjected, a hint of protective camaraderie in her voice. "We all have our reasons for coming back."

A heavy silence fell between us, filled only by the soft clinking of cups and the distant hum of conversations. I could sense the weight of their curiosity, each unasked question hanging in the air like a fragile spider web, ready to break at the slightest touch. The café felt both familiar and foreign, a microcosm of my life before I had stepped into the chaotic world of adulthood.

As I glanced out the window, watching the town buzz with life, memories fluttered back, vivid and haunting. The annual summer festival, where laughter intertwined with the scent of cotton candy, and late-night bonfires where we spun ghost stories under a blanket of stars. Yet, those memories were tainted with the bitterness of leaving.

"Tell me about the art scene in the city," Mia prompted, trying to lighten the mood. "Did you find your inner Picasso?"

"More like an inner kindergarten doodler," I chuckled, grateful for her efforts to redirect the conversation. "But I did manage to get a few pieces in a local gallery. Mostly abstract stuff, just me trying to make sense of... everything."

Carter's eyes sparkled with genuine interest. "I'd love to see them sometime. Art is all about expressing what's inside, isn't it?" His voice was smooth, an invitation wrapped in an unguarded moment, pulling me deeper into the orbit of his charisma.

"Yeah, I guess so," I replied, my heart fluttering. There was an electricity in his gaze that sent a rush of warmth coursing through me. We exchanged smiles, the kind that felt like a secret between us, igniting a flicker of possibility that I hadn't anticipated.

Mia, ever perceptive, leaned back and surveyed the two of us, her expression shifting into something akin to amusement. "You two have the same spark as in high school," she teased, waggling her eyebrows in exaggerated fashion. I felt my heart quicken again, but this time, it wasn't from anxiety. It was a heady mix of excitement and fear—an intoxicating cocktail I hadn't tasted in years.

But just as quickly as that spark ignited, the shadows of my responsibilities reared their ugly heads. My phone buzzed in my pocket, a reminder of the caretaker role I had reluctantly embraced. I excused myself, the familiar weight of duty settling heavily on my shoulders as I pulled out my phone to check the notification. It was a message from my younger brother, an update on our family's business—a constant reminder of the chaos I was trying to escape.

"Duty calls?" Mia asked, her voice tinged with sympathy. I nodded, forcing a smile that felt more like a grimace.

"Just a little family stuff," I said, but the way her eyes searched mine suggested she wasn't buying my half-hearted excuse. Carter remained quiet, his gaze fixed on me, offering an unspoken understanding that made my heart ache for more time in this moment, this café, with these two people who anchored me to a simpler past.

"I should probably get going soon," I said, my voice steadier than I felt. "But it was great seeing you, Mia. And you too, Carter. I hope I can catch one of your shows soon."

"Let's not make it a farewell," Mia said, her voice firm with resolve. "You're back, at least for a little while. We'll have plenty of chances to catch up."

Carter nodded in agreement, his smile disarming. "Absolutely. I can show you some of my latest pieces. I'd love your feedback."

Just as I was about to stand, the door swung open, letting in a gust of cool air that sent a shiver down my spine. I turned to see a group of familiar faces, classmates I hadn't thought of in years. Their laughter cut through my moment of warmth, and I suddenly felt very small and exposed, like a piece of art on display in a gallery.

"Look who's back!" one of them shouted, their voice echoing across the café, pulling my attention sharply from the warmth of the moment. The atmosphere shifted, a palpable wave of curiosity crashing around me. My past was standing right before me, and I felt the familiar sting of embarrassment as their eyes settled on me, filled with questions I wasn't ready to answer.

With a quick glance at Mia and Carter, I realized I was about to be swept up in a tide I wasn't prepared to face. I took a deep breath, the warm air filled with the scent of coffee and baked goods. The layers of my past peeled back like the petals of a flower, and I could feel the weight of their collective gaze pressing down on me, challenging my resolve.

As I opened my mouth to respond, ready to weave my way through this unexpectedly complicated reunion, I sensed the electricity still crackling between Carter and me, a promise of what could be if only I could free myself from the chains of my obligations.

And with that thought, I stepped forward, preparing to embrace whatever came next, determined to reclaim my story amid the whirlwind of old friends and unresolved feelings.

The laughter of my former classmates rang in my ears like the persistent chime of a clock, marking each second of this strange reunion. Their presence felt like stepping onto a stage I hadn't auditioned for in years, the spotlight glaring as they approached with curiosity written across their faces. Memories I'd tucked away surged forward, demanding attention, pulling me back into a world where my past mistakes were both a part of the landscape and the people who populated it.

"Look who's back in town!" one of them exclaimed, breaking through the noise with an enthusiasm that felt both comforting and suffocating. "It's the girl who made a dramatic exit!"

I felt a jolt of embarrassment rise, my cheeks flushing as I grappled with the duality of my situation. Here I was, in the café that had witnessed my youthful dreams and reckless ambitions, confronted by the very ghosts I had hoped to escape. Mia glanced at me, her expression a mix of encouragement and sympathy.

"Don't let them get to you," she whispered, leaning in conspiratorially. "We've all made choices. Some more questionable than others."

Her attempt at levity was met with chuckles from our old friends, a reminder that even in their mirth, they held the power to poke at the raw edges of my insecurities. They had each crafted their narratives—Mia, the driven mayor; others, successful in their careers, marriages, and lives, while I had been on a detour through self-doubt and disappointment.

As the conversation swirled around me, I felt the weight of their curiosity pressing down like a heavy blanket. They peppered me with questions, their faces a blend of nostalgia and intrigue. "Did you really leave to chase some big city dream?" one asked, feigning incredulity, while another chimed in with a teasing grin, "Or did you just run away from the reality of being a Montgomery Springs local?"

"I was just... exploring," I said, my voice quieter than I intended. I glanced at Carter, who remained nearby, an anchor in the shifting tides of the past. His eyes flickered with understanding, and I caught a hint of amusement dancing in them, as if he were relishing my discomfort with this spotlight on my former life.

"Exploring? Or hiding?" the first voice shot back, a playful smirk plastered on her face.

The comments were meant to be light-hearted, yet they felt like barbs, reminding me of all the ways I had not measured up. I could feel my defenses crumbling beneath the barrage of friendly fire. Just as I was about to retreat further into myself, Carter stepped forward, his presence commanding enough to draw attention away from me.

"Let's not forget the time you all nearly burned down the science lab," he said, laughter lacing his voice. "That was an impressive display of chaos."

The group erupted into laughter, and I felt the tension shift, the focus lightening. The shared memory painted a picture of innocent mischief—those moments of youthful exuberance when life was less about expectations and more about shared experiences.

Carter's laughter was infectious, and I found myself relaxing, allowing the warmth of the café to wrap around me again. It felt familiar yet strange, a reminder of how quickly life could change. I had once been one of them, a part of this vibrant tapestry woven from shared moments and youthful dreams, and now I felt like a frayed thread, still seeking to find its place.

As the conversation turned back to me, I summoned a smile, determined to reclaim the narrative of my return. "You know, I came back to help my family with the business," I said, injecting a note of certainty into my voice. "I figured it was time to contribute instead of just wandering."

"Oh, the family business!" another friend exclaimed. "The place with the kitschy souvenirs and summer camp vibes?"

"Hey, there's nothing wrong with a little kitsch," I replied, injecting humor into the moment. "It's a staple of Montgomery Springs. But yes, I guess I'm sort of the designated caretaker now."

Mia's eyes sparkled with mischief as she chimed in, "She's like our town's superhero, swooping in to save the day!"

"More like a reluctant sidekick," I retorted, laughter spilling from my lips, a welcome reprieve from the weight of expectations. I could feel Carter's gaze lingering on me, a quiet appreciation that made my heart flutter. The air between us crackled with unspoken possibilities, but I pushed those thoughts aside, focusing on the present, on the friends surrounding me.

As the chatter resumed, I felt a surge of determination course through me. This was my town, my story. I could write the next chapter however I chose. I could be the girl who returned, not to the ghost of her past but to a future ripe with potential.

With the sun dipping behind the skyline of Montgomery Springs, casting long shadows across the café, I reveled in the fleeting moments of connection. The walls, adorned with local art and framed photographs of the town's history, felt alive, breathing alongside the tales being shared. My heart warmed at the thought of belonging again, of reconnecting with a community that had shaped me, even as I'd tried to escape it.

Yet beneath the laughter and the surface-level camaraderie, I could sense the undercurrents of unfulfilled dreams and expectations. Some of my friends were trapped in lives they hadn't chosen, their aspirations dulled by the weight of conformity. But as I glanced at Carter, his passion for art radiating from him like a beacon, I was reminded that it was possible to forge a new path, to reclaim my story and chart my own course.

As the evening drew closer, the café buzzed with life, voices overlapping in a symphony of nostalgia and laughter. I felt a pull to linger, to delve deeper into this renewed connection, yet the threads of responsibility tugged at my heart. My family's business awaited, its needs demanding attention, yet the allure of the past and the promise of the future intertwined in a delicate dance.

In that moment, I made a silent promise to myself—to navigate this return with intention, to embrace the complexity of relationships and the messy beauty of life. I would no longer be the girl who fled; I would be the woman who returned, ready to embrace whatever adventures awaited me in Montgomery Springs, with Carter and Mia by my side.

As the last rays of sunlight faded and the café lights flickered to life, I felt a sense of belonging wash over me. I wasn't just back in Montgomery Springs; I was home, and that was a feeling I hadn't dared to hope for until now. With laughter bubbling around me and possibilities shimmering in the air, I stepped forward into this vibrant tapestry, ready to weave my story anew.

Chapter 3: Stitches of the Past

The door swung open with a muted creak, the familiar scent of fabric and dust greeting me like an old friend as I stepped back into "Stitch & Thread." The little boutique, nestled between a coffee shop that always smelled of roasted beans and a bakery that tempted passersby with the scent of fresh pastries, felt like a second home, albeit a home that had seen better days. Dim light filtered through the lace curtains, casting delicate patterns on the wooden floor, but the vibrancy of the past felt like a ghost lurking in the corners, whispering tales of former glories.

I stood there for a moment, absorbing the remnants of my parents' dreams, which had been woven into this space like the intricate stitches of a hand-sewn garment. The walls were lined with bolts of fabric in every hue imaginable—emerald greens, cobalt blues, and rich maroons, colors that once sparked joy but now lay dulled by neglect. I brushed my fingers against a roll of fuchsia satin, its glossy surface cool to the touch, a reminder of the glamorous dresses my mother had once created, each piece an ode to elegance and artistry.

It was clear that chaos had taken residence in my absence. Sketches fluttered on the floor like forgotten butterflies, some pinned to the corkboard in a jumbled array that seemed to mock the very idea of order. My mother's designs, once the lifeblood of this place, were now buried beneath a mountain of dust and disarray. It was disheartening, a physical manifestation of the fraying connections I felt with my parents. Every sketch told a story, a fragment of a life I had once been proud to be part of.

I dropped my bag beside the counter, its thud echoing in the silence. The little bell above the door tinkled, almost as if it too felt the weight of the moment. With a deep breath, I rolled up my sleeves, ready to plunge into the overwhelming task before me. Each piece I touched told a story, but it was my mother's old sketches that drew me in like a moth to a flame. An old trunk, half-hidden under a pile of discarded fabric, caught my eye. My heart raced at the thought of what might be hidden inside—memories, dreams, and possibly a spark of inspiration.

I knelt beside it, my fingers fumbling with the latch. With a gentle tug, the trunk creaked open, revealing a trove of neatly folded papers and the faint scent of aged leather. I drew out the first sketch, my breath catching in my throat as I recognized my mother's delicate handwriting labeling it "Summer Ballgown." The design was breathtaking, adorned with intricate floral patterns that danced across the page. Each stroke of her pencil seemed to hold a piece of her spirit, a reminder of the passion that had once ignited this boutique.

As I rifled through the trunk, a bittersweet pang of nostalgia washed over me. There were sketches for bridal gowns, children's outfits, and even a collection inspired by the changing seasons. My heart swelled with pride, yet a gnawing sadness accompanied the realization that my parents were struggling to keep this dream alive. I felt as though I had been running away from my roots, burying myself in my own world while they fought tooth and nail to sustain a legacy that had once brought so much joy.

I stood, my mind buzzing with possibilities. This wasn't just about salvaging the boutique; it was about rekindling the love that had once infused this space with life. I could envision vibrant displays of my mother's designs, new fabrics dancing alongside the old, each telling a story that intertwined with my own. I could breathe new life into "Stitch & Thread," not just for my parents but for myself, reclaiming my place in a world that had felt increasingly alien.

Just as I began to formulate a plan, the door swung open once more, and in walked Carter. He was a familiar presence, one that brought a warmth I hadn't realized I needed. His tousled hair fell over his forehead, and that easy smile he wore instantly melted away the tension that had been coiling in my chest. "What have you gotten yourself into this time?" he teased, his voice laced with a playful lilt as he took in the disheveled state of the boutique.

"Just a little spring cleaning," I replied, a smirk playing at the corners of my lips. "You know how it is—dirt and memories go hand in hand."

Carter chuckled, moving deeper into the boutique, his gaze falling on the trunk I had just uncovered. "Looks like you found a treasure trove. Is that your mom's work?" His eyes widened as he studied the sketches spread out before him, genuine admiration lighting up his features.

"Yeah," I admitted, my heart fluttering as I watched him appreciate the beauty of her designs. "She had a gift for turning fabric into dreams. I just wish I could revive that magic."

"Why not?" Carter stepped closer, his presence radiating encouragement. "You have the talent. Let's brainstorm some ideas. I mean, I'm not a fashion expert, but I've seen how you work. You could breathe new life into this place."

His words ignited a spark within me, a reminder of the connection we shared—our banter, our laughter, and the underlying current of something deeper that had always flickered just beneath the surface. "Are you sure you want to help?" I asked, feigning innocence while I felt a rush of excitement at the thought of collaborating with him.

"Absolutely," he replied, his gaze steady and sincere. "Besides, watching you transform this place will be worth the effort. It'll be like watching a flower bloom."

In that moment, I felt a shift within me, as if a tapestry woven with threads of hope and determination was beginning to take shape. The chaos around me faded, replaced by a sense of purpose that felt almost tangible. With Carter by my side, I was ready to dive into the challenge ahead, ready to stitch together the pieces of my past and present into something beautiful.

The laughter between Carter and me floated through the air like a melody, threading through the chaos of fabric and forgotten dreams. As he grabbed a broom from the corner, I couldn't help but smile. His presence had a way of softening the edges of my worries, turning the overwhelming task ahead into a light-hearted challenge.

"You know," he began, sweeping aside a cascade of colorful scraps, "this place is like a treasure map. Every corner you turn, you find something unexpected. It's practically an adventure." He gestured to the whimsical spools of thread spilling over from a neglected shelf, their vibrant hues a stark contrast to the layers of dust that had gathered on everything.

"Adventure, huh?" I raised an eyebrow, watching him with a mix of amusement and admiration. "Is that what you call it? More like a chaotic scavenger hunt, if you ask me."

He chuckled, that low, contagious laugh that seemed to bounce off the walls and wrap around me like a cozy blanket. "Well, consider me your trusty sidekick. What's the first treasure we're uncovering?"

With a determined nod, I stepped toward the rack of fabrics, my fingers brushing against the textured surfaces. "I think we should start with the display window. If we can make that inviting, maybe we can lure in some customers." The thought of revitalizing the boutique sparked a rush of adrenaline, and I felt a renewed sense of responsibility wash over me. This was more than just a store; it was a piece of my family's history, a tapestry of memories woven into every stitch.

"Alright, then," Carter said, rolling up his sleeves with exaggerated flair. "Let's create a window display that even the most indifferent passerby can't resist."

As we sorted through bolts of fabric, I explained the stories behind each one. There was a light blue cotton that had once been transformed into a little girl's dress for a summer wedding, and a bold floral print that had adorned a vibrant jumpsuit my mother wore to a family reunion. Each piece held a narrative, and as I shared these tales, Carter listened intently, his dark eyes sparkling with curiosity.

"I love how you light up when you talk about your mom's creations," he remarked, tying a bow with a remnant piece of ribbon. "It's like you're channeling her spirit."

A flutter of warmth bloomed in my chest at his observation, but I also felt a pang of sadness. "I wish I had the confidence she did," I admitted, my voice dipping into a softer tone. "She had this way of making every person feel beautiful, like they were the star of their own show. I'm just... lost."

Carter paused, his gaze steady and encouraging. "You're not lost; you're just on a different path. You have your own light to shine." He picked up a pastel pink fabric, holding it against the window as if envisioning its potential. "Besides, look at you. You have the same passion. You're just waiting for your moment to burst through."

His words ignited a spark of determination within me. I took a breath, summoning the courage I often felt slipping through my fingers. "Alright, let's do this. Let's make something that honors her and reflects who I am."

As the day unfolded, we transformed the boutique window into a vibrant canvas. We draped the fabrics like cascading waterfalls, layering textures and colors that sang in harmony. I lost track of time, immersed in the rhythmic motion of creating, feeling Carter's presence beside me like a steady drumbeat.

He held up a hand-painted sign, "Stitch & Thread: Where Dreams Are Sewn." "This needs to be the first thing people see," he declared, his enthusiasm infectious. "It's catchy and invites curiosity."

I couldn't help but laugh. "It's also a bit cheesy, don't you think?"

"Cheesy can be good," he replied with a grin. "It's memorable. People love a good story."

I had to admit he was right. The more we worked together, the more our laughter intertwined, weaving a fabric of camaraderie and understanding that felt comforting. It was in those moments I caught glimpses of a deeper connection between us, one that sparked like an electric current, drawing me closer to him even as I fought the urge to analyze it too deeply.

By the time the sun began to set, casting a golden hue across the boutique, our creation was complete. The window shimmered with life, a tapestry of hope and dreams. I stepped back, feeling a swell of pride that made my heart race. This was more than just a display; it was a reflection of my determination to breathe life back into "Stitch & Thread."

"Wow," Carter said, stepping beside me and placing a reassuring hand on my shoulder. "We really did this."

I turned to him, my smile radiant. "We did. Thank you for believing in me. I couldn't have done it without you."

He shrugged, a slight blush creeping across his cheeks. "What are friends for? Besides, I had fun." There was a softness in his voice that resonated within me, a reminder of the laughter and connection we had forged throughout the day.

As we stood side by side, admiring our handiwork, the silence settled in comfortably, wrapping around us like a shared secret. I caught myself glancing at him, and in that moment, something shifted. The air between us grew charged, and for the first time, I allowed myself to imagine the possibilities that lingered just beyond the boundaries of friendship.

But as the last rays of sunlight slipped away, casting the boutique into soft shadows, I felt a wave of uncertainty crash over me. The past loomed large, filled with familial expectations and the weight of my parents' struggles. Could I truly step into my own light without losing sight of them? Would rekindling my passion for this place mean severing ties to the people I loved?

I sighed, pulling my thoughts back to the present, where Carter stood, patiently waiting for me to speak. "What if... what if I fail?" I asked, my voice barely a whisper.

He turned to me, his expression earnest. "What if you don't? Every journey starts with a single step, right? Just take it one day at a time. You can't predict the future, but you can create it."

His encouragement felt like a lifeline, a thread pulling me back into the moment. I took a breath, feeling more grounded. "You're right," I said, a newfound resolve bubbling up within me. "I have to try, not just for them but for myself."

The darkness began to settle around us, but instead of feeling isolated, I felt emboldened. The boutique was a reflection of my heart, and as long as I was willing to fight for it, I knew I could carve out my own space in this world. With Carter by my side, the fear of failure faded, leaving only the thrill of possibility.

As the last embers of sunlight surrendered to twilight, the world outside "Stitch & Thread" transformed. The soft glow of streetlamps flickered on, casting a warm glow through the boutique's windows, illuminating the eclectic mix of colors and textures we had so carefully arranged. The laughter and camaraderie with Carter had woven a new energy into the space, and as I stood back to admire our work, I felt a swell of hope flutter within me like the wings of a freshly hatched butterfly.

"What do you think?" I asked, a hint of anxiety threading my voice.

Carter leaned against the counter, his arms crossed, his expression thoughtful. "It's inviting. It feels like a place where stories are born. I'd stop here just to see what you're creating." His words were both a compliment and a gentle push, urging me to embrace the potential that lay ahead.

The boutique had always felt like a sanctuary to me, filled with the spirit of my mother's creations. Each dress, each stitch held memories, and now, with Carter by my side, I felt that same spirit beginning to breathe anew. "I think we should celebrate this," I suggested, a spark of mischief lighting my eyes. "How about we hold a small event? Invite some locals, showcase my mother's designs, and let people know we're back in business?"

Carter raised an eyebrow, a playful grin spreading across his face. "You mean a 'come see what we've done and remember how great we are' party? I like it."

"Exactly!" I exclaimed, excitement bubbling over. "We can have refreshments, maybe a fashion show of sorts. Just something to bring the community back into this place."

He nodded, the enthusiasm between us palpable. "I can help with the planning. Maybe I could even model. You know, show off some of those stunning fabrics."

I laughed, picturing Carter strutting down a makeshift runway, his charm and easy confidence turning heads. "I don't know if my mother's creations were meant for your kind of runway."

"Ah, but the element of surprise is key," he countered, his eyes twinkling with mischief. "What's a little boldness if not the perfect accessory?"

As we planned into the night, our conversations began to weave a tapestry of dreams and ambitions, the kind that felt exhilarating and terrifying all at once. The boutique had transformed into a brainstorming haven, where every idea felt like a stitch pulling us closer together. I couldn't ignore the simmering undercurrent of attraction between us, but I pushed it aside, focusing instead on the tangible steps ahead.

With a tentative sense of purpose igniting in my chest, I started jotting down ideas for the event. As I wrote, the memories of my parents' struggles flickered at the edges of my mind. My father's deep lines of worry, etched like the patterns on a well-worn fabric, and my mother's relentless passion now felt like threads of the past demanding attention. I knew I had to confront my parents—not just about the boutique but about our family's future together.

The next morning, I summoned the courage to sit my parents down. The kitchen was bathed in morning light, the soft aroma of freshly brewed coffee mingling with the scent of pancakes sizzling on the griddle. My mother was flipping pancakes with her usual flair, her eyes crinkling into a smile as she caught sight of me. "Good morning, sweetheart! I made your favorite!"

"Thanks, Mom." I accepted the plate with a sense of warmth that briefly masked the nervousness coiling in my stomach. My father sat at the table, newspaper spread before him, his brow furrowed in concentration.

"Dad," I began, my voice trembling slightly, "I think it's time we talked about the store."

His head snapped up, eyes narrowing slightly. "What about it?"

"The boutique needs a revival. I have some ideas," I said, taking a deep breath. "I want to host an event. Show off Mom's designs and get the community involved again."

My mother's expression shifted from delight to concern. "Honey, it's not that easy. We're struggling, and we can't afford to make mistakes."

"I know," I replied, the sincerity in my voice underscoring my words. "But we can't keep waiting for things to change. We need to make the change ourselves. This place has so much potential, and it's been a part of our lives for so long. We owe it to ourselves—and to you, Mom."

The silence hung thick in the air as my father's gaze pierced mine, his gruff demeanor softened by the flicker of something I couldn't quite place. "You really believe we can pull this off?" he asked, skepticism evident.

"I do," I affirmed, feeling a rush of determination. "Together. If we pool our strengths, we can breathe life back into this place. I'm ready to put in the work, and I know Carter will help."

A heavy pause followed, filled with the weight of unspoken fears and hopes. Finally, my father nodded slowly, his walls crumbling just a bit. "Alright, let's hear your plan."

With that simple acknowledgment, the floodgates opened. I poured out every idea, every vision that had filled my mind, watching as my parents' expressions shifted from concern to cautious interest. Each detail brought them a little closer, each revelation bridging the gap that had widened over the years.

As we sat together, the kitchen slowly transformed into a brainstorming haven. Ideas bounced around like the sizzling pancakes, and for the first time in a long while, I felt a sense of unity forming among us. It was as if we were stitching together a new fabric of our lives, one that could withstand the fraying edges of doubt and fear.

By the time we had finished, my heart soared with hope. I could feel the spirit of my mother lingering in the air, guiding us toward a future that, while uncertain, felt worth pursuing.

Afterward, Carter joined us in the boutique, his presence a buoy in the waves of my swirling emotions. "So, what's the verdict?" he asked, leaning against the counter with that familiar casual charm.

I couldn't help but smile, the relief palpable in my voice. "They're in. We're going to do this together."

Carter's grin was wide and genuine, his excitement matching my own. "That's fantastic! Let's get to work."

As we dove into the preparations, our laughter rang through the boutique, echoing off the walls like a symphony of rebirth. We painted signs, crafted invitations, and gathered supplies, the energy between us palpable.

In those moments, amidst the colorful chaos of fabric and ideas, I allowed myself to embrace the spark igniting between us. Carter's support, his unwavering belief in my vision, felt like the wind beneath my wings. As the days passed and the event drew closer, I found myself drawn to him in ways I had tried to suppress. It was as if every stitch we crafted together intertwined our destinies, drawing us closer to a connection that could not be ignored.

The evening of the event arrived, and the boutique pulsed with life, filled with the laughter and chatter of familiar faces. The air was thick with anticipation, and as I stood among the vibrant displays, a wave of pride washed over me.

"Look at this place," Carter said, his voice a low murmur beside me as we surveyed the crowd. "You've done something incredible here."

I turned to him, feeling the weight of his gaze. "I couldn't have done it without you."

"Then let's make sure this is just the beginning."

In that moment, amidst the flutter of fabrics and the warmth of community, I felt a sense of belonging. Not just to the boutique or my family, but to something larger—a vision, a purpose that transcended my fears and insecurities. And as I stood beside Carter, our laughter mingling with the music in the air, I couldn't help but believe that the threads of our lives were finally beginning to weave a tapestry that was uniquely ours.

Chapter 4: Fabric of Life

The evening sun dipped low over the bustling streets of Charleston, painting the historic architecture with hues of gold and amber. As I walked the cobblestone streets, the aroma of fresh magnolia mixed with the salty air from the nearby harbor, creating a sense of nostalgia that wrapped around me like a warm shawl. This city was a tapestry of history and charm, its quaint boutiques nestled between grand antebellum homes, each whispering stories of love and resilience. Yet, at that moment, my heart raced not for the city's beauty but for the challenge that lay ahead.

Determined to rebrand my family's boutique, a quaint little shop known as "Fabric of Life," I had enlisted the help of Mia and Carter, two of my closest friends and fellow dreamers. With their creative sparks igniting my own ambition, we transformed our late-night brainstorming sessions into a vibrant concoction of laughter and determination. The scent of coffee and freshly baked pastries filled the air as we gathered around a cluttered table in the back of the store, which was strewn with sketches, swatches, and half-empty cups, remnants of our imaginative chaos.

Carter, with his tousled curls and a mischievous glint in his eye, leaned over the table, his finger tracing the outline of a vibrant fabric swatch. "What if we played with contrast? This bold floral print could dance beautifully with that vintage lace." His enthusiasm was infectious, his artistic flair illuminating even the most mundane fabric.

Mia, ever the realist with a knack for marketing, chimed in, "Yes! But we need a story to go with it. Every piece has a history; we should weave those tales into our marketing strategy. Imagine if customers knew the story behind each fabric. It'll give them a reason to choose us over the big box stores." Her voice held a conviction that urged us to delve deeper, to discover the emotional connections each fabric held, and to convey that intimacy to our customers.

As we tossed around ideas, I felt an exhilarating sense of freedom wash over me. I envisioned vibrant displays, inviting window arrangements, and a launch party that would be the talk of the town. Each idea felt like a stepping stone toward breathing new life into the shop that had been in my family for generations. Yet, beneath the excitement lay an undercurrent of apprehension, whispering of old family tensions that threatened to surface as I pushed forward.

My father, a man of tradition and steadfast beliefs, often reminded me of the boutique's legacy, echoing the sentiments of his own father before him. He had spent years building the shop's reputation, and any deviation from his vision felt like an affront to his hard work. I could sense the skepticism in his voice whenever I shared my plans. "It's not just a shop, you know. It's part of our heritage. People come here for the familiarity, not the flashiness," he would say, his brow furrowing in that way that made me feel small and uncertain.

With every fiber of my being, I wanted to honor our family's legacy while also forging my own path. Balancing these two opposing forces felt like trying to walk a tightrope strung between two skyscrapers. The thought of disappointing my father gnawed at me, yet the thought of stagnation made my heart ache. I could feel the weight of my family's expectations pressing down on me like the sultry Southern humidity, thick and suffocating.

As our brainstorming sessions continued, the synergy between us ignited new ideas, sending us spiraling into delightful tangents. I remember one evening in particular when Mia suggested we host a "Fabrics & Friends" night, inviting local artisans and crafters to showcase their work alongside ours. The thought of a community gathering sparked a warmth within me, igniting a sense of belonging that I craved. This could be more than just a launch; it could be a celebration of creativity and connection.

Under the soft glow of string lights, we envisioned tables adorned with vibrant fabric samples and art displays, the air filled with laughter and the sound of fabric scissors snipping away. The thought of inviting the community into our store, of creating a space where creativity could flourish, filled me with an unshakeable excitement. Perhaps this was the key to bridging the gap between my father's vision and my own.

As we planned, I found myself lost in the texture of the fabrics surrounding us. Each bolt held a story, a history waiting to be told. The buttery-soft cottons whispered of summer picnics, while the rugged burlap echoed tales of farmers' markets. I wanted our customers to feel these connections, to experience the joy of crafting something beautiful from our offerings. I imagined a family gathered around a sewing machine, laughter bubbling over as they created a quilt from our fabrics, threading together their own memories.

Yet, as the days passed and our plans took shape, I noticed an unsettling shift in the atmosphere. My father's skepticism grew palpable, lurking in the corners of our discussions like an uninvited guest. It was evident in the tightness of his smile when I excitedly shared updates, a flicker of disappointment hidden beneath his well-practiced facade. My heart ached at the thought of letting him down, and I found myself wrestling with doubt.

I knew I needed to confront this tension, to find a way to reconcile my vision with the legacy he held dear. One late evening, after Mia and Carter had left, I found myself standing alone in the store, surrounded by the soft glow of the pendant lights illuminating the fabric-covered walls. The shadows danced around me, and I inhaled deeply, savoring the familiar scent of the shop—the cotton, the linen, the dreams woven into every corner.

The walls seemed to echo my fears, urging me to confront the very essence of what Fabric of Life represented. With a deep breath, I whispered to the empty room, "I want to honor our past, but I also need to embrace my future." My voice trembled, the words hanging in the air like fragile strands of silk. It was time to bridge the gap between my ambition and my family's traditions, to weave my own story into the fabric of our lives.

The following week unfolded like the delicate fabric of a hand-stitched quilt, each day layered with new ideas, challenges, and moments of joy. The anticipation hung in the air like the sweet scent of blooming jasmine wafting through my open window. I could feel the energy crackling between Mia, Carter, and me as we immersed ourselves in our plans, each brainstorming session infused with laughter and bursts of creativity. Our late nights, illuminated by twinkling fairy lights strung around the boutique, became our sacred space—a cocoon of inspiration where dreams collided with reality.

Mia had taken it upon herself to curate a collection of local artists and craftspeople, each offering unique perspectives on fabric and design. We spent hours poring over their portfolios, our discussions lively as we debated whose work resonated most with our vision. "Look at this," Mia exclaimed one evening, holding up a vibrant watercolor print by a local artist, her eyes sparkling with enthusiasm. "This could be our centerpiece! Imagine it as a backdrop for our launch party—a splash of color to attract the eye!"

Carter chimed in, sketching furiously on a nearby notepad, the pencil flying across the page as he visualized how to incorporate the artwork into our displays. "We can layer this with some of that vintage lace you found. It will create a stunning contrast, bridging the old with the new. It's like telling a story through fabric," he said, his voice laced with passion. I watched them, feeling a swell of gratitude for their unwavering support. Their enthusiasm fueled my resolve to make Fabric of Life more than just a store—it would be a community hub, a haven where creativity thrived.

Yet, even amid this burst of creativity, shadows loomed. My father's skepticism nagged at the edges of my excitement, a persistent whisper that echoed in my mind during our brainstorming sessions. Each time I shared an update, I could sense the subtle tightening of his jaw, the barely concealed worry in his eyes. I knew he loved me and wanted the best for our family's legacy, but his doubts felt like a weight on my shoulders, threatening to stifle the dreams I was determined to breathe life into.

As the days turned into a blur of preparation, I spent countless hours in the shop, surrounded by the comforting chaos of fabric rolls and unfinished projects. The sunlight streamed through the windows, casting warm golden rays across the hardwood floors, illuminating the intricate patterns of the fabrics. I relished these moments of solitude, lost in the textures and colors, imagining the possibilities that lay ahead. With every snip of the scissors and every stitch I practiced, I felt a connection to the generations before me, an unbroken thread that tied me to my family's history.

One particularly humid afternoon, as the cicadas buzzed lazily outside, I found myself rearranging fabric swatches, contemplating how to display them for the launch party. The store was filled with the rich aroma of fresh coffee brewing in the corner, mingling with the earthy scent of cotton and linen. I was absorbed in the task when I heard the familiar chime of the doorbell, signaling a customer's arrival.

Turning to greet the newcomer, I was met with the sight of Ms. Ethel, a local seamstress and beloved figure in our community, who had been a loyal customer since the shop's inception. Her silver hair was pulled back in a tidy bun, and she wore a brightly colored apron that looked as if it had seen countless creative adventures. "Hello, dear! I heard whispers of a launch party. I simply had to see for myself!" she said, her voice warm and inviting.

I felt a rush of excitement. "Yes, Ms. Ethel! We're planning something special, a celebration of local talent and creativity." I eagerly shared our vision with her, describing the artists we were featuring and our hopes for the future. As I spoke, I saw her face light up with each detail, her eyes twinkling with genuine enthusiasm.

"Darling, you're doing wonderful things," she said, placing a reassuring hand on my shoulder. "Your father may not understand your vision, but trust me—people crave change. They want to feel connected, especially in a world that often feels so disconnected. You're weaving something beautiful here, and I can't wait to see it unfold."

Her words wrapped around my heart like a warm embrace, soothing the anxieties that had taken root. Encouraged by her support, I felt a renewed sense of purpose. If Ms. Ethel believed in me, perhaps I could find a way to bridge the gap between my ambitions and my father's traditions.

As the launch party drew closer, the excitement buzzed like a summer storm on the horizon. The shop transformed before my eyes, each detail lovingly curated to reflect our new vision. Mia and Carter helped hang vibrant artworks and organize fabric displays, their laughter echoing through the store, punctuating the air with joy. The combination of modern flair and vintage charm created an inviting atmosphere, one that whispered promises of creativity and community.

Yet, amid the preparations, I sensed a shift in my father. One evening, as I put the finishing touches on a display, he entered the shop with an air of gravity that set my heart racing. The moment our eyes met, I knew this conversation was inevitable. He cleared his throat, and the weight of unspoken words hung in the air between us. "I appreciate your enthusiasm, but I worry you're straying too far from what this shop represents."

I opened my mouth to protest, but his raised hand silenced me. "I know it's important to you, and I want to support you. But you must understand that this place has always been about tradition. Our customers come here because of our history, not just what's trendy."

His words pierced through my excitement, igniting a storm of frustration and confusion within me. I wanted to defend my vision, to explain how it wasn't about discarding our past but rather enriching it, weaving it into something new. But standing there, faced with the weight of his expectations, I faltered. "I'm just trying to honor what we've built while also reaching out to new customers. I want Fabric of Life to thrive, Dad."

He sighed, the lines on his forehead deepening. "I understand, but you have to be careful. Change can be dangerous. It can lead to losing what we hold dear." The sadness in his voice resonated within me, tugging at my heartstrings. I didn't want to hurt him; I wanted him to see the beauty of my dreams.

In that moment, I realized the true challenge wasn't just about rebranding a boutique. It was about navigating the delicate balance between my aspirations and my family's legacy, finding a way to weave our histories together into something that would stand the test of time. The path forward was uncertain, but the strength of my convictions stirred within me, urging me to forge ahead with both passion and purpose.

The day of the launch party arrived with an air of palpable excitement that hung over Fabric of Life like the sweet scent of peach cobbler cooling on a windowsill. The sun peeked through the sprawling oak trees, casting playful shadows across the boutique's entrance, and I could feel the energy thrumming in my veins. Mia and Carter had arrived early, their faces alight with the promise of creativity realized. We had spent the past weeks pouring our hearts into this moment, and I was determined to see it unfold beautifully.

As I stepped into the shop, the space felt transformed, alive with the vibrant colors and textures we had carefully curated. Art pieces adorned the walls, each telling its own story, while fabric swatches hung like flags of our collective aspirations. The familiar scent of fabric mingled with the rich aroma of freshly brewed coffee, and a table laden with pastries beckoned invitingly in the corner, ready to satisfy the sweet tooth of every guest.

Mia was arranging the last few pieces of artwork when I joined her, adjusting a particularly striking canvas—a depiction of swirling colors that evoked the feeling of summer. "This is it," she said, her voice brimming with excitement. "People are going to love this!" Her enthusiasm was infectious, and I couldn't help but smile as I caught a glimpse of her vision manifesting in front of us.

Carter, his artistic flair shining through as usual, added finishing touches to the fabric displays, artfully layering textures to create an inviting tableau. "You know, we should have an art corner where kids can come and create," he suggested, a mischievous glint in his eyes. "Imagine little hands painting while their parents browse. It could make the whole experience interactive!"

"Brilliant!" I exclaimed, already picturing the laughter of children and the chatter of parents filling the air. This was precisely the kind of connection we wanted to foster—a sense of community that extended beyond mere transactions.

As the clock ticked closer to the event's start time, I felt a swell of anticipation mixed with anxiety. The community had been invited, a diverse mix of familiar faces and new ones, and I longed for their acceptance. Would they embrace our vision, or would they cling to the comfortable familiarity of what had always been?

When the first guests trickled in, the atmosphere shifted from quiet anticipation to vibrant engagement. Ethel was among the first, her warm smile instantly putting me at ease. "Look at this place! You've turned it into a wonderland," she beamed, her eyes sparkling with genuine delight. Encouraged by her enthusiasm, I engaged her in conversation, sharing our plans and the artists we had invited.

As the crowd grew, laughter and chatter filled the space, weaving a rich tapestry of sound that enveloped me. Mia and Carter flitted through the boutique like butterflies, welcoming guests and guiding them through our displays. I watched as a group of young girls excitedly gravitated toward the art corner Carter had envisioned, their giggles rising above the hum of conversation.

But as I basked in this atmosphere of camaraderie and creativity, I couldn't shake the uneasy feeling gnawing at my heart. I spotted my father near the entrance, his brow furrowed as he surveyed the scene. He stood apart from the festivities, his arms crossed over his chest, an embodiment of skepticism amidst the jubilant crowd. I felt a pang of longing for his approval; it had always been a driving force in my life.

Summoning my courage, I made my way toward him, weaving through clusters of laughter and the intoxicating aroma of baked goods. "Dad, what do you think?" I asked, my voice barely above the bustling chatter.

He hesitated, his eyes lingering on the vibrant displays before turning to meet my gaze. "It's certainly... colorful," he remarked, his tone measured, the hint of a frown still etching lines across his forehead. "But do you think it's sustainable? What about the people who came here for the fabrics they've always known?"

The question hung between us, a heavy anchor that threatened to drag me down. "I believe this is what they need," I replied, my voice steadier than I felt. "They crave connection, Dad. This isn't just about fabrics; it's about community and creativity. I want to honor our past while also evolving with the times."

He opened his mouth to respond, but before he could speak, Ethel's voice chimed in, cutting through the tension like a warm breeze. "You're doing a marvelous job, dear! The community needs this spark. Change is what keeps us alive!" She beamed at him, and for a moment, I saw the corners of my father's mouth twitch upward, a flicker of understanding amidst his uncertainty.

Encouraged, I stepped back, letting the moment unfold, hoping my father would see the beauty of this transformation. The evening progressed, and as more guests filtered in, the atmosphere grew more electric. We laughed, shared stories, and engaged in animated discussions about art, design, and the intricate beauty of fabric. It felt like a renaissance, a celebration of everything Fabric of Life could be.

Later, as the night deepened, I caught sight of Mia and Carter sharing a laugh with a group of attendees, their faces illuminated by the soft glow of string lights. I marveled at how far we had come, how this space had become a canvas for dreams and connections. My heart swelled with pride as I moved to join them, feeling like I was finally stepping into the role I was meant to play.

Just then, the door swung open with a jingle, and in walked a figure I recognized instantly—my father, now surrounded by a handful of customers who had joined him. Their faces were animated as they engaged him in conversation, curiosity shining in their eyes. For a brief moment, I held my breath, uncertain of what this might mean.

Then, to my astonishment, I saw him gesturing toward one of our fabric displays, laughing at something one of the customers had said. A wave of relief washed over me, and I couldn't help but smile. Perhaps he was beginning to see the world we were building together.

As the evening wound down, and the last guests trickled out, I felt a profound sense of accomplishment. We had crafted not just a successful launch but a gathering of souls eager to connect with one another through creativity. The boutique was alive with possibilities, a beacon of hope for what could be.

Exhausted yet exhilarated, I turned to Mia and Carter, who were busy packing away the remnants of pastries and decorations. "We did it," I breathed, my voice a whisper filled with disbelief and gratitude. They exchanged knowing smiles, their eyes sparkling with the shared triumph of our efforts.

In that moment, surrounded by the warmth of friendship and the echoes of laughter still lingering in the air, I knew I had found a way to honor my family's legacy while forging my own path. The fabric of life, both in the boutique and in my heart, was beginning to weave together in a tapestry of dreams realized and connections made. I felt ready to face whatever came next, knowing that the threads of creativity and community would guide me forward.

Chapter 5: Unraveling Threads

The air crackled with excitement, a charged current that seemed to pulse through the brightly lit venue as I stood behind the curtain, peering out at the gathering crowd. The grand hall of the historic Spencer Theater, with its ornate chandeliers glistening like a thousand tiny stars, buzzed with chatter and laughter. It was the kind of place where dreams felt tangible, where ambition could be woven into the very fabric of the evening. My heart raced in time with the melodic strains of the jazz trio playing softly in the background, their smooth rhythms wrapping around the guests like a warm embrace.

As I adjusted the hem of my dress, a striking navy blue that hugged my curves just right, I took a moment to breathe deeply. The scent of fresh flowers mingled with the faint aroma of the hors d'oeuvres being served, and I imagined each fragrant note blending into a symphony of celebration. This was my night, my launch party for the line of hand-crafted textiles I had poured my soul into over the last year. Yet beneath the vibrant surface of anticipation lay an undercurrent of anxiety that threatened to unravel me.

My father's presence loomed like a dark cloud, his brow furrowed as he observed the festivities from a distance. I could almost feel the weight of his disappointment pressing down on me, an invisible tether anchoring me to the ground. The glances he shot my way—half-hearted smiles laced with skepticism—were enough to send tremors of doubt through my core. I had always craved his approval, but tonight felt like a precarious tightrope act between fulfilling my dreams and living up to his expectations.

"Just breathe," I whispered to myself, shaking off the chill that crept into my bones. With a deep inhale, I stepped out into the spotlight, determined to command the room rather than let it swallow me whole. The sea of faces turned toward me, and I managed a smile, the corners of my mouth trembling as I fought against the tide of unease.

"Welcome, everyone!" I announced, my voice steady despite the quaking of my heart. The crowd erupted into applause, a wave of encouragement that momentarily stilled my doubts. I spotted Carter weaving through the guests, his easy charm illuminating the room. He caught my eye and flashed me a reassuring grin, his presence a steady anchor amidst the swirling chaos.

As I mingled, I couldn't help but take note of the various reactions from my guests. Some marveled at my designs, their fingers gliding over the rich textures and intricate patterns like caressing old friends. Others nodded appreciatively, their polite smiles masking any real enthusiasm. But then there was Janine, a specter from my past who floated through the crowd like a breath of fresh air, drawing attention without even trying. She had always been the epitome of success, her sharp wit and striking beauty a potent combination that made her the center of attention wherever she went.

I felt the weight of her gaze even before I saw her. She was there, a vision in a fitted emerald green dress that accentuated her every curve, her laughter ringing out like a musical chime, drawing the eyes of everyone in the room. I swallowed hard, my heart pounding with a mix of admiration and jealousy that curled in my stomach like a bitter serpent. I couldn't help but compare our paths—hers, paved with accolades and success; mine, a winding road littered with uncertainty and self-doubt.

"Isn't this place magnificent?" Carter's voice broke through my spiraling thoughts, grounding me once more. He gestured toward the grandeur of the theater, his enthusiasm infectious. "You've truly outdone yourself, and everyone can see it."

I forced myself to smile, knowing that Carter was right. The room was alive with possibilities, and yet my gaze remained locked on Janine. She moved with the grace of a gazelle, effortlessly charming everyone she encountered. A knot tightened in my chest as I watched her engage in animated conversation, her laughter infectious as it echoed against the ornate walls.

"What's eating you?" Carter's voice turned serious, pulling me from my reverie. "You're missing the best part of the night, and it's right in front of you."

I sighed, glancing back at my father, who was deep in conversation with an influential local designer. "It's just—she's so perfect," I admitted, my voice barely above a whisper. "I can't help but feel like I'm drowning in her success."

"Perfection is overrated," Carter replied, his eyes gleaming with mischief. "Trust me, she's just as insecure as you are. You think she's got it all figured out? She's probably just as scared of failure as you are. We all are."

His words struck a chord deep within me, echoing in the cavern of my self-doubt. Perhaps Janine wasn't as untouchable as I perceived her to be. Perhaps her own path was fraught with shadows, as mine was. But as I watched her sparkle, I couldn't help but wonder if I'd ever find the courage to shine that bright.

As the evening wore on, the music swelled, a symphony of hope and uncertainty. I forced myself to engage with my guests, and slowly the evening began to weave a tapestry of connection. Yet each time I glanced at Janine, a tumult of emotions surged within me—envy, admiration, and the nagging whisper of inadequacy. With every laugh that bubbled from her lips, I felt myself shrinking, retreating into the shadows of my own insecurities.

I turned my attention to the bustling crowd, the vibrant energy of the party drawing me in, but the ghosts of my past lingered like shadows. Each interaction reminded me of the fierce competition that had colored my high school years, each success and failure a thread in the tapestry of my life. Tonight was supposed to be a celebration, yet it felt more like an unraveling, as if the very fabric of my confidence was being pulled apart thread by thread.

Yet amidst the swirling doubts, Carter's unwavering support was like a beacon in the darkness. He flitted between guests, connecting with them effortlessly, while I struggled to reclaim my footing. But then, in a moment that shifted the very axis of the evening, he gestured toward the stage, a glimmer of mischief dancing in his eyes.

"Let's make this memorable," he said, drawing me along as he hopped onto the small platform. I followed, hesitantly, as the crowd's attention shifted toward us.

"Ladies and gentlemen!" Carter announced, his voice booming with playful energy. "Let's give a round of applause for the mastermind behind tonight's creations, the one and only... my partner in crime, the incomparable Grace Parker!"

The room erupted into applause, and I felt my cheeks heat up with a mix of embarrassment and pride. Carter's infectious enthusiasm was just what I needed. As I stepped forward, I couldn't help but smile, the warmth of the crowd igniting a flicker of confidence deep within me. For a fleeting moment, the weight of my father's disapproval, the sting of Janine's presence, and the uncertainties of my journey faded away. In that moment, I was simply Grace Parker, a young woman standing at the precipice of her dreams, ready to embrace whatever came next.

The applause rippled through the theater, a wave of sound that seemed to wrap around me like a comforting blanket, banishing the chill of self-doubt that had crept in during the earlier moments of the evening. Carter beamed at me, a twinkle of mischief in his eye as he stepped back to give me the floor. The spotlight, once blinding and intimidating, now felt like a warm sunbeam, illuminating the vibrant colors of my designs scattered around the room.

"Thank you, thank you!" I exclaimed, waving my hands in mock humility, the laughter and cheers igniting a spark within me. "I'm thrilled to see so many familiar faces here tonight. Your support means the world to me."

I let the energy of the crowd fuel my words, the thrill of sharing my passion for textiles weaving a tapestry of connection with those gathered. I shared stories of late-night sewing sessions, the scent of freshly dyed fabrics still clinging to my memories, and the laughter shared over failed experiments that turned out to be delightful surprises. Each anecdote was met with nods and smiles, and for the first time that evening, the weight of expectation lifted, allowing me to simply enjoy the moment.

But just as I was starting to find my footing, I felt a sharp gaze settle on me. Janine stood at the edge of the crowd, her posture elegant and poised, a magnetic aura of confidence radiating from her. She was surrounded by admirers, their laughter ringing like chimes as they hung on her every word. It was as if she were a constellation, drawing all light toward her while leaving me feeling like a fading star in the background.

Carter noticed my distraction, his brow furrowing slightly. "Don't let her get to you," he whispered, leaning in close. "You're the one in the spotlight tonight."

I nodded, forcing a smile that felt more like a grimace as I turned my attention back to the crowd. But the image of Janine's flawless exterior lingered, a haunting reminder of my own insecurities. I had known her in high school, a fierce competitor who always seemed to have it all. While I struggled to find my voice, she was already on the path to success, painting a picture-perfect life in vibrant hues that I could only dream of. The way she seemed to glide effortlessly through life ignited a tempest of emotions within me—jealousy, admiration, and a deep-seated fear that I would never measure up.

The party buzzed around me, but I felt trapped in a bubble of my own making. The laughter of friends mixed with the clinking of glasses and the swirls of vibrant conversation faded into a distant hum as I grappled with my swirling thoughts. It felt as though I were watching life unfold through a foggy window, my own reflection a distorted shadow of what I aspired to be.

But Carter wasn't one to let me dwell in my thoughts for long. He grabbed my hand, leading me away from the suffocating throng. "Let's go grab a drink," he suggested, his tone light and teasing. "You need to fuel up before you make your next move. I can see the gears in your head turning."

I followed him toward the bar, the soft glow of golden lights casting a warm ambiance over the area. The bartender greeted us with a grin, and I opted for a sparkling water with a splash of lime, needing something refreshing to clear my head. Carter ordered something more adventurous, a concoction of muddled mint and rum that looked as vibrant as the fabric swatches hanging around the room.

As we stood there, sipping our drinks, Carter kept the conversation flowing effortlessly, his charm wrapping around me like a soft scarf on a chilly day. He shared snippets of his own dreams, from grand travel plans to opening a café that blended art and food into a delightful experience. I could see the passion igniting his eyes, a fervor that resonated with my own aspirations.

"Do you ever think about the future?" he asked, a curious glint in his gaze. "What you want to create next?"

I took a moment, swirling the cool liquid in my glass, the bubbles dancing playfully against the sides. "I want to explore more sustainable fabrics," I replied, feeling a flutter of excitement as I spoke. "To create something that not only looks beautiful but also respects our planet. I want to leave a mark, you know?"

He nodded, genuinely interested, and for the first time that evening, I felt the embers of my ambition reigniting. The night was still unfolding, and though the shadows of my insecurities loomed, they didn't feel quite so daunting in this moment. It was the thrill of possibility, the idea that perhaps I could carve out my own place in the world, separate from the specter of Janine's success.

"Then let's make it happen," Carter encouraged, his voice filled with conviction. "You've already accomplished so much. This launch is just the beginning."

With those words, a spark ignited within me, a sense of determination that I hadn't felt in what seemed like ages. Maybe I didn't need to be Janine. Perhaps, instead, I could find strength in my uniqueness, weaving my own story into the fabric of this world.

But as we returned to the crowd, that resolve wavered. Janine was still there, now mingling closer, her laughter cascading like water over rocks, effortlessly drawing people in. I couldn't help but glance her way, the tide of emotions rising again. What was it about her that made everyone gravitate toward her, while I felt like I was still fumbling through the shadows?

As if sensing my gaze, she turned, locking eyes with me. For a moment, time seemed to freeze, the chatter around us fading into a muted blur. Her expression shifted—an unreadable mix of recognition and something else, perhaps sympathy? I was taken aback by the vulnerability that flickered across her face, a fleeting glimpse of a woman who, despite her polished exterior, might also be wrestling with her own fears and doubts.

"Grace!" she called out, her voice cutting through the haze. "Congratulations on your launch! I've seen some of your pieces; they're stunning."

I blinked, caught off guard by her sudden warmth. It felt like a gentle hand reaching out from the storm, and the genuine compliment settled over me like a soft blanket. "Thank you," I managed, my voice shaky yet sincere. "It means a lot coming from you."

The conversation flowed as we exchanged pleasantries, the initial tension easing as we talked about our creative journeys. I found myself surprised by her openness, her words painting a picture of someone who had also battled insecurities behind closed doors. It was an unexpected twist that made me question everything I thought I knew about our rivalry.

As the night wore on, I began to recognize the threads that intertwined our lives—strands of ambition, vulnerability, and the unyielding desire for acceptance. Perhaps, instead of seeing Janine as a rival, I could view her as a mirror reflecting my own aspirations and fears. The air between us shifted, and I felt a sense of camaraderie forming, a recognition that we were both navigating the treacherous waters of our dreams in this unpredictable sea of life.

With that realization came a new sense of freedom. I could celebrate my achievements without allowing comparison to taint my success. As the evening pressed on, laughter and music filled the air, and I embraced the connections blossoming around me, knowing that while the night had its challenges, it was also a tapestry woven with the threads of possibility.

The atmosphere in the Spencer Theater buzzed with life, a vibrant tapestry of voices and laughter that enveloped me like a cherished melody. With each passing moment, I felt the boundaries of my insecurities begin to dissolve, replaced by an unexpected sense of camaraderie with Janine. Our earlier competition was transforming into something more nuanced, a shared understanding that perhaps success wasn't a zero-sum game. I was beginning to see that behind her polished façade lay the same vulnerabilities that plagued my own heart.

As the evening unfolded, a gentle wave of warmth washed over me. I found myself moving between conversations, the earlier anxiety ebbing like the tide. My designs, proudly displayed on elegant mannequins, were now drawing admiration and interest. I caught snippets of conversation, phrases like "exquisite craftsmanship" and "innovative designs" floating through the air like confetti, sparking a sense of pride within me that I desperately clung to.

In one corner, a group of local boutique owners examined the fabric samples I had laid out. Their eyes widened with intrigue as they discussed potential collaborations, and I felt a thrill shoot through me at the thought of my work reaching a broader audience. Maybe this was my moment—a chance to weave my passion into the very fabric of the community I adored.

Carter appeared at my side, his earlier drink now a distant memory as he grabbed a flute of champagne from a passing tray. "You're killing it," he said, his voice laced with genuine excitement. "Look at them. They can't get enough of you!"

I glanced at the group, who were now pointing at my vibrant textiles and sharing ideas about how they might incorporate them into their stores. I couldn't help but grin. "I can't believe this is happening. It feels surreal."

"Good surreal or bad surreal?" Carter quipped, waggling his eyebrows.

"Definitely good," I laughed, the sound ringing through the crowd like a bell. Just as I began to savor the moment, a shift in the atmosphere caught my attention. Janine had maneuvered her way to the center of the room, her voice rising above the din as she shared her latest ventures in the fashion industry. It was a story of triumph, one that illuminated her journey from high school rival to successful entrepreneur, each word dripping with the kind of confidence that could light up the dimmest corners of the theater.

I watched, captivated yet envious, as she effortlessly commanded the attention of everyone around her. The smiles, the laughter—she was a maestro conducting a symphony, and I was left sitting in the audience, yearning for a chance to play my own note in the grand composition. As the applause erupted around her, I felt a pang of bitterness worm its way into my heart, uninvited and unwelcome.

"Hey," Carter's voice broke through my thoughts, his brow slightly furrowed with concern. "Are you okay?"

"Yeah, I just—" I hesitated, glancing back at Janine. "I don't know, she's just so... perfect. It's hard not to compare myself."

"Comparison is the thief of joy," he said, a sage-like grin appearing on his face. "You have to remember that she's only showing you her highlight reel. You don't know what goes on behind the scenes."

"True," I conceded, but even as I said it, I felt the weight of my own struggles pressing down on me. The long nights filled with uncertainty, the constant second-guessing of my choices—it all replayed in my mind like a familiar song. Would I ever feel like I belonged in this world, or was I destined to remain an outsider?

Carter must have sensed my hesitation because he leaned closer, lowering his voice conspiratorially. "You know, I overheard Janine talking to someone earlier. She was saying how she admires your creativity. She didn't have to say that, but she did. Maybe there's more to her than meets the eye."

I raised an eyebrow, a hint of skepticism creeping into my thoughts. "Really? That doesn't sound like the Janine I remember."

"People change," he replied, his expression earnest. "Sometimes it takes stepping back to see that competition can evolve into inspiration. You're both chasing your dreams. Why not lift each other up?"

His words resonated, sinking in like the final thread in a beautifully woven tapestry. Maybe I didn't have to view Janine as a rival, but as a fellow traveler on this winding road of ambition. The very fabric of my journey was shifting, and the fear that had once wrapped around me like a tight corset began to loosen.

With newfound resolve, I made my way across the room, Carter by my side. As I approached Janine, the room fell into a hushed murmur, eyes turning to witness the unfolding drama. My heart raced, but I couldn't turn back now. This was my moment to weave a new narrative, one that embraced solidarity rather than division.

"Hey, Janine," I called out, my voice steadier than I felt. She turned, surprise flitting across her features before she masked it with a polite smile.

"Grace! Nice to see you," she replied, her tone warm yet cautious. "You've really outdone yourself tonight."

"Thanks! I've been working hard," I said, the words spilling out as if a dam had broken. "I'm really impressed by everything you've accomplished. Your journey is inspiring."

Her smile softened, and for a brief moment, the competitive edge melted away. "I appreciate that. It hasn't been easy, but I believe we all have our unique paths to follow."

"Exactly!" I said, the warmth of connection igniting between us. "We're both carving out spaces in this industry. Maybe we can collaborate in the future?"

Janine's eyes brightened, and the tension that had crackled between us seemed to dissipate. "I'd love that. We could create something beautiful together."

As we exchanged ideas, the crowd around us began to chatter once more, the murmur of conversation rising to a crescendo. It felt like the world had opened up, expanding with possibilities. The specter of jealousy faded, replaced by the thrill of potential partnership, and I could finally see the tapestry of our experiences intertwining instead of competing.

As the evening continued, I basked in the camaraderie that enveloped me. Conversations flowed seamlessly, laughter echoed through the grand hall, and my earlier insecurities felt like distant echoes. The night transformed from a showcase of my accomplishments into a celebration of connection, where shared stories became the threads binding us together.

When the night finally began to wind down, I stepped outside onto the theater's balcony, the cool night air brushing against my cheeks. I looked out over the twinkling lights of the town, the glow of anticipation shimmering in the distance. My heart swelled with gratitude, a soft hum of satisfaction threading through my chest.

Carter joined me, leaning against the railing with a relaxed demeanor. "So, how do you feel now?"

"Better," I admitted, allowing the night's events to wash over me like a gentle tide. "I realized that competition doesn't have to mean animosity. We can lift each other up instead of tearing each other down."

"Exactly," he said, the pride evident in his voice. "You've got the spirit of a creator, Grace. Don't ever let anyone dim your light."

I turned to face him, the warmth of his support enveloping me like a comforting embrace. In that moment, surrounded by the night's quiet beauty, I knew that my journey was just beginning. I had the power to shape my own narrative, one thread at a time, weaving it into a tapestry that reflected not just my ambitions, but also the connections and collaborations that would carry me forward. As the stars shimmered above, I felt a sense of purpose ignite within me, a bright and unyielding flame guiding me into the future.

Chapter 6: Tangled Emotions

The evening air was thick with the sweet scent of magnolias and the distant sound of laughter from the gathering that had erupted just beyond the twinkling fairy lights strung across the porch. I slipped away, seeking solace in the quiet corner of our sprawling backyard, a place where the tall oaks loomed like ancient guardians, their leaves whispering secrets I was too young to understand. It was here, nestled in the shadows of the vibrant party, that I found Carter, his presence both grounding and electrifying.

His silhouette was a striking contrast against the softly glowing lanterns, and when our eyes met, a rush of warmth surged through me, mingling with the cool night breeze. The stars scattered overhead like diamonds tossed carelessly across a dark velvet cloth, each one twinkling with a kind of mischief that seemed to mirror the fluttering in my chest. I had known Carter since we were children, but this was different—there was an intensity now, an unspoken promise that hung in the air between us, shimmering like the stars above.

"Hey," he said, a hint of a grin playing at the corners of his lips, his voice smooth like honey. "I thought I'd find you here."

"Just needed a breather," I replied, my heart racing as I stepped closer, drawn to him like a moth to a flame. "It's a bit overwhelming, isn't it?"

He chuckled softly, the sound rich and warm. "A little. But I think the chaos makes it fun."

I leaned against the rough bark of the oak, the tree's strength a stark reminder of the fragility of my own situation. The world around us faded, leaving just the two of us wrapped in our own bubble. I could see the faint glow of the party lights flickering in his eyes, reflecting the excitement of the evening, but there was something deeper there too—a sincerity that both thrilled and terrified me.

"Do you ever feel like..." I paused, searching for the right words. "Like you're supposed to be someone else? Like everyone has these expectations, and you just want to break free?"

Carter's expression shifted, and for a moment, I saw a flicker of understanding. "All the time," he admitted, his voice dropping to a whisper, as if sharing a secret meant only for me. "My dad wants me to take over the family business, and it's like... that's not me. I want to travel, to explore the world. I want to make art, not spreadsheets."

The revelation hung between us, charged with a vulnerability I hadn't expected. It made him more human, more real, and my heart ached for him. "You should do what makes you happy," I urged, a fierce determination sparking within me. "You deserve that."

His gaze met mine, and the air crackled with unspoken words, the kind that linger just at the edge of a confession. We stood there, wrapped in our shared secrets and dreams, each pulse of my heart resonating with the intensity of the moment. I could feel the pull between us, a magnetic force that drew me closer, daring me to take that leap.

Just as I felt ready to surrender to the tide of emotions crashing over me, my phone buzzed in my pocket, shattering the fragile moment. The brightness of the screen illuminated the darkness, and my heart sank as I read my mother's name flashing insistently. Anxiety twisted in my stomach like a coiling serpent.

"Sorry, I have to..." I murmured, stepping back, the connection between us severed, if only for a moment. As I glanced at the message, my heart plummeted. A health scare—just a routine check-up that had spiraled into something more. My mother had always been the anchor of my life, her laughter the lighthouse guiding me through stormy seas. The thought of her being unwell sent a rush of panic through me, a cold wave that drowned out the warmth of the evening.

"What is it?" Carter asked, concern etching lines on his forehead.

"It's my mom," I whispered, fighting back the surge of emotions threatening to overwhelm me. "She's having some health issues. I... I need to go."

The excitement we had shared moments ago dissolved into a heavy silence, the reality of my family's expectations crashing over me like an icy wave. The tightrope I walked, balancing my budding feelings for Carter and my responsibilities at home, seemed more precarious than ever.

"Do you want me to come with you?" he offered, his voice steady, grounding me amidst the chaos.

I shook my head, the weight of my mother's condition pressing down on me like a leaden cloak. "No, I'll be okay. I just... I need to figure things out."

As I turned to leave, I caught one last glimpse of him—his expression a mixture of worry and something else, something more tender that made my heart ache. I wanted to reach out, to tell him that this wasn't the end, that our connection was real, but the shadows of my obligations loomed large, casting a pall over the budding relationship I desperately craved.

The journey back to the house felt like walking through a fog, the vibrant world I had just stepped out of muted and distant. I entered the house, where the laughter and music of the party still thrummed in the background, a sharp contrast to the dread pooling in my stomach. My family needed me, and the weight of that responsibility hung heavily on my shoulders.

As I stepped inside, the chaos of the party faded, leaving only the echo of Carter's voice, the promise of what could have been slipping through my fingers like sand. I had a choice to make—one that felt as daunting as crossing a chasm on a tightrope, my heart split between the desire for freedom and the duty I couldn't escape. The path ahead was uncertain, but in that moment, I knew that love, with all its complications, would forever linger in the air around me, waiting for the right moment to make its presence known once more.

The next morning, the sunlight streamed through my window, casting a warm glow that felt both comforting and intrusive. It was a stark contrast to the turmoil swirling in my mind, where worry tangled with the remnants of the night before. I lay there, cocooned in my blankets, staring at the ceiling as my thoughts spiraled, caught between the echoes of laughter from the party and the looming shadow of my mother's health. I felt like a jigsaw puzzle with pieces that didn't quite fit, and no matter how hard I tried, the picture remained incomplete.

Eventually, I dragged myself from the cocoon of sheets and faced the day, the scent of fresh coffee wafting through the house like an inviting hug. My father was already at the kitchen table, his laptop open and papers scattered around him like leaves blown by an autumn wind. He looked up when I entered, his expression a blend of concern and determination.

"Morning, sunshine," he greeted, trying to inject some cheer into the air. "You look like you wrestled a bear last night."

I forced a smile, though it felt more like a grimace. "More like I wrestled my own thoughts."

"Want some breakfast? Your mom's still sleeping in," he said, his voice tinged with an unspoken worry. The thought of my mother lying in bed, possibly sick, made my stomach twist into knots.

"I think I'll grab something later," I replied, pouring a cup of coffee that smelled like hope, even as it fueled my anxiety. I needed to gather my thoughts, but I also longed for a moment of escape, a brief reprieve from the heaviness of reality.

After a quick shower, I decided to step outside, the late summer morning still holding onto the remnants of the previous day's warmth. The garden was a riot of colors, blooming in a joyous dance that felt almost mocking in its vibrancy. I wandered through the flowers, their petals brushing against my fingers like soft whispers, as if they were trying to soothe my frayed nerves. The birds chirped a lively symphony overhead, a stark contrast to the storm brewing in my heart.

As I walked, my mind drifted back to Carter—the way he'd looked at me under the stars, the way his laughter had wrapped around me like a familiar blanket. It was a feeling I hadn't allowed myself to fully embrace, not since I'd felt the pressure of family expectations tighten around my chest. I found myself wishing for a world where I could lean into that feeling, where love didn't come burdened with responsibilities and heartaches.

I pulled my phone from my pocket, hesitating for just a moment before tapping out a message to Carter. The screen lit up with his name, a jolt of excitement mingling with trepidation. Hey, how are you today? It was a simple question, but it held a thousand implications, a thousand hopes for connection that I wasn't sure I was ready to explore.

The response came almost instantly. Feeling a bit better now. How about you?

Relief washed over me. He was alive and well, and I felt my heartbeat synchronize with the moment. A smile crept across my face as I typed back, Trying to wrap my head around everything. Want to hang out later?

The three dots on the screen danced for what felt like an eternity before his reply came. I'd love that. How about we meet at the park around four?

A wave of warmth washed over me, a delicious thrill that chased away some of my worries. I texted back a quick confirmation and tucked my phone away, a lightness now in my step. The idea of being with him again felt like the first hint of spring after a long winter. But just as quickly, a heavy thought crept back in: my mother. What if she needed me? What if I was being selfish, focusing on my feelings when she was going through something potentially serious?

The rest of the day was a blur of chores and half-hearted conversations. Each sound felt amplified in my head, the clatter of dishes, the ticking of the clock, each noise resonating like a reminder of the weight I carried. As I helped my father prepare dinner, I caught glimpses of my mother's empty chair at the table, and it felt as if the air itself was heavy with expectation and unsaid words.

Around three, I decided to check in on her. I tiptoed into her room, the door creaking softly. She lay there, the sheets pulled up to her chin, her face pale against the white pillow. My heart tightened at the sight. "Mom?" I called gently, not wanting to startle her.

Her eyes fluttered open, a smile breaking through the haze of fatigue. "Hey, sweetheart," she murmured, her voice raspy but warm. "I was just resting."

I perched on the edge of her bed, my heart racing. "How are you feeling?"

"I'm okay, just a little tired," she reassured me, but I could see the worry lurking in her eyes. "You don't need to worry about me, love. I just need to take it easy for a bit."

But her words felt inadequate, a flimsy barrier against the wave of dread crashing over me. I wanted to protect her, to take away any pain or fear she might be feeling. "I'm here if you need anything," I promised, my voice trembling with emotion. "I'll always be here."

She reached out, taking my hand in hers, squeezing gently. "I know, and that means the world to me. Just promise me you won't forget to live your own life, too. You're young, and there's so much out there waiting for you."

Her words struck a chord, resonating deep within me. The conflicting emotions swirling inside felt like an endless loop—my responsibilities, my desire for independence, and the burgeoning connection I felt with Carter. I needed to find balance, a way to honor my family while also honoring my heart.

As I left her room, I felt the weight of the world on my shoulders, but also a flicker of hope igniting within me. I had a choice to make, a way to weave my desires and obligations together without losing myself in the process. Maybe, just maybe, I could carve out a space for love amidst the chaos of my life.

When the clock struck four, I slipped on my favorite sneakers and headed toward the park, my heart racing with each step. The vibrant green grass stretched out before me, dotted with families enjoying the sun, the atmosphere alive with laughter and chatter. I spotted Carter leaning against a tree, his relaxed posture exuding an effortless charm.

As our eyes met, a smile broke across his face, and for a brief moment, the world around us faded. All the chaos, all the worries fell away, leaving only the possibility of connection lingering in the air. I took a deep breath, steeling myself for whatever came next. I could feel my heart opening, ready to embrace whatever tangled emotions lay ahead.

The moment I approached Carter, the world around us seemed to dissolve into a blur, fading away like an old photograph left too long in the sun. He stood under a majestic oak tree, its branches arching overhead like the protective arms of a guardian. The late afternoon light filtered through the leaves, casting dappled patterns on the ground, and for a heartbeat, the heaviness in my chest lifted, replaced by a sense of exhilarating possibility.

"Hey," I said, my voice slightly breathless, as if I had sprinted the last few steps to him. He looked up, his expression transforming into one of warmth and welcome, and the flutter of anticipation danced in my stomach.

"Hey yourself," he replied, leaning back against the rough bark, effortlessly cool in a way that made my heart race. "I'm glad you made it."

"Wouldn't miss it," I quipped, attempting to match his laid-back demeanor, though I felt like a tightly coiled spring ready to unravel. The truth was, this was more than just a meet-up; it felt like a step into a new chapter, a chance to reclaim the pieces of myself that had been overshadowed by worry and obligation.

We began to stroll along the winding path that cut through the park, bordered by wildflowers that danced in the gentle breeze. The vibrant colors painted a backdrop that felt almost surreal, every bloom a reminder of life's beauty amidst the chaos. I caught the scent of lilacs wafting through the air, their sweet fragrance twirling around us like an invisible ribbon binding our shared moments.

As we walked, we shared stories that unfolded like the petals of the flowers surrounding us. I learned about his passion for painting, how he'd spent countless afternoons sketching in the park, capturing the world around him in strokes of vibrant color. His voice softened as he spoke, revealing an artist's soul beneath the confident exterior. "It's my escape," he confessed, his eyes lighting up with enthusiasm. "When I paint, it's like I can breathe freely. Everything else fades away."

I found myself leaning closer, entranced by the rhythm of his words. "What do you paint?" I asked, genuinely curious.

"Mostly landscapes, but lately I've been trying to capture emotions," he admitted, his expression turning serious. "I want to paint feelings, not just scenes. It's harder than it sounds."

"Feelings are messy," I mused, my thoughts dancing between the vivid imagery he conjured and the chaos swirling in my own life. "They're like paint splatters on a canvas—beautiful but unpredictable."

He nodded thoughtfully, and for a moment, our eyes locked in a shared understanding. There was something profound about that moment, an unspoken connection that made the air between us vibrate with possibility. Just as I felt the urge to step closer, to close the distance and breach the walls we had both carefully constructed, a nagging thought tugged at my consciousness. My mother, her well-being still an omnipresent shadow in my mind, clouded my moment of clarity.

Carter broke the silence, a playful grin spreading across his face. "You seem lost in thought. Are you plotting my demise?"

I laughed, the sound bubbling up like a brook after the thaw, warm and carefree. "No, just trying to figure out how I ended up with such a charming distraction instead of planning my next move with my family."

"Family?" he asked, tilting his head slightly, his curiosity piqued.

"It's complicated," I replied, my heart heavy again as I recalled my mother's weary smile. "My mom's been having some health issues, and I feel like everything's just... shifting. I'm not sure how to handle it."

He paused, the playful spark in his eyes dimming momentarily as he processed my words. "That sounds really tough," he said softly. "You don't have to go through it alone, you know."

His kindness wrapped around me like a warm blanket, igniting a flicker of hope. But that hope was quickly snuffed out by the realization that I might not have the luxury of time to figure everything out. I wanted to share more, to reveal the tangled web of emotions that twisted through my heart, but fear held me back. Fear of vulnerability, of revealing too much, and perhaps, fear of stepping into a deeper connection with Carter that could ultimately lead to heartache.

The sun began to dip lower in the sky, painting the horizon in hues of gold and amber. It was beautiful, yet tinged with a bittersweet realization that time was fleeting, and our moments together were like the setting sun—radiant, but slipping away.

"Let's sit," Carter suggested, leading me to a bench that overlooked a small pond, where ducks paddled lazily through the water, leaving ripples that danced across the surface. We settled onto the bench, the wood warm from the sun, and I let out a slow breath, attempting to release the tension coiling inside me.

"Tell me more about your art," I prompted, eager to redirect the conversation to something lighter. His enthusiasm was contagious, and I found myself smiling as he animatedly described his latest project—an abstract piece inspired by the feeling of longing.

As he spoke, I watched the way his hands moved, gesturing and illustrating his thoughts in the air, a canvas brought to life by his passion. His voice, rich with emotion, wove a tapestry of dreams and aspirations, and for a while, I let myself be swept away by it, allowing the worries of my own life to fade into the background.

But just as the warmth of connection enveloped us, a sudden gust of wind rustled through the trees, carrying with it the weight of my reality. I could almost hear the ticking of the clock in my mind, reminding me that every moment spent here was a moment I wasn't with my mother, and I struggled to reconcile that internal conflict.

"Carter," I began, hesitating, my heart racing as I prepared to share the truth that gnawed at me. "I really like spending time with you, but I need you to understand something."

He turned to me, his expression serious, the playful banter replaced by genuine concern. "You can tell me anything."

"I'm afraid," I admitted, my voice trembling slightly. "Afraid of getting too close. My family is... complicated, and I don't want to pull you into it."

He reached out, his hand brushing against mine, a gentle anchor in the turbulent sea of my emotions. "You don't have to face everything alone. We all have our struggles. Just because life gets messy doesn't mean you have to shut everyone out."

His words struck a chord deep within me, resonating with the desire to break free from the chains of obligation and fear. For the first time, I allowed myself to contemplate the possibility of balance, of embracing both my family and the chance for love without feeling like I had to choose one over the other.

As we sat there, hands intertwined, the world around us faded into a soft blur, and I felt an exhilarating sense of freedom wash over me. I realized that I could open my heart to Carter while still being present for my family. I didn't have to let go of one to embrace the other. Life was, after all, an intricate dance of intertwined threads, and perhaps it was time to weave a few more into the fabric of my existence.

In that moment, surrounded by the gentle rustle of leaves and the soft quacking of ducks, I felt a renewed sense of hope. The sun continued its descent, casting a golden hue over everything, and as I gazed into Carter's eyes, I understood that maybe love was worth the risk, even amidst the chaos. We could create our own little universe, even if just for a moment, where tangled emotions became beautiful, vivid strokes on the canvas of our lives.

Chapter 7: Draped in Shadows

The soft glow of the vintage chandeliers in my mother's boutique flickered gently overhead, casting dancing shadows that mingled with the scent of lavender and old leather. Each piece of clothing, draped meticulously on antique mannequins, seemed to carry a story. I had grown up in this space, where my mother poured her heart into every garment she designed, and yet, in this moment, it felt heavy with unspoken words. It was the third week since my mother had been hospitalized, and every thread of fabric, every touch of silk, felt suffocatingly tied to the weight of our family's unravelling history.

As I adjusted a beaded dress that shimmered like starlight, I couldn't help but glance at Carter. He stood across the room, organizing the shelves, his brows furrowed in concentration. His tousled hair fell into his eyes, giving him an air of boyish charm that made my heart ache in ways I could barely comprehend. It wasn't just his physical presence that drew me in; it was the way he seemed to occupy the space around him, filling it with a warmth that made the boutique feel like home even when everything else felt chaotic.

"Do you think this color works for the fall collection?" I asked, forcing a nonchalance I didn't quite feel as I draped a deep burgundy scarf over my shoulder.

Carter paused, looking up from the shelf with a mix of admiration and something else—an emotion I couldn't quite place. "It's perfect, but it doesn't need to compete with what you're dealing with right now," he replied, his voice steady, yet filled with an underlying concern that made my stomach twist. I hated how he could read me so well, how he could see through my carefully constructed facade.

I smiled weakly, the corners of my mouth barely lifting. "It's just fabric, Carter. It's what I do." I turned away, folding the scarf back onto the display, not wanting to confront the truth hidden behind my words. This was more than just fabric; it was a distraction, a way to bury the turmoil that churned in my heart like a storm ready to break.

Carter stepped closer, the sound of his footsteps muffled against the plush carpet. "You're not just trying to keep the boutique afloat, are you? You're using it to hide. You can't keep running from this." The softness in his voice contrasted sharply with the piercing truth of his words. "You can't keep running from me."

I swallowed hard, the knot in my throat tightening as the shadows of my parents' marriage loomed in the back of my mind like ominous clouds. Memories of whispered arguments, the tension crackling in the air like static electricity, flashed through my thoughts. Their struggles felt so heavy, weighing down the delicate balance of our family, leaving me feeling like a ghost in my own home. I feared that if I opened up about my feelings, I would shatter the fragile remnants of what I believed love could be.

"Carter, I—" I started, but he held up a hand, interrupting me.

"Just let me in, please," he implored, his eyes searching mine. There was a vulnerability in his gaze that made my heart ache. "I know you're scared, but shutting me out won't help either of us."

His words struck a nerve, igniting a spark of recognition. My heart raced as I realized how much I had been avoiding the truth of my feelings—not just for him, but for the precarious state of my family. I was terrified of repeating their mistakes, of letting love turn into something twisted and burdensome. I had watched my parents navigate a minefield of expectations and disappointments, their love fading into a mere shadow of what it once was. The thought of being consumed by such darkness made me recoil.

"Maybe I need more time," I said, the words tasting bitter on my tongue. "I've seen how love can hurt people. I don't want to be the reason you're unhappy."

"Is that what you think this is? That I'll be unhappy because of you?" he challenged, stepping closer until there was barely a breath between us. "You're not your parents, Claire. You're so much more than the weight of their choices."

His hand brushed against mine, and for a moment, I felt a flicker of warmth—an invitation to lean into the connection we shared. But as quickly as the moment ignited, fear doused the flames. I jerked my hand away, my heart thundering in my chest. "I can't. I can't do this right now."

"Then when?" he pressed, his voice softer now, almost pleading. "When will you let me in? When will you let yourself be happy?"

I looked away, unable to meet his gaze. My heart felt like it was in a vice, squeezing tighter with each moment I avoided the truth. I felt trapped between the desires that surged within me and the fear that threatened to engulf me. There was something inherently beautiful about Carter's faith in me, but it felt like a double-edged sword, pushing me to confront everything I had kept hidden.

"I don't want to hurt you," I finally managed, my voice barely above a whisper. The air between us crackled with unspoken tension, and I could feel the shift in our dynamic, as though we stood on the precipice of something monumental. My fears seemed to wrap around me like a vine, squeezing tighter with each passing second.

"I'm not fragile, Claire. You're not going to break me," he assured me, determination etched across his features. "You just have to trust me. Trust that I won't let you fall."

The sincerity in his voice pulled at my heartstrings, igniting a flicker of hope amid the shadows of doubt. Maybe I didn't have to walk this path alone. Maybe, just maybe, I could allow myself to embrace love without the fear of repeating the past. The thought felt foreign yet tantalizing, like sunlight breaking through the clouds after a relentless storm.

But the memories of my parents' struggles lingered like specters, casting a pall over the warmth of his words. Would I really be able to trust myself? Would I be strong enough to break the cycle, to choose love without fear? The answers danced just out of reach, tantalizing and terrifying all at once.

A soft hum of music filled the boutique, weaving through the air like a comforting embrace. The melody, familiar yet distant, mingled with the clinking of hangers and the rustling of fabric as I meticulously arranged the new arrivals. Each piece was a testament to my mother's artistry, her soul stitched into every seam. Yet, beneath the vibrant colors and intricate patterns lay an undercurrent of tension, a reminder of the storm brewing just beyond the glass doors.

The boutique had become a sanctuary, a refuge where I could immerse myself in creativity and avoid the gnawing worries about my mother's health. The rhythm of my hands sorting through clothes felt almost meditative, allowing me to forget—if only for a moment—the weight of my family's secrets. But even as I lost myself in the task, the shadows of doubt loomed larger, whispering fears that clung to my heart like a persistent fog.

Carter's presence remained a constant source of comfort, though I sensed a shift in the air between us. He had always been my anchor, a steady force that kept me grounded amidst the chaos. But now, with each passing day, I could feel his frustration simmering beneath the surface. He was growing weary of my evasiveness, of the emotional walls I had constructed to shield myself from the pain I refused to confront.

"Claire," he said, breaking the fragile silence that enveloped us, his voice tinged with an urgency that caught me off guard. I looked up to find him leaning against the display case, arms crossed over his chest, a mixture of determination and concern etched across his features. "You can't keep burying yourself in this work. You have to talk about what's happening. You're not going to magically make it go away."

His words hung in the air, heavy with truth. I opened my mouth to protest, but the sincerity in his gaze silenced me. Deep down, I knew he was right. The longer I avoided the conversations that needed to happen, the more they festered like an untreated wound. I had watched my parents dance around their issues for years, their silence a wall that only grew taller with time. Yet here was Carter, urging me to confront the shadows head-on, and for the first time, I felt the stirrings of resolve within me.

"Maybe you're right," I admitted, my voice barely above a whisper. The acknowledgment felt like a fragile thread connecting us, binding my insecurities to the undeniable truth that lay before me. "But what if I can't do it? What if I fall apart?"

"Then we'll put you back together," he said, a hint of a smile breaking through his intensity. "You won't be alone in this."

His words sparked something inside me—an ember of hope flickering beneath the layers of fear. Maybe there was a way forward that didn't involve retreating into the shadows. Maybe I could confront my past without letting it define me.

As the evening sun filtered through the windows, casting golden hues across the boutique, I felt a sudden surge of courage. "Alright," I said, taking a deep breath as I steadied myself. "Let's talk. Not just about my mom, but everything. About my parents, about... everything."

Carter's expression softened, and he stepped closer, closing the distance that had felt insurmountable just moments before. "I'm here, Claire. Whatever you need to say, I'm ready to listen."

I could feel the tension melting away like ice under the sun, and as I began to share my fears, it felt like I was peeling back the layers of my heart for the first time. I spoke of the memories that haunted me—the late-night arguments, the silence that filled the space where love once flourished. I laid bare the insecurities that clung to me, the fears of becoming my mother, of repeating the cycle of heartache and disappointment.

"Sometimes it feels like I'm standing on a precipice, and I can't decide whether to jump or hold back," I confessed, my voice trembling as I fought to keep the tears at bay. "I want to love, but I don't want to drown in it."

Carter listened intently, his eyes never leaving mine. He nodded, understanding illuminating his expression as he absorbed my words. "It's okay to feel that way. Love can be terrifying, especially when you've seen it break before your eyes. But it can also be beautiful—an adventure worth taking."

His belief in the beauty of love felt like a lifeline thrown into my turbulent sea of doubt. I could see the glimmer of possibility in his eyes, a reflection of the hope I had buried so deeply within me. The idea of stepping into the unknown, of embracing love despite the risk, began to feel less like a threat and more like a challenge.

"Tell me what you want, Claire," he urged, his voice low and steady. "What do you want for yourself?"

The question hung in the air, heavy and laden with potential. I took a moment to gather my thoughts, to sift through the chaos of my heart. The truth, raw and unrefined, bubbled to the surface, demanding to be acknowledged. "I want to break free from this fear," I finally admitted, the weight of my confession hanging between us. "I want to love without hesitation, to trust that I can build something real, something lasting."

His smile was slow but genuine, igniting a warmth in my chest that felt foreign yet exhilarating. "Then let's do it together. We'll figure it out, one step at a time."

In that moment, the shadows that had loomed over us began to dissipate, replaced by a growing sense of possibility. The boutique, once a sanctuary of avoidance, transformed into a space of empowerment—a canvas upon which I could paint a future free from the constraints of my past.

As we resumed our work, the atmosphere shifted, filled with the soft cadence of laughter and shared glances. The walls of emotional distance began to crumble, replaced by a newfound intimacy that surged between us. Carter's presence became a source of strength, a reminder that love didn't have to be a burden—it could be a partnership, a journey taken hand in hand.

The sun dipped lower on the horizon, casting elongated shadows that danced across the boutique floor. Outside, the world continued to bustle, oblivious to the small revolution unfolding within the four walls of our little haven. But for me, it felt like the beginning of something profound—a chance to rewrite my story, to embrace love with open arms and a willing heart.

The gentle jingle of the boutique's door announced the arrival of a familiar face, slicing through the thick atmosphere of unresolved tension that had begun to dissipate between Carter and me. I looked up to see Jenna, my childhood friend and the embodiment of sunshine with her golden curls bouncing around her shoulders and an easy smile that could brighten the gloomiest day. She breezed in, her eyes sparkling with mischief as she expertly sidestepped a rack of dresses.

"Look at you two, working hard or hardly working?" she teased, throwing a playful wink our way. "I thought I'd find you buried in fabric swatches, not having a heart-to-heart!"

Carter chuckled, the sound rich and warm, and my heart swelled with a mix of gratitude and relief. Jenna had a unique ability to lift spirits, her laughter like the sweet ringing of chimes in the wind, refreshing and infectious. As she strolled over to me, her presence provided a sense of grounding, a reminder that the outside world continued to spin regardless of my internal struggles.

"Hey, Jenna," I replied, brushing my hands on my apron. "You caught us in the middle of some serious deep thinking."

"Oh, I can see that," she said, arching an eyebrow. "Let me guess: you're debating the existential crisis of fabric? Or perhaps discussing how to cure world hunger with a new line of dresses?"

Her sarcasm was like a breath of fresh air, a stark contrast to the heaviness I had been carrying. I couldn't help but laugh, the sound bubbling forth and chasing away the remnants of my earlier tension. "Something like that," I admitted, exchanging a glance with Carter, who nodded as if to say, "Yes, she's not wrong."

"Good, because I was about to start the 'Jenna Lecture' on how to enjoy life and stop taking things so seriously," she said, hands on her hips, her expression playfully stern. "Let's take a break. How about some ice cream? My treat!"

The idea of stepping away from the boutique, if only for a moment, sounded like a reprieve I didn't know I needed. I glanced at Carter, whose expression softened, the corners of his mouth lifting in a smile that urged me to let go of the weight I had been carrying. "Ice cream sounds perfect," I agreed, a rush of excitement flooding through me.

As we made our way to the nearby ice cream shop, the cool autumn air wrapped around us, the scent of fallen leaves and pumpkin spice wafting through the streets. The sun hung low in the sky, painting everything in a golden hue that felt almost ethereal. The small-town charm of Crestview came alive in the twilight, lights flickering on in shop windows and laughter bubbling up from nearby cafes. Each step felt lighter, as if the burdens of the day were being shed with every stride.

Inside the ice cream shop, the air was thick with sweet, creamy aromas, and I could feel the nostalgic pull of childhood memories flooding back. I scanned the colorful array of flavors, my mouth watering at the sight of cookies and cream, mint chocolate chip, and the seasonal favorite—pumpkin pie swirl. Carter stood beside me, his hand resting casually on the counter, his relaxed demeanor easing my lingering apprehensions.

"What are you thinking?" he asked, tilting his head toward me. I could sense a shift in him, an eagerness to understand not just my choices in ice cream but the deeper layers of who I was beneath the surface.

"I think... I think I'm ready to start really talking about things," I said slowly, as if testing the waters of my own resolve. "Not just with you, but with everyone. I don't want to keep avoiding what's happening. I want to understand my mom's health and the impact it has on all of us, including my parents."

Carter's expression shifted, surprise mingling with pride. "That's a big step, Claire," he said, his voice steady and sincere. "And it's okay to feel nervous about it. Just know that I'll be right here, whatever you decide."

We ordered our ice cream, and as we found a small table by the window, I couldn't shake the feeling that this was a turning point. Jenna animatedly shared her latest adventures at college, recounting the awkward encounters and late-night study sessions, and I found myself laughing along, savoring the sweetness of the moment. But amidst the laughter, the thought of my parents crept back in—what had they gone through in silence, and how had it shaped the family I was trying so desperately to hold together?

"Claire," Jenna said, her voice cutting through my thoughts. "I know things are a bit tense with your mom, but don't forget about your dad, too. He must be going through a lot. Have you talked to him?"

The reminder struck a chord deep within me. My father had been a silent sentinel throughout my mother's illness, his own burdens hidden beneath a stoic exterior. "I haven't really had the chance," I admitted, the weight of guilt resting heavily on my shoulders. "I've been so focused on what's happening with Mom that I didn't stop to think about how Dad is handling it."

Jenna nodded, her expression softening. "Sometimes we get so wrapped up in one person's struggle that we forget how it affects everyone else. You need to reach out to him. Maybe he's waiting for you to make the first move."

Her words resonated like a bell tolling in the distance, echoing the very sentiments that had been buried within me. Maybe it was time to break down the walls of silence that had been built over the years, to have the conversations that needed to be had—not just with Carter, but with my father as well.

After we finished our ice cream, the three of us stepped back outside into the vibrant evening. The streets glowed with the warmth of the setting sun, casting long shadows that danced like whispers of the past. "Let's head back to the boutique," I suggested, a newfound determination swirling within me. "There's a lot more to talk about."

The walk back was filled with a lighter air, laughter spilling from our lips as we exchanged stories. I could feel the currents of change swirling around me, an exhilarating mix of hope and fear. The familiar surroundings of the boutique welcomed us back like an old friend, each fabric and garment a reminder of the legacy I was slowly beginning to confront.

As we settled back into our routine, a sense of clarity washed over me. It was time to embrace the chaos and uncertainty that came with opening up, to peel away the layers of fear that had suffocated me for so long. With Carter by my side, and with Jenna's unwavering support, I felt ready to face the challenges ahead.

I glanced at Carter, who was busy arranging the accessories with meticulous care, and I knew in that moment that I was not alone. Together, we would unravel the threads of our intertwined histories, forging a path that honored the past while embracing the future. As the last light of day faded into twilight, I felt the shadows recede, leaving room for the light of understanding, compassion, and love to take their rightful place.

Chapter 8: Seams of Healing

The air in "Stitch & Thread" buzzed with a creative energy that felt almost tangible, wrapping around me like a soft, comforting blanket. The shop, nestled between a vintage bookstore and a trendy coffee shop on a bustling street in downtown Asheville, overflowed with a colorful array of fabrics—floral cottons, shimmering silks, and textured linens that whispered tales of both tradition and innovation. Sunlight streamed through the tall, paned windows, casting a warm glow on the wooden floorboards that creaked gently underfoot, each sound a reminder of the countless footsteps that had tread here before me.

My fingers danced over the fabric swatches like a pianist coaxing a melody from a beloved grand piano. With each touch, I felt the pulse of the shop, a heartbeat of dreams woven into every stitch. The familiar scent of freshly cut fabric mixed with a hint of lavender from the potpourri my mother insisted on keeping by the register. It was these small comforts that made this place a sanctuary, one that I was determined to modernize while respecting the roots my parents had planted.

Mom sat at her sewing machine in the corner, the rhythmic hum echoing through the shop, a soothing counterpoint to the vibrant chaos around us. After her health scare, I had witnessed the spark slowly rekindling in her eyes as she resumed her role as the heart of our business. Each time I looked at her, stitching together the seams of fabric and memory, I felt an overwhelming sense of gratitude that she was here, that we were here together. Our hands, once divided by years of stubbornness and miscommunication, began to find common ground. The delicate threads of our relationship wove tighter, each shared laugh and moment of understanding a stitch in the fabric of our healing.

I had recently proposed a collection that blended classic patterns with contemporary styles, a mash-up that mirrored my own journey—a tapestry of past influences and future ambitions. Mom had raised her brows in surprise but slowly nodded, her enthusiasm blooming like the bold poppies we had picked out together. Our discussions transformed into brainstorming sessions, filled with laughter and nostalgia as we recalled past collections and the stories behind each piece. I could see her spirit returning, bolstered by the shared excitement of creating something new.

Carter had reentered my life like a breeze stirring leaves in the early morning. The very mention of his name sent a flurry of butterflies to my stomach, each one a reminder of our past—a past laden with unspoken words and missed opportunities. We had been friends once, bound by the shared dreams of our youth, but the complexities of life had frayed our connection. Now, he was a constant presence in the shop, stopping by under the pretense of needing fabric for a project. But I knew better; I could see the way his gaze lingered on me, filled with warmth and an unspoken promise.

Our shared moments were like snippets from a well-worn film reel, familiar yet refreshingly new. I often caught him watching me with a softness that made my heart flutter. The way his fingers brushed against mine as we reached for the same bolt of fabric ignited sparks that crackled in the air, an electric connection that felt both thrilling and terrifying. With every laugh, every playful argument about colors and patterns, I felt the walls I had built around my heart begin to crumble. We discussed ideas for our upcoming showcase, his creativity intertwining with mine, a beautiful choreography of thought and expression.

But as the days passed, I found myself wrestling with a duality—joy intertwined with an undercurrent of anxiety. My father, a man rooted deeply in tradition, remained unconvinced by my ideas. Each suggestion I made felt like an unwelcomed gust of wind rattling the shutters of his carefully constructed world. Our conversations often morphed into debates, his frustration pouring forth like a deluge, clouding the warm glow of our family bond.

I watched him one evening, silhouetted against the fading light of the setting sun, as he stood in the back of the shop, arms crossed tightly over his chest. His brows were furrowed in deep concentration, his lips a thin line. I felt the tension in the air, thick as the fabric draped over the mannequins around us. "This isn't how we do things, Emma," he said, his voice tinged with disappointment, the weight of his words heavy enough to press down on my heart.

The room fell silent, the hum of the sewing machines faded into the background. "Dad, I'm not trying to erase what you've built. I just want to build something new alongside it," I replied, my voice barely above a whisper. His gaze remained locked on the floor, as if the cracks in the wooden boards held all the answers to our conflicting dreams.

In that moment, I realized that my father's fears ran deeper than mere disagreements over fabrics and patterns. He felt threatened, as if my ambitions cast a shadow over his legacy. I understood the weight of that legacy—our family's history stitched into every seam of the shop. But it was mine to carry forward, to infuse with my voice, my vision.

As I turned to leave, my heart ached not only for the frustration between us but also for the love that lay beneath it. I wanted him to see that I wasn't just a rebellious daughter chasing fleeting whims. I was his daughter, with dreams anchored in the very foundation he had laid. I resolved then to navigate the intricacies of our relationship with grace, determined to mend the seams of our bond just as I would mend a frayed piece of fabric—carefully, with intention, and love.

The evening air felt cooler as I stepped outside, the crispness awakening my senses. The bustling street was alive with laughter and chatter, the vibrant pulse of Asheville spilling into my world. I inhaled deeply, allowing the fragrance of fresh pastries from the nearby café to swirl around me. In that moment, I recognized the threads of my life intertwining—the warmth of family, the flicker of a rekindled romance, and the promise of creativity. Each element added color to the canvas I was painting, a tapestry rich with potential, one that was uniquely mine to craft.

Evening light draped itself over Asheville like a cozy quilt, casting long shadows that danced playfully across the cobblestone streets. The chatter of pedestrians mingled with the soft strains of a nearby street musician, the lilting notes of a guitar weaving seamlessly into the fabric of the bustling atmosphere. "Stitch & Thread" was a world unto itself, a sanctuary where the outside noise faded, replaced by the comforting sounds of sewing machines whirring and fabric rustling. I savored these moments of creativity, feeling them wrap around me like a well-worn scarf—familiar, yet filled with the promise of new beginnings.

With each passing day, my role at the shop grew more defined, my vision merging with the rich tapestry of our family legacy. I had laid out my ideas for a new line that married vintage designs with modern aesthetics, an exploration of contrasts that echoed my own journey. My mother's enthusiasm was infectious, her hands moving deftly over fabric, guiding my choices with a gentle wisdom that resonated deep within me.

We worked side by side, the air around us thick with the scent of thread and creativity. I cherished these moments, each shared laugh punctuating the space between us. The rhythmic clatter of our sewing machines became a melody of collaboration, each stitch a note in a symphony that was uniquely ours. Mom would occasionally glance up, her expression filled with a mix of pride and nostalgia, as if she were watching her past fold seamlessly into her present.

Carter continued to be a constant presence, his laughter weaving through the fabric of my day like a bright thread among neutral colors. He had taken to dropping by unannounced, often with a goofy grin and some absurd reason for needing my expertise. Whether it was an ill-fitted shirt he claimed he needed for an upcoming "business meeting" (which was really just a gathering of friends) or an elaborate scheme for a costume party, he managed to charm his way into my heart each time he walked through the door.

One evening, as the sun dipped low, casting a golden hue across the shop, Carter arrived with a bundle of fabric clutched tightly in his hands. "I need your help, Emma. I'm being forced to attend a themed party, and the theme is '90s nostalgia. I can't just show up in jeans and a T-shirt!" His eyes sparkled with mischief as he presented his treasure—a gaudy neon fabric that screamed of eras gone by.

A chuckle escaped me as I took the fabric from him, feeling the synthetic texture beneath my fingertips. "You're absolutely right. Jeans and a T-shirt would be a crime against fashion." I held the fabric up, the bright colors practically glowing in the dim light. "You need a windbreaker, perhaps? Or a pair of those truly awful cargo shorts?"

"Cargo shorts it is!" he declared, throwing his hands up in mock defeat. "If you help me with this, I'll never doubt your fashion sense again."

As we worked together, our playful banter filled the shop, a soundtrack of warmth and camaraderie. The playful teasing melted away any lingering tension between us, and I found myself stealing glances at him, his focused expression framed by the chaotic beauty of the shop. I could see the remnants of our shared history reflected in his eyes, the remnants of a friendship that had once flourished before life's intricacies tangled our paths.

Every so often, our fingers brushed as we reached for the same tools or fabric, each contact igniting a spark that was both thrilling and terrifying. I could feel the unspoken words hanging in the air, thick with possibility. It was a delicate balance, this dance of reconnection; I wanted to leap forward, but the fear of stumbling held me back.

Later that night, as we sat amidst a sea of fabric scraps and thread spools, Carter looked up, a more serious expression replacing his playful demeanor. "You know, I've been thinking about how much you've changed since I first came back to town. It's like you've found your voice again, Emma." His words wrapped around me, both a compliment and a reminder of the shadows I had fought against.

"I'm still figuring things out," I admitted, my voice barely above a whisper. "But I'm learning to embrace it. This place, my family... everything feels different now."

He nodded, his gaze steady and unwavering. "It shows. And I admire that you're taking risks. Not everyone can do that."

I felt my cheeks warm under his scrutiny, the intensity of his gaze both comforting and unnerving. "I couldn't do it without my mom," I confessed. "She's the one who taught me how to sew, how to embrace imperfections. We're in this together now, rediscovering our bond."

Carter leaned back, a thoughtful expression crossing his face. "It's inspiring to see how you're navigating all of this. Your parents have built something special, and you're breathing new life into it. But... what about your dad?"

The question hung in the air, heavy with unspoken fears. I sighed, the weight of my father's disapproval pressing down like a lead blanket. "He's struggling with the changes. I think he feels threatened, like I'm trying to overshadow what he's created."

"Have you talked to him about it?" Carter's voice was gentle, urging me to confront the discomfort.

I hesitated, the thought of that conversation sending a shiver down my spine. "I've tried, but it always seems to end up in a fight.

He just doesn't see my perspective. I want to honor his legacy, but I also want to forge my own path."

As I spoke, I felt the knot of anxiety in my stomach tighten. The shadows of doubt loomed larger, threatening to eclipse the progress I had made. But in that moment, as I sat surrounded by remnants of fabric and laughter, I found solace in the truth that Carter had offered—there was strength in vulnerability, a power in sharing one's struggles.

"I'm here for you, Emma," Carter said, his voice steady, anchoring me in the storm of uncertainty. "Whatever you decide, you're not alone in this."

The warmth of his words wrapped around me, a protective cloak against the fears that had begun to rise again. It was a promise, a gentle reminder that sometimes, amidst the chaos of life, we can find our footing again, one step at a time. The vibrant world of "Stitch & Thread" pulsed around us, filled with the whispers of fabric, laughter, and the delicate threads of healing that bound us all together.

The days at "Stitch & Thread" flowed like the colorful threads we sold, intertwining with moments of laughter, creativity, and the complexities of family dynamics. With each new project, my vision took shape, a vibrant tapestry of modern flair woven through my parents' traditional craftsmanship. I reveled in this newfound freedom, my heart racing with the excitement of possibility.

One afternoon, while experimenting with bold patterns, I glanced up to see my mother smiling softly as she expertly stitched a delicate floral pattern. Her eyes sparkled with a mix of pride and nostalgia, and for a moment, the fabric of time seemed to blur. "You've got quite the eye, Emma," she remarked, her voice warm like the sun filtering through the windows. "This fabric is just screaming to be turned into something beautiful."

Her words wrapped around me like a comforting embrace, reinforcing the bond that had been slowly mended through our shared passion. Together, we began creating a line that not only honored the shop's legacy but also infused it with fresh energy. We chose vibrant colors and unexpected combinations—an elegant navy lace paired with a fiery orange taffeta, or a soft lavender silk juxtaposed against a geometric print. Each piece became a dialogue between us, an exploration of art and emotion that deepened our connection.

As we launched our new collection, I couldn't help but feel a surge of excitement that mirrored the lively pulse of the street outside. We hung our creations in the window, the fabrics catching the light and drawing in passersby like moths to a flame. I relished watching their faces light up with curiosity and delight as they stepped inside the shop, the air thick with the scent of fresh cotton and possibility.

But amid the joy of our creative revival, I felt the looming presence of my father's discontent. His disapproval, like a storm cloud, threatened to overshadow our blossoming relationship. One evening, as we gathered around the dinner table, I sensed the tension creeping in like an unwelcome guest. My mother's laughter echoed around the table, but I could see the flicker of concern in her eyes, a silent plea for peace.

"Emma, you've been spending a lot of time with Carter," my father began, his tone steady but edged with something sharper. "You should focus on the shop and not get distracted by... boys."

I bristled at his words, my fork hovering mid-air. "Dad, Carter is a friend. He's been a huge help with the new line, and honestly, I need his perspective." My voice trembled slightly, a blend of frustration and defensiveness bubbling to the surface.

He shook his head, the lines on his forehead deepening. "I just worry that you're losing sight of what's important. This shop is your heritage, Emma. You can't let your ambitions cloud that."

The table fell silent, the weight of his words hanging like a heavy quilt. I could feel my mother's eyes darting between us, a silent mediator in this delicate dance. I wanted to scream, to unleash the torrent of emotions swirling inside me. Did he not see the passion that fueled my every decision? The desire to breathe new life into our family legacy was not a rejection of it; it was an evolution.

"Dad, I'm not trying to overshadow anything," I said, my voice firmer this time. "I want to honor what you've built, but I also want to create my own place within it. Can't you understand that?"

He opened his mouth, but words failed him. The tension cracked like static electricity in the air, and I felt a mix of anger and sadness boiling within me. Just when I thought we were making progress, his fears resurfaced like a shadow lurking at the edge of my happiness.

Later that night, after the stormy dinner had settled, I found solace in the shop. The soft glow of the lights illuminated the fabrics and patterns that had become a second home to me. I stepped behind the counter and grabbed a bolt of soft, sea-green fabric. Running my fingers over it, I imagined the possibilities it held—the flow of a summer dress, the drape of elegant curtains, each potential project whispering to me like an old friend.

Carter appeared just as I was lost in thought, his silhouette framed by the door. "You okay?" he asked, stepping inside. His presence was a balm for my frayed nerves, a reminder that amid family conflicts, there were still moments of joy to be found.

I managed a half-smile, gesturing for him to join me. "Just the usual. Dad's worried I'm going off the rails with this new direction."

Carter leaned against the counter, his expression thoughtful. "He wants what's best for you, even if it doesn't feel that way." He paused, his eyes searching mine. "But you're finding your voice, Emma. Don't let anyone drown it out."

His words struck a chord, and I felt the tension in my chest begin to loosen. "It's just hard," I admitted. "I want to make him proud, but I also need to be true to myself. It feels like walking a tightrope."

"Maybe you need to find a way to show him that your vision doesn't conflict with his." He crossed his arms, contemplating. "What if you invited him into the process? Show him how your ideas can complement what he's built?"

The suggestion flickered like a candle in the darkness, illuminating a path forward. "You think he'd be open to that?" I asked, a sense of hope threading through my doubts.

Carter shrugged. "It's worth a shot. If he sees how passionate you are, maybe he'll come around."

We spent the next few hours brainstorming ideas on how to bridge that gap. Together, we sketched designs, merging classic styles with modern elements, each stroke a step toward reconciliation. The excitement we felt as we crafted our vision was palpable, each laugh and shared glance further igniting the spark between us.

As the night wore on, I felt lighter, the weight of my father's expectations easing as I focused on what truly mattered. I knew that forging a new path wouldn't be easy, but with Carter by my side, I felt emboldened to take that leap.

The following day, I decided to invite my father to the shop. "Dad, I'd like to show you what I've been working on," I said, my heart pounding as I hoped to find a glimmer of understanding in his eyes.

He hesitated but nodded, curiosity flickering in his gaze. I led him to the back, where we had laid out our newest designs, the fabrics vibrant and alive with potential.

As we stood together among the swatches and sketches, I began to explain my vision, weaving in stories of inspiration and how each piece was a reflection of both our past and future. I watched as his expression shifted from skepticism to intrigue, the lines on his forehead softening as he listened.

"This... this is interesting," he said slowly, his eyes scanning the fabrics. "You're really putting thought into this."

Encouraged, I pressed on. "It's about finding balance, Dad. Your traditional styles and my modern touch—they can coexist, just like we do."

He nodded, his gaze settling on a particularly bold print. "I see what you mean. It's not so much about losing the past as it is about evolving it."

In that moment, as the air filled with the scent of fabric and possibility, I felt the cracks in our relationship begin to mend. The fears that had once stood between us started to dissolve, replaced by a newfound understanding. Perhaps we could both find our voices in this tapestry of life, intertwined yet distinct, each thread vital to the overall design.

As we worked together, the boundaries that had once seemed insurmountable began to blur, and I couldn't help but feel that in this small shop filled with fabric and dreams, we were weaving a future together—one stitch at a time.

Chapter 9: Frayed Connections

The late afternoon sun hung low in the sky, casting a warm golden hue over the community park, where families gathered for the annual Harvest Festival. Laughter mingled with the scent of caramel apples and fresh popcorn, the air thick with the anticipation of a day filled with homemade pies and local crafts. I stood near the entrance, clutching a paper cup of cider, watching as children darted past me, their faces painted with vibrant colors of pumpkins and ghosts. A part of me wanted to join in their innocence, to forget the weight pressing down on my shoulders like an unwelcome visitor.

"Emily!" My father's voice cut through the chatter, sharp and commanding, pulling my focus away from the swirling chaos. I turned to find him striding toward me, his expression a mixture of authority and disappointment. The sight of him, with his tailored blazer and neatly combed hair, reminded me of the expectations he wore like armor. In that moment, I felt the world around us blur, the festival fading into an indistinct hum.

"Have you finalized the arrangements for the winter fundraiser?" he asked, his tone brooking no argument. It was not a question; it was an assertion. I could feel the familiar burn of frustration simmering in my chest, a fire stoked by years of feeling inadequate under his watchful gaze.

"I've been working on it," I replied, forcing a smile that felt more like a grimace. "I thought we could do something different this year. Maybe a silent auction or a holiday gala?" My suggestions hung in the air, fragile and trembling, waiting for his approval.

He scoffed, shaking his head slightly. "That's not how we do things, Emily. Tradition matters. The board expects the same format as last year. Don't fix what isn't broken." His words sliced through the vibrant atmosphere, drawing the attention of those nearby. I felt their gazes, a mixture of pity and curiosity, prickling against my skin.

Hurt swelled within me, rising up like a tide I couldn't hold back. I'd put my heart into planning something new, something that could breathe life into our stale fundraising events. "But what if we want to innovate? What if we want to inspire?" The plea in my voice seemed small, dwarfed by the weight of his authority.

"Emily," he began, his tone more controlled now, a warning wrapped in a veneer of calm. "This isn't just about you. It's about our family legacy, our reputation in this community. You need to understand that." Each word landed like a stone in my chest, each syllable tightening the knot of resentment I had carried for far too long.

"Understand?" I echoed, incredulous. "You mean conform? To live in the shadow of what you think is best?"

The crack in my composure was like a dam breaking, and I could feel my cheeks flush with anger and embarrassment. I turned, ready to flee the judgmental eyes of our community, but he reached out, his hand gripping my arm with a firmness that felt more like a shackle than support.

"Emily, wait—"

I jerked away, a storm of emotions swirling within me. "I can't do this right now." My voice trembled, a precarious mix of rage and sorrow. I stormed away, my heart pounding in my chest as I pushed through the crowd, the noise fading into a muffled roar behind me.

Outside the confines of the festival, I broke into a run, the crisp autumn air filling my lungs as I darted toward the edge of the park. The world around me felt like a kaleidoscope of colors, the leaves rustling like whispers of forgotten dreams. I sought solace beneath the old oak tree that stood sentinel at the park's border, its gnarled branches a testament to resilience. Here, away from the cacophony, I could breathe, but the ache in my heart remained.

"Emily!" Carter's voice broke through the silence, warm and familiar, pulling me from the depths of my spiraling thoughts. He approached, concern etched across his features, his dark hair tousled by the breeze. "What happened?"

"Did you see that?" I blurted, my anger spilling over. "He humiliated me in front of everyone! All I wanted was to bring something fresh to our events, and he acted like I was a child playing dress-up!"

Carter stepped closer, the softness in his gaze calming the storm within me. "I'm sorry. That sounds really tough."

"I just..." I trailed off, fighting against the swell of emotions that threatened to consume me. "I don't want to disappoint him, but I'm so tired of feeling like I'm not good enough. It's like I'm walking a tightrope, always trying to balance his expectations with what I want."

He nodded, understanding flickering in his eyes. "It's okay to want more for yourself, you know? Your vision is worth something, even if he doesn't see it."

A wave of vulnerability washed over me, and I found myself leaning against the tree, its rough bark grounding me. "What if I fail? What if I mess everything up? I can't bear the thought of disappointing my family... again." The confession hung in the air between us, raw and unfiltered.

Carter moved closer, his warmth wrapping around me like a shield against the chill in the air. "You're not going to fail, Emily. You have a vision, and that matters. You have the power to shape your own path, to carve out a space that feels right for you." His voice was steady, unwavering, as he spoke the words I desperately needed to hear.

In that moment, I felt the knot in my chest begin to loosen, the suffocating weight of expectation starting to lift. Maybe I didn't have to live solely in my father's shadow. Maybe there was a way to embrace my truth and still find joy in the journey.

As we stood together, the world around us faded, and I realized that in Carter's eyes, I could see the promise of something beautiful. Something that went beyond expectations and disappointments—a connection woven with the threads of understanding and hope.

The leaves crunched beneath my boots as I wandered away from the festival, the vibrant hues of autumn casting a warm glow that only seemed to deepen my melancholy. Each step away from the laughter and lights felt like a small act of rebellion against the carefully curated life my father had laid out for me. I found solace beneath the sprawling branches of the oak, its leaves whispering secrets of strength and endurance as I leaned against its sturdy trunk. The cool air carried the faint scent of damp earth, grounding me amidst the tempest of my thoughts.

Carter leaned against the tree beside me, his presence a calming balm against my inner turmoil. "What do you really want, Emily?" he asked, his voice low and inviting. The sincerity in his gaze made me pause, forcing me to confront the swirling desires I'd buried under layers of obligation and expectation.

"What do I want?" I echoed, as if tasting the words for the first time. I looked out at the park, where children chased each other in a game of tag, their laughter ringing out like chimes in the gentle breeze. A small part of me longed to join them, to feel the unfiltered joy of youth again. "I want to make a difference, to create something meaningful. But every time I try, it feels like I'm fighting against this wall my father built, brick by brick, with his expectations."

Carter nodded, his eyes unwavering. "Then maybe it's time to start chipping away at that wall. You have to find a way to break through, even if it's just one small crack at a time." His words ignited a flicker of determination within me, a spark that dared to dream beyond the confines of my father's vision.

But as the warmth of hope wrapped around me, the weight of doubt quickly followed. "What if I fail?" I admitted, my voice barely above a whisper. "What if everything I try ends up being a disaster? I've seen how hard my dad works to maintain this business, and I can't bear the thought of letting him down."

Carter stepped closer, his presence enveloping me like a protective shield. "Failure isn't the end, Emily. It's just part of the process. You're not alone in this; you have people who believe in you. You just have to let them help."

As I looked into his eyes, I felt a warmth unfurling in my chest, an undeniable connection that felt both comforting and terrifying. In the midst of my chaos, Carter was a beacon of understanding, encouraging me to step beyond the safe confines of my fears. "You're right," I said, my voice steadier now. "I've been so caught up in my father's expectations that I forgot to listen to my own heart."

Carter grinned, a genuine smile that lit up his face, and for a moment, the shadows of my worries lifted. "There's the Emily I know. You've got fire inside you, and it's time to let it burn bright."

We lingered there, the world around us fading as I felt the tension in my shoulders begin to ease. I had spent so long wrapped in the layers of my family's expectations that I had forgotten what it felt like to simply be. In that moment, standing beneath the sprawling oak tree, I could feel the first tendrils of liberation take root. It was frightening, yet exhilarating.

"Let's make a plan," Carter said, a playful glint in his eyes. "What's the first thing you want to do for the fundraiser? Something bold. Something that screams Emily."

The challenge in his tone sparked my imagination, and suddenly, ideas flowed through me like the rushing river at the edge of town. "What if we organized a themed event? Something that incorporates local artists, music, and maybe even a food truck festival? We could make it a celebration of the community, rather than just another fundraiser."

Carter's eyes widened with excitement, his enthusiasm contagious. "Now we're talking! That could be amazing! We can get people involved, have them share their talents. It could bring the town together in a way that feels fresh and alive."

The vision began to crystallize in my mind, the pieces falling into place like a puzzle I had long neglected. "And we could hold it at the old mill by the river," I added, my voice gaining momentum. "It has that rustic charm, and the view is breathtaking. We could turn it into something magical, something that people will talk about for years to come."

I could see Carter's mind racing, his fingers drumming against the bark of the tree. "I can help you organize it, reach out to local businesses, and get the word out. We can make it a whole weekend event, maybe even include some workshops!"

The excitement coursed through me, fueling a fire I hadn't realized had been extinguished for so long. The thought of doing something my way, of stepping into the light rather than remaining in my father's shadow, felt liberating.

As we plotted and planned, the sun began to dip lower in the sky, painting the horizon in brilliant shades of orange and pink. The laughter from the festival continued to echo, a distant reminder of the world outside our bubble. For the first time in what felt like ages, I could envision a future where I shaped my destiny rather than simply accepting the path laid out for me.

"Thank you, Carter," I said, sincerity woven into every word. "For believing in me. For reminding me that I can be more than just my father's daughter."

He shrugged, a charming smile playing at the corners of his lips. "What are friends for if not to help you find your spark? I've always believed you had it in you; it just needed the right moment to ignite."

As the sun set, casting a warm glow around us, I felt a renewed sense of purpose surging within me. Together, we could bring this idea to life. It was a chance to reclaim my narrative, to create something beautiful from the tangled threads of my past. And for the first time in what felt like an eternity, I dared to believe in the possibility of joy.

As the golden hour melted into twilight, the park transformed into a mosaic of shimmering lights and vibrant colors, the festival carrying on in a lively blur. Yet here, beneath the comforting canopy of the oak tree, I felt cocooned in a sense of purpose I hadn't known I was missing. Carter and I began to brainstorm, each idea sparking like fireworks in the gathering dusk.

"What about local musicians?" I suggested, my excitement growing with each word. "We could feature them throughout the day, and maybe even have a dance floor set up near the river. Imagine it—people swaying under the stars, the sound of laughter mingling with the music. It could turn into a celebration of community, a festival where everyone feels involved."

Carter grinned, his enthusiasm infectious. "And we could invite the farmers' market vendors to set up booths. Fresh produce, handmade goods—the town could rally around it." He paused, his brow furrowing slightly. "But we'll need a way to promote it. Social media, flyers, maybe even a local radio station."

I nodded, the vision expanding like a canvas beneath our brushstrokes. "Yes! We can create a hashtag for it—something catchy that will resonate with everyone. We can engage with the community before the event, make them feel like they're part of the process."

Ideas flowed freely now, our laughter mixing with the sounds of the festival as we crafted our dream into reality. Each suggestion led us deeper into a world where my vision could thrive, a world where I could finally step into the light instead of lurking in the shadows of my father's expectations.

As we sketched our plans, I couldn't help but notice the way Carter leaned closer, his excitement mirroring my own. Each shared glance sparked a thrill that coursed through me, something deeper than mere friendship. Yet, amid the exhilaration, a flutter of fear danced in my stomach. Would he still feel the same once the event was over? Or would this bond, like so many others in my life, unravel under the scrutiny of reality?

"Hey," Carter said, breaking through my spiraling thoughts. "Let's grab some food before we get too carried away. I'm starving."

We walked toward the nearest food stall, the air rich with the aromas of fried dough and spiced pumpkin soup. As we stood in line, the warm glow of string lights overhead made everything feel enchanting. I felt lighter than I had in ages, the burdens of my father's expectations fading into the background.

"Do you remember when we used to sneak out to the old abandoned barn on the edge of town?" he asked, a grin spreading across his face. "You used to be so scared of the ghosts, but you always insisted we go there at night."

A laugh bubbled up from my chest, a sound I hadn't heard in a long time. "I swear I heard the floorboards creak, and I was convinced we'd meet some spectral farmer who'd shoo us away!"

Carter chuckled, the warmth of his laughter wrapping around me like a blanket. "And yet, there we were, both terrified and exhilarated. It felt like our own little adventure, didn't it?"

"Yeah," I replied, my heart swelling at the memory. "Those moments meant everything. It was like we were the only two people in the world, and nothing else mattered."

The words hung between us, heavy with meaning. I wanted to dive deeper into that connection, to explore the edges of what lay unspoken, but the moment slipped away as we reached the front of the line.

After securing our plates of food, we found a small table beneath the twinkling lights. The laughter and music of the festival enveloped us, creating a sense of intimacy amidst the chaos.

"I can't help but think about how far we've come since then," Carter said, his gaze intent on mine. "We've both grown up a lot, but some things haven't changed, have they?"

The weight of his words settled into my chest, resonating with the unspoken truths that lingered in the air. "No, they haven't," I admitted softly, feeling vulnerable yet empowered in his presence.

"Your dreams are still there, waiting for you to chase them. And I want to help you," he continued, his voice steady and earnest. "You deserve to have your vision come to life, to stand up and say, 'This is who I am.'"

I looked at him, gratitude swelling within me. "Thank you, Carter. I've spent so long feeling like I'm not enough, like I have to fit into someone else's mold. But you..." I hesitated, searching for the right words. "You make me feel like I can be more than just an extension of my family."

His gaze softened, and for a moment, I could see the reflection of my own struggles mirrored in his eyes. "You're not alone, Emily. You never were. We all have our battles to fight, but that doesn't mean we have to do it by ourselves."

The sincerity of his words ignited a flicker of hope in my heart, dispelling the shadows that had long loomed over me. As the festival continued around us, I felt a renewed sense of determination surging through my veins. Maybe, just maybe, I could carve out a space for myself—a vibrant world where my ideas could flourish.

After we finished eating, the two of us wandered back toward the festivities, our spirits buoyed by the possibilities that lay ahead. The dance floor was beginning to fill with couples swaying under the soft glow of lights, and the laughter of children echoed through the air, creating a symphony of joy.

Carter caught my eye, a playful smile dancing on his lips. "What do you say we join in? Let's show everyone how it's done!"

I laughed, surprised by the rush of exhilaration that followed. "Dance? Are you sure? I'm not exactly the best dancer."

"Neither am I," he replied with a shrug, the mischief in his eyes infectious. "But that's the beauty of it. We can be terrible together."

With that, he took my hand, leading me toward the makeshift dance floor. The moment our fingers intertwined sent a thrill coursing through me, igniting the flicker of possibility that had blossomed earlier.

As we joined the throng of people, laughter mingling with the music, I felt an exhilarating sense of freedom wash over me. No longer was I just the girl standing in the shadow of her father; I was a part of something bigger, surrounded by the warmth of community and friendship.

With each step, each twirl, I let go of the remnants of doubt that had clouded my mind. The weight of expectation seemed to lift, and in its place, a sense of belonging bloomed. Carter and I danced like nobody was watching, our laughter echoing through the night as we embraced the moment, lost in the magic of connection and newfound hope.

In that swirling sea of lights and music, I understood that I had the power to reshape my destiny. The world was full of color and possibility, and for the first time, I was ready to dive in headfirst.

Chapter 10: Unraveled Threads

The bell above the door jingled as I stepped into "Stitch & Thread," the familiar sound wrapping around me like a well-worn quilt, a reminder of the warmth that this small fabric store had always provided. The scent of freshly cut fabric mingled with the faint hint of lavender from the potpourri my mother insisted on placing near the register. Sunlight streamed through the large front windows, illuminating the colorful chaos of spools, bolts, and swatches that filled the store, casting playful shadows on the hardwood floor. I inhaled deeply, letting the comforting aroma seep into my lungs, but it did little to quell the storm brewing in my chest.

As I arranged a set of floral prints, each one a riot of color and pattern, I could hear my father's booming voice from the back room, punctuated by the soft replies of my mother. Their conversation was muffled but carried an urgency that prickled at the edges of my consciousness. It wasn't unusual for them to argue over the direction of the business; my father's vision was rigid, like the thick canvas he favored for his projects, while my mother preferred a more fluid approach, believing creativity should flow freely, like the delicate silks she adored. I had seen their differing opinions clash too many times, and I had learned to navigate the battlefield with caution, adopting a strategy of silence that often felt more like surrender.

Today, however, the stakes seemed higher. I could hear my mother's voice rise above the other sounds, a melody of worry that twisted in my gut. "Martin, we can't keep doing things the way we always have. The market is changing, and if we don't adapt, we risk losing everything."

Her words settled in my mind, heavy as lead, and I felt a lump form in my throat. I had been so focused on transforming the shop into a reflection of my vision that I hadn't fully grasped the precariousness of our situation. The laughter and creativity I sought to infuse into the space felt trivial compared to the weight of my parents' concerns. What was the point of pouring my heart into this store if it might slip through our fingers like grains of sand?

I busied myself with the fabric swatches, arranging them by hue—blues and greens to evoke the calm of a tranquil lake, vibrant reds and yellows to spark joy and energy. The tactile sensation of the fabric under my fingertips soothed me, yet my mind raced. Would my father ever see the value in my ideas? Or was I merely an intruder in a business that had been his lifeblood for so long?

As I turned to reach for another bolt of fabric, I caught sight of my father's tall silhouette through the doorway. He stood with arms crossed, his expression hard and set. His usual jovial demeanor had been replaced by an unyielding façade, the kind of look that made me feel like I was staring down the barrel of a loaded gun. I steeled myself, ready to confront the unease that crackled between us like static electricity.

"Are we out of the paisley prints?" I asked, trying to keep my tone light, as if the sun-drenched space we occupied hadn't suddenly turned cold.

He grunted in response, not bothering to meet my eyes. "We'll restock next week. We've got bigger problems to deal with right now."

His words landed with the weight of a hammer hitting steel, and I felt a spark of anger flare inside me. "Bigger problems? Like what? The store is doing well! I'm revamping everything. I've got new ideas—"

"New ideas that you don't have the experience to back up!" he snapped, finally turning to face me, his brows knitting together in a storm of frustration. "You want to run this place like a trendy coffee shop, but we sell fabric! People come here for quality, not gimmicks."

His dismissal stung, but I refused to back down. "But isn't it possible to combine quality with creativity? We can attract a younger crowd, bring in fresh energy. You taught me that passion is what makes something great."

His eyes softened for a moment, a fleeting glimpse of the father who had once encouraged my creativity, but it was quickly overshadowed by the steel wall he had constructed. "This isn't about passion; it's about survival."

Before I could respond, the door swung open, and the warmth of the afternoon sun spilled into the store, momentarily banishing the tension. My mother stepped in, her face flushed and breathless. She was the embodiment of vibrant energy, with her curly auburn hair bouncing as she moved.

"Did I miss something?" she asked, her smile faltering as she sensed the charged atmosphere.

"No," my father replied curtly, turning back toward the back room, the shadows reclaiming his features.

I watched him go, disappointment flooding my senses. My mother caught my eye and gave me a reassuring smile, but it felt hollow. The weight of unspoken words settled between us, a bridge we both knew needed to be crossed but were hesitant to traverse.

"I overheard a bit of your conversation," I confessed, my voice barely above a whisper. "Are we really in that much trouble?"

Her eyes softened, filled with a mixture of concern and love that made my heart ache. "We're just feeling the pressure, sweetie. The market is changing, and we have to adapt to survive. Your father is worried."

I nodded, the realization hitting me hard. We were standing on a precipice, the ground beneath us shifting, and I was terrified of the fall. "I want to help. I really do. But I need him to listen."

"Then we need to show him that your ideas matter," she encouraged, her voice steady as if she had already been formulating a plan in her mind. "Let's work together, find a way to bring your vision to life. If we can show him the potential in your ideas, he might just see the light."

The fire within me reignited, a flicker of hope amid the uncertainty. I could feel the threads of my family's legacy tangling around me, pulling me into a tapestry of loyalty and love. It wouldn't be easy, but as long as we were together, I was determined to mend the fabric of our family before it unraveled completely.

The afternoon sunlight streamed through the shop windows, illuminating the array of colors that lined the walls like a vibrant quilt. As I stood behind the counter, inhaling the familiar scent of cotton and linen, I felt a renewed sense of purpose swell within me. My mother was already sketching plans for the upcoming community craft fair, her pencil moving swiftly across the paper, the tip leaving behind trails of creativity that mirrored the excitement bubbling inside me.

"What if we set up a little corner dedicated to handmade items?" I suggested, leaning over to get a glimpse of her drawing. "We could feature local artisans and maybe host some workshops. It would draw people in and keep them coming back!"

Her eyes lit up, a spark of enthusiasm igniting the air around us. "That's a brilliant idea! We could teach sewing classes or even DIY sessions for kids. Imagine the smiles on their faces when they create something from scratch."

The excitement was infectious, and I could feel the creative juices flowing, pushing aside the weight of my father's earlier dismissal. Together, we began to brainstorm, our voices intertwining as we layered one idea upon another. It felt as though we were weaving the very fabric of our dreams into something tangible, something that could breathe life back into "Stitch & Thread."

But just as the momentum built, the front door swung open with a jingle, and in walked my father, his brow furrowed and his posture stiff. The warmth that had enveloped the room seemed to evaporate, leaving behind a cold draft of uncertainty. I could see the tension in his jaw, the way his fists clenched at his sides as he took in the sight of us. It was as if he were a storm cloud, threatening rain on our parade.

"What's all this?" he asked, his tone more curious than angry, though the edge was still there. "What are you two plotting now?"

I took a deep breath, fighting the instinct to retreat. "We're brainstorming ideas for the craft fair! I think we could attract a bigger crowd by showcasing local talent and offering classes."

He shifted his weight, his gaze flicking between my mother and me. "Classes? We've always focused on selling quality fabric, not teaching people how to sew. We don't have the time or resources for that."

The disappointment washed over me like a cold wave. "But, Dad, isn't it worth trying? The world is changing, and so are our customers. We can't just stick to the same formula. We need to evolve."

He stared at me, and in that moment, I felt as though I was standing at the edge of a cliff, daring to leap while he remained anchored to the ground. "I appreciate your passion, but this isn't a hobby; it's our livelihood. We can't afford to take risks right now."

The weight of his words hung in the air, suffocating the hope I had tried to cultivate. My mother shot me a sympathetic glance, and I could sense her desire to defend my ideas, but she hesitated. This wasn't just about me; it was about the delicate balance of our family dynamics, and I knew she was trying to navigate that tightrope carefully.

"Martin," she interjected, her voice soft yet firm, "what if we view this as an opportunity rather than a risk? It could attract new customers and boost sales. We've always said we want to build a community here."

For a moment, it felt as though the air crackled with possibility, the tension in my father's shoulders easing ever so slightly. But then the storm returned, his expression hardening once more. "Community is all well and good, but we can't pay the bills with goodwill. We need to focus on what sells."

I felt the bitterness rising in my throat, a mix of frustration and disappointment. "And what if what sells isn't enough anymore? What if it all falls apart because we refuse to adapt?"

He opened his mouth to respond, but the sound of the bell above the door interrupted us as a group of customers filed in, laughter spilling over like a burst dam. I quickly shifted my attention to them, my heart racing as I plastered on a smile, trying to mask the turmoil beneath the surface.

The group, mostly women, fawned over the new fabric collection, their chatter filling the space with a lightness that was almost palpable. I immersed myself in their excitement, guiding them toward the swatches and offering suggestions based on their preferences. Each time I caught a glimpse of my father watching from the corner of my eye, I felt a pang of resentment, the distance between us feeling insurmountable.

As the day progressed, I threw myself into my work, organizing fabrics, rearranging displays, and helping customers. Each moment spent in the shop was a distraction from the growing chasm between my father and me. But as the sun began to set, painting the walls with hues of orange and pink, that distraction faded. I caught sight of my father deep in conversation with one of our loyal customers, and the sight stirred something in me.

He was passionate when discussing fabric choices and project ideas, his face lighting up in a way I rarely saw outside of those walls. It was a reminder of the man I had always admired, the father who had taught me the beauty of creativity, the magic woven into every stitch. The image conflicted with the stern figure he had been lately, and I felt a glimmer of hope flicker within me.

"Maybe he just needs to see the potential in my ideas," I murmured to myself as I wrapped up the day, determination settling in my bones like a warm embrace. "I can bridge this gap. I can remind him why we started this journey together."

That evening, as the shop closed and the streets of our quaint town grew quieter, I gathered my courage and approached my father in the workshop. The air was thick with the smell of sawdust and fabric, and the walls seemed to hum with the echoes of our family's history.

"Dad, can we talk?" I asked, my voice steady despite the fluttering in my stomach.

He looked up from his workbench, surprise flickering across his features before he nodded. "Sure. What's on your mind?"

I took a breath, summoning the courage that had eluded me throughout the day. "I know you're worried about the business, and I understand where you're coming from. But I really believe that embracing change could breathe new life into 'Stitch & Thread.' I want us to succeed together, as a family."

His gaze softened, just for a moment, and I seized that opportunity. "Let's brainstorm together. I want to hear your thoughts, too. What do you envision for our shop moving forward? I want us to collaborate, not just argue over different visions."

For the first time in what felt like ages, I saw a flicker of the man who had encouraged my creativity, the father who believed in possibility. And in that moment, as I shared my dreams and ideas with him, I felt the threads of our family beginning to weave together once more, strong and resilient against the storms that threatened to pull us apart.

The moment stretched between us, suspended like the vibrant fabrics that hung in the shop, each one a potential masterpiece waiting for hands skilled enough to craft it into something beautiful. My father studied me, a myriad of emotions flickering across his features. I could sense the walls he had built around himself beginning to crack, the cold exterior yielding ever so slightly to the warmth of familial connection.

"I know you care about this place," I continued, the words tumbling out in a rush, each syllable infused with my hope for the future. "But we can't keep doing things the same way forever. Change is scary, but it's also necessary. Let's find a way to blend your experience with my ideas. We can make this shop a community hub—something that brings people together."

He ran a hand through his salt-and-pepper hair, a gesture that I had come to recognize as a sign of his inner turmoil. "You really think people want to come here for classes? To learn how to sew or craft?"

"I do," I insisted, my voice firm yet gentle. "This town has a wealth of talent waiting to be tapped. If we can harness that, we could create something special. Besides, people crave connection. They want to feel like they're part of something bigger."

A beat of silence hung in the air, thick with unspoken thoughts. I could feel the uncertainty radiating off him, a palpable tension that echoed the very fabric of our lives. Finally, he nodded, albeit hesitantly. "Alright, let's hear your plan. But I'm not promising anything."

That small concession felt like a victory, igniting a fire within me. I launched into a whirlwind of ideas, painting a picture of what "Stitch & Thread" could become—a vibrant space bursting with life, creativity, and community spirit. I envisioned workshops filled with laughter and the sound of scissors snipping through fabric, children's eyes lighting up as they crafted their first projects, and adults bonding over shared interests.

As I spoke, I noticed my father's expression shifting. The rigid lines of concern began to soften, the shadows in his eyes lifting, and I felt as though I was breaking through the fog that had enveloped our family. I brought up the craft fair again, suggesting we set up a booth not just to sell our fabrics, but also to promote our classes and showcase local artisans. My mother chimed in, supporting my ideas, and together, we crafted a plan that felt tangible, alive.

As the evening wore on, the initial tension gave way to a tentative excitement. We sketched out our ideas on scrap paper, our conversation punctuated by bursts of laughter and the occasional glance at my father's proud smile. It was the first time in a long while that I felt a genuine connection with him, a moment that hinted at healing. The sense of camaraderie filled the space, wrapping around us like a comforting embrace.

That night, as I prepared for bed, my mind raced with possibilities. I could already envision the vibrant banners we would hang, the colors of the fabric dancing in the sunlight as we welcomed customers in. Each workshop I dreamed up felt like a thread weaving into the fabric of our lives, binding us together in a tapestry of shared experiences and memories. I was no longer just a daughter in a family business; I was a partner, an architect of our future.

But as dawn broke the next day, a sense of reality crept in, accompanied by the weight of expectations. The potential for success felt intoxicating, yet the fear of failure loomed larger. I found myself grappling with doubts as I arranged the store that morning, the sunlight illuminating every nook and cranny. Was it foolish to believe that our small-town fabric shop could transform into something grand? Would our loyal customers embrace this new vision, or would they cling to the familiarity of what had always been?

My thoughts were interrupted by the chime of the doorbell as a familiar face stepped inside. Clara, a long-time customer and local quilter, greeted me with her warm smile. "Good morning! I've been looking forward to coming by today. I hope you have something special for me to work with."

I returned her smile, grateful for the opportunity to share my excitement. "Actually, Clara, we have some new ideas brewing for the shop that I think you'll love!"

As I guided her through the aisles, showing her the latest fabrics and chatting about my vision for upcoming classes, I felt a swell of pride. Clara's eyes sparkled with interest, and she eagerly shared her thoughts, her enthusiasm contagious. It was moments like these that reminded me of why I loved this place—why I had fought so hard to carve out a space for creativity and community.

"Are you going to teach classes?" Clara asked, her voice brimming with excitement. "I'd love to come! I always wanted to learn how to quilt but never had the time."

"Yes! We're hoping to host workshops, and I'd love for you to join us. It's all about sharing the love of crafting and connecting with others in the community," I replied, the joy in my voice palpable.

As Clara thumbed through the fabric swatches, a light bulb went off in my head. "What if we host a quilting bee? We could gather locals, share stories, and create something beautiful together. I can already picture the quilts hanging in the shop, showcasing our community's talent!"

Her eyes widened in delight. "That sounds like a wonderful idea! I know a few people who would love to participate. You'll have to let me know when it happens!"

Just as Clara and I were deep in conversation, my father appeared from the back, his demeanor unexpectedly relaxed. "I'm glad to see the shop buzzing with excitement. Clara, would you be interested in helping us organize the quilting bee?"

Her face lit up, and she nodded enthusiastically. "Absolutely! I have some ideas already."

Watching them collaborate filled me with a sense of purpose, a warmth that enveloped the room like a soft blanket. As they exchanged ideas, I stepped back, absorbing the moment. My father was beginning to embrace change, and with each passing interaction, the shop morphed into something greater than just a business—it became a hub for creativity and connection.

Over the next few weeks, we poured our hearts into transforming "Stitch & Thread." My mother and I filled the store with vibrant displays, while my father began to take a more active role, participating in brainstorming sessions and bringing his invaluable experience to the table. We reached out to local artisans, inviting them to showcase their work and join our workshops, and the response was overwhelming. The sense of community grew stronger with each passing day, and I felt a renewed sense of hope.

Then came the day of the craft fair. The sun shone brightly, casting a golden glow over the town square, and as I set up our booth, I felt a mixture of nerves and excitement bubbling inside me. The atmosphere was alive with laughter, the scent of fresh-baked goods wafting through the air, and vibrant colors surrounded us, each one a reminder of the beauty that lay in creativity.

As people began to flock to our booth, I shared stories of our journey and the vision we had for the shop. Clara, along with a few other familiar faces, joined in, sharing their own excitement about the quilting bee. The connection between us all felt electric, a tapestry of shared experiences unfolding right before my eyes.

The day unfolded in a whirlwind of joy, and as I stood behind our booth, I couldn't help but smile. This was what I had hoped for—a community coming together, each person contributing a unique thread to the fabric of our lives. And as I caught my father's eye from across the bustling square, a smile broke across his face, one that spoke volumes about the journey we had embarked upon together.

"Stitch & Thread" was no longer just a shop; it was a sanctuary, a vibrant space that mirrored the love and creativity woven into our family's legacy. I felt a profound sense of gratitude as I watched my father mingle with customers, sharing laughter and ideas, his earlier reservations now seemingly a distant memory.

Together, we had unraveled the threads of doubt and fear, weaving them into something beautiful—a community united in creativity, laughter, and love. And as the sun began to set, casting a warm glow over the day's events, I knew that this was only the beginning of a much larger story, one where every stitch mattered, and every person played a vital role in the tapestry of our lives.

Chapter 11: Patterns of Regret

The sun hung low over Montgomery Springs, casting a warm, golden hue across the quaint town. I could almost feel the heartbeat of the place in the rustle of the leaves and the gentle hum of chatter wafting from the local café. This town had always been a patchwork of memories, with its cobblestone streets and charming boutiques, each one steeped in its own history. Yet today, there was a different kind of energy coursing through me, a thrill that seemed to dance just beneath the surface as I set my sights on a new horizon. My mind buzzed with vibrant fabrics and daring designs, each stitch a heartbeat of my aspirations. I had decided to host a fashion show, not merely to display our collection but to breathe life into my vision for the boutique—an ambitious fusion of tradition and modern flair.

Mia, my best friend and the fiery soul behind our marketing strategy, burst into the studio, her laughter ringing like a bell. She was a whirlwind of color and charisma, her hair a cascade of dark curls, always bouncing with the rhythm of her thoughts. "We're going to make this happen," she declared, her enthusiasm infectious. I could almost see the sparkles of her dreams glimmering in her eyes, igniting a fervor within me that I hadn't fully acknowledged until now. Carter, my steadfast partner and a master at turning my sketches into reality, nodded in agreement, his calm demeanor a comforting anchor amid the chaos brewing in my mind.

We spent the following weeks entrenched in a whirlwind of creativity. The boutique transformed into a hive of activity, swathed in bolts of fabric that spilled like vibrant waterfalls across the floor. Each piece was meticulously crafted, reflecting not just our talent but our collective spirit. The air was thick with the scent of fresh cotton and the sweet tang of creativity, a heady mixture that drove us onward. As I draped the fabric on the mannequin, I imagined the audience's gasps as they witnessed our collection—a tapestry of colors and textures that whispered tales of both heritage and innovation.

Yet, as excitement grew, so did the weight of responsibility. I couldn't shake the lingering anxiety that hung in the air, particularly when it came to my father. He had poured his soul into the boutique, a legacy built on the foundation of tradition and family. His skepticism loomed like a shadow, a silent but palpable presence that threatened to stifle my ambition. While Mia and Carter believed in the new direction, my father's gruff exterior often seemed impermeable, his fears a fortress that I struggled to breach.

One rainy afternoon, as the droplets tapped against the studio windows like a persistent chorus, I summoned the courage to confront him. The atmosphere was thick with unspoken words, and as we stood among the spools of thread and sketches strewn about, I felt the tension crackle between us. "Dad, I need you to understand," I began, my voice steady despite the storm brewing in my chest. "This fashion show isn't about abandoning our roots; it's about celebrating them while also evolving. We can't just stand still."

He crossed his arms, his brow furrowed as he leaned against the wall, an immovable wall of tradition. "You think this is easy for me? You think I want to see the business I built change into something unrecognizable? The world isn't what it used to be; I've seen trends come and go, but our values—those are what keep us alive." His voice was low, almost a growl, but beneath it, I could detect the underlying passion, the sacrifices he had made over the years, the late nights and early mornings, the countless decisions that weighed heavily on his shoulders.

In that moment, I saw him not just as my father but as a man molded by years of struggle, his dreams etched into the very fabric of Montgomery Springs. I stepped closer, my heart aching with the weight of understanding. "I know you've worked hard to protect what we have, but don't you see? We can blend tradition with innovation. The world is changing, and we need to change with it. We can honor our past while embracing our future." My voice trembled slightly, the truth of my words hanging between us like a fragile thread.

He looked at me, and for a fleeting second, I thought I caught a glimpse of something vulnerable in his eyes. It was the fear of change, the anxiety of losing what he held dear, but also a flicker of hope, the possibility that I could carry forward the legacy he had built. "You think it's that simple?" he replied, his tone softening. "This isn't just a business to me; it's family. Every piece we sell, every design we create carries a part of who we are."

I felt my own resolve harden, a fierce determination rising within me. "And that's why this fashion show is so important. It's not just my vision; it's ours. I want to honor what you've built while paving the way for what's next." I took a breath, letting the moment stretch, allowing the gravity of my words to settle in the space between us.

As the rain continued to patter against the windows, I could see the walls around my father's heart begin to crack, the rigidity of his stance slowly giving way. "Maybe... maybe there's room for both," he finally murmured, a hesitant smile creeping across his lips. "But you better be ready to fight for it, because this is a test of your resolve."

I nodded, a wave of relief washing over me. This was more than just a fashion show; it was a crossroads, a chance to merge the patterns of our past with the threads of our future. With renewed vigor, I returned to the fabric, each piece resonating with the echoes of our conversation—a testament to our shared dreams. Montgomery Springs, with its picturesque streets and vibrant community, was ready to witness the birth of something extraordinary. The stage was set, and I felt the pulse of possibility surge through me, igniting my passion and determination to prove that tradition and innovation could indeed coexist, hand in hand, as we stepped boldly into the unknown.

The days leading up to the fashion show unfolded like a tapestry, each moment woven with anticipation and a dash of trepidation. The studio had transformed into a vibrant workshop, brimming with the energy of creativity. Swathes of fabric in every imaginable hue cascaded from shelves, a kaleidoscope of inspiration that invited my imagination to run wild. Mia was our cheerleader, darting between piles of fabric, draping swaths over mannequins like an artist splashing paint on a canvas. Her laughter bubbled up like a sparkling brook, infusing our days with a lightness that often masked the weight of the stakes we were gambling.

Carter, ever the pragmatist, balanced Mia's exuberance with his grounded perspective. He meticulously cut patterns, his fingers moving with a practiced precision that made every snip of the scissors sound like a promise. "Remember, this isn't just about the clothes," he would remind us, pausing to let the weight of his words settle. "It's about the story we tell. Each piece has to resonate, to echo our vision." His focus was an anchor, a reminder that while the fabric shimmered under the studio lights, it was the emotion behind it that would truly capture our audience.

As I immersed myself in the creative whirlwind, I found solace in the act of designing. Each stitch I sewed felt like a declaration, a statement of my identity woven into the fabric of our collection. I envisioned the show as not just an exhibition but a celebration—a merging of past and future, a vibrant dialogue between the roots that grounded us and the branches that reached for the sky. The thought of the audience gasping at our designs filled me with exhilaration, igniting a fire deep within.

Yet, as the show date drew near, I could feel a growing tension simmering beneath the surface. My father's skepticism loomed large, an invisible weight pressing down on me as I worked. The boutique represented not just a business to him but a lifeline—a family legacy that had weathered storms, both metaphorical and literal. I often caught him watching me from the doorway of the studio, his arms crossed, his brow furrowed as if he were trying to decipher a puzzle he couldn't quite solve.

The day before the show, I knew I had to address this tension head-on. The air was thick with the scent of freshly cut fabric, and the soft hum of sewing machines surrounded me, but my thoughts were elsewhere. I found him in the back room, poring over old invoices and receipts, a familiar frown etched deep into his features. "Dad," I said, my voice steady despite the anxiety thrumming in my chest, "can we talk?"

He glanced up, his expression a mix of curiosity and apprehension. "What's on your mind?"

"I want to understand what you're afraid of," I pressed, stepping closer. "Is it the show, or is it something more?"

His gaze shifted to the window, where the evening light filtered through the glass, casting golden patterns on the floor. "It's not just the show, Jess," he finally admitted, his voice low. "It's what it represents. This boutique has always been about community, about knowing our customers by name and creating pieces that resonate with their lives. I fear that if we start chasing trends, we might lose sight of that."

His words hung heavy in the air, a testament to the values he held dear. I had always known my father was fiercely protective of the boutique, but hearing him articulate his fears struck a chord deep within me. I thought of the countless hours he had spent at the shop, the way he knew the regulars by heart, the stories woven into the very fabric of our business. "I get it, Dad. But innovation doesn't mean we have to forget our roots. We can honor them while also embracing new ideas."

He sighed, his shoulders slumping slightly. "Change is a double-edged sword, Jess. I've seen too many businesses falter because they strayed too far from what made them special in the first place. I just don't want to see you hurt."

In that moment, I realized the depths of his love masked by his gruff exterior. He was afraid of losing me, of watching me chase a dream that could slip away from us both. I stepped closer, taking a breath to steady my racing heart. "I promise, I won't let that happen. This is my passion, and I want to share it with you, not distance myself from it."

The silence that followed was heavy with understanding, the walls between us beginning to crumble. Finally, he nodded, the tension in his shoulders easing. "Alright, let's see what you've got. Just promise me you won't lose sight of the people who matter."

His willingness to listen ignited a flicker of hope within me, and I felt a renewed sense of purpose as I returned to the studio. The atmosphere buzzed with creativity, a heady mix of excitement and nervous energy. As Mia and Carter finished the final touches on the garments, I could feel the heartbeat of the boutique pulsing around me—a blend of tradition and innovation that was finally taking shape.

The night before the show, we gathered for a final rehearsal, each piece hanging on the mannequins like silent sentinels awaiting their moment in the spotlight. The lights dimmed, and Mia took center stage, her voice ringing out with infectious enthusiasm as she described our vision to the small group of friends and family gathered. Carter stood behind her, adjusting the lighting to create the perfect ambiance.

My heart raced as I envisioned the audience's reactions, the blend of awe and admiration that would sweep through them as we unveiled our collection. Each model would walk not just as a representation of our designs but as an embodiment of our collective story. I could almost hear the applause, feel the rush of adrenaline as the fabric swirled around them, a symphony of color and texture in motion.

As the evening stretched into the early hours of dawn, we worked tirelessly, laughter punctuating our efforts as we shared stories and dreams. I could see the nervous excitement mirrored in Mia's eyes and the quiet determination in Carter's movements. Together, we were not just preparing for a show; we were embarking on a journey that would define us, blending our individual passions into a vibrant mosaic.

With every stitch and every laugh, I felt the weight of my father's fears transform into something lighter—a shared understanding that rooted us deeper in our commitment to each other and to our community. This was our moment to shine, to weave together the patterns of our past with the vibrant threads of our future, and I was ready to embrace it all. The echoes of our conversations reverberated in my heart, igniting a fire that would carry us forward as we prepared to unveil our dreams to the world.

The day of the fashion show dawned bright and clear, the sky stretching above Montgomery Springs like a perfect canvas, unmarred by clouds. The sunlight streamed through the windows of the boutique, illuminating the carefully arranged collection that now filled the space with a vibrant energy. Each piece seemed to breathe, alive with the hopes and dreams stitched into their very seams. As I stood in the middle of the studio, I felt a mix of exhilaration and anxiety dance in my stomach—a wild tango of emotions that seemed to echo the vibrant hues of our collection.

Mia buzzed around like a bumblebee, her excitement palpable as she checked off lists, ensuring every detail was accounted for. "We're ready to make history, Jess!" she exclaimed, her eyes sparkling with mischief. I couldn't help but smile at her enthusiasm, the weight of the world lightened by her infectious spirit. She had poured her heart into promoting this show, crafting social media posts that captured the essence of our designs and drawing attention from far beyond our little town.

Carter, the ever-reliable cornerstone of our team, was busy adjusting the lighting in the makeshift runway that we had set up in the boutique. He had transformed the space into something out of a dream—a sea of flowing fabric, softly lit with strategically placed spotlights that bathed the garments in ethereal glow. "You ready for this?" he asked, his brow slightly furrowed in concentration as he tinkered with the settings.

"Ready as I'll ever be," I replied, attempting to inject confidence into my voice even as my heart raced. I caught a glimpse of my reflection in the polished mirrors lining the walls—hair pinned up haphazardly, a few strands rebelliously escaping, and my fingers stained with traces of fabric dye. Yet there was a spark in my eyes that felt undeniable, a glimmer of resolve that surged with each passing moment.

As guests began to trickle in, I felt a wave of anticipation wash over me. Friends and family filled the seats, their laughter and chatter creating a backdrop that added to the electric atmosphere. Among them sat my father, his expression a careful mask of neutrality, but I could see the glint of concern lurking beneath the surface. I caught his gaze, and he offered a small nod, a silent encouragement that fortified my resolve.

With the lights dimmed, Mia took center stage, her voice cutting through the air like a bell. She introduced the show with flair, her enthusiasm resonating with the crowd. "Welcome to a night of celebration! Tonight, you'll witness not just fashion but a story—a fusion of tradition and innovation that embodies the heart of Montgomery Springs!" The audience erupted into applause, and I felt a rush of adrenaline course through my veins. This was it. This was the moment I had been waiting for, the culmination of our dreams and hard work.

As the first model stepped onto the runway, my breath caught in my throat. The dress she wore flowed like water, each movement a dance that breathed life into the fabric. The vibrant colors mirrored the essence of our community, inspired by the sunsets over the local lake and the flowers blooming in every backyard. I watched as the audience leaned forward, captivated by the elegance that unfurled before them, a testament to the love and effort we had poured into our designs.

One by one, the models glided down the runway, showcasing the collection that was not only a visual delight but an emotional tapestry woven from the threads of our past. Each piece told a story—the flapper-inspired dress that whispered tales of bygone eras, the contemporary silhouettes that boldly challenged norms. I felt my heart swell with pride as applause echoed through the boutique, each clap a validation of our vision, a celebration of our journey.

Amidst the whirlwind of excitement, I caught a glimpse of my father in the audience, his demeanor shifting from skepticism to admiration. His eyes were fixed on the models, an imperceptible smile breaking through his usual stoic expression. In that moment, I understood that this show was more than just a display of clothing; it was a bridge, a connection between generations, a way to honor what had come before while paving the way for what was to come.

As the final model took her turn on the runway, showcasing the pièce de résistance of our collection—a breathtaking gown adorned with delicate embroidery that echoed the traditions of our boutique—the audience erupted into a standing ovation. The sound washed over me like a warm wave, enveloping me in the knowledge that we had achieved something extraordinary. I turned to Mia and Carter, tears of joy pooling in my eyes. "We did it!" I exclaimed, laughter spilling from my lips as the reality of our success began to sink in.

The show concluded, but the night was far from over. Guests mingled, the air filled with animated conversations and the clinking of glasses. I navigated through the crowd, grateful for the opportunity to connect with those who had come to support us. Each hug, each congratulatory remark reinforced the bonds of our community, the very fabric that had nurtured my dreams.

As the evening progressed, I found myself standing beside my father, a newfound understanding stretching between us. "You did good, Jess," he said, his voice gruff but warm. The sincerity in his words washed over me, a balm to the anxieties that had plagued me. I could feel the weight of his fears lifting, replaced by a cautious optimism that spoke of acceptance and hope.

"Thank you, Dad," I replied, my heart swelling with emotion. "This is just the beginning. We can do this together—honoring our roots while reaching for the stars."

He nodded slowly, his gaze reflecting a mixture of pride and contemplation. "Just remember, it's about more than just the designs. It's about the people who wear them and the stories we create together."

The evening drew to a close, and as we began to pack up, I felt a sense of fulfillment wash over me. The boutique, once a place of uncertainty, had transformed into a vibrant sanctuary of dreams and aspirations. I glanced around at my friends, my father, and the community that had supported us every step of the way.

In that moment, I realized that the fashion show was not merely a singular event; it was the beginning of a beautiful narrative that wove together the past and the future. The boutique was no longer just a business—it was a legacy, a living testament to the dreams we dared to chase. And as I stepped into the light of a new dawn, I knew that together, we would continue to write our story, one stitch at a time, embracing the patterns of both regret and triumph that defined our journey.

Chapter 12: A Stitch in Time

The gymnasium buzzes with a vibrant energy that crackles like static electricity. Banners hang from the rafters, each emblazoned with the name of my boutique, "Stitched Dreams," while the polished wooden floor reflects the eager faces of family and friends, all gathered for this pivotal moment in my life. I stand backstage, flanked by racks of dresses that shimmer under the bright lights, the fabrics a kaleidoscope of colors that mirror the emotions swirling within me. Each piece tells a story, a thread woven from the fibers of my hopes, fears, and aspirations.

As the first model steps onto the makeshift runway, a hush falls over the crowd, punctuated only by the swish of fabric and the soft click of heels on wood. I hold my breath, watching her strut with an effortless grace that makes my heart swell. She wears the very first design I created, a gown inspired by late summer evenings spent at the lake with my childhood friends, the golden hues reminiscent of the sun dipping below the horizon. I can almost hear the echoes of laughter, the splash of water, and the sweet scent of pine trees mingling with the salty tang of the air. I've captured that magic in the delicate layers of tulle and satin draping elegantly around her form, a reminder of simpler days.

Applause erupts as she makes her way back, and I bask in the sound, allowing it to wash over me like a warm breeze. But the moment is fleeting, and as the next model takes her turn, I glance towards the front row where my father sits. His face is a mask of stoicism, eyebrows knit together in a frown that tightens my chest. There's a world of expectations written in the lines of his face, a map of the dreams he carved for me long before I was even aware of my own desires. I can feel the weight of his disapproval draping over my shoulders like an ill-fitting coat, suffocating and heavy.

As the show progresses, I watch model after model showcase looks that embody the heartbeat of our community. Each outfit reflects the spirit of those who wear them—vibrant, resilient, and unapologetically unique. There's something cathartic about seeing my creations come to life, the colorful fabric twirling and flowing, like petals dancing in the wind. Yet, with each passing moment, my father's gaze feels like a reminder of the path I might have been expected to follow—a corporate job, a stable life—rather than the dream I've chosen to chase.

And then it strikes me. This show isn't just about the clothes; it's about unity, about family, about embracing the diverse threads that stitch us together. In that moment of clarity, inspiration bursts within me like a firework illuminating a dark sky. I need to make my closing look something that transcends the runway, a statement that speaks to the heart of who we are as a family, despite our differences.

I hurriedly wave over my assistant, Jenna, who's been a whirlwind of enthusiasm and support throughout this journey. Her bright blue hair matches the spark in her eye as she nods eagerly at my request. I adjust my plan, knowing that the final look needs to embody the essence of reconciliation and love—something that would resonate with everyone, especially my father.

As the final model preps backstage, I rush to the mirror, touching the fabric of the last ensemble I've prepared. It's a fusion of styles, a dress that incorporates elements from each of my previous designs, harmonizing them into one stunning piece. The bodice glimmers with delicate beadwork, a tribute to the craftsmanship passed down through generations. The skirt flows like water, layering different textures—soft cotton from my grandmother's apron, silk from my first prom dress, and the deep blue fabric I saved from my mother's old sewing box.

When the moment arrives, and my model steps onto the runway in my closing look, the audience is silent. I watch as she glides, her confidence radiating from her like a lighthouse guiding ships to shore. With every step, the layers of fabric swirl around her, weaving a tapestry of my family's history and my aspirations for the future. I can almost feel my heart beating in sync with the pulse of the crowd, the air thick with anticipation.

As she reaches the end of the runway, I'm compelled to join her, stepping out into the spotlight, my breath hitching in my throat. I clasp my hands together, feeling the warmth of the moment envelop me. This isn't just a showcase; it's a testament to who we are as a family, our struggles, and the love that binds us together despite the rifts.

The applause begins softly but swells into a cacophony of approval, a wave crashing over me, lifting me to new heights. I lock eyes with my father, and for the first time, I see a flicker of something other than disappointment—a glimmer of understanding perhaps? I step forward, heart racing, and address the audience, my voice trembling with emotion. "This collection is for all of us—our journeys, our stories. Each piece symbolizes our individuality, but more importantly, it reflects the unity we can find within our differences."

As I look at my father, I realize that the true essence of this moment isn't the applause or the beautiful designs but the connection to those I love. I hope he can see that I'm carving out my own path, one that might diverge from his dreams but still honors the love and support he has always given me.

With that thought blooming in my mind, I know that no matter the challenges ahead, I will navigate them with love as my compass. As the last model turns and the final notes of music drift into silence, I take a deep breath, ready to embrace whatever comes next with open arms.

The echo of applause still resonates in my ears, a comforting rhythm amidst the swirling emotions that envelop me. As the final model strides off the runway, I step back, heart racing, breathing in the scent of fresh flowers and polished wood mingling in the air. The gymnasium, once a space for gym classes and pep rallies, has transformed into a vibrant celebration of creativity and resilience. Strands of soft fairy lights crisscross the ceiling, twinkling like stars against the backdrop of the late afternoon sun streaming through high windows. It feels magical, and for a fleeting moment, I allow myself to bask in the success of the event.

Yet, the warmth of accomplishment is soon chased away by the chill of uncertainty. I scan the faces in the audience, searching for a familiar one that suddenly feels so distant. My father's expression weighs heavily on my heart, each flicker of disapproval tightening the knot of anxiety that has settled deep within me. I've spent countless hours pouring my soul into this collection, yet the echoes of his expectations cling to me like a shadow. I take a deep breath, steeling myself against the torrent of doubt that threatens to overwhelm me.

"Great show, huh?" Jenna's voice cuts through my reverie, her enthusiasm as palpable as the energy in the room. Her bright smile shines with an infectious zeal that momentarily lifts my spirits. I turn to her, trying to mirror her excitement, but I can feel the remnants of apprehension still swirling in my chest.

"Yeah, it was amazing," I reply, forcing the corners of my lips to curl upward, though my heart feels heavy.

Jenna claps her hands together, her blue hair swaying like a banner in the wind. "You did it! You really brought your vision to life! Everyone loved it!" Her exuberance is genuine, and I appreciate it, yet my mind drifts back to my father, still seated in the front row, his face unreadable.

"I just wish my dad felt the same way," I admit, my voice barely a whisper, as if speaking the words out loud might make the reality sting less.

Jenna's smile falters for a brief moment, a flicker of understanding crossing her features. "You can't let his expectations define you. This was your moment. You deserve to celebrate it."

Her words resonate within me, a gentle reminder that my journey is mine alone. I glance around the gym, the laughter and chatter of friends and family filling the space, and I feel a glimmer of hope breaking through the fog of doubt. I find solace in the joy of those who have supported me, who have cheered me on even when I struggled to believe in myself.

As the crowd begins to disperse, the excitement lingers like the scent of fresh cotton candy. I spot my mom making her way toward me, her eyes sparkling with pride. She embraces me tightly, enveloping me in warmth that chases away the shadows lingering in my mind. "You were incredible, sweetheart! I've never been more proud!"

"Thanks, Mom." I lean into her hug, letting the warmth of her affection wash over me. It's moments like these that remind me of the love that grounds me, even when the world around me feels chaotic.

As we pull apart, I catch sight of my father again. He's standing now, his arms crossed tightly over his chest as he watches the crowd mingle. The smile on my mother's face dims slightly as she catches my gaze, and I can feel the tension that simmers beneath the surface.

"I think I need to talk to him," I say, the words tumbling out before I can overthink them. My heart thuds heavily in my chest, the thought of confronting him both exhilarating and terrifying.

"Are you sure?" my mother asks, her brow furrowing with concern. "You know how he can be."

"I know," I reply, determination threading through my voice. "But I have to try."

With a deep breath, I move through the crowd, weaving between tables adorned with flowers and fabric swatches, each step closer to my father sending my heart racing. As I approach, the laughter and chatter fade, leaving only the sound of my pulse in my ears. His expression doesn't change, the same lines of disappointment etched into his face, but I refuse to let it deter me.

"Dad," I begin, my voice steadier than I feel. "Can we talk?"

He glances at me, his lips pressed into a thin line. "I'm busy."

But something shifts in his posture, a flicker of hesitation as I take another step closer. "Please. I just want to explain."

He hesitates, and the air thickens with tension, a taut string ready to snap. "Fine," he finally relents, gesturing for me to follow him to a quieter corner of the gym.

The distant sounds of celebration fade into a muted hum as we stand beneath the high arches of the gymnasium, a space filled with memories both good and bad. The lights cast long shadows that dance around us, amplifying the silence that stretches uncomfortably between us.

"I don't understand," he begins, his voice low and gruff, a mixture of frustration and concern. "You could have chosen a stable career. Something respectable."

"Dad, this is what I want," I reply, desperation creeping into my voice. "Fashion isn't just a dream for me. It's a part of who I am."

He shakes his head, the movement filled with disappointment. "You're throwing away your future on a whim. You could end up with nothing."

"No," I insist, feeling the heat rise within me. "This isn't just a whim. I've poured my heart into this. Every stitch, every fabric choice, it all represents me—my journey."

For a moment, silence hangs between us, heavy and charged. I search his eyes for any sign of understanding, any hint that he sees the passion that drives me.

"You need to understand that life is about stability and security," he says finally, his voice steady but weary. "This industry is cutthroat. You could fail."

I take a deep breath, the words I've rehearsed in my mind spilling out in a rush. "But what if I don't fail? What if I succeed? Isn't it worth taking a risk for something I love?"

His gaze softens just slightly, and I seize the moment. "I'm not asking for your approval, but I need you to see me for who I am—not just as your daughter, but as a person with dreams and ambitions."

For the first time, I see a flicker of something in his eyes—perhaps recognition, perhaps regret. The silence stretches, and I feel the weight of his expectations begin to shift, if only a little.

"I want you to be happy," he finally says, his voice softer now, the edge of frustration dulled. "I just... worry about you."

I step closer, the chasm between us narrowing. "Then support me. This is who I am, and I need you to believe in me."

As I speak, I feel the air between us begin to change, the tension easing as understanding seeps in. My heart races with hope, and in that moment, I realize that maybe, just maybe, I can bridge the gap that has grown between us. The journey ahead is uncertain, but I'm ready to face it with courage and love, fueled by the belief that my dreams can coexist with my family's expectations.

The air between us simmers with unspoken words, a fragile bridge constructed from shared memories and dreams. I watch my father's expression shift, his stern demeanor softening as my words hang in the air like tendrils of smoke, lingering long after they've been spoken. It's as if, for a fleeting moment, we exist in a space untouched by the noise of expectations, and I can almost hear the faint rustle of hope stirring between us.

He glances away, his gaze drifting over the remnants of the fashion show—the scattered flowers, the empty chairs still holding the warmth of those who once filled them. I can see him thinking, weighing my aspirations against the carefully crafted vision he has for my life, a vision rooted in the values he holds dear. It's a battle of love and fear, of dreams and realities. I take a step closer, emboldened by the vulnerability of the moment, hoping to break through the barriers he has built around himself.

"Dad," I say softly, "I don't want to let fear dictate my choices. I want to explore what this world has to offer, even if it's risky. Isn't that what life is about?"

He swallows hard, his eyes glistening under the fluorescent lights. "You think it's easy to watch you chase something uncertain? I've spent my life building stability, and I just want the same for you."

"Stability doesn't always mean happiness," I counter gently, searching for the right words to express the tempest of emotions roiling within me. "It can become a cage, and I refuse to be trapped in one just because it's safe."

In the silence that follows, I feel as though I'm standing at the edge of a precipice, peering into the vast unknown of our relationship. Will he leap with me, or will he retreat to the comfort of his familiar ground? My heart beats a frantic rhythm as I await his response, desperate to bridge the chasm that has grown between us.

After what feels like an eternity, he nods slowly, the lines of his face relaxing just a bit. "You're right," he concedes, his voice barely above a whisper. "But I still worry. I can't help it. It's my job to protect you."

"Protecting me doesn't mean smothering my dreams," I reply, my voice gaining strength. "I need your support, not your judgment."

For a brief moment, the weight of the world lifts from my shoulders as I see him process my words, his brow furrowing in thought. "I suppose it's time I learned to trust you more."

"Exactly," I say, relief flooding through me. "I'm still your daughter, and I'm still learning. But I need the freedom to find my way."

A smile breaks through his usual stoicism, a tentative connection forming in the air between us. The flicker of pride ignites something deep within me, a spark of possibility that flickers like a candle in the dark.

"I never doubted your talent," he admits, his voice gaining confidence. "I just wanted to protect you from the harsh realities of this world."

"And I appreciate that, Dad," I say, my heart swelling with gratitude. "But I also want to face those realities head-on. This is who I am. I hope you can accept that."

As we stand in this makeshift oasis of understanding, I feel a shift—a subtle but significant change that ripples through our relationship like the gentle waves of a calm lake. The fear that once loomed over me dissipates, replaced by the steady current of hope.

The sounds of celebration swell around us as family and friends gather to offer their congratulations, and I feel the buoyancy of excitement in the air. I know that the road ahead will be filled with its fair share of challenges, but for the first time, I feel a sense of unity with my father. Together, we're crafting a new path, one that honors our individual journeys while keeping the family bond intact.

As we step away from our heartfelt exchange, the world around me bursts back to life, the joy of the evening washing over us like a gentle tide. Friends envelop me in hugs, their laughter echoing through the gymnasium as they praise the show's success. Each word feels like a balm, soothing the frayed edges of my spirit and fortifying my resolve.

Among the familiar faces, Jenna bounds over, her energy infectious as she drags me towards a group of friends gathered by the refreshment table. "You're a star, you know that?" she beams, her eyes twinkling with admiration.

"It was a team effort," I say, humility brushing my cheeks with warmth. "I couldn't have done it without you."

"Oh, please! You were the heart of this show! Now come on, let's celebrate!"

I allow myself to be swept into the festivities, the rhythm of music and laughter weaving a tapestry of joy that envelops everyone. As I move through the crowd, I take in the smiles and chatter, the joy palpable in the air, igniting a sense of purpose deep within me.

Every face tells a story—a tapestry of struggles and triumphs, of dreams woven together like the threads of fabric that had graced the runway just moments ago. I look around, soaking in the beauty of this moment, the realization settling in that I am surrounded by those who have nurtured and believed in me when self-doubt threatened to overwhelm my spirit.

Jenna pulls me into the circle of friends, each voice rising in celebration as we toast to the success of the show, laughter bubbling like champagne. I feel a rush of gratitude, knowing that I'm not alone on this journey. Each person here has played a part in shaping my path, and together, we are forging ahead into uncharted territory.

As the evening progresses, the lights dim, casting a soft glow over the gymnasium, creating a cozy, intimate atmosphere. I find myself leaning against the refreshment table, watching as my friends dance and sway, their laughter filling the space with warmth. It's a kaleidoscope of joy, and I allow myself to get lost in the moment.

In the midst of this celebration, a figure catches my eye—a silhouette standing near the entrance, watching. My heart skips a beat as I recognize my father, his expression softened in the low light. For the first time, he seems at peace, a hint of a smile tugging at the corners of his mouth as he takes in the scene before him.

I know in that moment that we are both on a journey, one that will be filled with lessons, challenges, and growth. He is learning to let go, and I am learning to stand tall, grounded in my passion and my dreams.

With a renewed sense of purpose, I weave my way through the crowd, drawn towards him. The energy of the celebration flows around us, but in this moment, we exist in our own bubble, an unspoken understanding binding us together. I can feel the shift in our relationship, a bond strengthened by shared vulnerability and newfound acceptance.

As I approach, he meets my gaze, and I see pride shining in his eyes, a silent acknowledgment that he believes in me. The tension that once lingered between us begins to dissolve, replaced by a burgeoning hope for our future—a future where I am free to embrace my dreams while still carrying the love and support of my family with me.

Together, we step into the light, ready to face whatever challenges lie ahead, hand in hand, united by love and the beautiful tapestry of our lives. In this moment, everything feels possible, and I know that with every stitch I create, I'm weaving our stories together into something extraordinary.

Chapter 13: Torn Between Two Worlds

The spotlight faded, but the electric buzz of excitement still crackled in the air as I stepped off the stage, a whirlwind of emotions swirling within me. The local press was buzzing, their cameras flashing like fireflies in the twilight. People I'd grown up with, friends and neighbors, crowded around to share their enthusiasm, their faces alight with admiration. Each compliment felt like a feather-light touch, lifting me higher into the realm of possibilities I had always dreamed of, where the fabric of my ambitions intertwined seamlessly with the threads of reality. Yet, as the applause echoed in my ears, I felt an unsettling emptiness beneath the surface, a hollow echo that called me back to the foundation upon which this success was built: my father.

The moment I stepped into our boutique, the scent of fresh fabric and polished wood enveloped me, a familiar cocoon that usually brought comfort. Instead, it felt stifling, a heavy blanket woven with unspoken words. My father stood behind the counter, his brow furrowed as he arranged a colorful display of scarves with meticulous care. Each movement he made seemed deliberate, as though he were crafting not just a display but a shield against the world. I took a breath, steeling myself for the confrontation I knew awaited me.

"Dad," I began, my voice tentative. He looked up, and for a moment, the flicker of recognition crossed his face. But it was quickly replaced by a mask of neutrality, as though he were guarding his thoughts behind a fortified wall.

"What do you want, sweetheart?" he replied, his tone clipped, the warmth usually present now buried under layers of frustration.

I hesitated, searching for the right words, the ones that could bridge the gap growing wider between us. "Can we talk about the show? I know it was a little... unexpected."

"A little unexpected?" He chuckled, but there was no humor in his eyes. "It was a spectacle, Emily. A flashy display that took control out of my hands." His words were sharp, each one a dagger that pierced through the veneer of my happiness.

I felt my cheeks flush with embarrassment, a rush of heat that coiled in my stomach. "I thought you'd be proud. People loved it. It was innovative! It—"

"It was all about you," he interrupted, his voice rising. "What about the vision I've spent years building? It's like you've come in and taken over." His eyes, usually warm and inviting, now bore the storm clouds of disappointment.

I flinched, the sting of his accusation leaving a mark deeper than I'd anticipated. It was the first time I truly recognized the vulnerability beneath my father's hardened exterior. He had spent decades pouring his heart into this boutique, crafting a legacy brick by brick, and here I was, eager to leap into the spotlight without asking for his input.

"I didn't mean to undermine you," I murmured, my voice softer now, tinged with regret. "I thought we could modernize things together, bring in new ideas while still honoring what you've built."

He turned away, fingers trembling slightly as he adjusted the scarves, his back a fortress of rejection. I stepped closer, my heart pounding in the silence that stretched between us. I could feel the weight of our unspoken history pressing down on us like an anchor, and it dawned on me that our paths had diverged while I was busy dreaming.

"I want to be successful, Dad," I confessed, desperation creeping into my voice. "But I want to do it with you, not without you. You're my foundation. This is our dream, isn't it?"

At last, he turned to me, eyes wide and brimming with a mixture of surprise and a flicker of hope. "I've been scared, Emily. Scared that I'm not enough anymore."

His admission hung in the air, a fragile truth that sent a ripple of empathy through me. I approached him cautiously, crossing the invisible line that had separated us. "You're more than enough. You taught me everything I know about this business. I'm just trying to take it further, to honor what you've created."

He sighed deeply, a long exhale that released some of the tension coiling around us. "Maybe I've been too rigid," he admitted, rubbing the back of his neck as though trying to ease the knots formed by years of worry. "But I just... I don't want to lose what we've built together. This boutique has been my life's work."

"I get that," I said, my heart swelling with a mixture of pride and understanding. "I don't want to lose it either. Let's find a way to blend our ideas, to create something new without forgetting our roots."

Slowly, the corners of his mouth twitched upwards, a flicker of a smile breaking through the cloud of frustration. We began to sketch out a plan together, a new direction for the boutique that incorporated both of our visions. I could see the hope rekindling in his eyes, igniting a fire that had dimmed during our earlier confrontation.

With each suggestion we exchanged, the air felt lighter, as if the burdens we had carried were gradually lifting. The boutique became our shared canvas, a place where our dreams could intertwine, creating a masterpiece woven from threads of tradition and innovation. We brainstormed ideas for new lines that respected the timeless elegance of our existing inventory while daring to explore uncharted territories—bold patterns, sustainable fabrics, and styles that echoed the heartbeat of our ever-evolving world.

As we filled the shop with laughter and the scent of fresh ideas, I realized that our relationship was more than just a bond between father and daughter; it was a partnership, a collaboration that demanded not only trust but also vulnerability. We were crafting not just a business plan but also a bridge to connect our worlds—a blend of the wisdom of the past and the ambition of the future.

The warmth that enveloped us felt like a fresh breeze blowing through the boutique, rejuvenating our spirits. It was a reminder that together, we could navigate the stormy seas of uncertainty, forging a path that honored our shared history while embracing the possibilities that lay ahead.

As the days unfurled in the wake of our heart-to-heart, the boutique transformed into a vibrant hub of creativity. The walls, once mere canvases for our wares, began to breathe with the energy of collaboration. Each morning, I would step into the shop, greeted by the familiar scent of polished wood and fresh fabric, but now it felt charged with promise. My father had opened up, allowing his initial hesitation to evolve into a willingness to experiment. Our discussions morphed into brainstorming sessions filled with laughter, debates, and occasionally, playful disagreements.

One afternoon, as the sun streamed through the shop's large windows, casting golden light on the fabric swatches scattered across the counter, I proposed a pop-up event that would spotlight our new direction. The idea was to combine local artistry with our boutique's charm, showcasing not just our clothing but also handmade accessories crafted by artists in the community. I could almost see the cogs turning in my father's mind as he mulled it over, his brow furrowing with a mixture of excitement and trepidation.

"Are you sure we can pull it off?" he asked, his voice tinged with skepticism.

I laughed lightly, brushing a stray hair behind my ear. "Dad, if we can handle that show, we can handle anything. Plus, think about it. It's a way to bring people together, to remind them of the personal touch in fashion."

He nodded slowly, a spark of agreement lighting up his eyes. "You're right. The community could use something uplifting, especially after the whirlwind of the last few months."

As the plans began to take shape, I felt a surge of energy coursing through me. We crafted a vision for the event, from colorful flyers that would grace local coffee shops to a social media campaign that would draw in crowds. The boutique was no longer just a business; it was becoming a sanctuary for creativity, a space where people could gather, share stories, and perhaps even discover a piece of themselves through fashion.

The day of the pop-up event arrived, draping the town in a festive atmosphere that could be felt in the very air. Our boutique radiated warmth, its window displays a kaleidoscope of color, each garment telling a story waiting to be unraveled. The community buzzed with excitement, and as I stood in front of the boutique, my heart raced in tandem with the laughter and chatter of people filtering in and out.

My father was there, too, his hands busy arranging last-minute details while wearing an apron splattered with paint and glitter. His expression transformed throughout the day, evolving from cautious skepticism to visible pride as he watched our vision come to life. It was as if the boutique itself had shed its skin, revealing a vibrant soul that was an extension of both of us.

The atmosphere thickened with the mingling scents of artisanal coffee and freshly baked pastries as local vendors set up their stalls. I could see my friends mingling with customers, their laughter weaving through the air like a thread of joy. It felt surreal to witness our community come together, sharing not only the space but also their artistry and passion.

I spotted Sophie, my best friend since childhood, gliding over with her usual enthusiasm. "Emily! This is incredible!" she exclaimed, her eyes sparkling with excitement. "I can't believe how many people are here!"

I grinned, the adrenaline of the event making me feel invincible. "I know, right? It's all coming together!"

"Have you seen the new pieces we put out?" she asked, her voice conspiratorial. "I've already claimed a few for myself. I mean, you can't blame me; they're gorgeous!"

"Of course, you're a walking billboard for our brand," I teased, nudging her playfully.

As the day wore on, I took a moment to step outside, breathing in the crisp autumn air. The leaves crunched beneath my feet, a delightful reminder that change was all around us, echoing the transformation happening within our boutique. I looked back at the bustling shop, a kaleidoscope of faces—some familiar, others new, all drawn together by the common thread of community spirit.

That's when I spotted him—Ethan. He was leaning against the boutique's brick wall, his posture relaxed yet attentive, his eyes scanning the crowd. My heart fluttered at the sight of him, a welcome distraction amidst the chaos. He approached with that casual grace that always seemed to leave me breathless.

"Hey," he said, a warm smile breaking across his face. "I came to see what all the fuss was about."

I felt a flush creeping up my cheeks as I gestured to the boutique. "Just a little community gathering. Nothing too extravagant."

"Nothing too extravagant?" he chuckled, nodding toward the vibrant display behind me. "This is amazing, Em. I can't believe how many people showed up."

His praise felt like sunshine, warm and uplifting. "Thanks! It's been a lot of work, but seeing everyone here makes it worth it."

As we talked, a comfortable rhythm emerged between us, a dance of words that felt both familiar and exciting. I shared snippets about our plans, my father's involvement, and the reactions of the attendees, while Ethan listened, genuinely intrigued.

"I'm glad you're finding your footing," he said, his gaze steady and sincere. "You deserve this success. You've always had the drive."

His words wrapped around me, a gentle embrace that ignited a flutter of hope within. Just as I was about to respond, my father stepped out, wiping his hands on a cloth, and beamed at Ethan, a twinkle of appreciation lighting up his eyes.

"Ah, Ethan! You made it!" he exclaimed, the warmth of his tone surprising me.

"Hey, Mr. Reynolds," Ethan replied, shaking my father's hand. "This place looks fantastic. You've both done an incredible job."

My heart swelled as I witnessed the genuine connection blossoming between them. Ethan's presence seemed to bridge the gap that had lingered between my father and me, a testament to the power of community and support.

As the sun began to set, casting an amber glow over the boutique, I realized how deeply intertwined our lives had become. This was more than just a pop-up event; it was a celebration of our journey, a testament to the strength of our bond as a family and a community. The night air was filled with laughter, music, and the promise of new beginnings, weaving a tapestry of memories that would forever define this chapter of our lives.

The evening unfolded like a beautifully orchestrated symphony, each note resonating with the mingled scents of sandalwood and sweet pastries wafting through the boutique. As the sun dipped below the horizon, casting hues of lavender and peach across the sky, the atmosphere became electric. Customers, wrapped in a blend of curiosity and excitement, roamed through the displays, their laughter punctuating the gentle hum of music that filled the space. The pop-up event had transcended mere commerce; it had morphed into a celebration of creativity and community, a tapestry woven from the threads of our shared passions.

In this charged environment, I could see my father moving with a newfound vigor, his hands deftly arranging items on display while engaging with customers as if they were old friends. The hesitance that had once clouded his demeanor had lifted, revealing a man who had not only invested years in this business but had also forged connections that rippled through the community. His eyes sparkled as he recounted the stories behind each piece, from the vintage jackets that whispered tales of the past to the handcrafted jewelry that shimmered like starlight.

I mingled among the crowd, feeling the warmth of their appreciation enveloping me. Sophie had snagged a spot near the front, energetically promoting our latest pieces and drawing in a curious group of locals. I watched her with pride, knowing that our friendship had always been a source of strength, a reminder that I was never alone in this journey. She had a way of making people feel seen, her enthusiasm infectious.

As the night wore on, the laughter mingled with the soft notes of a live acoustic performance drifting in from the corner of the boutique. The musician, a local with a voice like honey, sang songs that resonated with the hearts of those gathered. I found myself drawn to the sound, captivated by the way music seemed to wrap around us, infusing the air with warmth and nostalgia. It was in this moment, amidst the laughter and melodies, that I realized how profoundly interconnected our lives had become, each thread contributing to the vibrant fabric of our community.

Then, as if summoned by an invisible thread, Ethan appeared at my side. He leaned casually against the wall, a faint smile gracing his lips as he absorbed the lively atmosphere. "You know, you're quite the magnet for good vibes," he said, his tone teasing yet genuine.

I laughed, my heart racing slightly at his presence. "I think it's the combination of good music and even better company," I quipped, tilting my head playfully.

His gaze flicked toward the stage where the musician continued to strum his guitar, the notes dancing like fireflies in the night. "Well, you've certainly brought the town together. It's not every day that I see this many people smiling."

"Just wait until the fashion show next week," I replied, my excitement bubbling over. "It's going to be even bigger. You should totally come."

"I wouldn't miss it," he promised, his eyes glinting with sincerity. There was something comforting about being in his presence, a kind of effortless understanding that seemed to flow between us.

Just then, my father approached, his expression a blend of pride and excitement. "Ethan! Glad you could make it," he said, clapping a hand on his shoulder. "Emily's done a fantastic job organizing everything."

Ethan nodded, his admiration for my father evident. "It's impressive to see the community rally around your work. I think you've struck a chord with them."

As they chatted, I stepped back slightly, allowing their conversation to blossom. It was fascinating to witness my father engaging so freely, sharing not just his expertise but also his heart. In this moment, it became clear that our partnership was becoming more than just a father-daughter dynamic; it was evolving into a true collaboration, with mutual respect and admiration.

As the evening continued, the atmosphere thickened with the mingling of voices and laughter, and I felt a sense of fulfillment wash over me. Each connection forged in the boutique that night was a reminder of the profound impact of community—a force that could lift us higher than any solitary ambition.

Then, as if drawn by the unspoken energy in the room, I spotted a familiar face. It was Mrs. Henderson, an elderly woman who had been a regular at the boutique for as long as I could remember. Her silver hair shimmered like moonlight, and her kind smile lit up her face. She approached me with an air of warmth, her eyes twinkling with wisdom.

"Emily, my dear," she said, her voice as soft as a whisper. "I just wanted to say how proud I am of you. This place has always felt like home, but tonight, it feels alive."

I felt a rush of gratitude. "Thank you, Mrs. Henderson. That means so much coming from you. I hope you're enjoying everything?"

"Oh, absolutely! I've picked out a few things already," she replied, holding up a lovely scarf adorned with delicate patterns. "You've got such an eye for beauty, dear. Your mother would be proud."

Her words struck a chord deep within me. It was the first time someone had mentioned my mother since the event had begun. The memory of her laughter echoed in my mind, a bittersweet reminder of the past. I swallowed hard, the ache in my chest sharpening, but I pushed it aside, focusing on the present and the connections being forged around me.

"Thank you, Mrs. Henderson," I said, my voice steady. "I'm trying to carry on her legacy."

Her eyes softened, filled with a mix of understanding and compassion. "You are, my dear. You're weaving something beautiful here, something that honors both your father and your mother."

As she wandered off, I returned my gaze to the room. It was alive with the vibrant energy of creativity, the embodiment of dreams manifesting before our eyes. The boutique had become a sanctuary for connection, a testament to the power of community and shared passion.

As the night wore on, laughter and chatter intermingled with the music, creating a symphony that resonated in my heart. I joined in conversations, weaving my way through familiar faces and newcomers alike, each interaction reinforcing the sense of belonging that wrapped around me like a warm blanket.

The evening climaxed when I took to the makeshift stage to thank everyone for their support. Standing before the crowd, I felt a blend of nervousness and exhilaration, my heart pounding in rhythm with the pulsing energy of the room. "Thank you all for being here tonight. This is more than just a pop-up event; it's a celebration of who we are as a community. Together, we're creating something beautiful, a space where we can all share our stories."

Applause erupted, filling the boutique with a palpable sense of unity. In that moment, I realized that the boutique was more than just a business; it was a living, breathing entity, a reflection of our shared aspirations.

As I stepped down from the stage, my father's eyes met mine, a silent affirmation passing between us. We were in this together, a team fueled by the love for our craft and the community we served.

In that bustling, laughter-filled boutique, I understood that I was not just carving out my path; I was honoring the roots from which I had grown. The journey ahead would be filled with challenges, but I was ready to face them, knowing that I had the strength of my father's support and the love of our community behind me. With each passing moment, I felt a renewed sense of purpose, a determination to nurture the dreams we had built together.

Chapter 14: The Fabric of Dreams

The soft chime of the bell above the door signaled Carter's arrival, a sweet sound that always made me feel like the day had suddenly brightened. The warm sunlight poured through the large windows of "Stitch & Thread," illuminating the vibrant fabrics hanging from the ceiling like colorful banners heralding the new life we were infusing into the old shop. I was busy arranging a display of handmade scarves—each piece a labor of love, crafted with intricate patterns that danced under the golden light—when he entered, and my heart skipped a beat.

Carter was just as I remembered: tall and slightly tousled, his dark hair framing a face that was somehow both rugged and soft. Today, he wore a charcoal gray shirt that hugged his broad shoulders, giving a glimpse of the artist hidden beneath his casual demeanor. It was in those moments, when he smiled and the corners of his mouth lifted slightly, that I could see the layers beneath. The laughter in his hazel eyes sparked a warmth within me, one that felt like coming home after a long journey.

"Hey there, ready to turn this place into a fashion-forward charity extravaganza?" he asked, his tone teasing yet warm.

I chuckled, trying to suppress the flutter in my stomach. "If by 'fashion-forward,' you mean making sure nothing falls off the racks and into a heap on the floor, then yes, absolutely." I motioned for him to come closer, and we began sorting through the myriad of ideas we had brainstormed.

As we sat together on the floor, surrounded by rolls of fabric, I felt the familiar comfort of our friendship wrap around us like a well-worn quilt. We tossed ideas back and forth—Carter would suggest a theme inspired by the colors of the sunset, and I would counter with a vintage flair, mixing eras and styles that reflected the heartbeat of our community. Each idea built upon the last, creating a tapestry of potential that began to weave our aspirations together.

The plans began to take shape, and with each detail, I felt a sense of ownership blossom. This event wasn't just a showcase; it was a vibrant call to the community, a celebration of creativity aimed at making a difference. I could already picture the townsfolk wandering through, sipping lemonade from mason jars, admiring the colorful displays of clothing and art, and sharing stories as laughter mingled with the music in the air.

We were so engrossed in our planning that I almost missed the flicker of tension in Carter's gaze when I mentioned our charity goals. "You know," I said, enthusiasm bubbling over, "we should really reach out to the local food bank. They're always in need of support, especially around the holidays. Plus, imagine how many people we could help."

Carter's smile faltered for a heartbeat, replaced by a shadow that slipped across his features. "Yeah, that would be great," he replied, but there was a hesitance in his voice, a subtle undercurrent that hinted at something unspoken. I noticed the way his fingers fidgeted with the fabric, absentmindedly twisting the ends of a vibrant blue scarf.

"What's wrong?" I asked, concern creeping into my voice.

He looked away, the sunlight catching the hint of worry in his expression, the laughter lines around his eyes dimming as he drew a breath. "It's just... I had some bad experiences with charity events before. It's complicated." His words hung in the air, heavy with untold stories.

I wanted to press him for more, to peel back the layers of his guardedness, but something held me back. I was learning that some stories needed to be shared in their own time. Instead, I placed a hand on his arm, trying to offer reassurance. "Whatever it is, I'm here for you," I said softly. "We're in this together."

His gaze returned to mine, and for a moment, I felt a connection crackling between us, electric and warm, like the first hint of spring after a long winter. It was as if the world faded away, leaving just the two of us in our little fabric sanctuary, surrounded by dreams and potential.

Carter's smile returned, but the underlying tension lingered like a ghost, reminding me that while our plans were blossoming, shadows were still present. As we continued to work, my heart felt lighter, buoyed by his laughter and the creativity flowing between us. I had no idea what past burdens he carried, but I hoped that our growing friendship could help lighten that load, just a little.

After hours of brainstorming and laughter, we stepped outside to take a break, the warm air wrapping around us like a comforting embrace. The streets of our small town buzzed with life, the scents of fresh bread wafting from a nearby bakery mixing with the earthy aroma of the blossoming spring flowers. Families strolled past, children darting in and out of shops, their giggles floating on the breeze.

I caught Carter watching a group of kids racing by, his expression softening. "You know, when I was younger, I loved painting murals for local schools," he reminisced, a hint of nostalgia coloring his voice. "It was like adding a splash of color to their world, making it brighter."

"Why don't you do it anymore?" I asked, genuinely curious.

His shoulders tensed momentarily before he shrugged it off. "Life gets in the way, I guess. But maybe I can try again. This event could be the perfect push."

I beamed at him, the thought of him reclaiming that passion igniting a flicker of hope within me. "Let's make it happen. We can showcase your work at the event, and you can even paint a mural at the shop!"

He looked at me, a mixture of surprise and delight dancing in his eyes. "Really? You think it could work?"

"Absolutely! It'll be the centerpiece of the event," I declared, the excitement bubbling over. "We'll pull the community together through your art. Just think of it—each brushstroke telling a story, every color speaking to someone."

As we stood there, bathed in the glow of the setting sun, I could see the gears turning in his mind. Maybe, just maybe, we were on the cusp of creating something beautiful, not just for ourselves, but for everyone around us. It was a chance to build a bridge from the past to a brighter future, woven together with threads of hope and creativity.

With each moment spent in Carter's company, I felt my own fears begin to dissolve. The world felt vibrant and alive, the possibilities endless, and I was grateful to be crafting my dreams alongside someone who shared the same passion. As the sun dipped below the horizon, casting a golden hue over our little town, I felt a new chapter unfurling before us—a chapter rich with promise, and perhaps a little romance.

Days melted into one another, blending seamlessly as we immersed ourselves in the preparations for the event. "Stitch & Thread" became a whirl of color and creativity, its corners filled with laughter and the scent of fresh coffee wafting through the air. Mia and I spent late nights at the shop, transforming it into a welcoming haven for our community. We draped elegant fabrics over old chairs, turning them into whimsical seating areas, and hung twinkling fairy lights that danced like fireflies, casting a soft glow that felt magical.

Carter was a constant presence, his easy laughter echoing through the shop like a beloved melody. He began bringing sketches each day, artful visions that captured the spirit of our town. One afternoon, he showed me a piece inspired by the vibrant murals that adorned the alleyways, a bright depiction of children playing in a park, their joy bursting from the page. "It's about community, right?"

he said, his brow furrowed in concentration as he put pencil to paper. "I want to reflect that."

I nodded, feeling a swell of pride in him. "Absolutely. Your work can remind everyone of the connections we share." As he spoke, I could see the light in his eyes grow brighter, an ember of hope igniting within him, urging him to reclaim the artist he had once been.

Between brainstorming sessions and late-night coffee runs, the lines between our friendship and something more began to blur. There were moments when our hands brushed while reaching for the same fabric, the contact sending delightful shivers through me. I noticed how he'd linger a little longer than necessary when he offered his help, his fingers brushing against mine as he passed a spool of thread. It made my heart race, the anticipation of something more weaving itself into the fabric of our collaboration.

Yet, with every fleeting touch, that shadow lingered in the background—Carter's past, shrouded in mystery. I found myself questioning what secrets lay beneath his charming exterior. Sometimes, when I caught him gazing out the window, a faraway look in his eyes, I wondered what memories haunted him. The laughter and camaraderie we shared felt like a delicate dance, teetering on the edge of something profound, yet held back by the weight of unspoken truths.

As the day of the event drew closer, I could sense the excitement building in the air. The community buzzed with anticipation, the local café displaying our flyers prominently, each colorful announcement drawing more eyes. It felt as though we were stitching together the very fabric of our town, uniting us in a shared purpose that transcended our individual lives.

One afternoon, as I hung the last of the fairy lights, I turned to see Carter leaning against the doorway, watching me with a soft smile. The way he looked at me made my stomach flutter; it was as if he could see straight through to my heart, teasing out the hopes and fears I harbored there. I couldn't help but tease him back. "You're not just going to stand there looking handsome all day, are you?"

His laughter rang out, rich and full, warming the room. "Well, it's a tough job, but someone has to do it."

I rolled my eyes, trying to suppress my smile. "Alright, Mr. Charming, how about you help me with these decorations instead?"

"Only if you promise to let me paint a mural on that blank wall over there." He gestured to a stark expanse that needed life. "I have this idea—something bright, something that speaks to the heart of this place."

"Deal," I replied, feeling a rush of excitement. As we climbed up on ladders and draped fabric over the last few bare spots, I could see the spark of inspiration igniting between us, transforming our collaborative energy into a creative force that was undeniable.

The night before the event, the shop transformed into a wonderland. The air shimmered with a kind of energy that vibrated through my veins. I stood back, taking in the twinkling lights, the vibrant displays, and the art pieces Carter had meticulously hung, each framed creation telling a story of its own. It was more than just a charity event; it was a love letter to our community, an invitation to come together and celebrate the very best of us.

As I prepared to lock up for the night, Carter stepped beside me, his presence a comforting weight. "You've done an incredible job," he said, his voice low and sincere. "I'm really proud of what we've created."

"Thanks to you," I replied, my heart swelling with gratitude. "I couldn't have done it without you."

His gaze lingered on me, and in that moment, the air grew thick with unspoken possibilities. My breath hitched as I felt the undeniable pull toward him, a magnetic force drawing us closer together. I wanted to bridge the gap between friendship and something deeper, to leap into the unknown.

But just as I gathered the courage to say something—anything—he stepped back, breaking the spell. "I should get going," he said, the familiar flicker of tension returning to his expression. "I have some last-minute details to wrap up."

The disappointment settled in my chest like a heavy stone. "Of course. I'll see you tomorrow, right?"

He nodded, but there was a hesitation in his smile, a fleeting moment where I could sense his internal struggle. "Absolutely. I wouldn't miss it."

As he walked away, I turned to face the now quiet shop, its vibrant colors seeming to dim in his absence. I couldn't shake the feeling that we were teetering on the edge of something significant, yet the shadows of his past loomed large. I resolved to be patient, to allow him the space he needed. Our journey was just beginning, and I had a feeling that tomorrow would be a turning point—a chance for both of us to embrace whatever was waiting for us beyond the curtain of uncertainty.

With the stars twinkling overhead and the air filled with the promise of new beginnings, I took a deep breath, allowing the thrill of anticipation to wash over me. Tomorrow was not just an event; it was an opportunity, and I was ready to seize it.

The day of the event dawned bright and promising, as if the universe itself conspired to paint the world in hues of hope. I arrived at "Stitch & Thread" early, the air buzzing with excitement and the scent of freshly brewed coffee mingling with the lingering aroma of cut fabric and paint. The shop was alive with energy, every corner transformed into a canvas of colors, textures, and stories waiting to unfold. Mia was already there, adjusting the seating arrangements and fluffing cushions like a dedicated stage manager prepping for a grand performance.

"Are you ready for this?" she asked, her eyes sparkling with enthusiasm as she stepped back to admire her handiwork.

"I think so," I replied, my voice barely above a whisper. The adrenaline coursed through me, setting my nerves alight. The space felt like a living entity, thrumming with possibilities, and I couldn't help but smile as I took in the vibrant decorations we had painstakingly crafted. "Just a little more tweaking, and we'll be good to go."

As the clock ticked closer to the event's start, the first attendees began to trickle in. I greeted each one with a warm smile, my heart swelling with gratitude for the community that had rallied around our cause. Familiar faces filled the room—friends, neighbors, and local artists all gathered to support us. Carter arrived soon after, carrying a large canvas under one arm and a few paintbrushes tucked into his back pocket.

His presence sent a thrill through me, as if the room brightened just by having him there. "I thought I'd give a live painting demonstration," he said, his voice steady, yet I caught a hint of nervousness beneath it. "Maybe I can inspire someone to take up the brush themselves."

"That sounds amazing," I replied, beaming at him. "You'll be the star of the show."

As he set up his easel in a cozy corner of the shop, I couldn't help but watch him, mesmerized by the way he transformed the blank canvas into something alive. The strokes of his brush were deliberate yet free, each color merging with the next in a joyful explosion of creativity. The soft melodies of a local band strumming in the background blended with the chatter of our guests, creating an atmosphere that felt electric with inspiration.

Mia and I floated among the crowd, engaging with attendees, sharing our vision, and explaining the cause we were supporting. The laughter and camaraderie were infectious, a reminder of why we were doing this. But amidst the joy, I noticed Carter's laughter had become a touch strained, as if he were balancing on a tightrope, caught between the exhilaration of the event and the weight of something unspoken.

As the afternoon wore on, I took a moment to step outside for a breath of fresh air, the sun dipping low in the sky, casting golden rays that turned the world into a watercolor painting. I leaned against the weathered wooden railing of the shop's porch, savoring the moment. I had never felt more alive than in that instant, surrounded by people who believed in the same dreams I did.

Carter emerged a few minutes later, his paint-smeared hands tucked into his pockets, his expression contemplative. "Hey," he said softly, joining me against the railing. "Everything looks incredible."

"Thanks to you," I replied, nudging him playfully. "Your mural is a hit. I can't believe how many people are drawn to it."

He smiled, but I sensed a flicker of hesitation behind his eyes. "It's just... nice to see everyone enjoying it," he said, his voice low. "But sometimes I wonder if they really understand the story behind it. There's a lot of pain and struggle in this community that goes unnoticed."

I turned to face him, catching the glimmer of vulnerability in his expression. "You mean your story?" I asked gently, hoping to coax him into sharing more.

He paused, his gaze drifting to the horizon, where the sun kissed the edge of the world. "It's complicated," he replied finally. "There were times when art was all I had, and I poured everything into it. But then life happened. The pressure to succeed, to fit into someone else's idea of what I should be—it almost crushed me."

"Carter, you're an incredible artist," I said, my heart aching for him. "You have so much talent, and more importantly, your work resonates with people. Don't let anyone dim that light."

He turned to me, a mixture of gratitude and something deeper flickering in his eyes. "Thank you for believing in me," he said, sincerity threading through his words. "It means more than you know."

Just then, the laughter of children reached us, pulling my attention back to the shop, where families were gathered, delighting in the colorful displays. The sight of those carefree moments reminded me why we were here. "Let's go inside," I said, taking his hand, feeling the warmth of his skin against mine. "We're making a difference today."

As we reentered the bustling shop, the atmosphere felt electric, and I could sense the magic in the air. The more people engaged with Carter's artwork, the more his spirit seemed to lift. I watched him chat with guests, his laughter returning, ringing out like the tinkling of wind chimes on a summer day. It was as if the joy of the community enveloped him, wrapping him in a warmth he had been missing.

At one point during the event, I looked around the shop and saw Mia animatedly discussing our charity goals with a group of local business owners. Her passion radiated, and I felt a swell of pride for her dedication. I was grateful to have someone like her by my side, someone who saw the potential in our dreams as clearly as I did.

As evening settled in, the fairy lights began to twinkle against the darkening sky, and we transitioned into a more intimate atmosphere. A local musician strummed soft chords on his guitar, and the guests gradually gathered around Carter as he prepared to unveil his latest work. My heart raced with excitement, a sense of pride swelling within me.

He stood before the easel, the flickering candlelight casting a warm glow on his face. "I wanted to create something that spoke to the heart of our community," he said, his voice steady and confident now. "This piece is for all of you, a reflection of the love, the struggles, and the resilience that binds us together."

With a dramatic flourish, he pulled back the cloth, revealing a vibrant mural that encapsulated the spirit of our town. There were swirling colors depicting a sun rising over the hills, children playing, and families gathering. It was a celebration of life—an explosion of joy that resonated with everyone present. Gasps of delight and applause erupted, filling the space with warmth and appreciation.

As I watched Carter, a sense of awe washed over me. In that moment, I saw not just an artist, but a man who had the power to heal through his creativity. I could feel the invisible threads of connection weaving us all together, drawing our community closer, and I knew that this event was only the beginning.

Carter turned to me, a radiant smile lighting up his face, and in that instant, everything shifted. The tension that had once loomed over us dissipated, replaced by a sense of clarity. The shadows of his past were still there, but they no longer defined him. Together, we were creating something beautiful, and I was filled with hope for what lay ahead.

As the night wore on, laughter mingled with music, and I felt a sense of belonging enveloping me. This was more than just a charity event; it was a tapestry woven from the dreams, struggles, and victories of the people I loved. I realized then that my journey with Carter was just beginning, and as we stood side by side, watching our community come together, I couldn't help but believe that we were both ready to embrace whatever lay ahead, together.

Chapter 15: A Palette of Possibilities

The day of the charity event unfurls like a vibrant canvas, every detail splashed with color and life, the air thick with anticipation and a hint of lavender from the fresh bouquets that dot the space. Sunlight streams through the boutique's wide windows, casting warm beams across the walls adorned with local artwork, each piece a window into the artist's soul. I take a moment to admire the eclectic mix: a swirling abstract that seems to dance with every flicker of light, a poignant portrait that captures a fleeting expression, and delicate watercolors that evoke a sense of calm. The boutique, usually so modest in its charm, has transformed into a gallery of possibilities, a sanctuary for creativity and community spirit.

Guests flow in like a gentle tide, each one contributing to the effervescent atmosphere. Laughter bubbles up, punctuated by the clinking of glasses filled with sparkling beverages. The sound is infectious, wrapping around me as I navigate through the crowd, my fingers grazing the edges of the art displays, each texture a tactile connection to the heart of this event. I can feel the thrill of the night pulsating through the room, an electric energy that ignites my spirit and makes me believe that anything is possible.

As I move deeper into the throng, my eyes drift toward the far corner where Carter stands. He is a focal point in this vibrant tableau, his presence magnetic as he interacts with a small group of art enthusiasts. There's an easy grace to his movements, the way he gestures with his hands while explaining the nuances of his work, a passion lighting up his features that makes my heart swell. The confidence he exudes draws others in, creating a small circle around him, captivated by his enthusiasm. I can't help but smile as I watch him—his laughter ringing out like music, his eyes sparkling with the thrill of connection and shared appreciation.

Yet beneath the surface of this joyful scene, an undercurrent of worry begins to stir in my heart. I am acutely aware of the weight of my insecurities, the whispers of doubt that seem to echo louder amidst the backdrop of his success. I remind myself that I've stepped into this world alongside him, a space filled with his dreams, but the shadow of comparison lurks in the corners of my mind. What if I am not enough? What if his past becomes a barrier I cannot breach?

In an attempt to shake off the feeling, I weave through the gathering, allowing the laughter and lighthearted conversations to wrap around me like a warm shawl. I sip a delicate lavender lemonade, the tartness refreshing against my lips, and force a smile as I exchange pleasantries with familiar faces. But my gaze often drifts back to Carter, who now stands in animated conversation with a woman I don't recognize. She has an effortless elegance, her laughter cascading through the air, and I can see how it draws Carter in like a moth to a flame.

I tell myself it's just the excitement of the event, but as I observe them, the tightness in my chest constricts further. There's an intimacy in their exchange, a familiarity that makes my stomach twist. The way her eyes linger on him, the softness of her tone, feels like a thread unraveling the fabric of our evening. I take a deep breath, willing myself to shake off the discomfort, to trust in the strength of what we have built together.

As the minutes stretch on, I can't ignore the gnawing feeling that pulls at me. It's as if the air thickens, becoming heavier with unspoken words and lingering doubts. Finally, I can't stand it anymore. The vibrant colors of the event swirl around me as I make my way over to them, each step feeling like a heavy weight on my heart. The laughter of the crowd fades, replaced by the rapid thump of my pulse as I approach.

"Carter," I interrupt, my voice steadier than I feel. He turns to me, surprise flickering in his eyes before melting into a welcoming warmth. But I can't shake the icy grip of jealousy that has crept into my thoughts. "Can we talk?"

His brows furrow with concern, and he glances at the woman before returning his gaze to me. "Of course. Just a minute," he replies, excusing himself. I feel her eyes on me, a scrutiny that only adds to my unease, and I force myself to meet her gaze, willing her to see the strength I'm trying to project.

Once we are a few steps away, I can't hold back. "Who was that?" The words spill out, sharp and immediate, betraying the vulnerability I feel underneath. I'm surprised by the tremor in my voice, the way it betrays my composure.

Carter's expression shifts, surprise fading into something more serious. "She's an old friend from art school," he replies, his tone gentle, as if trying to soften the blow of my insecurity. "We were just reminiscing about old projects."

I can feel the tension crackle between us, a fragile thread straining against the weight of my emotions. "It felt... familiar," I say, the bitterness seeping through despite my best efforts to keep it at bay. "I didn't realize I had to compete with your past."

He takes a step closer, the warmth of his presence flooding my senses. "You're not competing with anyone, especially not with my past. That was years ago, before I even knew who you were. What we have is something entirely different."

His sincerity wraps around me like a comforting blanket, yet the edges of my doubts still flicker in the back of my mind. "But what if—"

He cuts me off, his hands finding my shoulders, grounding me. "What if nothing. You're here now, and that's all that matters. I want to share my future with you, not chase shadows from the past."

With those words, he leans in, capturing my lips with his. The kiss ignites a spark, melting away the doubt, leaving only the warmth of his affection. It's passionate and sincere, a tangible connection that breathes life into my insecurities, banishing them like the dark clouds that sometimes hang over the sun. As I sink into the moment, I realize that this—this feeling—is the palette of possibilities we are painting together.

As the evening unfolds, the atmosphere buzzes with a delightful mix of chatter and laughter, a cacophony of voices blending seamlessly into a symphony of celebration. I lose myself in the crowd, letting the energy of the event wrap around me like a comforting shawl. The gallery, filled with art and heart, pulsates with life, each brushstroke on the walls whispering stories of the artists behind them. I catch snippets of conversations, laughter bubbling up like champagne, and my spirit lifts with each joyful exchange.

Yet even amidst this sea of smiles and goodwill, a part of me is still tethered to the weight of uncertainty. I spot Carter again, animated and radiant, his eyes sparkling with enthusiasm as he discusses his work with a small group. My heart swells with pride, watching him shine, but that prick of jealousy still lingers like a shadow, an unwelcome guest at the feast of joy.

The laughter of the guests around me turns into a gentle hum as I drift further into my thoughts, retreating slightly from the lively chatter. My fingers trace the outline of a striking piece of art nearby, the coolness of the frame grounding me, reminding me of the creative spirit that brought us all together. I take a deep breath, inhaling the sweet scent of fresh flowers and the rich aroma of artisan snacks wafting through the air, hoping to wash away my lingering doubts.

As I meander through the crowd, my eyes inadvertently search for the familiar silhouette of Carter. There's something about the way he moves, a rhythm to his steps that feels as if it were choreographed just for him. He captures the attention of those around him effortlessly, his charisma a magnetic force that pulls people in. Just then, a wave of laughter erupts from his corner, and I can't help but turn my head, drawn in like a moth to a flame.

There she is again—the woman from earlier. Her laughter rings like music, a melody that dances through the air. I squint to catch the full view, my heart racing slightly. They stand close, her hand brushing against his arm, and in that moment, a strange wave of heat washes over me, mingled with something deeper, darker. I remind myself of his reassurances, but the feeling coils tighter around my heart.

The evening stretches on, filled with small victories and heartfelt exchanges. I chat with friends, share smiles, and make sure to enjoy the event, yet my thoughts circle back to Carter and the enigmatic woman who seems to inhabit a space in his past. Every laughter I hear and every glance he shares with her chips away at the buoyancy of my earlier confidence, leaving behind an unsettling doubt.

As the evening winds down, the sky outside transitions into a soft twilight, painting the horizon in hues of pink and gold, a stark contrast to the turmoil brewing within me. I step outside for a moment, seeking solace in the cool breeze that dances through the air. The bustling sounds of the event fade into the background as I take a deep breath, welcoming the fresh air to fill my lungs and steady my racing heart.

I lean against the boutique's brick façade, absorbing the beauty of the setting sun. It feels as if the universe is playing a cruel trick on me, juxtaposing the beauty outside with the tempest inside. I'm drawn into my own thoughts, replaying every moment from the evening, dissecting each exchange, and wishing I could erase the unwelcome images of Carter with her.

Finally, the heaviness in my chest becomes too much to bear, and I decide to confront it head-on. With renewed determination, I push away from the wall and stride back inside, my heart racing as I navigate through the final remnants of the event. I find Carter alone, taking a moment to admire his artwork displayed in the boutique, a contented smile gracing his features.

"Carter," I say, my voice firm yet trembling with vulnerability, cutting through the hum of the evening. He turns to me, his smile faltering slightly as he senses the shift in my tone.

"Hey! Just taking it all in. It turned out really well, didn't it?" His eyes glimmer with warmth, but I can't shake the nagging sense of unease.

"It did. But we need to talk," I reply, the words spilling from my lips before I can second-guess myself. The sincerity in his expression deepens, a flicker of concern crossing his face.

"Of course. What's on your mind?" He steps closer, the warmth radiating from him inviting and yet intimidating.

"It's about her," I say, my voice low yet steady. "The woman you were talking to earlier. I couldn't help but notice the connection you two had."

His brow furrows, a flash of confusion marring his features. "Oh, you mean Mia? We go way back, but it was just a friendly conversation."

"Friendly, sure," I reply, an edge creeping into my voice. "But it didn't feel that way to me. I felt... excluded, like I was watching something intimate."

Carter's expression shifts, a mix of surprise and concern. "I didn't mean to make you feel that way," he says, his voice gentle yet resolute. "Mia and I have history, yes, but that was then. I'm here now, with you."

"History has a way of creeping back in," I counter, my insecurities bubbling to the surface. "What if it affects us? What if I'm not enough?"

He closes the distance between us, his hands finding my shoulders, grounding me in the moment. "You are more than enough," he says, his voice steady and reassuring. "You are my present and my future. My past with Mia doesn't diminish what we have. It enhances it, showing me just how special you are."

In that moment, his words wash over me like a balm, soothing the frayed edges of my heart. I search his eyes, looking for the sincerity that has always been there, and I find it—an unwavering connection that pulls me in and holds me close. "You promise?" I ask, my voice barely above a whisper, the vulnerability hanging in the air between us.

"I promise," he replies, his gaze never wavering. And as he leans in, capturing my lips once more, the kiss deepens, enveloping us in a world of our own creation. The weight of the night slips away, leaving only the warmth of his touch and the certainty of our bond—a bond that transcends the shadows of the past, illuminating a path forward filled with hope and possibility.

As the kiss lingers, time seems to stretch, encapsulating us in a moment where the chaos of the world outside fades into nothingness. The boutique, filled with laughter and art, recedes into the background, and all I can feel is Carter's warmth enveloping me, grounding me amidst my swirling doubts. It's a revelation that feels like the softest touch of sunlight breaking through a thick layer of clouds, illuminating the shadows that had threatened to engulf my heart.

I pull back slightly, searching his gaze for any hint of hesitation. Instead, I find unwavering sincerity and an intensity that makes my heart race. "So, what now?" I ask, my voice steadying as I regain my footing, the tumultuous emotions beginning to settle into something more manageable.

"We celebrate this night, and then we talk about the future," he replies, a grin breaking across his face that transforms the space around us. It's as if the boutique itself brightens, echoing the promise of new beginnings.

Together, we return to the bustling crowd, the energy palpable as guests mingle and share their thoughts about the artwork adorning the walls. I notice how Carter effortlessly draws people in, his passion illuminating the room like a beacon. It's clear that he doesn't just create art; he breathes life into it, imbuing each piece with his spirit. I admire the way his eyes sparkle when someone expresses genuine appreciation for his work. It's intoxicating, watching him thrive in his element, and it ignites a fierce sense of pride within me.

But as the night progresses, I can't shake the memory of that earlier conversation. Mia's laughter still echoes in my mind, a haunting reminder of the past that seems to hover just out of reach. I try to engage in conversations, but my thoughts keep drifting back to the connection they shared. It feels as if a small part of him still lingers with her, and the pang of insecurity resurfaces, making me question whether I am truly enough to fill the void.

"Hey," Carter's voice cuts through my thoughts, and I glance up to find him watching me with concern. "You okay?" His brow furrows slightly, and the warmth in his eyes invites me to share what's bothering me.

I take a breath, summoning the courage to speak. "I'm fine. Just thinking... about everything." I gesture vaguely to the crowd, my words veering away from the truth, the vulnerability I feel still raw and exposed.

Carter places a reassuring hand on my back, guiding me toward a quieter corner of the boutique, where the colors of the art seem to blend into a soothing backdrop. "You know you can talk to me about anything, right?"

His words wash over me, a gentle reminder that I'm not alone in this. I nod, feeling the comfort of his presence anchoring me as I gather my thoughts. "I guess I'm just... processing everything. I want to be part of your world, but sometimes it feels overwhelming."

He nods, his expression softening with understanding. "It's a lot, I get it. But remember, you're not just stepping into my world—you're creating a new one together. You bring something unique to it that I didn't even know I was missing."

His words, so earnest and sincere, ripple through me, calming the turbulent waves of my insecurities. I glance around, noting the vibrant interactions happening around us—an artist discussing the intricacies of color theory with a captivated listener, a couple admiring a breathtaking landscape that seems to transport them to another world. It dawns on me that this event isn't just about showcasing art; it's about building connections, forging relationships, and igniting the spark of creativity within each person who walks through those doors.

As I step back, I begin to see our relationship in a new light. Carter and I are not merely two individuals navigating the complexities of our pasts; we're co-creators of something beautiful, each brushstroke adding depth and dimension to our shared canvas. The realization hits me like a warm breeze on a cool evening—this moment, this connection, is our masterpiece.

With a renewed sense of clarity, I lean into Carter, resting my head against his shoulder as we watch the ebb and flow of the crowd. I take a moment to absorb the collective energy swirling around us, the warmth of the community enveloping us both. It's in these small, intimate moments that I feel the most at home.

"Thank you," I murmur, my voice muffled against him. "For being here. For understanding."

He tilts my chin up gently, forcing me to meet his gaze. "Always. And thank you for being brave enough to share your feelings. It means a lot to me."

A comfortable silence settles over us, a cocoon of shared understanding, and for the first time tonight, I feel at peace. The colors around us blur together in a mesmerizing dance, and as I watch the interactions happening around me, a sense of belonging fills the space where doubt once resided.

The evening continues to unfold, each moment weaving into the next like the threads of a tapestry, rich and intricate. As the event begins to wind down, I notice how Carter's artwork has sparked conversations, inspired creativity, and even rekindled old friendships among guests. The atmosphere is electric, a celebration not just of art but of human connection.

Eventually, as the last few guests begin to trickle out, I help Carter gather his paintings, each piece imbued with the essence of this beautiful night. Together, we share laughter and stories, our connection deepening with every shared moment. There's a sense of fulfillment that comes with being part of something greater than ourselves, a bond that is woven from vulnerability and trust.

As we step outside, the night air greets us like an old friend, cool and refreshing against our skin. I glance up at the star-studded sky, the twinkling lights reminding me of the possibilities that lie ahead.

"I've got an idea," Carter says, breaking the comfortable silence. "Let's celebrate our first event together. How about ice cream?"

My heart flutters at the thought of spending more time with him, free from the weight of expectations and past memories. "Yes, please! A scoop of something sweet sounds perfect right now."

With laughter bubbling between us, we walk side by side, the world around us blurring into a backdrop of vibrant colors and shared dreams. The ice cream shop is just a few blocks away, and as we stroll through the quiet streets, the buzz of the evening lingers in the air, echoing the excitement of our newly ignited relationship.

We arrive at the shop, the bright neon lights illuminating our path. The scent of freshly made waffle cones wafts through the open door, wrapping around us like a warm embrace. I can feel the thrill of anticipation building as we step inside, the vibrant decor and cheerful ambiance enveloping us. We take our time, browsing the eclectic selection of flavors, each one more enticing than the last.

"Mint chocolate chip or birthday cake?" I ponder aloud, my eyes dancing between the two options.

Carter chuckles, his gaze softening as he leans closer. "How about both? Life's too short to choose just one flavor."

With his playful suggestion, I can't help but smile. It feels like the perfect metaphor for our relationship—embracing all that life has to offer, together. I nod in agreement, excitement bubbling within me as we place our orders, two scoops piled high in crisp cones, vibrant colors reflecting the energy of the evening.

As we step back outside, the cool night air wraps around us, and I take a deep breath, savoring the moment. The weight of my insecurities dissipates like mist in the morning sun. We find a cozy spot on a nearby bench, the world around us a blur of color and sound, but in this moment, it's just us, the ice cream, and the sweet taste of possibility.

I glance at Carter, who takes a generous lick of his cone, his eyes sparkling with joy. There's something magical about this moment, a connection that feels unbreakable, forged through shared experiences, laughter, and a mutual desire to embrace whatever comes next. We may not know what the future holds, but for now, in this vibrant world filled with color and creativity, we are exactly where we need to be—together, painting our own masterpiece, one scoop at a time.

Chapter 16: Falling for Shadows

The storm arrived in Montgomery Springs like a shroud, draping the quaint town in a heavy, oppressive atmosphere. The familiar sound of rain tapping against the windowpane filled the room with a rhythmic percussion, each drop a reminder of the chaos stirring not just in the sky but within me. I rolled over in bed, attempting to reclaim the warmth of sleep, but the tension in my chest kept me wide awake, a restless energy thrumming beneath my skin. The air was thick with the scent of petrichor, a sweet, earthy aroma that typically grounded me, but tonight it only deepened my unease.

Carter's laughter echoed in my mind, an intoxicating melody that contrasted sharply with the storm outside. It had been a perfect evening—the charity event glowed with laughter, music, and the gentle clink of glasses filled with bubbly champagne. I remembered the way his eyes sparkled when he caught me gazing at him from across the room, the brief moments when our fingers brushed, igniting sparks of electricity that made me feel alive. Yet, as the night wore on, an undercurrent of dread snaked its way into my heart, a feeling I couldn't shake no matter how hard I tried.

The storm raged on, each clap of thunder shaking the walls of my small bedroom, mirroring the upheaval brewing within me. Carter's past—so full of shadows—loomed large in my mind. I had caught glimpses of it, whispered tales and hushed conversations that hinted at darkness, hurt, and mistakes he had made long before our paths crossed. It gnawed at my insides, the fear that those shadows could overshadow our blossoming connection, leaving only remnants of what might have been.

I threw the covers off, feeling the cool air wrap around me like a comforting embrace. The last thing I wanted to do was wallow in my insecurities. I padded to the kitchen, each step echoing in the silence of my home, the occasional rumble of thunder my only company.

The dim light from the streetlamps outside flickered through the window, casting elongated shadows that danced across the walls. I poured myself a cup of coffee, letting the warmth seep into my hands, the rich aroma a temporary balm for my frayed nerves.

The boutique awaited me like a blank canvas, and I realized I needed to pour my heart into something tangible, something I could control. As I dressed in a comfortable oversized sweater and leggings, I mentally prepared myself to face the day. The thought of diving into my designs felt like a lifeline, a way to distract myself from the whirlpool of doubt threatening to pull me under. I grabbed my notebook, the one filled with sketches, fabric swatches, and half-formed ideas, and headed out into the storm.

The boutique stood proudly on Maple Avenue, its charming façade a beacon against the darkening sky. As I unlocked the door, the chime of the bell rang out, a welcoming sound that momentarily soothed my worries. The interior was warm and inviting, with shelves filled with vibrant fabrics and the intoxicating scent of freshly brewed coffee wafting through the air from the little corner café that shared my space. I flicked on the lights, illuminating the carefully curated displays and revealing a world of color and creativity that felt like home.

The storm raged outside, the rain pouring down in sheets, but inside, I was safe. The chaotic rhythm of the raindrops against the roof became a symphony, one that I could weave into the fabric of my designs. I set to work, sketching feverishly, allowing the swirling patterns in my mind to take shape on the page. Each line flowed effortlessly, a reflection of my emotions, hopes, and fears.

But as the hours slipped away, I found myself wrestling with more than just fabrics and designs. With every stroke of my pencil, I confronted the truth—my feelings for Carter were deeper than I had allowed myself to acknowledge. The more I designed, the more I realized that I couldn't hide from my insecurities. Each dress I envisioned was tinged with the fear that perhaps, like my sketches, our relationship was beautiful but ultimately fragile, susceptible to the storms that life threw our way.

With the rain pouring outside, the world felt closed off, isolated from the worries that waited for me beyond the boutique's doors. Yet, as I poured my heart into every stitch and seam, I realized that this was not just an escape; it was a confrontation. I was crafting not just garments, but a future—my future—and I couldn't let fear dictate my choices any longer.

Just as the clock struck noon, the bell above the door jingled again, heralding a visitor. I looked up, my heart racing, hoping it would be Carter. Instead, it was Lila, my best friend, her hair soaked and clinging to her cheeks, a determined look on her face. "I figured you'd be here," she said, shaking off the rain like a puppy, her laughter filling the room with warmth.

"Did you swim here?" I teased, setting my sketchbook aside.

Lila stepped closer, her expression turning serious. "You've been hiding away, and I thought it was time for a little intervention. You've got a storm brewing inside you, and you can't just ignore it."

Her words cut through the tension in my chest, and I took a deep breath, the truth of her observation landing heavily between us. I knew she was right, but how could I open up about the whirlwind of emotions swirling within me, especially when it came to Carter?

Lila's presence was like a jolt of caffeine to my weary spirit. She shook off the rain, sending droplets flying, and her laughter rang through the boutique, pulling me from my tangled thoughts. The playful chaos she brought into my life was exactly what I needed, a refreshing counterpoint to the swirling storm inside me.

"Are you going to stare at those sketches all day, or are you going to let me help you breathe some life into them?" she asked, her eyes sparkling with mischief. Lila always had this knack for turning the mundane into an adventure, and I couldn't help but smile at her enthusiasm.

I leaned against the counter, crossing my arms and feigning indifference. "I'm perfectly capable of breathing on my own, thank you very much." But the truth was, I had become so engrossed in my work that I hadn't even realized how much I needed a distraction—a little chaos to balance the storm of feelings I was trying to navigate.

"Right, and I'm a flying unicorn," she retorted, rolling her eyes. "Come on, show me what you're working on."

Reluctantly, I led her to my drafting table, the surface cluttered with sketches and swatches of fabric that seemed to come alive in the light. As I flipped through my sketches, I couldn't help but notice how each design reflected a piece of my heart—some bold and vibrant, others delicate and fragile, just like my feelings for Carter. I felt a pang of anxiety as I hesitated, unsure of how much to reveal.

"Okay, this one is my favorite," I said finally, pointing to a flowing dress adorned with intricate lace and vivid floral patterns. "I envision it for a summer gala—something whimsical and elegant."

Lila leaned in, examining the details with a critical eye. "You've captured the essence of what you want," she said, her voice laced with genuine admiration. "But what's missing is your own flair. You're a hopeless romantic, and that needs to shine through. What's the story behind this dress?"

Her question sent my mind reeling. What story was I trying to tell? I opened my mouth to answer, but the truth felt tangled in my throat. It wasn't just about the dress; it was about the feelings I was grappling with—feelings I wasn't sure I was ready to confront.

"It's... complicated," I finally managed, my voice barely above a whisper.

Lila's brow furrowed with concern, her gaze piercing as she studied me. "Is this about Carter? Because if it is, we need to talk about it."

The storm outside intensified, the wind howling as if echoing my inner turmoil. I looked out the window, watching the rain streak down the glass, blurring the world outside. "I'm just worried that his past will come back to haunt us," I admitted, feeling the weight of my vulnerability. "I like him, Lila. I really do. But I can't shake the feeling that I'm not enough to withstand the shadows that follow him."

Lila stepped closer, her expression softening as she placed a reassuring hand on my shoulder. "You know, everyone has shadows. Carter might have his, but you have yours too. It's part of being human. What matters is how you choose to face them together. You have to trust that he wants to share his burden with you."

Her words sank in, but doubt still curled around my heart like a vine, refusing to let go. I wanted to believe that our connection was strong enough to weather the storm, but what if it wasn't? I glanced down at my sketches, the designs now feeling like echoes of my fears rather than expressions of hope.

"Let's do something about it," Lila said, her voice brightening with excitement. "Why don't we plan a little adventure? You need a break from all this introspection. Let's grab some coffee, and then we can go shopping for supplies. You need new fabric and maybe even some inspiration."

For the first time that day, a smile tugged at my lips. "You know how to lure me out of my funk, don't you?"

"Of course! Now, get those creative juices flowing and pick a few favorites. We'll make a day of it, and maybe while we're out, you can gather your thoughts about Carter too. You can't avoid him forever."

As we set to work sorting through the sketches, my heart felt lighter. Lila's energy was infectious, and I found myself laughing at her antics as she imitated the various customers we encountered in the boutique. With each quip, she chipped away at the walls I had built around my insecurities, and I could almost see the shadows receding, if only a little.

Once we had gathered everything we needed, we stepped outside into the storm. The air was charged with energy, the scent of rain and wet earth filling my lungs as I took a deep breath, letting it invigorate me. Montgomery Springs had a charm all its own, even in the pouring rain. The trees lining the streets swayed, their branches dancing like carefree spirits, while the rhythmic patter of raindrops created a soundtrack to our adventure.

We ducked into our favorite coffee shop, the aroma of freshly brewed coffee wrapping around us like a warm hug. The cozy interior was adorned with vintage furniture and local artwork, lending an artistic flair that always inspired me. I ordered my usual—a caramel macchiato—and Lila opted for a daring hazelnut mocha, a decision that resulted in her promptly sloshing half of it on her shirt.

"Oops!" she exclaimed, her cheeks flushed with embarrassment as she wiped the mess away with a napkin. "I'd say it's a sign of good luck, right?"

"Sure, let's go with that," I chuckled, finding comfort in her unshakeable optimism. We settled into a corner booth, the warm light creating a cocoon around us. The storm rumbled outside, but inside, we were safe—two friends surrounded by warmth, laughter, and the scent of coffee.

As I sipped my drink, I began to share my fears with Lila, the words flowing more freely in the cozy sanctuary of the café. "What if he's not ready to open up? What if I push him away?"

"Or," she countered, "what if he's just waiting for the right moment? Relationships take time, and if you give each other space to be vulnerable, it might strengthen what you have. You can't control everything, but you can decide how you want to handle it when those shadows creep back in."

Her words resonated deep within me, and for the first time that day, I felt a flicker of hope. Maybe embracing the uncertainty wasn't as terrifying as I had imagined. With every storm comes a chance for renewal, for growth. I just needed to trust Carter and myself, to step into the unknown with courage rather than fear.

Lila's laughter brought me back to the moment, and I smiled at her, grateful for her unwavering support. "Thank you for being my grounding force, Lila. I'm lucky to have you in my corner."

"Always, my friend. Now, let's finish our drinks and hit those fabric stores! We've got a world to create!"

Her excitement was contagious, and as we left the café, the rain seemed to lighten, a soft drizzle accompanying us as we ventured into the streets of Montgomery Springs. The shadows still lurked in the corners of my heart, but I was learning how to embrace them, how to dance in the rain rather than hide from it.

The rain softened to a gentle patter as Lila and I meandered through the fabric store, the inviting scent of cotton and linen filling the air. Rolls of vibrant fabrics lined the walls like a kaleidoscope, each hue telling a story of its own. I ran my fingers along the bolts of fabric, feeling the textures beneath my fingertips—the silks were smooth and luxurious, while the cottons had a comforting familiarity that beckoned creativity.

Lila, ever the whirlwind, grabbed a vibrant floral print that practically danced with color. "This one screams summer garden party," she declared, holding it up against her chest. Her enthusiasm was infectious, and I couldn't help but smile at her antics. "Imagine twirling in this. You'll be the belle of the ball!"

"Or the garden," I quipped, laughing as I caught a glimpse of my reflection in the nearby mirror. With my oversized sweater and leggings, I felt like a flower hidden beneath a blanket. "I'd need to add some flair to my wardrobe first."

"You've got the flair in your heart, my dear. Let's just bring it to the surface!" she replied, playfully tossing a bolt of deep burgundy fabric my way. I caught it with one hand, the weight of the material a comforting reminder that I was here, grounded in this moment, surrounded by colors and textures that inspired me.

As we wandered through the aisles, Lila continued to chatter about our plans for the boutique's upcoming summer collection. The excitement of new designs and fresh ideas coursed through me, each conversation nudging my insecurities further away. Still, the shadows of doubt lingered at the edges of my mind, waiting for the moment I would let my guard down.

"Okay, what about this?" Lila said, gesturing to a shimmering, silvery fabric that caught the light. "It could be the perfect base for something elegant yet daring. You could design a gown that would make even the stars jealous!"

As I studied the fabric, I imagined what I could create. Would it be a floor-length gown or a chic cocktail dress? The possibilities swirled around me, each one tugging at the threads of my imagination. The vision took shape, transforming into a stunning creation that could capture the essence of romance—the kind of piece that would make hearts race.

But just as I felt my spirit lift, a familiar voice cut through my thoughts. "I didn't expect to find you here."

I turned to find Carter standing at the entrance, a soaked figure framed by the doorway. The rain clung to his hair, droplets glistening like tiny stars against the dark fabric of his shirt. My heart quickened, an unexpected surge of joy mixed with apprehension flooding my veins.

"Hey," I managed, my voice barely above a whisper.

"Looks like the storm followed you," he remarked with a wry smile, stepping into the store and shaking off the rain like a dog after a bath. His eyes scanned the vibrant colors surrounding us, a playful smirk tugging at his lips. "You know, I always imagined you as the kind of person who'd be lost in a fabric store."

I shot Lila a quick glance, and she raised her eyebrows knowingly, her excitement palpable. "Oh, I was just telling her how we're planning a summer collection," she chimed in, her voice bubbling with enthusiasm. "You should totally give her some ideas, Carter! She's the genius behind the designs."

The warmth of their camaraderie brought a smile to my face, but I couldn't ignore the tightening in my chest as I felt the weight of his presence. Carter stepped closer, and I could sense the quiet storm brewing beneath his surface.

"I'm here to pick up some supplies for a project," he said, but his gaze lingered on me, his expression unreadable. "Thought I'd check in on you."

The air thickened with unspoken words, an invisible thread weaving us together in that moment. Lila, sensing the tension, excused herself to explore another aisle, leaving us in the eye of the storm.

"What project?" I asked, hoping to lighten the mood, but the moment felt too heavy, too fraught with potential pitfalls.

"Just some art for a community initiative," he replied, a shadow flickering across his features. "You know me—always trying to get involved."

I nodded, but doubt bubbled beneath the surface. "You have a lot on your plate, Carter. Are you sure you have time for more?"

His brow furrowed, and I could see the flicker of frustration in his eyes. "I'm fine. Really. Just... trying to keep busy. Keeps my mind off things."

The implication hung between us, heavy with significance. I wondered if his "things" were the same shadows that haunted me—his past, the mistakes that could erupt at any moment like a volcano spewing ash.

"I get it," I said slowly, my heart racing. "But you don't have to face it alone. You know that, right?"

Carter looked away, his gaze fixating on a bolt of navy fabric across the aisle. The shadows flickered again, and I knew I had touched on something delicate. "It's complicated," he said, his voice barely above a whisper.

"Everything feels complicated right now," I murmured, my pulse quickening as I searched for the right words. "But maybe we can figure it out together?"

He turned to face me, the storm in his eyes reflecting the tempest outside. "I want that, but I'm scared that my past will ruin whatever we have."

I took a step closer, my heart pounding in my chest. "Carter, I'm willing to embrace the uncertainty. I want to understand your past because I want to be part of your future."

The sincerity in my voice seemed to crack the ice that had formed between us. He stepped forward, the air electrifying as our eyes locked. In that moment, it felt like we were suspended in time, surrounded by the chaos of fabric and rain, two souls intertwined amidst a tempest of emotions.

Before I could process what was happening, Carter closed the distance between us, his hand brushing against mine. "I've never felt this way about anyone," he admitted, his voice thick with emotion. "But I don't want to drag you into my mess."

"Maybe I want to dive into that mess," I replied, my pulse racing. "Together, we can navigate it. Just like in life, sometimes you have to weather the storm to find the rainbow."

He smiled then, a genuine smile that illuminated his features. "You're something else, you know that?"

"And you're not so bad yourself," I teased lightly, relief washing over me.

Lila returned just in time, her eyes wide with curiosity. "What did I miss?"

Carter and I exchanged a knowing glance, the tension still lingering but somehow lighter, more bearable. "Just discussing some summer collection ideas," I said, forcing nonchalance into my tone.

"Right," Lila said, her expression unreadable. "Well, let's get back to it! I have a feeling this is going to be our best collection yet."

As we resumed our shopping, I couldn't shake the warmth of Carter's gaze from my mind, the way it ignited a fire within me, pushing aside the shadows that threatened to overtake us. With every bolt of fabric I picked, I felt more resolved to embrace whatever lay ahead. The storm outside might rage on, but within the confines of the boutique, I felt hopeful. The future felt vibrant, ready to be woven together with love, creativity, and the promise of what could be.

As we wrapped up our shopping, my heart swelled with anticipation. The fabric we had chosen was a blend of dreams and colors, much like the new path I was eager to walk with Carter. Whatever storms awaited us, I was ready to face them head-on, armed with the strength of my feelings and the support of my friends.

Chapter 17: Ripped Seams

The storm had swept through Lakewood with a ferocity that felt almost personal, twisting trees like pretzels and lashing rain against the windows of my father's boutique. The muted hues of the shop's façade—a gentle seafoam green—seemed dulled by the ominous clouds that hovered overhead. Inside, the faint scent of cedar mingled with the remnants of vintage perfume that clung to the dresses that hung on the racks like silent sentinels. My heart sank as I surveyed the chaos: mannequins lay toppled, their graceful forms now awkwardly strewn across the polished wooden floor. A ceiling tile had given in to the water's relentless assault, leaving a damp patch that threatened to expand like a stain on the very fabric of our dreams.

"Do you understand the magnitude of this?" My father's voice echoed through the space, thick with frustration. He stood at the back counter, his hands gripping the edge like it was the only thing keeping him upright. Lines of worry etched deeper into his forehead, contrasting starkly with the playful twinkle that used to light his eyes. I could feel the weight of his disappointment settling heavily in the air, an oppressive fog that made it hard to breathe.

"Dad, I didn't—" I began, but he cut me off with a wave of his hand, dismissing my words like autumn leaves caught in a sudden gust.

"You didn't think, is what you mean to say." His tone was sharp, and it sliced through my resolve, leaving me feeling exposed and vulnerable. "We made sacrifices to get this place running, and now look at it. The repairs alone are going to drain our savings—if we even have any left after this."

My heart raced as I glanced at the scattered remnants of the storm's wrath, my thoughts churning like the turbulent sky outside. Each word felt like a pebble thrown into an already turbulent pond, rippling out into every corner of my mind. This boutique was not just a business; it was a patchwork of my father's dreams and my own aspirations, stitched together over countless late nights filled with sketches and fabric swatches. It was where I had found myself, and now it felt like it was all slipping away.

"Maybe we can file an insurance claim?" I suggested hesitantly, knowing deep down that it wouldn't be nearly enough.

My father's eyes narrowed, a mixture of disbelief and anger washing over his features. "And what if they deny it? What if this is all for nothing? This is your fault for insisting we carry those designer lines. You pushed for them; now we're paying the price."

His words hung in the air, heavy and bitter. I could feel the tears prickling at the corners of my eyes, but I fought them back, unwilling to show weakness. "I thought they would attract more customers," I said quietly, the conviction in my voice faltering. "I thought we could stand out."

"Stand out? Look where standing out has gotten us!" His frustration boiled over, echoing through the boutique like the storm outside. I felt my chest tighten, every heartbeat a reminder of how fragile our partnership had become, how easily the threads that held us together were unraveling.

"Maybe I should just leave," I muttered under my breath, hoping he wouldn't hear the hurt laced in my words.

"What was that?" he snapped, but I couldn't look him in the eye.

I needed air—needed space. I pushed past him, my feet carrying me outside into the chaotic symphony of rain and wind. The air was thick, tasting of damp earth and petrichor, but as I inhaled, the weight of the world felt momentarily lighter. I stood on the cobbled sidewalk, my gaze drifting to the grey clouds that mirrored the turmoil in my heart. I had never felt so alone, yet the storm felt strangely comforting, a reminder that even nature could rage and still eventually find peace.

As I leaned against the boutique's weathered facade, a familiar warmth enveloped me. Carter appeared like a lighthouse in my stormy sea, his arms wrapping around me with a sense of safety that I desperately craved. "Hey," he murmured, his voice soft against the backdrop of the howling wind.

I closed my eyes, allowing myself to melt into his embrace. "I didn't expect to see you here," I whispered, my voice muffled against his chest.

"I couldn't leave you like this. I know how hard you've worked." There was a pause, a moment where the world seemed to hold its breath. "Want to talk about it?"

I hesitated, the walls I had built around my emotions whispering caution. But his presence was a soothing balm, coaxing out the fears I had been holding inside. "It's just... everything feels so fragile right now. One storm and it's like everything could come crashing down."

Carter's grip tightened, his warmth seeping into my bones. "You're stronger than you think," he said, a sincerity in his voice that made me want to believe him. Yet, lurking behind his encouraging words was the shadow of his past—an enigma I was terrified would always overshadow us.

He shifted slightly, creating space for honesty. "You know I've had my struggles too, right?" The vulnerability in his tone made my heart ache. I wanted to ask him to share, to unravel the layers of his story, but I was afraid. What if his burdens were too heavy for me to carry?

"I know," I admitted, my throat tightening. "But sometimes I wonder if... if they'll always come between us." The words tasted bitter, like burnt coffee in my mouth.

Carter sighed, the sound heavy with unspoken thoughts. "I can't promise my past won't affect us. But I can promise that I'm here, no matter what."

The sincerity in his gaze felt like a lifeline, yet I couldn't shake the nagging doubt. Could love truly withstand the weight of scars? As the storm raged on, I realized I had a choice to make—a leap into the unknown, or retreat into the safety of my fears.

But in that moment, standing against the storm with Carter beside me, I sensed a flicker of hope amidst the chaos. Perhaps we could weather this together, even if it meant facing our shadows head-on.

The storm continued to thrash against Lakewood, a cacophony of nature that matched the turmoil in my heart. As I stood there in Carter's embrace, the world around us felt muted, as if the chaos had been relegated to the background. His warmth enveloped me, a cocoon of safety that I desperately craved, yet doubt lingered in the corners of my mind. Did I deserve this moment of peace?

"Why don't we get away from here for a bit?" Carter suggested, his voice a soft murmur that contrasted with the tempest around us. "Somewhere where we can think without the weight of this storm hanging over us?"

The idea was tantalizing, a welcome escape from the suffocating expectations and looming deadlines that crowded my thoughts. "Where do you have in mind?" I asked, my curiosity piqued.

"Just up the road, there's a little coffee shop—The Roasted Bean. It's cozy and usually quiet, perfect for a stormy day like this." His suggestion painted a picture in my mind of warm light, the smell of coffee mingling with sweet pastries, and laughter lingering like an echo in the corners. I felt a flicker of hope, a sense that maybe we could carve out a moment of normalcy amidst the chaos.

"Okay," I replied, taking a step back to gauge his expression. I saw the flicker of relief in his eyes, and it eased the knot of anxiety tightening in my chest. Together, we hurried to his car, the rain drenching us as we dashed across the parking lot. I laughed as Carter playfully shielded me with his jacket, its fabric already soaked. There was a lightness in that moment, a fleeting respite from the weight of reality.

The drive was punctuated by the rhythmic patter of rain against the windshield, a soothing sound that filled the silence between us. Carter's presence next to me felt grounding, even as we navigated through streets turned into rivers. I stole glances at him when I thought he wasn't looking, tracing the line of his jaw and the way his hair fell just so, tousled but still charming. The way he gripped the steering wheel with confidence made me forget, if only for a moment, the turmoil that awaited us back at the boutique.

When we arrived at The Roasted Bean, the warm glow spilling from the windows drew us in like moths to a flame. Inside, the scent of freshly brewed coffee enveloped us, mingling with the sweetness of baked goods that tempted my senses. It was a sanctuary away from the storm, a pocket of warmth that felt almost magical. I breathed in deeply, feeling a sense of calm wash over me.

As we settled into a corner table, the small space filled with the gentle hum of conversation and the clinking of mugs. I felt the tension in my shoulders start to ease as I sipped my hot chocolate, the warmth seeping through me like a comforting embrace. It was as if the world outside had momentarily faded away, leaving just the two of us in this little bubble of tranquility.

"I've been thinking," Carter began, his brow furrowing slightly as he stirred his coffee. "About the things we carry with us. You know, the stuff from our past that doesn't just go away."

His tone shifted the atmosphere, and I set down my mug, suddenly aware that this conversation had the potential to crack the delicate surface of our budding relationship. "You don't have to talk about it if you don't want to," I offered, wanting to shield him from whatever memories lay heavy on his heart.

"No, it's okay. I need to share this with you," he insisted, his eyes locking onto mine with an intensity that made my heart race. "I just don't want you to think that my past won't affect our future."

The weight of his words hung between us like a storm cloud, threatening to burst at any moment. "I don't want to pressure you, but I'm here to listen. I promise I won't judge."

He took a deep breath, the steam from his coffee swirling around him like a halo. "When I was younger, my family faced some... financial issues. My dad lost his job, and my mom had to pick up extra shifts to keep us afloat. It was tough. I watched them fight, and that stress bled into everything—school, friendships, even my self-worth. I felt like I had to be the one to fix it all, to be perfect. But nothing I did ever felt good enough."

I listened, captivated by his vulnerability. The way he spoke revealed the raw edges of his soul, pieces of him that had been weathered and reshaped by life's storms. "That sounds incredibly hard, Carter," I said softly, my heart aching for the boy he once was, the burden he had carried alone.

"Sometimes I feel like that kid is still inside me," he confessed, his voice low. "I worry that if things go wrong—like they did with my family—I'll just fall apart again. That I'll mess this up and lose everything."

The fear in his voice mirrored my own anxieties, the doubts that lingered like shadows at the edges of my mind. "We're not our pasts, though," I said gently, reaching across the table to cover his hand with mine. "We can learn from them, but we don't have to be defined by them."

His gaze softened, and a small smile tugged at the corners of his lips. "You always know what to say to make me feel better."

"It's a gift," I replied with a playful grin, but inside, I felt a sense of pride swell. Maybe we were both learning to navigate the storms together, step by step. "But seriously, we can't let our pasts dictate our future. We have to trust in each other and in what we're building."

Carter nodded, and for a brief moment, the weight of his burdens seemed to lift. The connection we shared felt like a lifeline, and I realized that perhaps this was what it meant to truly be partners—not just in business, but in life.

"Let's make a pact," he said suddenly, a spark of mischief returning to his eyes. "No more letting our fears run the show. We face things head-on. Together."

"I like the sound of that," I agreed, squeezing his hand as a sense of warmth blossomed within me. In that little coffee shop, surrounded by the storm, we were carving out our own space, one built on trust, understanding, and a shared determination to move forward, no matter what the future held.

The warmth of the coffee shop faded, but the connection we had forged over those steaming mugs lingered like the sweet scent of cinnamon in the air. Carter and I emerged into the storm again, but this time it felt different—less suffocating, as if we were armed with new resolve. The rain drummed rhythmically on the pavement, a symphony that seemed to echo our unspoken promise. Hand in hand, we navigated the puddles that formed small lakes in the cracks of the sidewalk, our laughter punctuating the steady downpour like tiny bursts of sunlight.

"Let's check on the boutique," I suggested, my heart racing at the thought. I wasn't sure if it was excitement or dread, but the thought of facing my father with a fresh perspective filled me with determination. "Maybe we can start planning for the repairs together."

Carter nodded, a reassuring smile dancing on his lips. "I'm with you. Whatever we face, we face it together."

As we reached the boutique, the atmosphere shifted. The sight of the broken windows and debris scattered across the floor twisted my stomach into knots. I took a deep breath, steeling myself for the confrontation that awaited us inside. My father was likely still simmering with frustration, and the thought of navigating that tension felt overwhelming. Yet, I also knew that he needed to see that we were not just a pair of lost souls; we were a team, willing to weather the storm together.

Pushing through the door, the scent of damp wood and torn fabric enveloped us, the chaos echoing the tempest outside. My father stood at the back, his silhouette outlined by the dim light of the shop. He was on the phone, his voice low and strained as he barked into the receiver about estimates and timelines. The sight of him—stressed and weary—pulled at my heartstrings, and I wondered if he understood the depth of my commitment to this business, to our family.

"Dad," I said softly, hoping to catch his attention without adding to his frustration. He looked up, his eyes narrowing for a moment before softening as he recognized me.

"I'm on the phone," he said tersely before turning back to his conversation, leaving me standing there, caught between wanting to reach out and feeling the sting of his dismissiveness.

Carter stepped forward, an instinctive protector at my side. "We wanted to help with the repairs," he said, his tone steady but firm.

My father nodded absently, still focused on his call, and I exchanged a glance with Carter. There was something powerful in that moment—a silent understanding that we were both fighting for a shared dream, even if the battles were often personal.

Finally, my father hung up the phone and turned to us, his expression a mixture of relief and concern. "I'm sorry, but we need to get quotes for the repairs as soon as possible. I've got a couple of contractors coming by, but—"

"Dad, I know the repairs will be costly, but maybe we can brainstorm some ideas to offset those costs. We could run a sale or even reach out to some local businesses for collaborations." I felt the words spilling out of me, fueled by the hope Carter and I had just cultivated.

My father's brow furrowed, but I pressed on, buoyed by the support radiating from Carter beside me. "What if we hosted a charity event? We could invite local designers to showcase their work, and we could donate a portion of the proceeds to help the community recover from the storm."

There was a moment of silence, the tension thick in the air as my father considered my words. "That's... actually a decent idea." His expression softened, and I could see the wheels turning in his mind. "We could use the exposure. And it might help lift some spirits around here."

"Exactly," I said, my heart leaping at the glimmer of hope in his voice. "We could turn this around."

Carter's hand squeezed mine, and I felt bolstered by his presence, ready to tackle whatever else lay ahead.

As we discussed potential plans, the initial tension dissipated, and I could see my father starting to see the value in our partnership. Together, we brainstormed ways to reach out to the community, to not only mend our own wounds but to help others heal as well. The boutique began to feel like a hub of creativity and resilience again, the heart of Lakewood pulsing with new energy.

"I'll reach out to some of my contacts," Carter offered, his voice steady with determination. "We can get this event off the ground and maybe even draw in some press coverage."

With each suggestion, my father's mood improved, his frustrations easing as we found common ground in the shared mission of recovery. I caught glimpses of the man he used to be—the visionary, the dreamer—and it filled me with a newfound sense of purpose.

As we wrapped up our discussion, my father placed a hand on my shoulder, his expression sincere. "I appreciate you stepping up like this. I know it hasn't been easy, and I may have been a little harsh earlier."

"Just a little," I quipped, unable to resist the urge to lighten the mood.

He chuckled, and it felt like a victory to see that flicker of humor return to his eyes. "Well, let's get to work then. We've got a lot to do."

The storm had not only battered our boutique; it had stripped away the layers of misunderstanding that had built up between us. In its wake, we were left with raw emotions and a shared determination to rise above it all. Together.

Later that evening, as the sun began to set and the storm clouds cleared, the world outside transformed into a breathtaking watercolor palette of pinks and purples. The air felt fresh and invigorating, a promise of new beginnings. I stood by the window, watching as the first stars twinkled above, each one a reminder of the vast possibilities that lay ahead.

"Hey," Carter said, sidling up beside me. "I know things were rough earlier, but I'm really proud of you for how you handled everything."

"Thanks," I replied, feeling warmth spread through me at his words. "I couldn't have done it without you. You made me believe we could face this together."

The moment hung between us, charged with unspoken feelings. Carter leaned in closer, the space between us shrinking as the world outside faded into the background. Just as I thought he might close the distance, he pulled back slightly, a contemplative look crossing his face.

"Do you think we're ready for this?" he asked, the vulnerability in his voice echoing the uncertainty in my heart.

"Ready for what?" I asked, my brow furrowing in confusion.

"To really be in this together, to face everything—my past, your worries, the storms that come our way."

I took a moment to absorb his words, feeling the weight of our journey thus far. "I think we have to be. If we let fear dictate our choices, we'll never move forward."

He smiled, a genuine warmth spreading across his face, and I couldn't help but mirror it. In that instant, we forged an unbreakable bond, an understanding that whatever came next, we would tackle it side by side.

The storm had tested us, but it had also revealed the strength of our partnership. And as we looked out at the vibrant sky, filled with shimmering stars, I felt an exhilarating rush of hope, anticipation, and possibility—all wrapped up in the promise of what lay ahead.

Chapter 18: Reweaving Connections

The warm sunlight streamed through the open windows of the boutique, casting playful shadows on the polished wooden floors. Dust motes danced in the golden rays, swirling like tiny fairies celebrating our new beginnings. As I stood amidst the remnants of what had once been a thriving shop, the air was thick with the scent of fresh paint and fabric. It was a fragrance I had always loved, one that hinted at creativity and new possibilities. Montgomery Springs had a way of wrapping its arms around you, whispering stories through the gentle rustle of leaves and the laughter of its residents. Today, it felt particularly alive, as if the entire town had decided to breathe new life into our beloved boutique.

My heart raced with excitement and a hint of anxiety as I surveyed the space. The once-vibrant colors of the fabric and accessories were dulled by time and neglect, but I could envision what it could become again. I had invited the townspeople to join us for "Stitch & Share" day, hoping to spark a collective effort that would weave together not just the fabric of the boutique but also the threads of our community. I believed that together we could mend the past and create something beautiful anew.

One by one, faces began to filter in, each one carrying the unique stories of Montgomery Springs. Old Mrs. Hargrove, with her silver curls bouncing and her hands perpetually dusted with flour from her famous pies, arrived first, a wicker basket overflowing with spools of thread and an infectious smile that could warm the coldest winter day. "I brought my grandmother's sewing kit," she declared, her eyes twinkling with nostalgia. "I can't wait to see what you all are going to create!"

Her enthusiasm was like a spark in the air, igniting the spirits of everyone who walked through the door. Soon, the boutique was filled with the sounds of laughter and the soft hum of conversation.

I watched as neighbors gathered around tables, swapping stories and ideas while needles glided through fabric, each stitch a testament to the bonds we were forging.

In the midst of it all stood Carter, a figure I had been trying to understand since our first encounter. He moved with an ease that was both charming and intimidating, deftly threading a needle with the concentration of a seasoned craftsman. The sunlight caught the glint in his deep brown eyes as he glanced over at me, and for a moment, everything else faded. It was as if the chaos of the boutique had transformed into a backdrop for just the two of us, and the familiar warmth in my cheeks ignited again.

"Need a hand?" he asked, his voice a mix of playful banter and genuine interest. I could see the easy confidence he carried, and it made me feel both exhilarated and vulnerable. The vulnerability was a new sensation for me, one I was learning to embrace, especially in this moment filled with laughter and hope.

"Actually, I could use a lot of help," I replied, trying to sound casual despite the flutter in my stomach. "I thought we'd start by patching up the big holes in those display curtains. You in?"

"Consider it done."

As we worked side by side, I felt our chemistry spark with every shared glance and gentle brush of our shoulders. Carter's fingers danced over the fabric, turning mundane tasks into something beautiful. We talked about everything and nothing, sharing fragments of our lives as the afternoon slipped away. Each story I shared drew us closer, weaving a tapestry of our own that was slowly unfolding.

"Did you always want to own a boutique?" he asked, curiosity lacing his tone.

"I did," I confessed, feeling the warmth of nostalgia wash over me. "As a kid, I used to pretend my bedroom was a shop, displaying all my treasures for imaginary customers. I guess I've always wanted to create a space where people could find something special, something that speaks to them."

He nodded, his gaze intense as he took in my words. "That's beautiful. It's like you're curating joy for others."

"Curating joy," I echoed, letting the phrase roll off my tongue. It felt fitting, yet daunting. "But sometimes I wonder if I'm really good enough to do it."

Carter paused, his expression serious for a heartbeat before breaking into a soft smile. "Vulnerability is a strength, you know. It takes courage to put yourself out there."

His words resonated deep within me, filling the spaces that fear and doubt had occupied for far too long. "You think so?"

"I know so."

Just then, a burst of laughter erupted from the other side of the room, pulling us from our conversation. I glanced over to see Mrs. Hargrove sharing a funny anecdote about her baking misadventures. The sound of community enveloped us, a reminder that I wasn't alone in this endeavor. Together, we could overcome the challenges that had threatened to unravel everything we held dear.

As the day wore on, I realized that "Stitch & Share" was more than just a project to revive the boutique; it was a celebration of who we were as a community. Each stitch sewn held the promise of connection, a reminder that even in our struggles, we were woven together by shared experiences, laughter, and a collective will to rebuild.

With each passing moment, I felt a deeper bond forming not only with Carter but with the people around us. The intimate exchanges and shared vulnerabilities laid a foundation for something beautiful, something that would carry us into the future. As the sun dipped lower in the sky, painting the room with hues of gold and rose, I felt a renewed sense of purpose envelop me, urging me to embrace both the journey and the connections that would define it.

The sun began its descent, draping a warm golden blanket over Montgomery Springs. It cast long shadows through the boutique's wide windows, creating a mosaic of light and texture that felt almost magical. The chatter and laughter of my neighbors echoed around me like music, weaving a melody that lifted my spirits higher with each note. With Carter beside me, stitching curtains and crafting memories, I realized we were crafting something far more profound than fabric and thread. We were weaving a tapestry of shared experiences, vulnerable moments, and hopeful aspirations.

The hours melted away as our community settled into a rhythm. People gathered around tables strewn with colorful fabrics, needlework supplies, and half-finished projects. It was a beautiful chaos, filled with the sounds of clinking scissors, soft laughter, and the occasional exclamation of triumph when someone managed to pull off a particularly tricky sewing technique. I watched as the older generation, once cloistered in their homes, eagerly shared their skills with the youth, bridging gaps that had widened over the years. It was a sight that filled me with warmth, like a comforting hug on a chilly day.

As we worked, I felt a sense of pride swell within me. This was my vision coming to life, where everyone had a role to play, no matter how small. I moved from one table to another, offering encouragement and sharing ideas, my heart buoyed by the enthusiasm surrounding me. In the back corner, I spotted Mrs. Hargrove demonstrating how to embroider delicate flowers onto a patch, her eyes shining with excitement as a young girl named Ava leaned in, utterly captivated. "You see, darling? Just a gentle hand, and it blooms," Mrs. Hargrove said, her voice lilting like a song.

I chuckled softly, enchanted by the image of a flower coming to life under Mrs. Hargrove's careful touch, and it struck me: that's what we were all doing. Each of us was a flower, bringing color and life to the fabric of our community. But as beautiful as that thought was, a shadow lurked in the back of my mind. While we were patching up the boutique, could we really mend the emotional scars we carried?

With the sun casting rosy hues through the windows, I found myself stealing glances at Carter. He was focused, a small crease of concentration etched between his brows as he worked on a particularly stubborn seam. I admired the way he threw himself into the task, his passion for creation evident in every deft movement. It was infectious, a spark that ignited something within me. I felt as though I had stumbled upon a rare gemstone, one that illuminated the shadows of doubt that sometimes clouded my heart.

"Looks like you've got a knack for this," I said playfully, stepping closer to him, my voice low enough for only him to hear. The way he turned to me, a surprised smile lighting up his face, sent warmth flooding through my veins.

"I'm just following your lead," he replied, his tone teasing. "Besides, it's hard not to get inspired when you're around."

His words hung in the air, thick with unspoken meaning. I felt the heat rush to my cheeks as I attempted to gather my thoughts, my heart racing in response to his compliment. Was it merely a casual remark, or was there something deeper simmering beneath the surface? I chose to let it linger, a delicious secret shared between us amid the cheerful chaos.

As the afternoon rolled into evening, the atmosphere transformed, rich with the scent of baked goods wafting in from the makeshift kitchen area where some of the local bakers had set up shop. I could see platters of cookies, brownies, and slices of pie being passed around, the sweetness mingling with our labor to create an intoxicating blend.

"Hey, let's take a break," Carter suggested, stretching his arms overhead. "I could use a snack and a chance to soak in all this creative energy."

"Good idea," I agreed, grateful for a moment to step back and breathe. As we made our way to the snack table, I was struck by how effortlessly he moved through the crowd, exchanging jokes and nods with the people around us. It was as if he belonged to this tapestry of community, a thread woven deeply into its fabric.

We found a spot by the window, the golden light cascading over us as we picked at the assorted treats. I nibbled on a piece of pie, its flaky crust crumbling beautifully, and watched as Carter savored a chocolate chip cookie, his eyes lighting up with delight.

"This is amazing," he said, mouth half-full, a genuine grin stretching across his face. "I've never understood why people put their heart and soul into baking until now."

I laughed, loving how simple pleasures could brighten someone's day. "Baking is just like sewing," I mused. "Both require patience and a little bit of love. Plus, the end result is always worth the effort."

Carter leaned back, his eyes narrowing thoughtfully. "Is that why you do what you do? Because you believe in the end result?"

I paused, his question resonating deeply within me. "Absolutely. I want to create a place where people feel seen, where they can find beauty in the simplest things. Just like these cookies."

"And just like you," he replied, his tone softening. "You've created something special here."

I looked down, suddenly shy under the weight of his gaze. "It's not just me, you know. It's all of us. Today is proof of that."

"But you're the one who brought everyone together. You're the heart of this," he insisted, his voice earnest.

My pulse quickened at his words, and I dared to look into his eyes. For a moment, I could see the reflection of my own dreams mirrored there. In that moment, I felt a shift, as if the walls I had carefully constructed around my heart were beginning to crumble.

"Maybe it's time for us all to embrace our vulnerabilities," I said, surprising myself with my honesty. "To share not just our skills but our fears too."

He nodded, understanding hanging in the air between us like a tangible force. "Sometimes, it takes a little push from someone else to start reweaving those connections."

And there it was—the weight of what we were doing together, stitching together not just fabric but lives, relationships, and hidden fears. As we resumed our work, the sun dipped below the horizon, and the boutique glowed with a warm, inviting light, symbolizing the hope we had ignited. In that moment, I knew that we were not just rebuilding a shop; we were crafting a community that would endure through laughter, love, and a touch of vulnerability.

The evening settled around us like a soft, warm quilt, wrapping the boutique in a cocoon of coziness. The fading sunlight cast a tapestry of rich oranges and deep purples through the windows, illuminating the motley crew of volunteers who were now more like family than neighbors. As I glanced around, I marveled at how every corner of the space seemed to thrum with energy. Laughter bubbled like the gentle sound of a nearby stream, intermingling with the rustle of fabric and the rhythmic thumping of hammers as we repaired display shelves that had long seen better days.

Each of us was engaged in our little corners of creativity, yet we were all bound together by a single thread—an eagerness to breathe life back into our community. I watched as Ava, her face scrunched in concentration, attempted to thread a needle for the first time, her determination palpable. "You can do it!" I cheered, the words slipping out before I could stop them.

"Why is this so hard?" she groaned, her frustration erupting in a light-hearted pout.

"Because you're trying to thread it with all the finesse of a raccoon trying to pick a lock," I teased, and her giggles echoed through the room, an unmistakable note of joy amidst the hard work.

With every smile exchanged and every encouraging word, I felt the boutique begin to blossom again, a metaphorical flower unfurling its petals toward the sun. I stole another glance at Carter, who was leaning against a workbench, watching the scene unfold with an amused expression. His warmth was a constant comfort, like a favorite sweater that envelops you just right. As he caught my eye, his lips curled into that lopsided smile that sent my heart racing, a reminder that we were weaving more than just fabric today.

I was swept up in the moment, a rush of gratitude flooding through me as I pondered how this simple gathering had transformed into a celebration of hope. Yet, beneath the surface of this joyful camaraderie lay deeper currents, each person carrying their own stories, struggles, and dreams. I felt a twinge of sadness as I considered the loss and heartache many had endured, particularly after the recent difficulties that had shadowed our little town.

Just then, Mrs. Hargrove approached, her hands dusted with flour from the baking escapades that had ensued in the corner of the boutique. "We could use a fresh set of hands over by the pie table, dear," she said, her voice a melody of warmth. "I fear the cookies are starting to conspire against the pies, and we can't let that happen now, can we?"

"Of course, Mrs. Hargrove! Just let me finish this seam," I said, gesturing to the curtain I was working on.

As I sewed, I felt a rush of purpose, as if each stitch was stitching my heart back together. When I finally finished, I jumped up and made my way to the baking corner. The air was thick with the comforting scents of cinnamon and vanilla, the aroma wrapping around me like a long-lost friend.

"Ah, you've come to rescue me," Mrs. Hargrove proclaimed, her eyes sparkling with mischief as she thrust a rolling pin into my hands.

"Your mission, should you choose to accept it, is to flatten this dough to the perfect thickness before it runs away!"

I laughed, accepting the challenge. It was moments like this that made me realize how deeply interwoven our lives were; each thread represented a connection, a shared experience that could bring light even to the darkest corners. As I rolled out the dough, I couldn't help but think about how often we let our insecurities dictate our actions. Today, though, it felt different. Vulnerability was no longer a burden; it had become a strength that united us.

As I worked alongside Mrs. Hargrove, I noticed Carter wandering over, his expression curious as he leaned against the counter. "What are you cooking up over here?" he asked, his voice playful as he peeked at the swirling flour dust clouding the air.

"Just saving the world, one pie at a time," I quipped, flouring my hands with a flourish. "Care to join me?"

"I would love to, but I'm afraid my talents lie more in needle and thread than in baking." He raised an eyebrow, and I couldn't help but feel a rush of warmth at the way his gaze lingered on me.

"Is that so? I bet you're hiding a hidden talent," I said, pressing my palms against my hips, challenging him. "How about we make a deal? If you can help with the pie crusts, I'll teach you how to sew."

Carter chuckled, leaning closer. "You've got yourself a deal. Just don't expect me to create a masterpiece."

"Deal," I said, my heart dancing at the prospect of spending more time with him.

The atmosphere shifted, the energy crackling between us as we exchanged teasing banter while baking. We worked side by side, the rhythm of our movements echoing the camaraderie that had built around us. Every so often, our hands would brush against one another as we reached for the same spatula or flour-dusted rolling pin. Each accidental touch sent sparks shooting through me, igniting the tender embers of something that felt both new and terrifying.

Just as I was getting lost in our little world, the door swung open, and a wave of chill air swept through the boutique. A tall figure stepped inside, his presence instantly commanding attention. It was Maxwell Rowen, the patriarch of the Rowen family, and his arrival sent ripples of unease through the room. His reputation preceded him, a man known for his authority and sharp tongue, particularly when it came to the well-being of his family.

"Good evening, everyone," he announced, his voice deep and authoritative. "I trust I'm not interrupting anything too... frivolous?"

The cheerful atmosphere dimmed slightly, the laughter fading into an uneasy silence. I felt a sudden wave of protectiveness for the community that had opened its arms to me. This was our moment, our chance to rebuild and connect, and I refused to let it slip through our fingers.

With a steely resolve, I stepped forward, summoning every ounce of courage I had. "We're just working on some repairs, Maxwell. We're weaving our community back together, piece by piece."

His gaze narrowed, weighing my words. "Community is important, but let's not forget that some connections should remain unaltered."

The tension in the room was palpable as I glanced at Carter, who stood slightly behind me, his presence a reassuring anchor. I wasn't about to let fear dictate our choices anymore, not after everything we had built together. "Perhaps," I countered, my voice steadier than I felt, "but sometimes those connections need a little reweaving to grow stronger."

Maxwell's eyes flickered with surprise, perhaps even admiration, but he quickly masked it with his typical stoicism. "I hope you know what you're doing."

As he stepped back, a murmur of agreement rippled through the crowd. We were here for each other, and it was a bond forged in shared experiences, laughter, and moments of vulnerability. I could feel the warmth of support surrounding me, bolstering my resolve.

With the evening winding down and the laughter returning, I knew we had crossed an invisible threshold. The boutique was more than just a shop; it was a sanctuary where we could shed our fears and insecurities, embracing the beauty of our collective spirit. And in that moment, as Carter's hand brushed against mine, I felt a newfound sense of purpose bloom within me. Together, we were not just mending fabric; we were crafting a future brimming with hope, connection, and love.

Chapter 19: Woven Promises

The sun hung low in the sky, casting a golden hue over the sprawling fields that flanked the edges of our small town, Maplewood. As the final hammer struck the last nail into place, a symphony of cheers erupted from the crowd. I stepped back to take it all in, my heart swelling with an unexpected warmth. This wasn't just any community project; it was the culmination of countless hours spent laboring alongside neighbors and friends, transforming a once-neglected park into a vibrant space where laughter and life would bloom anew. The smell of freshly turned earth mixed with the rich aroma of barbecue wafted through the air, weaving its way through the mingling scents of cotton candy and popcorn.

Children raced around, their giggles ringing like chimes, as they darted between parents who held plates piled high with food. I could see Mrs. Thompson from across the way, her silver hair catching the sunlight as she expertly flipped burgers on the grill, while Mr. Harrison oversaw the pie-eating contest with the enthusiasm of a carnival barker. It was a slice of Americana that felt both nostalgic and invigorating. Each face in the crowd, every cheer and shared laugh, felt like threads weaving a tapestry of connection, binding us together in a way I had never experienced before.

My father stood nearby, his arms crossed, an uncharacteristic smile tugging at the corners of his mouth as he observed the festivities. He had always been a pillar of strength in our family, but the burdens he carried weighed heavily on him, making his expressions rare and fleeting. Today, though, a lightness seemed to flicker in his eyes, a promise that perhaps this day could shift the landscape of our lives. It was a small but significant victory, one that would take root in the heart of our community and, hopefully, in the heart of my father as well.

As the sun dipped lower, painting the sky with strokes of pink and orange, I made my way to where the food was served. The sound of sizzling patties mingled with the bubbling laughter, creating an atmosphere that felt almost magical. I filled my plate with an assortment of treats—hot dogs, corn on the cob slathered in butter, and a slice of cherry pie that looked like it belonged on the cover of a magazine. It was in these moments, surrounded by the comforting familiarity of my hometown, that I found a profound sense of belonging.

Later that evening, after the festivities had wound down and the laughter began to fade, Carter pulled me aside, his demeanor shifting from playful to serious. The shadows cast by the setting sun danced around us, creating a quiet space that felt charged with anticipation. I could see the conflict in his eyes, a tempest brewing beneath his usually easygoing exterior.

"I need to tell you something," he began, his voice steady but low, as if he feared the very air around us might betray his thoughts. "I've been thinking about my future—really thinking about it."

I felt a knot tighten in my stomach, a mix of excitement and dread. Carter had always been a dreamer, his mind swirling with visions of places far beyond the reach of our little town. His adventurous spirit had always captivated me, igniting a spark of wanderlust within myself. Yet, the idea of him leaving filled me with a palpable sense of loss.

"I want to travel," he confessed, his gaze dropping to the ground, as if the weight of his dreams were too much to bear. "I want to see the world, experience things that—" He paused, collecting his thoughts like a painter mixing colors. "Things that make me feel alive."

The words hung between us like a fragile web, intricate yet easily severed by the winds of change. I could feel my heart racing, caught in a tug-of-war between wanting to support him and the instinctive fear of losing the boy who had become my anchor. "Carter, that sounds incredible," I replied, searching for the right words. "But... what about us? What does that mean for us?"

He looked up, his expression a mixture of hope and uncertainty. "I don't want to lose what we have," he said, his voice thick with emotion. "But I also can't ignore this urge to explore. It's a part of who I am."

The truth of his words resonated within me, creating a poignant ache in my chest. Love, I realized, was not just about holding on tightly but also about allowing each other the freedom to chase our dreams, even when those paths diverged. I wanted him to be happy, to experience all the wonders this world had to offer, but the thought of being apart was a bitter pill to swallow.

"What if," I started, hesitating, "what if we made a promise? A promise to support each other no matter where we go? That way, we both know we're still in this together, no matter the distance."

He smiled, the tension in his shoulders easing as if my words had cast away the shadows that had been weighing on him. "I'd like that. I'd really like that."

In that moment, the air felt lighter, the weight of uncertainty shifting to something more hopeful. We stood there, two souls intertwined by dreams and promises, each vowing to support the other's journey, no matter how far apart our paths might lead. The world outside was vast and daunting, but here, in our little corner of it, we had built something beautiful—a bond woven with trust and love. As the stars began to twinkle above, I felt a renewed sense of purpose swelling within me, ready to embrace whatever lay ahead.

The following weeks settled into a rhythm that felt almost cinematic, the kind of predictability that made my heart swell with gratitude. As summer enveloped Maplewood in its warm embrace, I found myself immersed in the comforting chaos of community life. The park we had revitalized stood proudly at the center of town, a vibrant hub teeming with activity. Families picnicked beneath the shade of newly planted trees, children chased each other around the colorful playground, and laughter echoed through the air like a sweet melody.

One afternoon, as I sat on a weathered bench watching the world unfold around me, I felt a gentle nudge at my side. I turned to see Carter, his sandy hair tousled by the breeze, a wide grin illuminating his face. He flopped down beside me, a half-eaten ice cream cone in hand, its chocolate swirl dripping down the side as if it were desperately trying to escape. "I think I've found my next destination," he declared, an eager gleam in his eyes.

"Oh really?" I leaned in, my curiosity piqued. "Where to this time? The Eiffel Tower? The beaches of Bali?"

He chuckled, the sound light and infectious. "Close. The local art fair! There's an artist I've been dying to meet. She's supposed to be this genius with spray paint, and her work is breathtaking." He animatedly recounted his research, gesturing wildly, his excitement contagious.

"Sounds intriguing. Count me in," I replied, my heart fluttering at the prospect of spending more time with him. It felt essential to support his aspirations, to become a part of the journey he was so eager to embark upon. We made plans for the following weekend, and as we stood up to leave, I couldn't help but feel a thrill coursing through me, a shared energy that seemed to spark a new adventure.

As the days rolled on, I found myself captivated not just by Carter's dreams but also by the simplicity of our moments together. Each sunset we chased, the vibrant hues painting the sky, seemed to symbolize our blossoming relationship. We explored the nooks and crannies of Maplewood, discovering hidden trails and forgotten corners of the town that brimmed with history and secrets waiting to be unearthed.

One evening, we wandered along the banks of the Crystal River, the water glistening under the moonlight like a scattering of diamonds. The air was cool, filled with the sweet scent of honeysuckle that hung like an invisible thread, binding us to this enchanted moment. Carter tossed a pebble into the water, watching as it created ripples that faded into the darkness. "You know," he said, his voice contemplative, "sometimes I think about how small we are in the grand scheme of things. Just little dots on this spinning rock."

I contemplated his words, feeling the weight of them settle between us. "But even the smallest dots can create beautiful patterns," I replied, looking into his eyes, which shone with the reflection of the starlit sky. "Every choice we make, every path we take, adds to the tapestry of our lives."

He turned to me, a smile breaking across his face, illuminating the corners of his eyes. "You always have a way of making things sound profound." I felt warmth bloom in my chest, an appreciation for the connection we were forging.

Yet, beneath the surface of my budding affection, a current of anxiety lingered. I wrestled with the knowledge that Carter's dreams extended beyond the borders of our small town. Each adventurous plan he shared felt like a gentle tug on the thread of our bond, threatening to unravel the fabric of what we were weaving together. Could I bear the thought of him wandering off into the unknown, leaving me behind in the safety of Maplewood?

The art fair arrived with all the fanfare of a small-town festival, filled with vibrant stalls that lined the main street. The scent of freshly painted canvases mingled with the aroma of street food, creating an intoxicating blend that ignited the senses. Colorful flags fluttered in the breeze, and laughter danced in the air like confetti. I watched as Carter darted from one booth to another, his enthusiasm palpable as he engaged with local artists, his eyes lighting up with every new discovery.

I lingered at a nearby stall, admiring a piece of artwork that depicted a sprawling field of wildflowers beneath a cerulean sky. The colors were vivid, alive with energy, and I could almost feel the breeze rustling through the blooms. It struck me then—Carter's dreams of travel and exploration were like those wildflowers, vibrant and free, yearning to stretch their roots into foreign soil. I wanted to nurture that dream, to be the sun that fueled his growth.

Just as I was lost in thought, I felt a presence beside me. Carter stood there, a canvas tucked under his arm, grinning ear to ear. "Look at this!" He revealed a piece that showcased a breathtaking sunset, hues of orange and pink swirling together like a warm embrace. "I got it from that artist I wanted to meet. Isn't it stunning?"

"It's beautiful," I replied, genuinely impressed. "It captures everything we love about this town." A flicker of pride surged within me, not just for Carter's accomplishment but for the passion that radiated from him.

As the day wound down and the sun dipped low, casting a golden glow over the fair, I couldn't shake the feeling that this moment was pivotal. Surrounded by laughter and the aroma of fried dough, I glanced at Carter. He was in his element, living his dream, and I felt an overwhelming urge to say something meaningful, to weave our promises into the fabric of our shared journey.

"Carter," I began, the words tumbling out with a nervous energy. "No matter where you go, no matter what you see, I want you to remember that you can always come back to this place. To us. I'll always be here, cheering you on."

His expression softened, and for a moment, the noise of the fair faded into a gentle hum. "I want you to know that wherever I go, you're a part of me," he said, the sincerity in his voice wrapping around me like a cozy blanket. "I'll carry this town and you with me, no matter the distance."

In that moment, surrounded by the vibrancy of the art fair, I felt as if we were building a bridge, one that would carry us over the chasms of uncertainty. It was a promise woven with threads of love, hope, and the unyielding belief that we could navigate whatever lay ahead—together.

The weeks that followed unfurled like the pages of a well-loved book, each day rich with new experiences and the sweet fragrance of possibility. Maplewood was alive with the pulse of summer; vibrant hues spilled across the landscape, and the community buzzed with a sense of renewed connection. Festivals and farmers' markets brought everyone together, creating an intricate tapestry of shared stories and laughter. There was a palpable energy in the air, a reminder that life's most beautiful moments often sprang from the simplest of gatherings.

One afternoon, Carter and I strolled through the bustling farmers' market, the bright stalls overflowing with colorful fruits and vegetables, their hues nearly blinding in the sunlight. The chatter of vendors hawking their goods mingled with the laughter of children chasing one another through the aisles, and the sweet scent of freshly baked bread wafted through the air. I felt as if we were at the heart of a living painting, where every brushstroke told a story, and every color reflected the essence of our little town.

As we wandered from booth to booth, I marveled at the beauty of the everyday moments we shared—Carter's laughter, light and infectious, as he playfully dodged a wayward kid wielding a water balloon, and the way his eyes sparkled when he spotted the local artisan selling hand-painted ceramics. I watched as he engaged with the vendor, enthusiasm radiating from him like sunlight breaking through clouds.

"I think this one would look perfect in your kitchen," he said, holding up a delicate bowl adorned with intricate blue patterns reminiscent of waves. My heart swelled at the thoughtfulness behind his words; he had always known how to make the ordinary feel extraordinary.

"It's beautiful!" I exclaimed, imagining it filled with ripe, juicy strawberries or fresh herbs. "But how about we pick out something together? I mean, we both have kitchens to think about." The suggestion rolled off my tongue before I fully realized it, a quiet acknowledgment of how intertwined our lives had become.

He grinned, his eyes crinkling at the corners. "Alright, let's find the perfect piece, then! Something that represents us."

Our playful banter echoed through the market, and soon we had selected a charming, sun-kissed bowl, adorned with whimsical flowers that reminded us of our park project. As we paid the vendor, I felt a spark of something profound, as if this simple purchase marked a moment in time—a memory etched in the fabric of our shared life.

Later that evening, the sun dipped below the horizon, casting long shadows across the grassy expanse of the park. The golden hour bathed everything in warmth, and we settled onto a blanket spread out beneath a giant oak tree, its gnarled branches sheltering us from the encroaching night.

As we shared a picnic, laughter flowed freely, the remnants of our day spilling into our conversation. "You know, I was thinking," Carter said, pausing between bites of homemade sandwiches. "What if we documented our adventures together? Like a travel journal, but one that captures the little moments here too, not just the big trips?"

His idea resonated within me, igniting a flicker of inspiration. "That could be incredible! We could sketch, write, or even collect things—like leaves or ticket stubs." I imagined the pages filled with our adventures, the simple joys we encountered along the way, and the milestones that marked our growth.

"Exactly!" he replied, enthusiasm igniting his voice. "It'll be our way of holding onto this time, of remembering who we were as we chase our dreams."

I felt a swell of pride, knowing that we were both committed to weaving our stories together, acknowledging the inevitable changes that lay ahead. It felt vital, a binding promise that neither distance nor time could unravel.

As the stars began to twinkle overhead, a gentle breeze rustled the leaves, and we settled into a comfortable silence, the world around us transforming into a magical realm illuminated by moonlight. It was in this serene moment that I sensed an unspoken agreement—a mutual understanding that whatever paths we chose, we would carry a piece of each other with us.

As summer turned to fall, the first hints of change appeared in the air. The leaves transformed into fiery shades of red and gold, carpeting the ground in a beautiful tapestry. Yet beneath the vibrant exterior, I sensed the weight of impending decisions. Carter's aspirations loomed like storm clouds on the horizon, and the reality of his dreams weighed heavily on my heart.

One afternoon, while walking through the newly vibrant park, we stumbled upon a gathering of artists and musicians. The sounds of laughter mingled with the strumming of guitars and the melody of flutes, creating an atmosphere that felt alive with creativity. It was a festival celebrating local talent, an event where dreams were shared and nurtured.

As we wandered from booth to booth, I felt a mixture of excitement and apprehension brewing within me. Artists displayed their work with pride, showcasing the heart and soul they poured into their creations. I watched as Carter engaged with them, absorbing their stories like a sponge, his excitement bubbling over.

"Do you ever think about what it takes to really pursue your passion?" he asked, his voice laced with wonder. "To throw caution to the wind and just go for it?"

The question lingered in the air, drawing me into a deeper contemplation. "It's terrifying, isn't it? The idea of putting yourself out there, of risking failure," I replied, my voice softening as I considered my own fears. "But what if we never try? What if we stay safe, forever wondering what could have been?"

Carter nodded, understanding reflected in his eyes. "Exactly. I want to chase that feeling of being alive, even if it means stepping outside my comfort zone."

The words hung between us, charged with a shared vulnerability. I felt a surge of admiration for his courage, for his willingness to pursue his dreams despite the risks. And yet, a knot tightened in my stomach, an acknowledgment that every leap came with a price.

As the festival unfolded around us, I could see the beauty in the risks he wanted to take, yet I couldn't ignore the fear of losing him to those ambitions. I wanted him to soar, to chase the horizons, but part of me clung desperately to the safety of our shared world.

"Promise me something," I finally said, my voice steady despite the turmoil inside. "No matter where you go, you'll share those experiences with me. I want to be a part of your journey, even if it's from afar."

His gaze met mine, the sincerity in his eyes grounding me. "I promise. You'll always be my anchor, even when I'm chasing the wild winds."

With that, the world around us faded into a blur of colors and sounds, the festival alive with energy while we stood rooted in our moment of understanding.

Underneath the vast expanse of the sky, with its canvas of stars twinkling like distant dreams, I realized that love is not merely about holding on; it's about embracing the ebb and flow of each other's lives. As the laughter echoed through the night, I felt a sense of peace settle in my heart, a quiet acceptance that love could indeed flourish amidst the uncertainty of tomorrow.

Chapter 20: Frayed Edges

The vibrant clatter of hangers clinking against each other filled the air, mingling with the rich scent of lavender from the fresh bouquets I'd placed by the register. The boutique had begun to hum with life again, each customer a brushstroke in the lively painting that had once been dulled. Sunlight streamed through the wide windows, casting a warm glow over the carefully curated racks of dresses, blouses, and accessories, each a testament to the dreams and hard work woven into the fabric of our small-town charm. I had spent countless hours rearranging displays, adjusting the lighting, and infusing the space with a palpable sense of joy—an act of defiance against the shadows that had loomed over my life just weeks before.

Yet, despite the blossoming vitality surrounding me, a storm brewed just beneath the surface, twisting and tugging at my heartstrings. Carter had become an integral part of my daily routine, the echo of his laughter resonating like a familiar melody in the background of my bustling life. The connection we shared deepened with each passing day, our chemistry crackling like static electricity in the air. Yet, the closer we grew, the more my anxiety tightened its grip. His ambitions loomed like a cloud over our blossoming relationship, a constant reminder that what we had might not be enough to withstand the pressures of his dreams and my own burgeoning hopes.

On one particularly warm evening, as we sorted through a fresh delivery of fabrics—a delightful assortment of florals and polka dots—I felt the urge to voice the fears I had kept bottled up inside. The air was thick with the mingling scents of cotton and linen, the colors around us a dizzying array of hues that felt like a metaphor for our own complicated emotions. I hesitated, fingers brushing over a rich emerald fabric, its softness a stark contrast to the knot in my stomach.

"Carter," I started, my voice wavering slightly as I broke the comfortable silence that had enveloped us. He glanced up, his expression softening, his dark curls falling over his forehead in that charmingly disheveled way that never failed to make my heart skip. "I've been thinking..."

His brows furrowed with concern, and he set down the vibrant yellow fabric he'd been examining. "What is it? You know you can tell me anything."

Taking a deep breath, I forced myself to meet his gaze. The warmth in his eyes made the vulnerability I felt more tangible. "I'm scared, Carter. I know we're having fun, and it feels so good to be close to you, but what happens when your dreams take you away from here? What if you go off to chase them, and I... I can't follow?"

The words spilled out like the frantic notes of a symphony, the crescendo building within me until I could no longer hold it back. I watched his expression shift as he absorbed my confession, his brow smoothing out as he stepped closer, the distance between us shrinking. The air between us crackled with an intensity that sent shivers down my spine.

"I know how you feel," he said softly, the sincerity in his voice wrapping around me like a comforting embrace. "I've been thinking about it too, about how everything is changing. But it doesn't mean we can't make this work. We'll find a way. I promise."

His words ignited a flicker of hope within me, illuminating the dark corners of my doubts. Yet, a tiny voice in the back of my mind whispered that promises could be fragile, easily shattered by the harsh reality of life. Carter had dreams that stretched far beyond the quaint streets of our town, aspirations that painted pictures of bright lights and bustling cities where my name might never echo. I longed to be a part of his world, but the weight of uncertainty pressed heavily against my heart.

As we resumed sorting the fabrics, our hands brushed together, a fleeting connection that sent sparks dancing along my skin. I stole glances at him, noting the way his brow furrowed in concentration and how he bit his lip when deep in thought. The sight of him was a balm to my worries, but I couldn't shake the underlying fear that gnawed at me. The rhythm of our work fell into sync, a gentle back-and-forth that mirrored the ebb and flow of our growing relationship.

In the days that followed, I threw myself into my work with a fervor, determined to keep the boutique thriving while also pushing down the rising tide of anxiety. I created new displays, showcasing the vibrancy of our fabrics against the backdrop of the season's change. But as the weeks passed, the emotional rollercoaster I was riding with Carter left me feeling dizzy, my heart fluttering with exhilaration and dread alike.

We shared stolen moments between customers—quick, breathless conversations that felt like little slices of happiness amidst the chaos of our day. But with every laugh we shared, the echo of my fears grew louder. What if this was just a fleeting moment in time? What if we were destined to drift apart, like two ships passing in the night, forever out of reach?

One evening, after closing up the boutique, we lingered under the dim light of the porch, the gentle hum of cicadas wrapping around us like a soft blanket. I leaned against the railing, my heart racing as I watched him. Carter's presence grounded me, but the uncertainty of what lay ahead still cast a shadow over my thoughts.

"Let's not let fear dictate our story," he murmured, the sincerity in his tone softening the edges of my worries. "We're writing this together, one day at a time."

His words held a promise, a gentle reminder that we had the power to shape our narrative. Yet, the heaviness of potential loss still weighed on me. My heart was a fragile thing, so easily bruised and yet yearning to leap toward the unknown. Each moment with Carter was a delicious blend of hope and anxiety, and I couldn't help but wonder—was it worth the risk?

The next few days unfolded like a delicate tapestry, each moment weaving into the next, a mix of excitement and trepidation that echoed in the quiet corners of my mind. The boutique thrummed with a renewed energy, its polished wood floors reflecting the vibrant hues of summer, a kaleidoscope of colors splashing joy across every surface. The bright dresses danced on the racks, whispering tales of adventures yet to come, while the scent of freshly brewed coffee from the small café next door seeped through the door, filling the space with a warm familiarity.

Carter was my constant companion, his laughter mingling with the chatter of customers who filled the store, each one a reminder of the life we were building together. He had taken to helping out more often, his hands deftly sorting fabrics and adjusting displays, as if he were becoming a part of the very fabric of my life. I cherished these moments, yet they were tinged with a bittersweet awareness—the nagging thought that our paths might diverge when his dreams took flight.

One afternoon, the sun dipped low in the sky, casting a golden hue over everything. I caught Carter leaning against the counter, a playful smirk on his face as he joked with a customer. The warmth of his smile wrapped around me, and for a brief moment, I felt as if the world outside faded into oblivion. But as I watched him, my heart tightened. Beneath the laughter and easy camaraderie, I sensed an undercurrent of tension. The world was pulling him toward it, and I was left with the disquieting feeling that I might not be able to keep pace.

That evening, after the last customer had wandered out with a shopping bag filled with their own dreams, I found myself gazing out the window, the vibrant streetlights flickering to life as the sun surrendered to twilight. Carter approached, leaning against the window frame beside me. He glanced at me sideways, the light catching the flecks of gold in his eyes. "Penny for your thoughts?" he asked, a teasing lilt in his voice that I loved.

I hesitated, the weight of my worries pressing down on me. "Just thinking about how much I've missed this place," I said, forcing a smile that didn't quite reach my eyes. "And how wonderful it is to see it thriving again."

He nodded, but I could see the curiosity in his gaze. "I can tell there's more on your mind. You've been a bit... distant lately."

His observation stung, a reminder that my efforts to mask my feelings were not as effective as I hoped. Turning to face him fully, I took a deep breath, feeling the rush of honesty push its way to the forefront. "It's just... I worry about what happens next. You've got so many dreams, and I want you to pursue them. But what if those dreams lead you away from me?"

Carter's expression softened, and he stepped closer, the warmth of his body radiating against the cool evening air. "You think I would let that happen? You're a part of my dreams, you know."

The sincerity in his voice wrapped around me like a warm embrace, yet a part of me still felt tethered to that gnawing fear. "But what if it gets too complicated? I don't want to hold you back."

His gaze turned serious, and for a moment, I could see the conflict dancing behind his eyes. "You could never hold me back, Lily. I want you in my life, no matter what. We can figure this out together, one step at a time."

I wanted to believe him, to let those words wash over me and soothe the jagged edges of my anxiety. But the uncertainty loomed, and I felt like I was standing on the edge of a precipice, peering into the unknown.

With the night deepening, we decided to take a stroll along the riverside. The air was alive with the sounds of crickets and the soft rustling of leaves. The river glimmered under the moonlight, a ribbon of silver winding its way through the heart of the town. As we walked side by side, our fingers brushed occasionally, each gentle touch igniting a spark that made my heart race.

We found a bench overlooking the water and settled in, the silence between us comfortable yet charged with unspoken words. I watched the reflection of the moon ripple on the surface of the river, and suddenly, I felt the urge to push aside my fears and embrace the moment. "What do you want, Carter? Really want?"

His brows furrowed, and he turned to me, the weight of my question hanging in the air. "I want to build something—something meaningful. I want to make my mark, but I don't want to do it alone."

"What if what you build takes you far away?" I asked, the vulnerability in my voice matching the raw honesty in his gaze.

"Then I'll find a way to bring you along," he replied, his tone unwavering. "You're my anchor, Lily. I can't imagine my life without you in it."

The gravity of his words settled over me like a comforting blanket, and for the first time in days, I felt a flicker of hope break through the clouds of my doubt. We spoke long into the night, sharing dreams and fears, desires and uncertainties, our words weaving a tapestry of connection that felt both fragile and resilient. The more we talked, the more I realized how much I cherished this man standing beside me, how his presence ignited a spark within my soul that I had almost forgotten existed.

As we made our way back to the boutique, the moon casting a gentle glow over the streets, I found myself leaning into the idea of partnership, of shared dreams, and of navigating life together. With every step, the weight of my anxiety began to lift, replaced by a sense of determination to embrace the unknown.

Back in the boutique, I caught a glimpse of the vibrant fabrics hanging against the wall, a palette of colors that mirrored the emotions swirling within me. The boutique was not just a business; it was a testament to resilience and hope, a symbol of what could be achieved through hard work and community support. And as I stood there, my heart swelling with renewed purpose, I knew that whatever path lay ahead, I was ready to face it—together with Carter, no matter where the journey would take us.

Days turned into weeks, and with every sunrise that painted the sky in hues of pink and gold, the boutique thrived. I found myself waking up with the dawn, eager to embrace the day. The moment my feet touched the cool hardwood floor, I felt the familiar excitement thrumming through my veins. The quaint little shop that once felt like a heavy weight on my shoulders was now a sanctuary of creativity and connection. The locals buzzed in and out, their laughter and chatter mixing with the vibrant colors of the fabrics that adorned the racks. Each piece told a story, and I relished in helping my customers find the perfect outfit that spoke to their spirit.

Carter had become my partner in this whirlwind of colors and textures. He brought a warmth to the space, his easy smile and quick wit lighting up even the dullest days. His passion for design was infectious, and I often found myself lost in the excitement of brainstorming new ideas with him. We collaborated seamlessly, combining our visions into cohesive collections that reflected the eclectic charm of our small town. Each afternoon spent together was like weaving a tapestry of memories—every laugh, every touch, every glance layered with a deeper connection.

However, the thrill of our blossoming relationship was tempered by an ever-present shadow. The more I invested in our shared moments, the louder the whispers of doubt became in my mind. Carter was destined for greatness, and I was tethered to a life that felt both fulfilling and fragile. He had dreams that stretched far beyond the cozy walls of the boutique; I could feel the ambitions pulsing beneath his skin like a heartbeat, relentless and vibrant. What if one day those dreams pulled him away, like a tide that washes out to sea, leaving nothing but silence in its wake?

One balmy evening, as the golden sun dipped below the horizon, painting the world in soft pastels, we found ourselves nestled in the small café that had become our go-to retreat. The aroma of freshly brewed coffee mingled with the sweetness of pastries, wrapping around us like a warm embrace. We sat at our usual table by the window, the light casting a halo around Carter as he leaned back, laughter bubbling up as he recounted a story about a particularly clumsy customer who had tried to juggle three bags while leaving the store.

"I'm telling you, she looked like a one-woman circus act," he said, shaking his head, laughter dancing in his eyes.

I couldn't help but giggle, the sound bubbling up effortlessly. But as I watched him, my heart ached with the realization that these moments were fleeting. His ambition loomed over us, a silent giant that demanded attention. "You know," I began, my voice quieter, "it's amazing to see how passionate you are about all of this. I sometimes wonder if you'll find the need to chase bigger dreams elsewhere."

His laughter faded, replaced by a more serious expression. "Lily, this isn't just a job for me. It's about creating something that lasts. But I want to do that with you. You are part of my dreams too."

The sincerity of his words warmed me, yet the knot in my stomach tightened. "What if your dreams take you far away?" I asked softly, my vulnerability surfacing like a wave ready to crash. "What if you find opportunities in places where I can't follow?"

His gaze locked onto mine, and for a moment, the noise of the café faded away, leaving just the two of us in our bubble of uncertainty. "Then I'll make sure you're a part of those opportunities," he said, his voice steady, filled with conviction. "I won't let distance become a barrier between us. We can navigate this together."

A flicker of hope ignited within me, but shadows of doubt still lingered at the edges. The prospect of change was both thrilling and terrifying, a dance between the known and the unknown. I wanted to believe that our connection could withstand the winds of change, yet deep down, I feared the inevitable tug of fate.

As we finished our drinks, I noticed a small group of customers enter the café, their faces lighting up at the sight of us. They were familiar—friends and patrons of the boutique, a comforting reminder that our community was vibrant and full of life. Their presence wrapped around me like a warm blanket, and I felt a surge of gratitude for the support they had shown us. It was this very connection that had helped the boutique flourish again.

"Let's take a walk by the river," Carter suggested, breaking my reverie. "I want to show you something."

Intrigued, I followed him out into the warm evening air. The sun had set, leaving a canvas of twinkling stars above us, the moon casting a gentle glow on the path ahead. As we strolled along the riverbank, the soft murmur of the water provided a soothing backdrop to our conversation. The night felt alive, electric with possibility.

Carter led me to a secluded spot under a grand oak tree, its branches swaying gently in the breeze. The leaves rustled like whispers, and the sight of the shimmering water reflecting the stars made my heart swell. "This is where I used to come to think about my dreams," he said, his voice low and earnest. "It's peaceful here, and it reminds me that dreams are meant to grow, just like this tree."

I looked up at the tree, its roots firmly planted in the earth, branches reaching toward the sky. "It's beautiful," I said, the metaphor resonating within me. "But what if your dreams pull you away from your roots? From the people who care about you?"

Carter turned to face me, his eyes bright with conviction. "That's the thing. My roots are here, with you. You're the heart of this place for me. I don't want to lose that connection, no matter where life takes us."

His words washed over me like a gentle tide, and I felt my heart begin to mend the frayed edges of my anxiety. As we stood together, the cool breeze weaving through our hair, I realized that the uncertainty was part of life's tapestry—a vibrant mix of joy and fear, laughter and tears. The promise of tomorrow was uncharted, yet filled with endless possibilities.

I stepped closer to him, feeling the warmth radiating from his body. "So, what do we do now?" I asked, my voice barely a whisper, but filled with resolve.

"We embrace it all," he replied, a grin breaking across his face. "We take it one day at a time, knowing that we have each other. I'll work hard to make my dreams come true, and you'll continue to breathe life into this boutique. We can build something beautiful together."

In that moment, surrounded by the whispers of the night, I felt a shift within me. The worries that had once clouded my thoughts began to lift, replaced by a newfound sense of determination. Whatever the future held, we would face it hand in hand, weaving our stories into the fabric of our lives. Together, we could create a masterpiece, one thread at a time, and the fear of loss no longer felt insurmountable. The road ahead might be uncertain, but I knew that as long as we were together, we could weather any storm.

Chapter 21: Tapestry of Dreams

The sun dipped low over Montgomery Springs, casting a warm golden hue across the quaint storefronts that lined Main Street. I leaned against the window of my boutique, The Stitched Dream, watching the world unfurl outside. The annual Arts Festival was more than just an event; it was a chance for us to reclaim our corner of the art scene, to let our creativity burst forth like the blooms in the surrounding gardens. My heart raced with excitement, the kind that dances in your chest when you know you're on the brink of something extraordinary.

Inside the boutique, the scent of fresh paint mingled with the rich aroma of coffee from the corner café, weaving a tapestry of inspiration in the air. Carter was sprawled across the wooden floor, his sketchbook opened like a treasure chest, a whirl of colors and ideas splattered across its pages. His fingers, stained with paint, moved deftly as he sketched a vision for our collaborative piece. There was a certain magic in watching him work, the way his brow furrowed in concentration and then lifted in delight when a new idea took flight.

"Okay, picture this," he said, looking up with eyes gleaming with passion. "We create a dress that mirrors the landscapes of Montgomery Springs—flowing lines that mimic the river and bursts of color like the gardens in bloom. Your designs paired with my art could create something that captures the very essence of our town."

I felt a thrill race down my spine at the prospect. "Yes! And we could incorporate elements of nature—maybe fabric leaves that cascade down the train? It would be like wearing a piece of the festival itself."

As we delved deeper into our brainstorming, the boutique transformed into a sanctuary of creativity. The walls, once adorned with traditional mannequins dressed in last season's trends, now stood as canvases for our collaboration. I pinned sketches on corkboards, while Carter hung his vibrant paintings like stars against the night sky. Each brushstroke brought the boutique to life, infusing it with an energy that sparked hope and ambition.

We spent countless nights in that space, the hum of our laughter echoing through the quiet streets of Montgomery Springs. The festival approached with relentless speed, but in those moments, it felt like time stood still, as if the universe had conspired to keep us wrapped in our bubble of creativity.

With every conversation, I felt myself drawn deeper into Carter's world. There was a charm in his artistic chaos, a sincerity that stirred something within me. He was the spark that reignited my passion for design, and every moment spent together felt electric. We'd sit cross-legged on the floor, surrounded by a kaleidoscope of fabric swatches and paint tubes, fueled by caffeine and shared dreams.

One evening, as the sunset painted the sky in shades of lavender and gold, I received a call that sent my heart racing—a prestigious fashion magazine wanted to feature our work. The words washed over me like a warm wave, exhilarating and terrifying all at once. This was the validation I had craved for so long, the chance to shine in a way I had only dreamed of.

But with the excitement came an overwhelming pressure. My mind raced as I hung up the phone, thoughts spiraling around the implications of the feature. Carter sensed my sudden shift in energy and looked up from his canvas, concern etched across his face.

"Hey, what's wrong?"

"Nothing," I said too quickly, forcing a smile that felt more like a mask. "Just got a call from Vogue. They want to feature us."

"Wait, what?" His voice rose in disbelief, the corners of his mouth curving into an infectious grin. "That's amazing! We have to celebrate!"

"Yeah, but..." My excitement dulled as I thought of the looming deadline. The festival was right around the corner, and I couldn't shake the feeling that I was losing my grip on the project.

He moved closer, eyes locking onto mine with an intensity that made my heart flutter. "What's the but? This is a good thing!"

"I know! But now I feel like I have to prove myself, like if I don't meet their expectations, I'll let everyone down. This was supposed to be fun, Carter." My voice wavered, the weight of my anxiety creeping in like a fog.

Carter's expression softened. "Listen, we'll make it fun. Let's pour our heart and soul into this, and I promise it will be worth it. No one can take away the joy we've created, no matter what happens."

His words wrapped around me like a warm blanket, and I took a deep breath, allowing the tension to ease from my shoulders. He was right, of course. We had created something beautiful together, and I didn't want to let fear tarnish that.

As the days slipped by, our collaboration blossomed into a riot of colors and textures. I felt the spirit of Montgomery Springs seep into every stitch I made, each thread weaving our dreams into reality. We worked tirelessly, pulling late nights filled with laughter and fueled by inspiration.

I remembered the way the river sparkled under the summer sun and how the gardens danced with vibrant blooms, and I poured those memories into our designs. The night before the festival, I stood in the boutique, surrounded by the fruits of our labor, and for the first time in what felt like an eternity, I allowed myself to hope.

In that moment, I felt a stirring within me, a burgeoning belief that perhaps this was only the beginning of our story—one filled with creativity, friendship, and the unexpected turns of life that had the power to transform us all.

The morning of the festival dawned bright and clear, the sun streaming through the windows of The Stitched Dream, illuminating the boutique with a warm glow. It felt like the universe was conspiring to paint our world in the vibrant hues of excitement and possibility. I stood in front of the mirror, adjusting the collar of my vintage dress—a light, flowing creation adorned with pastel florals that echoed the beauty of the blooming gardens outside. Every thread felt like a celebration of the artistic spirit we had cultivated over the past few weeks.

As I busily added the final touches to my hair, the sound of laughter drifted in from the boutique floor. Carter was setting up our display, arranging the pieces we had crafted together with an artist's eye for detail. I couldn't help but smile at the sight of him, the way he danced around the room, his paint-stained fingers deftly moving from one canvas to another, turning each space into an extension of our shared vision.

"Could you hand me that light blue scarf?" he called out, his voice full of playful exuberance. "We need to add a touch of sky to our creation."

I reached for the scarf, feeling a twinge of excitement at how effortlessly we worked together. Handing it to him, I caught a glimpse of the installation—a dress mannequin draped in a tapestry of our work. Each fabric piece swirled with colors that mirrored the landscapes we loved; it was as if the spirit of Montgomery Springs itself had come alive and wrapped itself around the form.

"Perfect!" he exclaimed, adjusting the scarf with a flourish. "Now, it looks like it's ready to float down the river."

We both took a step back, a moment of silence enveloping us as we admired our handiwork. The installation felt like a living entity, a creature born of our late-night brainstorming sessions and creative storms. The thrill of sharing this piece with the world sent shivers of anticipation coursing through me.

"Are you ready for this?" I asked, my voice barely above a whisper, a mix of excitement and nervousness bubbling within me.

"Ready? I was born ready!" He flashed a cheeky grin, and I felt a rush of warmth at the playful confidence radiating from him.

As the hours slipped by, the festival began to unfold outside, transforming Montgomery Springs into a vibrant tapestry of color, art, and laughter. Street vendors lined the sidewalks, their tables bursting with handmade crafts, local delicacies, and fragrant flowers. The sounds of live music floated through the air, creating a backdrop that set my heart racing with the promise of possibility.

With each passing moment, more people gathered around our boutique. The energy of the festival pulsated through the streets, and I felt an invisible thread connect me to the crowd as they drifted past our window. I caught snippets of laughter and conversation, each one a thread woven into the rich fabric of the day. It was intoxicating, this dance of creativity and community, and I found myself swept along in its current.

When the doors swung open and the first guests entered, the atmosphere crackled with excitement. I greeted each visitor with a smile, eager to share the fruits of our labor. Carter stood beside me, his eyes sparkling as he animatedly described the inspirations behind our designs. There was a palpable energy between us, a rhythm that felt almost like a dance.

"Welcome! This is our collaborative piece," I said, gesturing toward the installation. "It's inspired by the landscapes of Montgomery Springs and the beauty of our local community."

"Oh my, it's stunning!" a woman exclaimed, her eyes wide with wonder as she stepped closer. "The colors remind me of the gardens in full bloom."

Carter leaned in, his enthusiasm infectious. "Exactly! We wanted to capture that essence. Each piece here tells a story, just like the town itself."

As the crowd swelled, the boutique buzzed with laughter and compliments. Each interaction felt like a thread, weaving connections between the people who admired our work and the passion that had gone into it. I couldn't help but feel proud, a sense of accomplishment swelling in my chest.

Then came the moment I had both yearned for and dreaded—the arrival of the fashion magazine editor. She swept through the door like a whirlwind, a vision of polished elegance. I felt a flutter of nerves as she scanned the boutique, her discerning gaze taking in every detail.

"Ah, there you are," she said, locking eyes with me and extending her hand. "I'm Clara Reynolds. I've heard so much about your work and couldn't resist seeing it for myself."

"Thank you so much for coming!" I stammered, shaking her hand with a mix of excitement and trepidation. "We're thrilled to have you here."

As we spoke, I could feel the pressure mounting. Clara was a force to be reckoned with, her sharp mind and keen eye assessing everything with an unyielding intensity. She inquired about the creative process, her questions probing deeper than I anticipated. Each response felt like a performance, a balancing act of authenticity and professionalism.

"Your designs have a distinct voice," she remarked, observing a piece that caught her attention. "I see a lot of potential here, especially in your choice of colors."

I felt the weight of her words, both validating and intimidating. Carter caught my eye, a reassuring smile on his lips, and I clung to that sense of camaraderie as Clara continued to explore our creations.

After a while, she turned her attention to our installation, her expression shifting from curiosity to intrigue. "This is where the magic happens, isn't it?" she mused, her fingers grazing the fabric. "Tell me about the story behind it."

As I recounted the inspiration behind the installation, I felt the nervousness begin to dissolve. Sharing our journey, the late nights filled with laughter and creativity, transformed the conversation into something more intimate. Clara nodded, her eyes lighting up with genuine interest.

"Your passion is palpable, and it's clear you've put your heart into this," she said. "That's what makes a piece truly resonate with people."

Her praise wrapped around me like a warm embrace, infusing me with renewed confidence. In that moment, I realized that while the pressure was undeniably intense, it was the very essence of creativity—the ability to connect, to inspire, and to share our stories. The festival was not just an event; it was a celebration of everything we had built together, a tapestry of dreams woven from the threads of our lives. And as I stood there, surrounded by art, laughter, and the hum of the crowd, I felt ready to embrace whatever came next.

The air pulsed with anticipation as the Montgomery Springs Arts Festival reached its zenith. Vibrant banners fluttered in the gentle breeze, their colors dancing against a backdrop of azure sky. My heart raced, caught in the effervescent rhythm of creativity that enveloped the entire town. As I stepped outside the boutique, I was greeted by the cheerful sounds of laughter, music, and the scent of cotton candy mingling with the fresh earthiness of nearby food stalls. It felt like the world had come alive, a kaleidoscope of color and sound that beckoned every resident and visitor to participate in this celebration of art and community.

Carter emerged from the boutique, adjusting his paint-splattered apron, a confident grin on his face. He looked every bit the artist—wild, free, and entirely captivating. "Ready to make magic?" he asked, his voice brimming with excitement as he gestured toward the festival grounds.

"Absolutely!" I replied, my nerves tingling with a combination of thrill and apprehension. Today was more than just an exhibition; it was a culmination of our hard work, our dreams interwoven with the threads of this small town.

As we strolled through the festival, we passed vendors showcasing their crafts: delicate pottery, intricate jewelry, and paintings that seemed to capture the very essence of Montgomery Springs. Each booth radiated passion, stories told through the hands of artisans. It reminded me of our boutique, a haven where creativity flourished and unique ideas blossomed. I felt a pang of pride at what we had created—a space that felt alive, a reflection of the artistic spirit that pulsed through the veins of this town.

We finally reached our installation, a centerpiece nestled in the heart of the festival. A small crowd had gathered, their faces alight with curiosity. The dress mannequin stood proudly adorned in the flowing fabric we had crafted together, each layer of color telling a story of the landscapes that shaped our lives. Carter and I exchanged a glance, the thrill of our shared accomplishment electrifying the air around us.

"Here goes nothing," I whispered, stepping forward to welcome our audience. "Welcome, everyone! We're excited to share our creation with you." The crowd leaned in, eager to soak in every word, and I felt a surge of warmth wash over me as I spoke about the inspiration behind the piece.

"This installation represents the beauty of Montgomery Springs—the winding river, the blooming gardens, and the vibrant community that supports us. Each element is crafted with love and intention, embodying the spirit of our home."

The audience responded with murmurs of appreciation, and as I pointed out the intricate details—like the delicate fabric leaves that cascaded down the dress, mimicking the trees lining the riverbank—I could see the joy spreading among them. Carter stepped in to share his artistic process, his passion palpable as he spoke. Together, we wove a narrative that connected us not just to each other, but to everyone standing before us.

As the festival continued, the editor from the fashion magazine drifted closer, her eyes sharp yet thoughtful as she absorbed every detail of our work. I felt a flutter of nerves once more, the weight of her gaze a reminder of the stakes we faced. Yet, as she watched the crowd's reaction, I noticed a flicker of interest spark in her expression, and I couldn't help but feel a sense of validation wash over me.

Hours melted into moments, laughter ringing through the air as children spun around in delight and couples strolled hand in hand. Carter and I mingled with our audience, answering questions and sharing the behind-the-scenes stories that had birthed our creations. Each interaction deepened the connections we were forging, and the joy radiating from the crowd felt like an embrace.

The sun began to set, casting a golden light over the festival, wrapping everything in a soft, warm glow. I glanced at Carter, who was lost in conversation with a couple admiring his work. There was something incredibly endearing about his unguarded passion. In that moment, I felt a quiet realization settle over me—a burgeoning admiration, something deeper than mere friendship.

"Excuse me," I said to the couple, gently interrupting. "Do you mind if I borrow him for a moment?"

Carter turned, a playful glint in his eyes. "What's up? Are we about to make a dramatic escape?"

"Maybe," I teased, pulling him aside to a quieter corner of the festival. "I just wanted to check in. How are you feeling about all this?"

He leaned against a nearby tree, the warm light framing his features. "Honestly? I feel amazing. This is everything I dreamed it could be. The response is unreal." He paused, glancing around at the festivities. "It's so much bigger than just us, you know?"

I nodded, feeling a swell of pride that mirrored his sentiments. "We did this together, Carter. I couldn't have imagined pulling this off without you."

His gaze locked onto mine, and for a moment, the laughter of the festival faded into the background. "You're incredible, you know that? I think we've tapped into something special."

Before I could respond, Clara approached us, her presence commanding attention. "I must say, I'm impressed," she stated, her tone professional yet warm. "The installation is a stunning representation of local artistry, and I believe it has tremendous potential."

My heart raced as I exchanged glances with Carter. Clara's approval was like a golden ticket, an affirmation that our hard work hadn't gone unnoticed. "Thank you! That means a lot coming from you," I replied, trying to sound more composed than I felt.

"I'd love to feature you both in our next issue. Let's set up a time for an interview," she continued, her smile genuine but her gaze unwavering, assessing. "There's a unique story here, and I think our readers would resonate with it."

As the words sank in, it felt like fireworks ignited within me. An interview! A chance to share our journey with a wider audience. Excitement bubbled to the surface, mingled with the reality that this moment marked a pivotal turning point in our lives.

"Absolutely! We'd be honored," I said, a thrill of gratitude and anticipation coursing through me.

As Clara took notes on her notepad, Carter squeezed my hand discreetly, a shared understanding passing between us. The journey ahead was unknown, yet this moment solidified our bond—a partnership steeped in trust, creativity, and a hint of something more.

As the festival came to a close, the glow of string lights illuminated our space, casting a soft ambiance that made the night feel like a dream. We gathered our things, hearts full, laughter spilling over as we reminisced about the day's highlights.

"Can you believe it? We did it!" Carter exclaimed, his voice bursting with enthusiasm.

"I never thought we could pull this off," I admitted, beaming at him.

But amid the joy, a new awareness settled within me, a realization that the tapestry of our lives was only just beginning to unfurl. With the festival behind us and the magazine feature ahead, I could sense that this was merely the first thread in a far more intricate design, one that would intertwine our paths in ways we could only begin to imagine.

As we packed up, laughter echoed in the distance, and I couldn't help but glance back at the installation, proud of what we had created together. It felt like the beginning of a beautiful adventure—an unfolding story filled with color, connection, and the promise of dreams yet to come.

Chapter 22: Seams of Discord

The summer air hung thick with the scent of popcorn and sweet funnel cakes, a syrupy sweetness swirling around me like a familiar embrace as I navigated the bustling streets of Riverton. Brightly colored banners fluttered overhead, painting the sky in vibrant hues of red and blue, while laughter bubbled up from every corner. The annual Riverton Festival was not merely an event; it was a rite of passage, a celebration of our community's spirit that drew families together like moths to a flame. As I walked through the throngs of people, my heart raced with the intoxicating blend of anticipation and dread.

Each booth and stall seemed to pulse with life, from the handmade crafts glinting in the sun to the children's delighted shrieks as they raced around, faces smeared with cotton candy. I could feel the festival's heartbeat beneath my feet, a rhythm that mirrored my own. It was a chaotic orchestra of colors and sounds, one that promised both joy and tension as the days ticked closer to the festival's grand opening.

But beneath the lively façade lay an undercurrent of discord. My father's skepticism echoed in my mind, a persistent refrain that began to dampen my excitement. He had always favored tradition, embracing the time-honored ways of our town, while I was a dreamer, eager to infuse new ideas and creativity into our community's fabric. The clash of our visions felt like a thunderstorm brewing on the horizon. I could feel it gathering strength with every passing moment, darkening the once bright sky of my hopes.

When we first began planning the festival, my vision had been bold and vibrant. I envisioned a celebration filled with local artists and musicians, showcasing the eclectic blend of talent our town possessed. But my father, with his strong, resolute stance, was less enthusiastic. "We've always done it this way, Emma," he'd said, his tone firm, a hint of frustration lacing his words. "Why change something that has always worked?"

The heat of our arguments simmered just below the surface, igniting as we discussed the festival. Each disagreement felt like a rift growing wider between us, and I was caught in the middle, wrestling with my desire to honor tradition while yearning to express my creativity. The walls of our small kitchen became the battleground for our debates, the familiar scent of brewing coffee now tainted with unspoken tension.

In the midst of this chaos, Carter's past emerged like an unwelcome specter, casting shadows over our fragile plans. He had always been an enigma to me, a boy with dreams that stretched far beyond the confines of Riverton. The whispers of his former relationships, of aspirations that once defined him, swirled around me like autumn leaves caught in a gust of wind. I had seen glimpses of his uncertainty, the way his laughter sometimes faltered, but I had never fully understood the weight he carried.

It was during one of our late-night talks, beneath the glow of string lights in my backyard, that he finally opened up about the opportunity looming before him. "I've been offered a chance to work in Seattle," he confessed, his voice low, almost swallowed by the night. "They want me to help with their new marketing campaign. It's everything I've ever wanted, but..." His words trailed off, the hesitation hanging in the air like a heavy mist.

The ground beneath me felt unsteady, the world shifting as I processed his words. Seattle. A city bursting with life, creativity, and possibility, beckoning him with promises of success and adventure. My heart raced at the thought of him leaving. Would he chase this dream, leaving Riverton—and me—behind? The excitement of the festival seemed to dim, overshadowed by the looming specter of his departure.

"I don't want to hold you back," I managed to say, my voice barely above a whisper, each word laced with the fear of losing him. The idea of Carter stepping into a future filled with opportunity while I remained in the familiar confines of our town felt like a dagger to my heart. I was terrified that I'd be left behind, watching him from a distance, forever wondering what could have been.

His eyes searched mine, the depth of his feelings reflected in their warmth. "Emma, this is my chance. But you... you're important to me," he said, his voice steady yet tinged with uncertainty. "I don't know how to balance this. I want to support you, especially with the festival, but I can't ignore this opportunity."

Each of his words resonated within me, a symphony of hope and despair. I felt like a tightrope walker, balancing precariously between supporting him and safeguarding my heart from the potential heartbreak. The festival had become a symbol of everything I wanted—community, creativity, and connection. Yet, it was also a reminder of what I stood to lose if he chose a different path.

As the festival's date drew nearer, my mind churned with questions. Could I convince my father to see the beauty in my vision? Could I help Carter understand that his dreams didn't have to come at the expense of ours? The weight of these decisions pressed heavily on my shoulders, and I found myself yearning for clarity amidst the turmoil.

With each day that passed, the festival felt both exhilarating and suffocating, a delicate balance of excitement and anxiety that mirrored my life's most significant choices. The whispers of change surrounded me, each decision I faced woven into the very fabric of Riverton's heartbeat, a reminder that even the most beautiful celebrations can carry the weight of unspoken fears.

As I prepared for the festival, I found myself clinging to the hope that amidst the chaos, I could forge a new path—not just for myself, but for Carter as well. I was determined to stand at the crossroads, to fight for my vision, while also cherishing the moments we shared, hoping that together we could weave a tapestry of dreams that would endure the tests of time.

The sun dipped low in the sky, casting a warm golden glow across Riverton, as I stood in the heart of the festival grounds, surveying my vision coming to life. The laughter of children, the cheerful chatter of families, and the rhythmic strumming of a nearby band filled the air, creating a backdrop of happiness that felt almost magical. Yet, beneath the vibrant exterior lay an unsettling tension, a churning knot in my stomach that refused to dissipate. With each moment, the shadows of doubt grew larger, threatening to overshadow my dreams.

I had poured my heart into this festival, imagining a tapestry of colors, sounds, and tastes that would resonate with our community. Artisans showcasing their crafts, local musicians filling the air with melodies, and food vendors enticing everyone with delicious aromas. It was more than just an event; it was a celebration of who we were, a reflection of the vibrant spirit that defined Riverton. But as the days ticked down, my father's skepticism gnawed at my confidence, threatening to unravel the fabric I had so carefully woven.

"Emma, are you sure about all this?" he had asked earlier, his brow furrowed in concern as we stood in our living room, the weight of his gaze heavy upon me. "What if people don't respond to your ideas? What if it doesn't go as planned?"

I could feel the heat rising in my cheeks as I struggled to articulate my thoughts. "But Dad, this is our chance to breathe new life into the festival! To show everyone that Riverton is more than just its traditions!" I had wanted to shake him, to make him see the beauty in my vision, but instead, I felt the familiar pang of frustration.

His silence spoke volumes, and the disappointment hung in the air like a thick fog, shrouding my hopes. My father had always been my rock, a man whose steady presence grounded me. Yet, as I fought for my dreams, I began to feel like I was challenging the very foundation of our relationship. The arguments felt endless, each clash revealing the rift growing between us, a divide that left me grappling for balance in a world that felt increasingly unsteady.

Then there was Carter, whose mere presence had the power to ignite a spark within me. Our late-night conversations had woven a bond that felt both thrilling and terrifying, the ebb and flow of our lives entwining in ways I had never anticipated. But as the festival drew closer, I found myself caught in a whirlwind of emotions, torn between the excitement of our plans and the gnawing fear of his potential departure.

The night he shared his opportunity, I had watched the moonlight dance across his features, illuminating the indecision etched in his expression. "Emma, it's a huge opportunity," he had said, his voice barely above a whisper, as if afraid the universe would overhear. "I don't want to leave Riverton, but this could be my chance to do something meaningful."

My heart had raced, not just with the fear of losing him, but with the realization that this wasn't merely about him; it was about us. The thought of Carter pursuing a dream in a city far away felt like a bittersweet melody playing in the background, the notes both uplifting and heartbreaking. My mind raced with the implications of his potential move, imagining the distance growing between us like an unbridgeable chasm, while simultaneously yearning for him to chase his aspirations.

As the days unfolded, our interactions became tinged with an unspoken tension. We would laugh and joke, yet beneath the surface lay a current of apprehension, a silent acknowledgment that everything was changing. I often caught myself watching him as he immersed himself in the festival preparations, his energy infectious. I admired the way his hands moved as he arranged decorations, the intensity in his gaze when he discussed ideas with the other volunteers. But then, the weight of his choice loomed over me, a dark cloud threatening to rain on my parade.

One afternoon, we found ourselves seated on a rickety picnic table, the scent of freshly cut grass mingling with the tantalizing aroma of nearby barbecue. I watched as he absentmindedly picked at the wood, his brow furrowed in thought. "I want to be here, but..." he trailed off, glancing toward the horizon, where the sun painted the sky in shades of pink and orange.

"Carter," I interrupted softly, "you deserve to pursue your dreams." My voice trembled, betraying the vulnerability I had tried to conceal. "But what about us? What if you leave?"

His eyes met mine, and for a moment, time stood still. "Emma, you're the best part of Riverton for me," he confessed, the weight of his words settling between us like a fragile promise. "But I can't ignore this opportunity. It could change everything for me."

His honesty struck me like a lightning bolt, illuminating the shadowy corners of my heart. I wanted to scream, to tell him that I would fight for him, for us, for everything we had built together. But I also understood the gravity of his dreams. They were powerful, palpable, and undeniably enticing.

As the festival unfolded, each moment felt charged with significance, the air thick with both excitement and dread. I threw myself into organizing the event, pouring my soul into every detail. With each colorful banner I hung and every vendor I recruited, I hoped to drown out the anxieties creeping in. The festival became my sanctuary, a place where I could lose myself in the chaos and creativity, if only for a little while.

But as the opening day approached, the familiar knot in my stomach tightened. I knew I had to confront my fears, to face the reality that loomed before me. The stakes were higher than ever, and as I looked around at the festival, at the smiling faces and twinkling lights, I realized that I couldn't simply sit back and let the currents of life sweep me away.

As I prepared for the grand event, I felt the weight of my decisions bearing down on me. The thrill of the festival buzzed around me like the excitement of fireworks, but deep within, I felt the tension, a haunting reminder of the choices I had yet to confront. With every beat of my heart, I steeled myself for the impending confrontation, knowing that whatever happened next could forever alter the course of our lives, pulling us in different directions or binding us even closer together.

The festival dawned bright and early, the sun's rays spilling over Riverton like warm honey, illuminating the vibrant decorations that adorned every corner of the town square. The buzz of excitement was palpable, a sweet tension in the air, mingling with the scent of fresh pastries and blooming flowers. My heart raced in sync with the thrumming music that filled the space, the rhythmic beat echoing the chaotic symphony in my mind. Each cheerful face I passed felt like a reminder of the stakes at play, my father's doubts still looming like a storm cloud, threatening to dampen the vibrant energy surrounding us.

As I moved through the bustling crowd, I could see the fruits of my labor beginning to blossom. The art installations I had envisioned were proudly displayed, each piece telling a story of our community's resilience and creativity. Local musicians strummed their guitars, their voices intertwining with laughter and applause. Children dashed about, their joyous shouts punctuating the air like firecrackers, while vendors showcased their culinary delights, offering everything from mouthwatering BBQ to delicate cupcakes adorned with swirling frosting.

Yet, despite the vivid tapestry of celebration around me, I felt a hollow ache in my chest. Carter's absence weighed heavily, and the conversations we'd shared about his future echoed in my mind. He had promised to help me with the festival, yet here I was, navigating the excitement without him by my side. I longed for his laughter, his playful banter, and the way he would tease me about my overzealous ideas while secretly supporting them. The thought of him chasing dreams in a city miles away stung, and I couldn't shake the sense of loss creeping in, like a shadow that refused to be chased away.

I spotted my father in the crowd, his brows furrowed as he examined the festival with a critical eye. I took a deep breath, steeling myself as I approached him. "Dad, look at how many people have come out today! This is what we wanted," I urged, gesturing toward the joyful scenes unfolding around us.

He looked at me, skepticism etched in every line on his face. "It's all well and good, Emma, but how long will it last? You're trying to turn this festival into something it's not. People come for tradition, not for... whatever this is."

I could feel the heat rising in my cheeks as his words pierced through the cheerful atmosphere. "But that's exactly it! We can embrace tradition and still allow room for new ideas. We don't have to be stagnant!" My voice wavered, but I refused to let him see my frustration.

Before he could respond, the sound of Carter's laughter reached my ears, and my heart leaped. I turned to see him weaving through the crowd, a smile brightening his face as he caught sight of me. The weight in my chest lifted for a moment, only to come crashing down again as I remembered the conversation we had the night before. His future was still uncertain, a pendulum swinging between what he wanted and what he felt he should do.

"Hey, you made it!" I exclaimed, relief flooding through me as he joined my side. "I was starting to think you'd forgotten about me."

"Not a chance," he replied, the light in his eyes momentarily banishing my doubts. "I wouldn't miss this for the world. It's amazing to see it all come together."

His presence was a balm to my frayed nerves, and for a brief moment, I allowed myself to bask in the warmth of his support. Together, we wandered through the stalls, sharing bites of food and engaging in playful banter. Yet, beneath the surface of our laughter, an unspoken tension simmered, an undercurrent that neither of us could ignore.

As the afternoon sun began to dip, casting a golden hue over the festival, I knew it was time to confront the inevitable. We found a quieter spot away from the throngs of people, the laughter and music fading into a soothing background hum. I turned to him, heart pounding. "Carter, we need to talk about... what you mentioned before."

His smile faded slightly, the light in his eyes dimming as he prepared himself for the conversation. "I know," he said quietly. "It's been on my mind, too."

"I don't want to hold you back," I began, the words tumbling out before I could reign them in. "But the thought of you leaving... it terrifies me. I don't want to lose you."

Carter sighed, running a hand through his hair, the gesture both familiar and unsettling. "Emma, you need to know that this opportunity means a lot to me. It's something I've dreamed about for so long. But..." He paused, looking down at his feet, as if searching for the right words in the grass beneath him. "You're important to me. Being here with you... it's what makes this festival feel real."

His confession sent a surge of hope coursing through me, yet it was tangled with the anxiety that had taken root in my heart. "What if you take the job? What happens to us?"

The question hung heavy between us, unspoken fears taking form in the silence. He stepped closer, the warmth of his presence wrapping around me like a lifeline. "I don't want to lose what we have, either. But I can't ignore this chance. It's not just about leaving Riverton; it's about finding myself, finding my place in the world."

His honesty struck a chord deep within me, a bittersweet reminder of the choices we faced. I could feel the edges of my heart fraying, but I also understood the pull of ambition, the desire to chase dreams that felt just out of reach. "What if we made it work?" I suggested, my voice trembling with the weight of hope. "What if you went to Seattle, and we figured out how to make it work long distance?"

Carter studied my face, a flicker of uncertainty passing through his expression. "I want to, Emma. But the reality is... it's hard. The distance, the time zones, the uncertainty. What if it changes everything?"

My heart sank at the thought. The very essence of our connection could shift, fracturing under the strain of separation. "I don't want to lose you. You mean too much to me," I admitted, my voice barely a whisper.

He took a step back, running a hand over his face, as if trying to wipe away the weight of the conversation. "Let's focus on today. The festival is important. We can think about the future later."

Though I nodded in agreement, the pit in my stomach grew heavier. As the sun dipped below the horizon, casting a soft twilight glow across the festival, I knew that today was just a temporary reprieve. The excitement of the festival was a fleeting distraction, a beautiful moment that would soon give way to the reality of our choices.

As the stars began to twinkle overhead, the festival lights illuminating the darkness, I understood that our paths were diverging, leading us down roads neither of us could predict. But as I stood by his side, feeling the warmth of his presence, I realized that whatever lay ahead, I would cherish these moments, the laughter, the shared dreams, and the connection that had blossomed amidst the chaos of life. We were at a crossroads, caught between the thrill of today and the uncertainties of tomorrow, but together, we would navigate the seams of discord that threatened to pull us apart.

Chapter 23: Beneath the Surface

The air inside the boutique is thick with the sweet scent of fabric softener and the faint aroma of lavender from the candles flickering on the shelves. My creations—each stitch, each pattern—dance around me like old friends, their vibrant colors glowing under the soft, golden light that bathes the room. I trace my fingers along the delicate fabrics hanging from the racks, feeling the threads beneath my fingertips, and yet a deep-seated doubt curls around my heart, whispering insidious thoughts that threaten to smother me. Am I truly enough? Have I poured all my hopes into this venture only to watch them wilt like flowers left too long in the sun?

The festival is tomorrow, and it feels as though the entire town of Willow Creek is holding its breath, waiting for the moment when the curtain will rise on my dreams. With each passing hour, the weight of expectation settles heavier on my shoulders, each pulse of my heart a reminder of the stakes involved. This isn't just a showcase of my work; it's a test of everything I've ever wished for. The boutique has become more than just a store; it's a reflection of my journey, my growth, my very essence woven into every seam. Yet, standing amidst the racks of colorful dresses and neatly arranged accessories, I feel like an imposter in my own creation.

As I grapple with my swirling emotions, the bell above the door jingles softly, breaking the tension in the air. I turn, and there he is—Carter. He strides in with an easy confidence that seems to light up the dim corners of the boutique. His messy curls frame his face, and his bright eyes, those soulful pools of warmth, instantly make the chaotic thoughts in my mind begin to settle. The way he carries himself, as if the weight of the world has never dared to touch him, draws me in like a moth to a flame.

"Hey," he says, his voice a calming balm. "I thought I might find you here." He glances around, taking in the chaos of fabric and ambition that fills the space. I can't help but smile at the way his gaze lingers on a bright yellow sundress, its hem fluttering slightly in the soft breeze from the open window.

"I just—" My voice falters, the tremors of my insecurity bubbling to the surface. "I'm scared, Carter. What if tomorrow doesn't go the way I hope? What if I fail?" The words spill out in a rush, as if they have been waiting for this moment to escape my lips. I can't hide the fear that lingers beneath my bravado.

He steps closer, his presence enveloping me in warmth and reassurance. "You won't fail," he assures me, his voice steady and firm, yet gentle, as if he's handling something precious. "You've worked so hard. You're not just showcasing clothes; you're sharing pieces of yourself. That's what makes it special."

But his words, while soothing, can't fully lift the weight off my chest. The anxiety coils tighter as I think about all the faces that will turn to me tomorrow—the friends, the critics, the strangers who might decide in an instant whether my dreams are worthy of their attention. I want to believe him, but the fear of falling short looms larger than my hopes. "What if I lose everything I've built? The boutique, the dreams, us..." My voice trails off, heavy with the unspoken fear that has gnawed at me for too long.

Carter's expression shifts, the light in his eyes dimming slightly as he absorbs my words. "You won't lose me," he says, taking my hands in his, grounding me in the moment. The warmth of his grip seeps into my skin, calming the storm within me. "I'm here for you, no matter what happens. I believe in you." His sincerity pierces through the fog of doubt, and I find myself leaning into him, seeking solace in his unwavering support.

The world outside feels distant, muted by the bubble of intimacy we've created in this small space. I can hear the faint sounds of Willow Creek—the laughter of children playing in the park, the soft chatter of neighbors preparing for the festival, the distant thrum of excitement filling the air. Yet, in this moment, nothing else exists but us. I close my eyes, letting the warmth of his presence wash over me like a soothing tide, calming the crashing waves of my fears.

As I open my eyes, I find him gazing at me, a playful smile dancing on his lips. "You're a force of nature, you know that?" he teases lightly, a mischievous glint in his eyes. "Even if the festival doesn't go as planned, you'll still be you. And that's what really matters."

His words wrap around my heart like a comforting blanket, infusing me with a newfound strength. I take a deep breath, the weight of doubt beginning to lift. Maybe it's not about the festival at all; maybe it's about the journey and the people I've met along the way. With Carter by my side, I feel the thrill of possibility rising within me, the spark of determination igniting once more.

As the shadows lengthen and the last light of day filters through the boutique's window, I know that whatever happens tomorrow, I will face it head-on. Carter's presence is a beacon of hope, a reminder that I'm not alone in this endeavor. We share a quiet moment, the atmosphere electric with unspoken promises, before he leans in, brushing his lips softly against mine. It's a kiss filled with warmth and reassurance, a tender promise that we'll navigate this together, no matter the outcome.

And as our lips part, I can't help but feel a flicker of excitement amidst my uncertainty. Tomorrow may be a test, but it's also an opportunity—a chance to share my vision, my heart, with the world. And with that thought, I pull back slightly, meeting Carter's gaze with renewed determination. The festival isn't just an end; it's a beginning, and I'm ready to embrace it with open arms, no matter where the path may lead.

Morning light spills through the boutique's window, illuminating the carefully arranged garments that hang like silent sentinels. Each piece reflects not only my artistry but also the weight of anticipation that has settled in my chest. The festival is here, and the streets of Willow Creek pulse with an electric energy, the promise of celebration intertwining with my anxiety. I watch as clusters of townsfolk drift by, their laughter carrying on the breeze, blending with the faint strains of music wafting from the town square. Yet, inside me, a storm brews—a mix of excitement and dread that leaves me feeling both alive and paralyzed.

I take a moment to gather my thoughts, allowing the morning's tranquility to wash over me. The boutique is quiet, save for the soft rustle of fabric and the distant chatter from the festival preparations. I run my fingers over the silky texture of a lavender sundress, its color reminiscent of the blooming lilacs outside. It feels like a tangible embodiment of my hopes, vibrant and ready to shine, yet the flicker of doubt lingers, gnawing at the edges of my confidence. I wonder if the townsfolk will appreciate what I've poured into my designs or if they will merely glance and move on.

Just then, the bell above the door jingles, and my heart skips a beat. Carter enters, his smile breaking through my trepidation like the sun breaking through clouds. He's wearing a crisp white shirt, the sleeves rolled up, revealing toned forearms, and his jeans are perfectly worn, hugging his frame in a way that makes my heart race. The sight of him brings an instant warmth, a reminder that I'm not in this alone.

"Ready for the big day?" he asks, his voice teasing yet filled with genuine excitement. I can't help but smile, the tightness in my chest easing slightly.

"I guess so," I reply, trying to sound more confident than I feel. "Just trying to remember that it's not the end of the world if things don't go perfectly."

"Exactly. It's about showcasing your passion. And from what I've seen, your creations are incredible." He walks further into the boutique, examining the pieces with admiration. I follow him, my heart fluttering as he stops in front of a deep emerald gown that I've worked on tirelessly.

"Wow, this is stunning. It looks like something out of a fairy tale," he says, his fingers brushing against the fabric as if it might come to life under his touch.

I can't help but blush at his compliment, the warmth of his approval wrapping around me like a comforting embrace. "I wanted it to feel magical," I admit. "Something that makes the wearer feel special."

His gaze meets mine, and for a moment, the world outside fades away. "You've done that and more. You have a gift, and I want you to know that I'm proud of you—no matter what happens today."

His words resonate deeply, soothing the frayed edges of my anxiety. I step closer, savoring the connection that seems to spark between us, charged with unspoken promises. "Thank you, Carter. Your support means everything." The sincerity in my voice is palpable, a quiet confession of the trust I place in him.

"Let's make a pact," he suggests, a playful glint in his eyes. "No matter what happens, we'll celebrate your hard work tonight. No second-guessing. Just fun."

I can't help but laugh, a genuine, bubbling sound that seems to lift the heaviness around us. "You make it sound so easy."

"It can be," he replies, his tone earnest. "All you need to do is embrace it. Let it unfold."

The moment hangs in the air, thick with possibility. I lean in closer, drawn to the warmth of his body, the magnetic pull between us undeniable. He lowers his voice, almost conspiratorially. "What do you say we grab some ice cream after the festival? Just you and me?"

The thought sends a thrill through me, the idea of celebrating our small victories together igniting a flicker of joy amidst the chaos of the day ahead. "That sounds perfect," I say, allowing a smile to dance across my lips.

As we talk, I feel the weight of my worries slowly dissipating. The sunlight filtering through the window casts a golden hue around us, illuminating the space and creating an atmosphere that feels almost dreamlike. The boutique transforms into a haven of creativity and friendship, where my insecurities seem a little less daunting in the face of Carter's unwavering support.

With each passing moment, we share laughter and stories, allowing the joy of the festival to seep into our conversation. I feel lighter, buoyed by the connection we're nurturing, one that has grown in depth and complexity since he first walked through the door of my boutique. It's comforting to know that he sees me, not just the designer but the person behind the fabric—the dreams, the fears, the hopes.

Eventually, the sounds of the festival outside grow louder, the chatter and music spilling in through the open door like an invitation I can no longer ignore. I take a deep breath, readying myself for the day ahead. Carter catches my gaze, his expression filled with warmth and encouragement, and I feel a surge of determination rise within me.

"Are you ready?" he asks, and his tone carries an air of anticipation that makes my heart race.

"I think I am," I respond, feeling the spark of confidence igniting once more.

With one last shared look, we step out into the vibrant world beyond the boutique. The festival is a tapestry of color and sound, the streets lined with stalls adorned in bright banners and strings of lights that dance in the gentle breeze. Children run past, their laughter echoing like sweet music, while vendors hawk their wares with cheerful calls, inviting townsfolk to partake in the festivities.

As we weave through the crowd, I can feel the energy thrumming in the air, an intoxicating blend of excitement and hope. I glance at Carter, who walks beside me, his presence grounding and reassuring. It's as if he knows that beneath the surface of the festivities lies the heart of my dreams, pulsing with life and possibility.

As we reach the center of the square, I spot my booth, the culmination of my hard work and creativity, adorned with my designs. The sight of it sends a thrill through me, and I can't help but feel a sense of pride swell within my chest. This is my moment, my chance to shine, and as Carter squeezes my hand, I know I'm ready to embrace whatever the day may hold.

The festival unfolds like a vibrant tapestry, each thread woven with laughter, music, and the scent of fried dough wafting through the air. As I stand behind my booth, my heart pounds with a rhythm that matches the pulse of the crowd, a medley of voices blending into a symphony of anticipation. Carter stands beside me, his presence a steadfast anchor amidst the whirlwind of colors and sounds. The sun hangs high, casting a golden light over everything, turning the ordinary into the extraordinary.

I take a moment to absorb the atmosphere, allowing the sights and sounds to wash over me. Vendors shout about their handmade goods, children dart past with painted faces, and couples stroll hand in hand, their smiles illuminating the day. My booth, adorned with my creations, gleams like a treasure trove—dresses fluttering in the gentle breeze, their vibrant hues competing for attention. Each piece is a story, a dream made manifest, and I can't help but feel a swell of pride as I watch people pause, their curiosity piqued.

"Look at how they're drawn to your work," Carter says, his voice warm and encouraging. I glance over to see a group of girls giggling as they examine a coral sundress embellished with intricate embroidery, their eyes wide with delight. The sight fills me with a sense of purpose, a reminder of why I embarked on this journey in the first place. I want to create joy, to infuse each garment with a piece of my heart.

"Do you think they'll like them?" I ask, my voice tinged with uncertainty. The shadow of doubt that crept in during the night threatens to resurface, but Carter is quick to dispel it with a reassuring smile.

"They'll love them," he assures me, stepping closer, his shoulder brushing against mine in a way that sends a shiver of warmth through me. "You've put your soul into every stitch. That passion shines brighter than any fabric." His words wrap around me, a shield against the anxieties that swirl in my mind.

With renewed determination, I turn my attention to the crowd, greeting familiar faces as they approach my booth. Old Mrs. Whitaker, the town's unofficial historian, peers at a floral wrap that I designed with her in mind, her eyes twinkling with delight. "Oh, my dear! This is simply exquisite! I can already envision it at the tea party next month!" she exclaims, her approval sending a rush of warmth through me.

Encouraged by her enthusiasm, I chat with her about the details of the fabric, the inspiration behind the design, and the countless hours spent bringing each piece to life. She listens intently, her appreciation evident, and I find myself growing bolder, sharing my vision and hopes for the boutique.

The festival continues around us, the vibrant energy infectious, and with each passing moment, I feel the weight of my earlier doubts lighten. Carter, ever the supportive presence, engages with the guests, making them feel welcome and at ease, his charm working like magic. I can't help but steal glances at him—his laughter, the way he leans in to listen intently, the way he gestures animatedly as he talks about my designs—it all reinforces my confidence.

As the sun begins its slow descent, casting a warm, amber glow over the festival, I notice a small crowd forming in front of my booth.

Heart racing, I straighten up, ready to greet the new customers. A couple of my classmates join the group, their eyes wide with admiration as they point out the pieces they find appealing. It feels surreal to have them here, supporting me, acknowledging my hard work.

"Wow, Lily! You've really outdone yourself!" Jenna, my bubbly friend, exclaims, her excitement infectious. "I've been hearing people rave about your booth all day!"

Her words wash over me like a soothing balm, a reminder of the community I've built around me. I spot other friends mingling among the crowd, each one contributing to a growing sense of celebration. I can hardly believe that this is my moment, my chance to shine, and I'm overwhelmed by gratitude for everyone who has supported me.

Just as I start to catch my breath, I see Ethan walk toward the booth, his presence cutting through the crowd like a magnet. He radiates an air of confidence and ease, but there's a flicker of uncertainty in his eyes as he approaches. A flutter of nerves dances in my stomach; he's part of the Rowen family, and I wonder what he's thinking.

"Hey," he says, a hint of nervousness in his tone. "I heard you were here. I just wanted to check it out."

His eyes scan my booth, and I can see the flicker of admiration in them. "You've done an incredible job, Lily. This all looks amazing."

"Thanks, Ethan," I reply, feeling a warmth spread through me. It's not lost on me that his presence adds a layer of complexity to this day. "What brings you here? I didn't think you were into fashion."

He chuckles softly, the sound reminiscent of a summer breeze. "I'm not, but I do appreciate creativity. Plus, I wanted to see how you were doing."

As we chat, I notice Carter watching us from the corner of my eye, a subtle tension threading through the air. I can sense the unspoken questions simmering beneath the surface, and a knot tightens in my stomach. But before I can delve deeper into my thoughts, a flurry of activity breaks out in the square as a local band starts to play, drawing a crowd eager to dance.

"Want to join me?" Ethan asks, nodding toward the lively gathering that's forming. There's a genuine excitement in his voice, an invitation I find hard to resist.

"Sure!" I say, glancing back at Carter, who is still standing at the booth, a slight frown creasing his brow. "Just for a moment, though."

As I step away from the booth, I can feel the thrill of the music coursing through my veins, mixing with the heady excitement of the festival. Dancing with Ethan is both exhilarating and nerve-wracking. He moves effortlessly, guiding me through the crowd with a natural rhythm that pulls me in.

We sway and twirl, laughter bubbling between us like champagne. I lose myself in the moment, the worries of the day fading as I embrace the joy around me. Ethan's smile is contagious, and I can't help but mirror it, feeling lighter than I have in weeks. The music weaves its way through the air, igniting a fire within me that urges me to fully embrace the experience.

After a few songs, I catch a glimpse of Carter, standing a few feet away, his expression inscrutable. The easy camaraderie between Ethan and me seems to draw a line in the air, one I didn't intend to cross. My heart races, a mix of exhilaration and uncertainty swirling within me.

I dance one last spin with Ethan before pulling away, the sudden distance leaving me breathless. I weave through the crowd, returning to the booth where Carter waits, his expression a mix of pride and something else—something I can't quite place.

"Enjoying yourself?" he asks, a hint of teasing in his tone, but I can sense an undercurrent of something deeper.

"Yeah, it was fun," I say, trying to keep my voice steady. "Ethan just wanted to dance."

"I saw," he replies, crossing his arms as he leans against the booth. "He seems to be quite the dancer."

There's a note of protectiveness in his voice that makes my heart skip. "Carter, it was just a dance. You know how festivals are."

"I know," he replies, but his gaze is still fixed on Ethan, who is now mingling with other festival-goers. "I just want to make sure you're happy, that's all."

I step closer to Carter, desperate to bridge the gap that seems to have formed between us. "I am happy, but this day isn't just about me. It's about all of us. The boutique, the community... It's everything I've ever wanted."

His eyes soften, and for a brief moment, the tension dissipates like mist in the morning sun. "I get it," he murmurs, stepping back slightly as if acknowledging the weight of my words. "I just want you to know that I'm here for you—always."

The sincerity in his voice warms my heart, and I realize how lucky I am to have someone who believes in me, who stands by my side through the chaos of dreams and insecurities. The festival continues around us, the vibrant sounds swirling together in a celebration of life, but all I can focus on is the connection we share.

With renewed determination, I turn my attention back to the crowd, my heart full of gratitude for the moment, for the people who have shown up to support me. The festival is alive with possibilities, and as I look around, I know I'm ready to face whatever comes next. Together, we'll embrace the adventure, the uncertainty, and the joy that life has to offer.

Chapter 24: Colors of Ambition

The day unfolds in a kaleidoscope of vibrant hues, wrapping the town of Montgomery Springs in a festive embrace. The sun stretches its golden arms over the main square, igniting the colorful banners fluttering in the gentle breeze like the joyous whispers of children. Everywhere I look, laughter dances through the air, accompanied by the rhythmic pulse of music that seems to weave itself into the very fabric of the day. The scent of caramel popcorn and sizzling hot dogs wafts past, teasing my senses and heightening the thrill that courses through my veins.

With each step I take, my heart pounds in harmony with the energetic beats of the festival. My hands tremble slightly as I adjust the placement of my installation, a mosaic of recycled materials transformed into an explosion of color and creativity. The shimmering glass reflects the sunlight, casting playful patterns on the cobblestones beneath my feet. I step back to admire our work, a collaborative effort that symbolizes both my vision and Carter's artistic prowess. Together, we've poured our souls into this piece, and it stands proudly amidst the hustle and bustle, begging for attention.

Carter's laughter rings out like a melody, drawing me closer to him. He's standing beside the installation, his infectious smile illuminating the surroundings even more than the summer sun. There's a spark in his eyes that ignites something deep within me, and for a moment, I lose myself in the warmth of his presence. It's as if the chaos of the festival fades away, leaving just the two of us in a bubble of creativity and connection. The world around us blurs, and I can feel the energy surging between us, a current that pulls me closer and makes my heart race.

As we share ideas and visions, I watch as children run by, their faces painted like exotic animals, their laughter echoing through the square. The festival is alive, a living tapestry woven from the dreams and ambitions of everyone in our community. In this moment, I feel an overwhelming sense of belonging, as if the fabric of this town is stitched together with threads of hope, and I am woven tightly into it.

But as the day unfolds like a flower in bloom, I catch sight of something that shatters my moment of bliss. Across the bustling square, I see Carter engaged in conversation with Mr. Thompson, my former mentor, whose sharp suit and polished demeanor have always radiated authority. The man's gestures are animated, his brow furrowed with intensity as he leans in closer to Carter. I can't hear their words, but the way Carter's face shifts—his smile falters, his eyes darting nervously—sends a chill down my spine. My heart sinks, heavy with the weight of fear that threatens to unravel everything I've built in my heart.

Mr. Thompson has always been a powerful figure in the art community, his influence spreading like ripples on water. The thought of him steering Carter towards a corporate job sends panic coursing through me. I've watched so many artists become swallowed by the corporate machine, their creativity dulled by the weight of expectations and stability. The reality is harsh and unyielding, and I can't shake the feeling that today could be the day everything changes.

Carter and I had shared late-night conversations filled with dreams of galleries and art shows, of creating pieces that spoke to the heart of humanity. We've envisioned traveling to far-off places, collecting stories like treasures to infuse into our art. Now, as I watch him talk with Mr. Thompson, I fear that those dreams are slipping through my fingers like grains of sand. What if this is the moment that pulls him away from me, away from the artistic path we've both cherished?

The festival swirls around me, a blur of colors and laughter that feels distant and hollow. I force myself to breathe deeply, to steady my racing heart, but it's as if the ground beneath me has shifted. I can't allow fear to dictate my actions, nor can I stand idly by while someone else shapes Carter's future. I must reach him before he's swept away, before the world takes him in a direction that might lead him far from me.

With determination igniting my resolve, I navigate through the throng of festival-goers, the sounds of joy fading into the background as I focus on Carter. My heart beats fiercely against my ribcage, an urgent reminder of what's at stake. As I draw closer, I can see the tension in Carter's posture, the way he shifts slightly as if he's being cornered. I won't let that happen. I refuse to lose him to the corporate world that has already claimed so many.

"Carter!" I call, my voice cutting through the noise, carrying a mix of urgency and hope. His head turns, and in that moment, our eyes lock, a tether formed between us.

For a heartbeat, the world around us dissolves into a muted background, leaving only the electric connection that has always existed. I rush forward, weaving through the crowd, my heart pounding not only with fear but with the fierce desire to stand by his side.

He looks relieved, and that spark of connection flickers brighter, igniting a warmth that wraps around us, reminding me that our dreams are intertwined. With every step I take, I feel the weight of possibility surge within me, urging me to fight for what we've created together. Today is not just a festival; it is a testament to our dreams, our passions, and the future that we dare to imagine.

As I reach him, I grasp his hand tightly, feeling the warmth of his skin beneath my fingers. Together, we stand before Mr. Thompson, ready to confront whatever challenges lay ahead. In this moment, I know that our love, fueled by ambition and creativity, can withstand the forces that threaten to pull us apart.

The vibrant chaos of the festival envelops me, wrapping me in its lively embrace. I can hardly breathe without inhaling the scents of kettle corn and fried dough, each tempting whiff drawing me deeper into the heart of Montgomery Springs. Children dart past, their faces smeared with ice cream and joy, while musicians strum cheerful tunes that echo through the streets, creating a soundtrack for the unfolding celebration. But amid the laughter and the clamor, a storm brews within me, a tempest stirred by the sight of Carter deep in conversation with Mr. Thompson.

I squeeze his hand tighter, my fingers intertwining with his, grounding myself in the warmth of his presence. Carter's expression shifts, a mix of curiosity and uncertainty flickering across his face as he exchanges words with my former mentor. I can't help but feel like an intruder in their conversation, standing at the precipice of a chasm that threatens to widen between us. It's as if the world around us fades, the colors of the festival dulling against the vivid hues of my anxiety.

"Are you okay?" Carter asks, glancing at me with concern. His brow furrows, and the corners of his mouth tug downward, the worry etched into his features like a painting that has begun to fade.

"I am now," I manage to say, though the lie sits uncomfortably on my tongue. My heart races not only from the adrenaline of the festival but also from the gnawing fear that clings to my thoughts. What if Mr. Thompson is selling Carter on the idea of a stable job, a life built on safety rather than the wild freedom we had dreamed about? I can almost hear the gears of corporate machinery grinding in the distance, a foreboding sound that threatens to drown out our aspirations.

As if sensing my turmoil, Carter leans closer, and the warmth of his body radiates against mine. "What did I miss?" he asks softly, his eyes dancing with a mixture of humor and sincerity.

I take a breath, letting the momentary comfort of his presence wash over me. "Just the usual chatter about what you're doing next. You know how Mr. Thompson can be." I force a laugh, hoping it will lighten the mood, though the tightness in my chest remains.

He nods, understanding flickering in his gaze. "He means well," he says, but the doubt in his voice betrays his uncertainty. I see the flicker of ambition in his eyes, a fire ignited by the prospect of art, but there's also the shadow of doubt, of societal expectations that loom like dark clouds over the brilliant blue sky of our dreams.

The festival hums around us, a world filled with possibility and vibrant energy. Yet, my thoughts drift toward a future that feels less certain, each heartbeat echoing with questions that circle my mind like a moth drawn to a flame. The installation we created together symbolizes more than just a moment of collaboration; it embodies the very essence of our aspirations, a beautiful representation of the dreams we dared to chase. But will that installation remain an aspiration, or will it fade into a memory eclipsed by the weight of responsibilities and expectations?

"Let's go check out the other booths," I suggest, my voice a fragile thread weaving through the noise. Carter's eyes light up at the idea, and he grins, a spark of mischief igniting his features.

"Are you trying to distract me?" he teases, his playful nature breaking through the tension like sunlight piercing through dark clouds.

"Maybe," I reply, nudging him gently with my shoulder. "Besides, I think I saw a booth selling those giant pretzels. You can't resist a good pretzel."

With a reluctant chuckle, he agrees, and together we navigate the bustling crowd, our fingers still entwined. Each step away from Mr. Thompson's looming presence feels like shedding a layer of anxiety. The energy of the festival wraps around us like a protective cloak, shielding us from the encroaching shadows of adulthood and responsibility.

We pause at a booth filled with hand-painted ceramics, each piece bursting with colors that rival the festival itself. I pick up a small vase adorned with swirling patterns reminiscent of the ocean, my fingers brushing against the cool, smooth surface. "Look at this!" I exclaim, turning it in my hands, captivated by the artistry.

Carter leans closer, his shoulder brushing against mine, sending a ripple of warmth through me. "It's beautiful," he agrees, his voice low and earnest. "Just like the art we created."

My heart swells at his words, the sincerity radiating from him like the sunshine spilling over the landscape. In this moment, surrounded by the laughter of children and the enticing aroma of food, it's easy to forget the worries that linger in the back of my mind. I momentarily lose myself in the way he looks at me, as if I hold the universe within my hands.

But that moment is fleeting. Just as I'm about to voice my thoughts, a voice cuts through the atmosphere, jarring me back to reality. It's Mr. Thompson again, his smooth tones slicing through the festival's joy. "Carter! There you are," he calls out, his voice commanding attention like a conductor summoning an orchestra.

Carter's shoulders stiffen imperceptibly, and I can feel the tension creeping back into the space between us. I can't let this happen; I can't allow the fabric of our connection to fray before my eyes.

"Let's go over there," I say, gesturing to a nearby tent that promises face painting and carnival games. "I want to see you covered in sparkles."

He laughs, the sound a balm to my nerves, and we head toward the tent, but not without glancing back at Mr. Thompson, who watches us with a scrutinizing gaze, as if assessing our every move. The games are lively, filled with laughter and playful shouts as children compete for the biggest prizes. I watch as a little girl triumphantly holds up a stuffed bear, her face radiant with joy.

"Let's play!" I declare, pulling Carter along, determination shining in my eyes. The day may be tumultuous, but I refuse to let it define us.

As we engage in the festivities, tossing balls at pyramids of cans and attempting to knock them down, the weight of my worries lifts, if only for a moment. Each laugh we share, each playful challenge we engage in, feels like a small rebellion against the uncertainty that threatens to loom over us.

With each prize we win—a small plush toy here, a colorful bracelet there—I feel a little more hopeful, a little more emboldened. Maybe we can carve out our own path amid the expectations, maybe we can create a future that honors our dreams rather than stifling them. As I turn to Carter, his eyes gleaming with mischief, I know that no matter what, I will stand by his side, ready to face whatever the world throws our way.

The festival pulses around us, each moment a flicker of joy, laughter, and vibrant colors that seem to dance in the air. I am reminded of the way we poured our hearts into the installation, channeling our dreams into a physical form, and I can't help but feel a swell of pride and defiance. Carter and I share this creation, a manifestation of our artistic spirits, yet I can sense the subtle riptide of doubt that runs beneath the surface. We are both teetering on the brink of a precipice, balancing between the future we aspire to and the world's expectations that threaten to pull us back.

We find ourselves in the face-painting tent, and I can't help but laugh at the whimsical chaos that unfolds before us. Children sit in brightly painted chairs, their faces transforming into fantastical creatures. A girl with butterfly wings giggles as the artist dabs color onto her cheeks, while a boy with a cheeky grin becomes a fierce tiger, stripes cascading down his forehead. "You should totally do it," I say, nudging Carter, who is momentarily distracted by the enchanting spectacle.

"Absolutely not," he laughs, shaking his head. "I'm an artist, not a canvas."

"Come on! What's the worst that could happen? You could come out looking like a fierce dragon!" I tease, knowing full well how easily I could coax him into it. His mock horror is adorable, and I find myself grinning at the sight of his animated expressions.

As we wait our turn, I catch sight of Mr. Thompson out of the corner of my eye, his sharp gaze still fixed on us. I can feel the tension in my chest tighten once again. What if he comes over? What if he confronts Carter about the corporate job again? The thought clings to me, an unwelcome shadow lurking just beyond the bright colors of the festival. My heart races not from the thrill of the festivities but from the fear of losing Carter to the very world we've both resisted.

But then, just as I think the day might take a turn for the worse, a little girl runs past, her painted face lighting up with delight as she clutches a balloon shaped like a puppy. It's a simple moment, yet it carries the weight of pure happiness. The innocence and freedom radiate from her, and it reminds me that perhaps I, too, can embrace this day without the encumbrance of worry.

"Alright, alright, you've convinced me," Carter relents, his voice laced with mock resignation. I clap my hands in excitement as we approach the artist, who greets us with a warm smile. "What do you want?" she asks, her hands covered in a spectrum of paint.

"I want to look majestic," Carter declares, a playful glint in his eye. I watch as he sits down, and I can't help but admire his willingness to dive into the spirit of the festival, to momentarily shed the weight of expectations and just enjoy the moment.

As the artist paints, I lean against the tent's frame, watching the strokes of color transform Carter's face. With each brush of paint, he seems to become more at ease, a bright and whimsical version of himself emerging. I can't help but laugh when the artist asks him what animal he would like to be, and he answers without hesitation: "A lion, of course. A fierce lion ready to conquer the world."

I'm struck by how fitting that is, how closely it mirrors the man I know him to be—a creative soul with ambitions as wild as his dreams. His laughter is infectious, and I can feel the tension beginning to dissolve like sugar in warm water. Maybe today can still be a celebration of who we are, without the looming shadow of tomorrow's responsibilities.

After the painting is complete, Carter stands to reveal his face, and I can't help but burst into laughter at the sight. His cheeks are adorned with golden rays and a mane painted around his eyes, giving him the appearance of a lion ready to take on the savanna. "I can't believe you went through with it," I say, wiping a tear of laughter from my eye.

"Hey, I promised I'd look majestic, and I think I've achieved that," he grins, a twinkle of mischief lighting up his eyes.

With renewed energy, we dive into the games, tossing rings, trying our luck at dart throwing, and indulging in the sweet taste of cotton candy that melts on our tongues. It's a simple joy, but it feels monumental in the context of everything swirling around us. Each win is a small victory, a reminder that there are still moments to be cherished, even in the midst of uncertainty.

As the sun begins to dip lower in the sky, casting a golden hue over the festival, I catch glimpses of other booths filled with art and handmade crafts, each a testament to the creative spirit that thrives within our community. The installations speak to the heart of Montgomery Springs, each one telling a story woven with passion and ambition.

But just as I allow myself to get lost in the beauty of the festival, I spot Mr. Thompson approaching again, his sharp silhouette cutting through the crowd like a hawk seeking prey. My heart races anew, a wild flutter that pulls my focus from the festivities. Carter seems to sense the change in the air, his expression shifting slightly as he catches sight of the approaching figure.

"Stay close," he murmurs, his voice barely above a whisper, as if sharing a secret.

I nod, determination coiling in my stomach. Whatever he has to say, we'll face it together. Carter's presence is a beacon of strength, and I'm resolved to stand by him, unwavering.

"Carter!" Mr. Thompson calls, his voice ringing out, authoritative and demanding attention. My heart sinks at the way it slices through the laughter and music around us. Carter glances at me, and I can see the slight hesitation in his eyes as he steps forward, our fingers reluctantly separating.

"Hey, Mr. Thompson," Carter replies, his tone casual, though I can feel the tension radiating from him. The world feels heavy, the laughter fading into a muted backdrop as I stand to the side, a spectator to this critical moment.

"Congratulations on your installation; it looks impressive," Mr. Thompson begins, but I can sense the underlying motive in his words, the sharp edge of an agenda beneath the veneer of praise. "I've been speaking with some contacts who are very interested in your work, Carter. You should really consider the opportunities available to you."

"Thanks, but I'm happy where I am," Carter replies, a hint of defiance creeping into his voice. My heart swells with pride, but I can see the doubt flickering behind his confident façade.

"Happy?" Mr. Thompson's tone shifts, a slight edge creeping in. "You're an artist with potential, Carter. Don't waste it on something that won't benefit your future. You need stability, and a corporate position would offer you that."

The words hang in the air like an unwanted storm cloud, and I can feel the tension build between them, an electric charge sparking as they stand face-to-face. Carter's brow furrows, and I know the battle raging within him. I want to step in, to defend our shared dreams, but I hold back, knowing this is a conversation he needs to navigate.

"I appreciate the concern, but I want to make art that matters, not just fit into a mold," Carter replies, his voice steady, but the flicker of uncertainty in his eyes betrays the turmoil underneath.

"Art is a luxury, not a necessity," Mr. Thompson counters, his voice a smooth blade cutting through the moment. "You need to think about your life after the festival, what will sustain you. You have to choose wisely."

I can see the frustration mounting within Carter, the fire in his spirit igniting. My heart races with a fierce desire to support him, to remind him that art isn't just a career; it's a lifeline, a part of who we are.

As they exchange words, I notice the crowd around us has started to drift, their attention drawn to the unfolding tension. The joyous festival atmosphere now feels fragile, like a glass ornament that might shatter with a single wrong move.

"Carter, you've worked so hard for this. Don't let him take that away from you," I whisper, but my words are lost in the noise.

Just then, Carter meets my gaze, and in that moment, it's as if time stands still. There's an understanding that passes between us, a silent agreement forged in the fires of shared ambition. He nods subtly, a flicker of determination igniting in his eyes.

"I'm not ready to give up on my dreams, Mr. Thompson. I want to create something that lasts, not just something that pays the bills," he states firmly, the resolve in his voice resonating through the air.

As the sun sinks lower, painting the sky in hues of orange and purple, I feel the tension between them dissolve slightly, replaced by a sense of camaraderie that springs from mutual respect for creativity. Carter stands tall, anchored by his dreams, and I can see Mr.

Thompson's expression soften just a fraction, as if he's starting to understand.

"Very well," Mr. Thompson concedes, though his tone remains slightly clipped. "Just know that the world outside these streets is waiting for you."

With that, he takes a step back, nodding curtly before turning to leave. I can feel the tension evaporate like steam, replaced by the exhilaration of Carter's courage.

As he steps back toward me, I can't help but let out a breath I didn't realize I was holding. "You did it," I say, beaming at him

Chapter 25: Echoes of the Past

The festival buzzes like a swarm of bees, each sound and sight vibrating with an electric energy that seems to pulse through the air. Neon lights flicker above the makeshift stalls, casting colorful reflections on the faces of the people milling about—each person lost in their own stories, their own hopes, and fears. The smell of fried dough mingles with the sweetness of cotton candy, wrapping around me like a comforting blanket, even as the chaos whirls around. I stand in the midst of it all, my heart beating a chaotic rhythm that feels out of sync with the joy surrounding me.

My gaze drifts over the crowd, searching for something familiar amid the sea of strangers. It lands on Carter, his tall frame easily distinguishable against the backdrop of cheerful chatter and laughter. He stands with his mentor, animatedly discussing the future that seems so tangible for him—so far out of reach for me. The way his hands move, punctuating each point with enthusiasm, reminds me of the passion he brings to everything he does. It's infectious, and I can't help but feel a flicker of pride, even as a heaviness settles in my chest.

I shift my weight from one foot to the other, the gravel beneath my sneakers crunching softly, a grounding sound amid the vibrant chaos. The lights overhead cast a halo around Carter, illuminating the earnestness in his eyes, and for a moment, I let myself be swept away in the admiration I have for him. But then a wave of insecurity crashes over me, pulling me under, reminding me of the chasm that seems to widen between us. What if his dreams pull him away from me, like leaves carried off by a brisk autumn wind?

"Hey," my father's voice breaks through my reverie, warm and reassuring. He slides up beside me, and I can feel the steady presence of his strength. Together, we stand at the booth decorated with hand-painted signs and vibrant banners. The festival is in full swing around us, but in this moment, the world outside fades into a gentle hum.

"I'm proud of you," he says, his eyes gleaming with sincerity. "You've come so far." His words, simple yet profound, settle within me, igniting a flicker of confidence. I offer him a smile, though it feels somewhat forced. The pride in his eyes contrasts sharply with the turmoil swirling in my heart. I know I should be celebrating this moment with him, but the shadows of my fears loom larger than the brightness of the festival.

As we share this brief interlude, Carter approaches us, the energy around him palpable. "Hey, what are you two talking about?" he asks, a playful grin spreading across his face. His smile is magnetic, drawing me in even as my stomach tightens with a cocktail of emotions. I want to be the girl who lights up when he's near, but instead, I feel more like a black hole, sucking the joy from the air around us.

"Just enjoying the festival," my father replies, his tone light. "How about you? Have you spoken with your mentor about the opportunity?"

Carter nods eagerly, his excitement spilling over. "Yeah, I think I'm going to take it. It's a huge step, but it feels right. I just can't wait to see where it leads."

Each word he utters reverberates through me, the truth of his ambition sinking deep, creating an ache that mingles with my pride. I want to share in his enthusiasm, to be the supportive friend I know I should be. Yet, as I stand there, an undercurrent of fear thrums in my veins, threatening to drown out his joy.

We begin walking through the festival together, the thrumming bass of music from a nearby stage vibrating in our chests. Colorful lights dance around us, and laughter bubbles up from the crowd like a sparkling fountain. I watch as families and friends enjoy the simple pleasures—a game of ring toss, the spin of the Ferris wheel, the delight of cotton candy being spun fresh.

"Are you excited about this?" Carter asks, breaking the silence that hangs between us. I catch a glimpse of his earnestness, the way his eyes search mine for a connection. I feel the warmth of the moment, but the doubt creeps in, clouding my response.

"Yeah, it's...great," I manage, though my heart feels heavy with the weight of unspoken fears.

We pass a booth with intricate handmade jewelry, each piece more captivating than the last. Carter stops to admire a delicate silver bracelet adorned with tiny charms. "Look at this one," he says, pointing at it. "It's beautiful, isn't it?"

"It is," I agree, my voice barely above a whisper. "But it's not as beautiful as the future you're building."

He turns to me, his expression shifting, a flicker of uncertainty crossing his face. "What do you mean?"

My pulse quickens, the moment stretching between us like a taut wire. It's now or never. "Carter, I'm... I'm worried about what this means for us. Your future looks bright, and I don't want to hold you back."

His eyes widen slightly, surprise etched across his features. For a brief moment, the noise of the festival fades, leaving only the two of us suspended in this fragile bubble. "You could never hold me back. You're part of that future, whether you see it or not."

But his words feel like a soft pillow, not the solid ground I need. I force myself to meet his gaze, to show him the turmoil swirling within. "But what if we end up on different paths? What if you go after your dreams and I'm just here, stuck?"

He opens his mouth to respond, but the silence stretches, heavy and uncertain. It's an unsatisfying pause that only amplifies the doubts gnawing at me. I can almost feel the weight of my insecurities pressing down, threatening to drown out everything else. The kaleidoscope of colors and sounds feels muted, the laughter of friends becoming a distant echo.

"Look, I don't know what the future holds," Carter finally replies, his tone steady but laced with concern. "But I do know that I want you in it. You're not just a part of my life; you're the one who makes it all worthwhile."

The sincerity in his voice sends a tremor through me. I want to believe him, to hold on to that belief like a lifeline, but the shadows of my fears creep closer, whispering doubts into my ear. I want to be the girl who supports him, who embraces his dreams. I want to bask in the glow of his ambition, yet the shadows cling stubbornly to my heart, reminding me of the fragility of everything I hold dear.

The vibrant chaos of the festival seems to pulse like a living organism, alive with the laughter of children darting between booths, the scent of warm pretzels drifting through the air, and the chatter of families soaking in the joy of the evening. The lights twinkle overhead like stars scattered across a dark sky, illuminating the smiles and the excitement that radiates from every corner. Yet, despite the spirited atmosphere, I feel as if I'm walking through a fog, the thrill around me muffled and distant, overshadowed by the weight of my insecurities.

Carter walks beside me, his presence both comforting and unnerving. I can see how much this moment means to him, how the festival encapsulates everything he's worked for, and I can't help but feel like an anchor tied to his dreams. The flickering lights play across his face, highlighting the determination etched in his features, and I find myself wishing I could share in that same zeal, yet a tide of doubt crashes over me.

"Want to try that?" he asks, gesturing towards a booth festooned with colorful balloons and a spinning wheel of prizes. His enthusiasm is contagious, a spark in the heavy atmosphere, and for a fleeting moment, I consider how exhilarating it would be to just dive into the fun, to spin that wheel and let fate decide my fortune for the evening.

But as we approach, the noise grows louder, and my heart races with the realization that I might be stepping too far into his world—one where I feel increasingly out of place. "Maybe later," I say, the words tasting bittersweet on my tongue. I wish I could be carefree, but the impending reality of our lives pulls at my heartstrings like a puppeteer with strings made of worry.

"Okay, but you can't keep avoiding the fun forever," he teases, nudging my shoulder playfully. There's a brightness in his eyes, a fierce light that I wish I could reflect. "You have to indulge a little, you know?"

I give a half-hearted laugh, but it feels more like an echo of the joy I want to feel rather than genuine delight. Instead, I nod and force a smile, a fragile mask that hides the storm of emotions brewing within.

As we continue walking, the festival unfolds before us like a canvas painted with laughter and vivid colors. Families gather around the dunk tank, the splashes punctuating the air with shouts of excitement. Children clutch their cotton candy like treasures, their faces sticky with sugar and laughter. Everywhere I look, the world seems to be moving forward, while I stand frozen, caught in a moment of indecision and fear.

"Do you think you'll go for it?" I finally ask, breaking the silence that has wrapped itself around us. The question feels heavy, a boulder dropped into a serene pond, creating ripples of uncertainty.

Carter glances at me, a flicker of surprise in his expression, and then his gaze drifts back to the crowd. "Go for what?" he replies, though I know he understands.

"Your offer. This... big opportunity."

He pauses, his brows furrowing slightly. "Of course. It's a chance to do something meaningful. I can't let it slip away." The conviction in his voice is like a flame, illuminating the corners of my doubt, but it also burns a little too bright, searing into my heart a realization I've been trying to avoid.

"What about us?" The question escapes my lips before I can reel it back in, a wild card thrown into our conversation. I can see his resolve falter for just a moment, and in that hesitation, my heart twists painfully.

"Us?" he echoes, and I can feel the tension in the air thickening like fog before a storm.

"Yeah. I mean, if you're pursuing this opportunity, what does that mean for... what we have?" I search his face for an answer, my heart pounding in my chest as I try to navigate the treacherous waters of our friendship.

"Nothing changes that," he insists, though his tone carries a note of uncertainty that sends my stomach into a tight knot. "You're still important to me. Always will be."

But those words, though sweet, feel too simplistic in the face of what's unfolding before us. The truth is, I can't help but envision him soaring into his dreams while I'm left grappling with my own insecurities. The image of him moving on, of him being embraced by new experiences and new people, feels like a chasm opening beneath me.

We meander through the festival, and the sounds of laughter echo around us, yet I feel a swell of anxiety threatening to drown out the joy. As we pass a group of friends laughing and taking selfies, I watch Carter's eyes light up, and I can't help but feel a pang of jealousy for the carefree delight they embody. They're the people who would share in his triumphs, the ones who would celebrate him while I lingered in the shadows, unsure of my place.

"Why do you look so serious?" Carter's voice cuts through my thoughts, his brow knit in concern. "It's supposed to be fun!"

I force a laugh, trying to mask the turmoil inside me. "Just thinking," I reply, the words tasting hollow. "About the future, I guess."

His expression softens, and for a moment, I think he might reach for my hand, but then the moment slips away, leaving us standing together at an emotional precipice. "You don't have to worry about that," he reassures me, but I can see the tension lingering beneath his words. It's a dance of unspoken fears swirling around us, an intricate choreography that neither of us knows how to navigate.

"Maybe I do," I counter, my voice tinged with an edge I hadn't intended. "You're going to be busy with your new life, and I'll just be... me. Stuck in the same place."

He steps closer, his gaze intense. "You're not stuck. You have your own path, and I want to be there to support you."

"But what if our paths diverge?" I challenge, my heart racing with the vulnerability of laying bare my fears. "What if I end up holding you back?"

Carter's expression shifts, and in his eyes, I see a storm brewing. "You could never hold me back," he states firmly, but the conviction in his voice doesn't fully reach his eyes.

We pause near a booth offering handmade jewelry, a rainbow of beads and stones glittering under the festival lights. "Look," he says, pointing to a delicate silver chain with a single, shimmering charm. "What if we got matching ones? Something to remind us that no matter where we go, we're still connected?"

The gesture warms me, a flicker of hope amidst the swirling doubts. "That sounds nice," I murmur, my heart fluttering at the thought of carrying a piece of him with me, a talisman against the fears that threaten to pull us apart.

As we approach the booth, the vendor greets us with a smile, and I watch as Carter examines the charms, each one a story waiting to be told. I wonder what kind of charm would represent our journey—maybe a compass, a reminder that no matter the distance, we're still navigating this path together.

But as I stand there, the weight of my uncertainty presses down on me again. What if, despite these small tokens, the world changes too much for us to hold on? As the laughter and music swirl around us, I can't shake the feeling that this festival—this moment—might just be the calm before the storm.

The shimmering lights of the festival cast a kaleidoscope of colors across the ground, illuminating the dust that dances in the air, suspended in the warm evening glow. As Carter and I move deeper into the throng of people, the cacophony of laughter, chatter, and distant music swirls around us like a tide, pulling us into its rhythm. Yet, beneath the surface of this joyous celebration, an undercurrent of tension threads through my thoughts, whispering fears I wish I could silence.

Carter's infectious enthusiasm propels him forward, but I feel like I'm treading water, struggling against the waves of my uncertainty. He stops to admire a caricature artist sketching lively portraits, his laughter ringing out like a melody that lifts the spirits of everyone nearby. I catch glimpses of the sketches—exaggerated noses, whimsical expressions, and bright colors—that perfectly capture the playful essence of the festival. A pang of longing swells within me, a yearning to join in the lightness of the moment, but instead, I feel tethered to the weight of my worries.

"Come on, let's get a caricature!" he urges, his eyes sparkling with mischief. The thought of it sends a flutter through my stomach, and I contemplate the absurdity of capturing this moment—a blend of joy and uncertainty—on paper. Yet, I can't shake the feeling that I would somehow dilute the magic with my insecurities.

"Maybe later," I reply, my voice trailing off as I watch him bound toward the artist, his enthusiasm contagious. I force a smile, wanting to appear engaged, but the smile feels brittle, a fragile facade masking the turmoil inside. As I stand there, watching him, I can't help but feel the distance growing, the invisible wall between us made of my doubts.

"What's the worst that could happen?" Carter calls over his shoulder, glancing back at me, his grin wide and inviting. "We could end up looking ridiculous together, and then at least we'd have a story to tell!"

The playful banter momentarily eases my worries, and I can't help but chuckle at the thought. "Ridiculous is a solid plan B," I retort, my heart lightening just a fraction.

He continues toward the booth, the distance between us shrinking as he pulls me along. The artist greets us with a warm smile, gesturing to a couple of chairs in front of a colorful backdrop. I find myself settling into the chair beside Carter, the moment feeling surreal as I prepare to engage in this lighthearted venture.

As the artist begins sketching, I steal glances at Carter, noting the way he leans into the caricature, his eyes twinkling with laughter and warmth. The artist captures his essence effortlessly, transforming his exuberance into strokes of ink. A small part of me wishes I could feel as carefree, as unencumbered by the shadows of my worries. I watch as the lines begin to take shape, a whimsical representation of the joy surrounding us.

In the midst of the laughter and banter, a flicker of uncertainty steals through my thoughts again. What if this moment is fleeting? What if I can't keep up with the world he's stepping into, a world filled with opportunities and ambitions I'm not sure I fit into? As the artist turns the paper to reveal our portraits, I can't help but cringe at the exaggerated features staring back at us—Carter's smile broad and buoyant, mine a caricature of uncertainty.

"Look at us!" Carter exclaims, his laughter ringing out in delight, and despite my initial apprehension, I can't help but join him, laughter bubbling up from somewhere deep inside.

"Ridiculous indeed," I reply, shaking my head, but the warmth of his joy envelops me, even as the weight of my worries lingers just beneath the surface.

As we step away from the booth, I find myself instinctively reaching for his hand, a small gesture of connection that momentarily dispels the shadows hovering at the edges of my thoughts. The warmth of his grip reassures me, a reminder that despite the swirling chaos, there's comfort in our bond.

We continue to wander through the festival, the vibrant energy swirling around us like a dance. Carnival games beckon with promises of plush toys and oversized candy, while the sweet notes of music drift from the stage where local bands take turns performing. My heart swells with the enchantment of the moment, even as the uncertainty persists like an uninvited guest.

"Let's try that!" Carter suddenly exclaims, pointing to a booth where a ring toss game glitters under the lights. The sight of the game triggers a spark of spontaneity within me. "I bet I could win you something," he teases, and before I can process it, he's pulling me along with him, excitement radiating from his every pore.

As we approach the booth, I feel the thrill of competition igniting in my chest, a surge of adrenaline that momentarily banishes the shadows lurking in my mind. "Oh, really? You think you can beat me?" I challenge, a playful grin spreading across my face.

"Challenge accepted!" His determination is palpable, and I watch as he hands over a few tickets to the vendor, who promptly hands him three colorful rings.

With an exaggerated concentration, Carter takes aim, his brow furrowing in focus as he tosses the first ring. It lands with a soft plop around a bottle neck, and his grin widens. "One down!"

Encouraged by his success, I take my turn, tossing the ring with careful precision. It spins through the air, arcing perfectly, only to fall just short of its target. "Close, but no cigar," I murmur, feeling a rush of competitive spirit swell within me.

Carter and I take turns tossing rings, our laughter mixing with the din of the festival, creating a melody of shared joy that envelops us. Each ring that lands perfectly ignites a rush of triumph, while the ones that miss evoke playful groans. It's a delightful distraction, a bubble of normalcy amidst the swirling thoughts that threaten to pull me under.

After several rounds, I finally succeed, the ring encircling a bottle with a satisfying thunk. "Yes! I knew I could do it!" I cheer, exhilaration coursing through me like a jolt of electricity. Carter erupts into laughter, the sound bright and genuine, echoing around us.

"You win! What do you want?" he asks, his eyes glimmering with excitement.

"I'll take the giant panda!" I declare, pointing to a plush toy that looms over the rest.

"Of course you want the biggest one," he teases, but he's already waving to the vendor. The plush panda is handed to me, its soft fur warm against my skin as I cradle it close, and for a moment, everything feels right.

Yet as we step away from the game, the reality of our lives begins to creep back in. The plush toy feels like a placeholder, a sweet distraction that only serves to amplify the silence around the bigger questions looming between us.

As we walk side by side, I look up at Carter, the soft glow of the festival lights reflecting in his eyes. "What if we both get too caught up in our own worlds?" I finally voice, the fear bubbling to the surface. "What if this... all of this—" I gesture to the vibrant scene around us, "—changes everything?"

His expression shifts, a seriousness settling over his features. "It won't," he assures me, though the conviction in his voice falters slightly. "We'll make it work, no matter what."

"But how?" The word slips out, tinged with desperation. "What if you're off chasing your dreams and I'm stuck here, feeling like I'm fading into the background?"

"I won't let that happen." His voice is steady, but I can sense the uncertainty beneath it.

The festival hums with life around us, yet I feel suspended in this moment, caught between fear and the warmth of his presence. The crowd ebbs and flows, laughter echoing in the air like a sweet melody, but my heart thrums with a dissonance I can't shake.

"Let's promise," I say suddenly, my voice barely a whisper. "Let's promise to always stay connected, no matter what."

Carter meets my gaze, his expression softening, and in that moment, I can almost see the future stretch out before us, a winding path filled with possibilities. "Always," he promises, and as he takes my hand in his, the warmth of his grip soothes the ache in my heart.

For a brief moment, the festival fades away, and it's just the two of us standing there, surrounded by a world full of light and laughter. The fear still lingers, but as we make our promise, I hold on to the hope that perhaps we can weather any storm together. The path ahead may be uncertain, but with him by my side, it feels a little less daunting, a little more vibrant.

Chapter 26: Woven Paths

The vibrant hum of the boutique echoed in my ears like a melody, woven from laughter and the clinking of hangers as I hung the last of the dresses, their fabric shimmering under the soft lights. The recent festival had injected new life into the shop, transforming it from a quiet haven into a bustling epicenter of creativity and camaraderie. Each dress told a story—floral prints that danced like whispers of spring, sleek lines reminiscent of a summer's sunset, and textures that invited the fingers to explore. Every morning felt like unwrapping a gift, a new opportunity to embrace the world outside the glass doors, where the sun painted shadows on the pavement of our small town.

But beneath the surface of my burgeoning excitement, an unsettling current churned. Carter, my partner in this venture and my heart's compass, had always been my anchor. His laughter filled the boutique, and the way he twirled fabric between his fingers made every piece feel alive. We had crafted this space together, each corner infused with our dreams and aspirations. Yet now, as I stood amidst the cascade of colors and fabrics, the very air crackled with a tension that suffocated me. He had received an offer—a promising position in a city brimming with opportunities. A leap into a world where he could thrive, where his talent would shine like the stars he always aimed for.

The conversation had started innocently enough, with Carter casually sharing his excitement about the opportunity. But as the words spilled from his lips, they morphed into heavy stones, sinking into my heart. The air thickened, wrapping around us like a shroud. My initial smile faltered, replaced by a sense of impending doom. How could he even consider leaving? This place—this boutique—was more than just a shop; it was our dream, our labor of love. I watched as his excitement twisted into something else, a glimmer of uncertainty clouding his bright eyes.

"Carter, wait," I had pleaded, the desperation creeping into my voice. "We've worked so hard for this. Don't you see? This is our moment!"

He leaned against the display, the soft rustle of the fabric draping around him a stark contrast to the storm brewing in his eyes. "It's an incredible opportunity, and you know that," he replied, his tone measured but firm. "I need to think about my future, my career."

And just like that, the words struck like lightning, igniting a fire of emotions I couldn't control. Anger, fear, and betrayal wove together in a tangled mess, spilling out in a heated argument that felt more like a tragic play than a discussion between lovers. With every passionate plea I made, I could see him retreating, as if I were pushing him away with the weight of my expectations.

"It's not just about you, Carter! What about us?" I shouted, the volume of my voice echoing against the walls, the vibrant colors now feeling like they were closing in on me. "What about everything we built together?"

He shoved a hand through his hair, the frustration radiating off him like heat from a summer pavement. "It's not about abandoning you! This is my chance to prove myself, to be more than just your sidekick in this boutique."

With a final, heart-wrenching look, he stormed out, leaving behind a silence that felt deafening. The door jingled softly as it closed, a haunting reminder of his absence. I stood in the middle of the boutique, surrounded by the very fabric of our dreams, feeling more alone than ever. Each item seemed to mock me, remnants of our late-night brainstorming sessions, the laughter we shared, the designs sketched on napkins in cozy cafés. Had I been too selfish, too blinded by my own desires to support him?

Sleepless nights ensued, each hour stretching endlessly into the next, the darkness settling around me like a thick fog. I threw myself into my work, pouring every ounce of energy into perfecting our upcoming collection, a new line inspired by the festival's vibrancy. The scent of fresh fabric filled the air, and the rhythmic snip of scissors became my only solace. I painted my emotions into every piece, infusing them with the joy I had once felt in this creative sanctuary. Yet, beneath the hustle and bustle of my routine, a gnawing ache of uncertainty clawed at my insides, a relentless reminder of what I might lose.

As I draped fabric over mannequins, their silent forms seemed to whisper secrets of my despair. I wondered if love was enough to bridge the chasm that had opened between us. Could our dreams coexist without one overshadowing the other? With each passing day, I found myself entangled in a web of questions, the answers as elusive as the spring blossoms that began to peek through the thawing earth.

The boutique thrummed with a new energy, customers flowing in and out like the tide, their enthusiasm infectious. I welcomed them with a smile, my heart racing with the thrill of connection, yet the laughter felt hollow. I envied their ease, their uncomplicated desires. Each cheerful customer reminded me of the warmth I once felt in Carter's presence, the way his eyes sparkled when he shared his ideas, his passion for life spilling over into everything he touched.

The fabric swayed gently from the racks as I worked late into the night, the fluorescent lights casting a soft glow around the shop. I could see the vision of our future slipping through my fingers like sand. And yet, with every snip of the fabric, I clung to hope, believing that love could indeed find a way, even through the most tangled of paths.

But as the days turned into weeks, the weight of uncertainty pressed down harder, threatening to suffocate the joy that had once bloomed within me. I longed for Carter's return, for the laughter and camaraderie we had shared, but more than that, I yearned for clarity—a sign that our dreams could remain intertwined, a patchwork of ambition and love that would endure, despite the challenges we faced.

The early morning sun streamed through the large windows of the boutique, casting a warm glow over the vibrant displays that seemed to dance with the promise of a new day. The air was laced with the lingering scent of fresh cotton and a hint of lavender from the candles I kept burning to create a welcoming atmosphere. As I opened the door and stepped into the space, it felt like entering a different world—one where the struggles of the previous weeks could be momentarily forgotten, wrapped in the soft fabric of hope.

But the moment my eyes landed on the half-finished dress draped over the mannequin, a familiar pang of sorrow twisted in my chest. I could still see the reflection of Carter's laughter in the folds of that fabric, the way he would playfully tug at it while discussing design ideas. We had envisioned something stunning together, a piece that would capture the spirit of the festival and our dreams. Now, it felt like an unfinished story, one with a disheartening cliffhanger that had left me hanging in limbo.

Each day blurred together, a cacophony of customers filtering in and out, their excitement contagious yet simultaneously unbearable. I plastered on my most cheerful smile, greeting each patron as though I were not drowning in a sea of confusion and heartache. They marveled at the new arrivals, exclaiming over the colors and styles I had meticulously chosen, but I felt like a ghost gliding through the fabric-laden aisles, my heart a heavy weight tethered to a past that seemed to slip further away with every passing moment.

As I adjusted the displays, the door swung open, and a gust of fresh air filled the room, bringing with it a rush of energy. Jess, my ever-enthusiastic best friend, burst through with her usual flair, her bright eyes scanning the boutique as if it were a treasure trove of secrets. "You won't believe the new café that just opened up across the street! It's adorable, with pastel walls and the most decadent pastries. We should totally go!"

Her enthusiasm was infectious, and for a fleeting moment, I allowed myself to be swept away in her excitement. "That sounds amazing! But I really should—"

"Oh, come on!" she interjected, a playful smirk dancing on her lips. "You've been holed up in here for ages. Besides, how do you expect to find inspiration in all this... beautiful chaos if you don't take a break?"

I couldn't argue with that. The walls of the boutique had begun to close in on me, each bolt of fabric and every shimmering bead becoming a reminder of the distance growing between Carter and me. I hesitated for only a moment before relenting. "Okay, let's go. I could use a pastry or two."

As we made our way to the café, the warm sun kissed my skin, and the bustling sounds of the town enveloped us like an embrace. I took a deep breath, inhaling the sweet aroma of blooming flowers and freshly baked bread that wafted from the café. Stepping inside was like entering a whimsical wonderland, with pastel-colored walls adorned with eclectic art and shelves lined with sweet confections that looked like miniature works of art.

Jess and I settled at a cozy table by the window, our laughter mingling with the soft jazz music playing in the background. As we perused the menu, my mind drifted back to Carter. Was he thinking of me? Did he feel the chasm that had grown between us? The thought gnawed at me, relentless and unsettling.

"I've been meaning to ask," Jess began, her voice cutting through my swirling thoughts. "How are things with Carter? You two seem... well, a bit off lately."

A lump formed in my throat as I met her concerned gaze. I could see the genuine worry in her eyes, the way she cared so deeply for me. I sighed, letting the weight of my emotions spill over. "I don't know,

Jess. He's considering that job offer, and it feels like he's pulling away. It's like... like I'm losing him, and I don't know how to fight for us when he's got one foot out the door."

Her brow furrowed, and she reached across the table, her hand resting gently on mine. "You both want different things right now. It's tough, but maybe this is an opportunity for you both to grow. Sometimes, distance can help you realize what you truly want."

"I know that logically, but it's hard to accept," I replied, my voice barely above a whisper. "We built this dream together, and now it feels like it's unraveling before my eyes. What if he leaves, and I'm left here alone with nothing but... everything we've created together?"

Jess squeezed my hand, her grip steady and reassuring. "You won't be alone, you know that. You have me, and the boutique will still be here. Just focus on what you can control, and let him figure out what he wants. You're strong, and I believe in you."

Her words wrapped around me like a warm blanket, easing some of the anxiety that had been constricting my chest. We talked and laughed over pastries—flaky croissants filled with rich chocolate and creamy vanilla éclairs that melted in my mouth. For those brief moments, the world outside faded away, leaving only the warmth of friendship and the sweet taste of indulgence.

Yet, as we finished our treats and prepared to return to the boutique, the reality of my situation loomed large once more. Jess noticed the shift in my mood and tilted her head, her expression softening. "You know, sometimes when things feel heavy, it helps to create. Why don't you channel that energy into a new project? Something that embodies your feelings, something fresh and exciting."

I nodded, the idea sparking a flicker of inspiration within me. "You're right. I need to focus on something that makes me feel alive again. Maybe a collection that captures the essence of where I am right now—everything I'm feeling."

As we walked back, my mind raced with ideas—bright hues clashing against soft pastels, fabrics that whispered of both struggle and triumph. I felt a spark of determination igniting within me, a reminder that even amidst uncertainty, creativity could serve as both refuge and a path forward.

The boutique welcomed us back, and I threw myself into the task of drafting designs, allowing my emotions to seep into every stroke of the pencil. Hours passed as I lost myself in the rhythmic dance of creation, each new piece a reflection of my heart—a heart that yearned for Carter yet longed to carve out my own identity amidst the chaos.

As the night deepened, the lights in the boutique twinkled like stars, and I felt a renewed sense of purpose enveloping me. Though the road ahead remained uncertain, I would weave my dreams into fabric, channeling my heartache into something beautiful. Each stitch would carry my story, and with it, a hope that perhaps love, too, could find its way back through the tangled paths we were forging.

The following days unfolded like a series of colors swirling together on an artist's palette, each one vibrant yet laden with an unsettling hue of uncertainty. I immersed myself in the creative process, pouring my heart into the designs that had become both my refuge and my expression. The boutique transformed into a sanctuary where every stitch and seam echoed my desires, fears, and the flickering hope that perhaps Carter and I could still find a path back to each other.

I filled the walls with sketches—some bold and playful, others tender and delicate. The soft strains of indie music floated through the air, a backdrop to my thoughts as I worked late into the night, fueled by a mixture of coffee and determination. As I draped fabric over mannequins, each silhouette began to tell a story of resilience and longing. The deep emerald greens and blush pinks danced together, a visual representation of my conflicting emotions, intermingling with memories of laughter shared with Carter in this very space.

But even as I poured my soul into this new collection, a sense of emptiness lingered. The boutique, once filled with his infectious enthusiasm, felt quieter. I missed the way he would stand beside me, offering insights that would make my heart race with excitement. Every time the bell above the door jingled, I would glance up, half-expecting to see him walk in, his eyes sparkling with new ideas and plans. Instead, it remained an echoing reminder of the distance that now stretched between us.

One afternoon, as I sat amidst the colorful chaos of the boutique, the door swung open, and in walked Mrs. Thompson, a loyal customer and the town's unofficial style guru. Her presence always brought a refreshing energy, like a burst of sunshine breaking through the clouds. Today, however, she wore an expression that danced between concern and curiosity.

"Sweetheart, I've been hearing whispers around town," she said, her voice warm yet tinged with a hint of seriousness. "Is everything alright? You seem a bit... off lately."

I took a deep breath, trying to piece together my swirling thoughts before responding. "It's just... things have changed. Carter's considering a job in the city, and I'm not sure what that means for us. I feel like everything we've worked for is hanging in the balance."

Mrs. Thompson nodded, her brow furrowed in understanding. "Ah, young love. It can be so tumultuous, can't it? But let me tell you something, dear. Sometimes, the path isn't straight. Sometimes, you have to go around the bends to find where you truly belong."

Her words resonated deep within me, echoing the very sentiments I had been grappling with. Perhaps it wasn't about holding onto a singular path but rather finding a way to navigate the detours together. With renewed resolve, I shared my plans for the new collection, my excitement growing as I described each piece, allowing her to envision the vibrant tapestry of emotions I was weaving.

"Darling, it sounds magnificent!" she exclaimed, her eyes sparkling. "You must showcase these designs. They're a reflection of you—your struggles, your hopes. Host a small event here; invite everyone! It could bring the community together, and who knows, perhaps it'll spark something beautiful."

The idea ignited a flicker of hope in my chest. An event would not only celebrate my new collection but also serve as a bridge—perhaps even a bridge to Carter. It could create a space for connection, not just for the boutique but also for us. With a determined smile, I began to map out the details, eager to infuse every aspect with the love and creativity we had shared.

The day of the showcase arrived, the air buzzing with excitement as I transformed the boutique into a whimsical paradise. Strings of fairy lights twinkled overhead, illuminating the carefully arranged displays of my latest designs. Colorful flowers adorned every surface, their fragrances mingling in the air, creating an inviting atmosphere that drew people in like moths to a flame. I wanted it to feel like a celebration of life and art, a joyous reunion of creativity and community.

As the first guests trickled in, I felt a mixture of exhilaration and nervousness wash over me. The soft chatter of conversation filled the air, punctuated by delighted gasps as attendees marveled at the designs. With each compliment, a piece of my heart felt lighter, a reminder that despite the turmoil in my personal life, I was still capable of creating something beautiful.

Amidst the sea of familiar faces, my heart raced as I caught sight of Carter standing near the entrance, uncertainty etched across his features. He looked as handsome as ever, the light from the boutique casting a soft glow on his face, illuminating the emotions swirling in his deep-set eyes. He shifted nervously, a stark contrast to the confident man I had once known.

"Hey," I greeted, my voice barely above a whisper, caught between hope and apprehension. "I didn't think you'd come."

He shrugged, his hands shoved deep into his pockets, a familiar nervous habit. "I had to see what you've created. Jess wouldn't stop talking about it."

Our eyes locked, and in that fleeting moment, time seemed to stand still, the noise around us fading into a distant hum. A thousand words danced unspoken between us, heavy with meaning.

"I'm glad you're here," I said, stepping closer, feeling the warmth radiating off him. "I've missed you."

"I've missed you too," he admitted, his voice softer, tinged with vulnerability. The sincerity in his gaze melted some of the tension that had built between us over the last few weeks. "Things have been... complicated."

"Tell me about it," I replied with a wry smile, trying to lighten the mood. "But for tonight, let's just enjoy this."

He nodded, a hint of a smile creeping onto his lips. Together, we wandered through the boutique, sharing laughter and lighthearted banter as we explored each piece. I watched as his eyes sparkled with recognition, the memories flooding back of the dreams we had woven together.

As the evening wore on, I felt the atmosphere shift, a sense of reconnection blooming between us. We moved from conversation to conversation, mingling with our friends and neighbors, each moment weaving us closer together.

Then, as I stood in front of a mirror displaying the final piece of my collection—a breathtaking gown that captured both elegance and spirit—I felt Carter's presence beside me. "You've really outdone yourself," he murmured, admiration lacing his tone. "This is stunning."

I turned to face him, my heart racing. "It's a reflection of us," I said, gesturing to the gown. "All the ups and downs, the dreams and fears—it's all there."

He nodded slowly, his expression thoughtful. "I want you to know that I'm still figuring things out. This job... it's a big decision. But tonight, seeing this, seeing you, it reminds me of why I wanted to create this with you in the first place."

The weight of his words settled around us, wrapping us in a cocoon of shared understanding. It was a moment suspended in time, a promise woven into the fabric of our dreams. Perhaps this night, this celebration of creativity, could be the turning point we needed.

As the event drew to a close and the last guests filtered out, the boutique felt different, charged with renewed energy. We stood amidst the remnants of the night—empty glasses, crumpled napkins, and, most importantly, a lingering hope that our paths could intertwine once more. I could feel the weight of my uncertainty beginning to lift, replaced by a tentative optimism.

Together, we began to clean up, each movement a silent testament to our willingness to navigate this new chapter, whatever it may hold. As we worked side by side, I glanced over at Carter, a smile tugging at my lips. In that moment, the boutique wasn't just a space filled with fabric and dreams; it was a tapestry of possibility, a reminder that even in the face of uncertainty, love could still weave its magic through the threads of our lives.

Chapter 27: Fractured Reflections

The boutique buzzes with life, a symphony of chatter mingling with the soft melodies wafting from the vintage record player in the corner. Sunlight streams through the large windows, casting a golden hue over the vibrant fabrics and delicate accessories that adorn the shelves like jewels waiting to be discovered. Each garment tells a story, woven with threads of ambition and dreams, but today, I find myself lost in the chaos of color and fabric rather than creating my own narrative. I tug at the hem of a flowing bohemian dress, its fabric whispering against my fingers, reminding me of the warmth of summer days spent wandering through flea markets, yet my heart remains tethered to the storm of emotions brewing within.

Mia, with her ever-enthusiastic spirit, hovers nearby, her brows furrowed in thought. She flips through a rack of clothes, her vibrant red curls bouncing with each movement. "You need to let it out, you know," she suggests, her tone casual yet pointed. "Holding it all in isn't going to help. You're not a one-woman show."

I shake my head, a gentle smile playing on my lips despite the weight in my chest. "You know I thrive on the chaos, Mia. It's when I create best." But the truth lies buried deeper, where I can't quite reach. My fingers graze the fabric of a long-sleeved top, its texture evoking memories of comfort, of moments spent wrapped in Carter's embrace. The thought sends a shiver down my spine, a fleeting reminder of what we've lost amid the loud arguments and hurtful words that echoed between us.

Mia meets my gaze, her deep brown eyes sparkling with a mix of understanding and concern. "This isn't just chaos, Ella. It's heartbreak. You need to face it. Write it down, talk to someone, just—don't pretend it isn't happening."

I nod, but the truth is I'm not ready to confront the jagged edges of my feelings just yet. Instead, I retreat into the sanctuary of my work, surrounding myself with fabric swatches and sketches, pouring my soul into our upcoming collection. Each stitch becomes a release, a form of therapy, a way to stitch my fragmented heart back together, if only momentarily. I imagine the look of the new pieces: flowing silhouettes that embrace the wearer's shape, colors that sing with the vibrancy of an autumn sunset, each design telling its own story of resilience and beauty.

Hours melt away as I lose myself in the patterns and textures, the boutique transforming into a realm where I can control my creations, where I can escape the emotional chaos swirling outside. But even here, the absence of Carter looms like a shadow, reminding me of the laughter we shared, the late-night conversations that made the world seem infinite. His voice, once a soothing melody, now echoes like a haunting refrain in my mind, the memory of his laughter mingling with the bitterness of our last encounter.

As evening approaches, the boutique grows quiet. The last of the customers trickle out, leaving me in a cocoon of silence punctuated only by the soft crackle of the record player. I take a deep breath, the air thick with the scent of freshly printed fabric and a hint of lavender from the candles scattered around the shop. It's time to confront the emotions I've been avoiding. I grab a pen and a crisp sheet of paper, the blank canvas daring me to spill my heart.

My thoughts flow like water, unfiltered and raw. I write about the ache in my chest, about the way his absence feels like a missing piece of myself. I reflect on our love—the moments that ignited joy, the laughter that bubbled over like a champagne cork, and the warmth of his hands intertwining with mine. But I also acknowledge the fractures, the arguments that left scars, the hurtful words that flew like daggers, cutting deeper than I ever anticipated.

"I can't cling to you if it means losing myself," I write, the pen gliding across the page with a fervor fueled by clarity and resolve. "You're not just the love of my life, Carter; you're also my biggest distraction. I need to find my path again, even if it means walking it alone for a while."

I read and reread my words, feeling the weight of the message sink in. Leaving the letter on the counter, I take a moment to admire the boutique, this sanctuary that has cradled my dreams and frustrations. The soft glow of the lights casts a warm ambiance, and for a fleeting moment, I feel a sense of peace wash over me.

Stepping outside, the cool evening air wraps around me like a comforting blanket, but I can't shake the lingering uncertainty. The streets of the city are alive with energy, vibrant lights flickering like stars against the deepening twilight. I wander down the sidewalk, feeling the pulse of the city thrumming beneath my feet. Each step takes me further away from the boutique, and I can't help but feel a mix of nostalgia and longing for the days when everything felt uncomplicated.

Lost in thought, I find myself at the edge of the river, where the water flows steadily, reflecting the glimmer of the city lights. The breeze carries whispers of dreams and hopes, and as I watch the current dance beneath the moonlight, I realize I must also find my own rhythm. Life isn't meant to be static, nor is love. It ebbs and flows, like the river, carving its own path regardless of the obstacles in its way.

Turning to leave, I resolve to focus on the future. My dreams are not dependent on Carter, and in that realization lies a glimmer of freedom. With every stitch I sew, I'll create a future that reflects my aspirations, my heart, and the strength I carry within. As I walk away from the river, the weight of my decision settles into a comforting lightness, a promise to myself that the journey ahead will be filled with possibility.

The following days drift by, each one a blend of purpose and longing. Mornings find me in the boutique, surrounded by fabrics that feel like second skin, each piece echoing with the potential of new beginnings. The shop hums with a warmth that feels almost tangible, its walls adorned with splashes of color and playful patterns that invite creativity. Mia often hovers, her fingers deftly rearranging accessories while casting me sidelong glances, as if gauging the weight of my thoughts. The laughter and banter of customers becomes a background score, a reminder of the world outside my turbulent heart.

I sink into the rhythm of designing, lost in a dance of swatches and sketches, each creation a thread in the fabric of my aspirations. Yet, even amid the bustle, there's a persistent shadow of Carter's absence, lurking in the corners of my mind like an unwelcome ghost. I can almost hear his teasing laughter, a melody I once took for granted. On the days when the ache feels particularly sharp, I close my eyes and envision our last moments together—the rawness of our argument echoing in the hollowness of the boutique.

One late afternoon, as I meticulously pin a hem, the bell above the door jingles, pulling me from my thoughts. I look up, heart racing for an instant, only to find a familiar face stepping into the warmth of the boutique. It's Hannah, a longtime friend and fellow designer. She exudes an effortless confidence, her long chestnut hair flowing freely as she enters, a swirl of energy.

"Ella! I was in the neighborhood and thought I'd pop in," she exclaims, her eyes sparkling with mischief. "I've been meaning to catch up and see what you're cooking up over here."

I can't help but smile as I wipe my hands on my apron. "Oh, you know me—always brewing something. Want to see?"

Her enthusiasm is infectious as I lead her to the back room, where the chaos of fabric and sketches creates a whirlwind of color. "This is gorgeous!" she marvels, picking up a swatch of deep emerald silk that seems to shimmer with a life of its own. "What's the inspiration behind this collection?"

Taking a deep breath, I plunge into an explanation of the themes I've been exploring: resilience, femininity, the essence of freedom found in self-expression. It feels good to articulate my thoughts, to share the vision that has consumed me. Hannah listens intently, nodding as I reveal how I want to create pieces that empower women, that allow them to feel fierce yet elegant, soft yet strong.

"That's incredible, Ella," she replies, her voice full of admiration. "You have a gift for turning your emotions into something beautiful. I can see the passion behind every stitch."

Her words wrap around me like a comforting shawl, momentarily easing the ache left by Carter's absence. We talk for hours, sharing laughter and ideas, the boutique buzzing with renewed energy. It feels like a long-overdue reminder of the joy that can be found in friendship, and for the first time in days, I feel a spark of hope igniting within me.

As the sun begins to set, painting the sky in hues of pink and orange, we step outside together, our shadows dancing on the pavement. "Let's grab a drink," Hannah suggests, her eyes alight with excitement. "You need a break, and I know the perfect place."

Before I can protest, she's already leading the way, and soon we find ourselves in a cozy little bar tucked away from the main streets, its exterior adorned with fairy lights that twinkle like stars. Inside, the atmosphere is warm and inviting, a mix of soft jazz and laughter filling the air.

Settling into a corner booth, we order drinks—Hannah opts for something fruity, while I stick with a classic gin and tonic. As we sip, the conversation flows effortlessly, touching on everything from fashion trends to personal dreams. Each moment spent with her feels like a balm for my soul, soothing the remnants of tension that had taken residence in my heart.

"Have you thought more about that internship offer you received?" Hannah asks, leaning in with genuine interest. "You know, the one in New York? It could be a huge step for you."

The question hangs in the air, a delicate thread connecting my past and future. I take a moment, swirling the ice in my glass as I consider it. "I have. But there's this part of me that's scared to leave everything behind. The boutique, the city, and... Carter."

Hannah's expression shifts to one of understanding, her gaze steady. "Ella, you have to prioritize your own growth. If Carter isn't supportive of your dreams, then maybe he's not the one who should be holding you back."

Her words resonate deeply, stirring the embers of determination within me. I've spent so long trying to navigate the murky waters of our relationship that I've neglected to chart my own course. I can't allow fear to tether me to the past. I deserve to chase my dreams, to see what lies beyond the familiar confines of my current life.

As the night unfolds, the laughter and warmth of friendship wrap around me like a soft blanket, filling the void that had threatened to swallow me whole. I can't help but feel a renewed sense of purpose blossoming within me, a desire to explore the possibilities that await.

By the time we leave the bar, the city glows under the stars, a tapestry of lights and life that feels invigorating. I take a deep breath, allowing the crisp night air to fill my lungs, feeling the weight of my indecision slowly begin to lift. I may not have all the answers, but I know that moving forward is the only option. As Hannah and I walk side by side, I find comfort in the realization that I can embrace the unknown, even if it means stepping away from the familiar.

With each step, I feel the tremors of change surging through me, a quiet whisper urging me to embrace the new journey ahead. The world stretches out before me, vibrant and full of potential, and I can't help but smile, imagining the future that awaits, one that I will create on my own terms.

The following weeks unfold like a delicate dance, each day weaving together threads of discovery and reinvention. The boutique feels alive, not merely as a place of work but as a canvas upon which I paint my emotions and aspirations. As I immerse myself in the creative process, the vibrant fabrics and eclectic designs begin to mirror my journey of self-rediscovery. I'm surrounded by shelves of pastel cottons and bold silks, their colors a kaleidoscope that draws me in. Each fabric becomes a tactile reminder of the beauty of my craft and the importance of embracing change.

I work tirelessly on our upcoming collection, its theme rooted in the idea of metamorphosis—how life can pivot and shift, often unexpectedly, much like a butterfly emerging from its cocoon. The designs evolve with each passing day, blossoming into intricate silhouettes that echo my own transformation. I envision flowy dresses that sway with movement, sharp blazers that convey confidence, and accessories that pop with personality. Each piece encapsulates not just style but the resilience I've cultivated in the wake of heartbreak.

One crisp morning, as I prepare to open the shop, I notice a small package on the counter. Curiosity piqued, I unwrap it to find a vintage brooch—a delicate silver butterfly adorned with tiny gemstones that glimmer like dewdrops in the morning sun. Attached is a note in Mia's familiar handwriting, encouraging me to embrace the notion of transformation. A smile creeps onto my face, the warmth of her friendship filling the space.

"Perfect," I murmur to myself, pinning the butterfly to my apron as a reminder of the beauty that can arise from change. The boutique hums to life with customers, laughter echoing off the walls as I assist them in finding their own unique styles. The familiar sounds of fabric rustling and cheerful chatter create a comforting backdrop, one that feels like home.

Yet, beneath the surface, I can still feel the echoes of my unresolved feelings for Carter. The reality of our situation hangs over me like a dark cloud, though I've resolved to focus on my path. On particularly quiet afternoons, I find myself gazing out the window, watching the world outside bustle by, my thoughts slipping back to him. I miss our late-night conversations, the way he could effortlessly make me laugh even on my worst days. But I remind myself that I cannot dwell in a space that doesn't nurture my spirit.

As the collection begins to take shape, I decide to organize a small showcase at the boutique—a way to celebrate not just the new designs but the community I've come to cherish. I invite local fashion enthusiasts, artists, and friends, hoping to create a lively atmosphere that breathes life into the shop. The anticipation builds as I prepare for the event, transforming the boutique into a whimsical display of creativity. Fairy lights drape from the ceiling, casting a warm glow, while arrangements of fresh flowers create bursts of color throughout the space.

The night of the showcase arrives, a perfect blend of excitement and nerves coursing through me. Guests trickle in, the shop buzzing with energy as laughter fills the air. I move from one group to another, sharing stories about the designs and the inspiration behind them. It's exhilarating to see others respond positively to my work, their eyes lighting up as they run their fingers over the fabrics.

Amidst the crowd, I catch sight of Mia, her radiant smile cutting through the commotion as she raises her glass for a toast. "To Ella," she calls out, her voice ringing clear. "For following her heart and creating something beautiful!" The applause that follows feels like a warm embrace, a reminder that I am supported, cherished, and not alone in this journey.

In that moment, the weight of my decisions lifts, replaced by a sense of belonging. I am not defined by my past with Carter; instead, I am carving out my own identity through my work and the relationships I've nurtured. I scan the room, taking in the laughter, the joy, the shared moments, and for the first time, I feel truly free.

As the night deepens, I step outside for a moment of solitude, relishing the crisp air on my skin. The stars twinkle above, a vast canvas that stretches endlessly, mirroring the limitless possibilities ahead of me. I lean against the boutique's doorframe, letting the serenity wash over me, when I hear footsteps approaching.

I look up, surprised to see Carter standing there, his expression a blend of apprehension and hope. "I got your letter," he says, his voice low and hesitant. The air thickens with tension, and I feel my heart racing.

"Carter," I breathe, unsure of how to navigate the emotions bubbling to the surface. "I didn't expect to see you here."

"I know," he replies, stepping closer. "I've had some time to think. I'm sorry for how things ended. I was angry, and I didn't really listen to you."

His words hang in the air, a fragile peace settling between us. There's an openness in his eyes that I hadn't seen before, and it pulls at the remnants of my heart. "It's okay," I find myself saying, my voice steady. "I've been working on myself, on my dreams. I can't lose sight of what I want."

He nods, understanding etched across his features. "I want to support you, Ella. I miss you, but I also realize I have to respect your space."

A flood of emotions washes over me, the realization that I'm not ready to abandon the journey I've embarked upon. "I miss you too," I admit, my heart racing at the vulnerability of my confession. "But I need to do this for me."

In that moment, we stand suspended in time, the past and future colliding in a delicate balance. Carter reaches for my hand, his touch sending a jolt of warmth through me. I don't pull away; instead, I allow the connection to linger, a reminder of the love that once felt so vibrant.

"Maybe we can find a way back to each other," he suggests softly. "But I understand if it takes time."

I smile, feeling the weight of possibility settling in my chest. "Let's take it one step at a time. I want to focus on this journey, but I'm open to whatever happens next."

As we share that tentative moment, the stars seem to shimmer brighter above us, mirroring the promise of new beginnings. In the embrace of uncertainty, I realize that while the path ahead may be uncharted, it's one I'm eager to explore. Hand in hand, we step back into the warmth of the boutique, ready to embrace whatever unfolds—together, yet apart, as we both carve our own paths toward the future.

Chapter 28: Patterns of Choice

The late afternoon sun poured into my studio, casting a warm glow over the chaos of fabric swatches and half-finished garments scattered across the worn wooden table. The air was thick with the scent of freshly cut cotton, a reminder of the transformative power of fabric. Each bolt held potential, whispers of the stories waiting to be sewn into existence. I reveled in the familiarity of this space, the walls adorned with sketches that chronicled my evolution as a designer—a journey marked by threads of tenacity and imagination.

As I sat cross-legged on the floor, a patchwork of colorful fabrics spread around me like a quilt of memories, I felt a surge of inspiration. This collection wasn't merely a showcase of my skills; it was a celebration of my independence, a declaration that I was no longer just a designer caught in the shadows of others' expectations. With every stitch, I poured my heart into the garments, stitching together tales of resilience and hope. There was something profoundly liberating about letting my hands guide me, trusting my instincts rather than adhering to the rigid rules of the fashion world. The designs flowed effortlessly, like words tumbling from my lips when I spoke of my dreams.

It was during one of those moments, lost in the rhythm of my sewing machine, that I heard the unmistakable sound of a familiar knock on the door. My heart skipped a beat, and I paused, thread hanging limply from the needle. Carter. The name alone conjured a mix of excitement and apprehension, an emotional cocktail that left my stomach swirling. He had become a constant presence in my thoughts, his absence a palpable weight that I carried with me. What would he say? Would he be different, or would we once again find ourselves circling the same unresolved tension that had shadowed our last encounter?

I inhaled deeply, steadied myself, and opened the door. He stood there, bathed in the afternoon light, his messy hair catching the golden rays, casting him in an almost ethereal glow. The intensity in his deep brown eyes held a hint of vulnerability, an invitation to explore the depths of unspoken feelings. I couldn't help but notice the way the sunlight illuminated the contours of his face, accentuating the sharp line of his jaw and the slight curl of his lips, which, until that moment, had only existed in my memory.

"Hey," he said, his voice a mix of warmth and uncertainty.

"Hey," I replied, stepping aside to let him in.

The moment he crossed the threshold, the air felt charged, as if the space itself recognized the unresolved tension between us. We settled into a tentative silence, the hum of the sewing machine a distant echo as I shifted uncomfortably on the chair. The familiar cacophony of my studio suddenly felt foreign, each stray bolt of fabric serving as a reminder of the distance that had grown between us. I couldn't avoid it any longer; I needed to share my thoughts, to lay my heart bare, even if it terrified me.

"Carter," I began, my voice shaky yet determined, "I've been thinking a lot about us."

He leaned forward, his gaze unwavering. "Yeah, me too."

I hesitated, weighing my words carefully. "I wrote you a letter."

He looked intrigued, the corners of his mouth twitching upward in a faint smile. "A letter? You really went old-school on me, huh?"

I chuckled softly, the warmth of our shared memories momentarily easing the tension. "I figured it was the best way to express everything I've been feeling."

I reached for the envelope resting on the table, my fingers brushing against the delicate paper as if it held the weight of my emotions. With a deep breath, I handed it to him. Watching him read my words felt like peeling back layers of my heart, exposing the raw vulnerability I had hidden beneath my bravado. Each sentence I had penned echoed the realization of my own strength, my desire to carve my path without losing sight of the love we had shared.

As he read, I observed the subtle shifts in his expression—the furrowing of his brow, the flicker of understanding in his eyes. When he finally looked up, the silence between us was laden with meaning.

"I've been struggling too," he admitted, his voice low and sincere. "It's like I've been pulled in two directions—my dreams and... us."

His words resonated with me, a symphony of our intertwined lives. I knew the weight of ambition, the longing for independence, and the fear of losing something precious. We both stood at a crossroads, teetering between the familiar comfort of love and the unpredictable path of individual aspirations.

"Maybe," I suggested gently, "we need to confront what that means. What it means to let go."

He exhaled slowly, the tension visibly leaving his shoulders. "I don't want to lose you," he confessed, his eyes earnest.

"Neither do I," I replied, my voice barely above a whisper. "But holding on might mean sacrificing our dreams. We have to ask ourselves what truly matters."

As we sat together in the fading light of my studio, surrounded by the remnants of my creations, I felt a profound sense of clarity. It was a bittersweet realization that love sometimes meant letting go, even if it felt like the hardest thing in the world. Our journey had been filled with laughter and shared dreams, but it was now tangled in the intricate patterns of choice—each thread pulling us in different directions, shaping our destinies in ways we couldn't yet comprehend.

In that moment, I understood that we were more than the sum of our choices; we were the architects of our futures, standing at the precipice of a new chapter.

The sun dipped lower on the horizon, casting long shadows across the studio as I immersed myself in my work. Each design I sketched was a fragment of my soul laid bare—a tapestry of emotions woven together by the fabric of my experiences. I reveled in the process, allowing my creativity to spill onto the page, each line guiding me closer to the essence of who I was becoming. My fingers, stained with the colors of my vision, danced across the materials, as vibrant as the emotions that fueled me.

The soft sound of music filtered through the room, a gentle backdrop to the whirlwind of thoughts in my mind. The melody felt like a companion, urging me to explore deeper, to embrace not only the joy of creation but also the catharsis it brought. I turned my attention to a deep cerulean blue fabric, its smooth texture reminiscent of the ocean waves crashing against the rocky shores of Maine. It was a color that whispered of adventure and untold stories, begging to be transformed into something beautiful.

Lost in this creative reverie, I barely noticed when the door creaked open again. The familiar scent of cedar and musk drifted in, and my heart fluttered at the prospect of seeing Carter once more. This time, he stepped in with a tentative smile, his eyes searching mine for a spark of the connection we had shared. I could see the shadows of doubt lingering behind his gaze, a reminder of the weight we both carried.

"Hey," he said, his voice breaking through my thoughts like a gentle breeze.

"Hey," I replied, my pulse quickening as I studied him. The way he stood there, slightly unsure but undeniably magnetic, sent a thrill down my spine. I motioned for him to sit, the chair creaking slightly as he settled across from me.

We exchanged small talk, but the air crackled with an unspoken urgency. The tension that had once felt like a comfortable blanket now hung between us like a storm cloud, thick and electric. I could see the storm brewing in his eyes, and it mirrored the tumult within my own heart.

"I've been thinking about what we talked about," I finally said, breaking the silence that felt like it was stretching into eternity.

His expression turned serious, the lightheartedness fading as the weight of our reality settled back into place. "Yeah, me too. It's hard to know what to say sometimes."

He leaned back in his chair, running a hand through his hair, a gesture I had come to associate with his unease. I could see him wrestling with the words, battling against the desire to hold on and the need to let go.

"I want to be honest with you," I continued, my heart pounding. "I've poured my heart into this collection, and it feels like a turning point for me. I want to own my independence and everything that comes with it."

Carter nodded slowly, his brow furrowing. "I get that. But... I'm struggling too. I love what we had, but I also feel like I'm at a crossroads with my own dreams."

I could see the sincerity in his eyes, the conflict etched in the lines of his face. It was a sentiment that resonated deeply with me, the delicate balance of love and aspiration weighing heavily on both our shoulders. "What if we're not meant to follow the same path? What if letting go is what we need to grow?"

He was quiet for a moment, lost in thought, and I could feel the air between us thicken with the enormity of our conversation. "Maybe it is," he said finally, his voice laced with uncertainty. "But the thought of losing you... it's hard to bear."

I reached across the table, my hand brushing against his, an electric spark igniting at the contact. "It's hard for me too, Carter. But I can't pretend that everything is okay when it feels like we're both fighting against ourselves."

His gaze fell to the table, tracing the lines of my sketches, each design a silent testament to my journey. "I just wish things were simpler," he murmured, his tone heavy with the weight of our realities.

"Don't we all?" I replied softly, feeling the ache of truth in my own words. Simplicity felt like a distant dream, a luxury we could no longer afford in the intricate web of our lives.

As we sat in silence, I could feel the clock ticking away the moments, each second a reminder of the choices we faced. The warmth of his hand lingered on mine, but it was a fleeting connection, a reminder of what was at stake. I wanted to hold on, to grasp this moment and keep it alive, but I knew the truth was a double-edged sword.

"I've been working on some pieces for the collection that represent this," I said, a spark of inspiration igniting within me. "They're about transformation and letting go. It's a part of the journey, right?"

He lifted his gaze, curiosity flickering in his eyes. "How do you mean?"

"Each piece is a reflection of the process," I explained, my enthusiasm building. "Like how the fabric transforms into something entirely new. It's not just about what we lose; it's also about what we gain in the process. We have to embrace the change."

Carter leaned forward, interest piqued. "I'd love to see what you've created."

With renewed energy, I guided him through my sketches, explaining the inspiration behind each design. As I spoke, the atmosphere shifted, the tension dissolving into a shared passion for creativity. In that moment, the world outside my studio faded away, leaving only the vivid colors of possibility swirling around us.

"There's beauty in the unknown," I said, gesturing to a flowing gown made from iridescent fabric that shimmered like a dream. "It symbolizes the idea that, while we may not know what lies ahead, we can still find grace and elegance in the journey."

Carter's eyes sparkled with admiration as he took in the garments, his appreciation evident in the way he leaned closer, captivated. "You've truly captured something special here."

A warm flush spread across my cheeks at his words, a sense of pride blooming within me. "Thank you. It's a part of me, and sharing it feels like stepping into the light."

For a fleeting moment, we were wrapped in a cocoon of creativity, the outside world fading into insignificance. But as the sun continued its descent, casting a soft glow that bathed the room in golden hues, I felt the weight of our conversation begin to creep back in.

"Whatever happens," I said, my voice steady yet tinged with emotion, "I want you to chase your dreams. I want you to find what makes you feel alive."

Carter's expression shifted, a mix of longing and resolve washing over him. "And I want you to do the same. You're meant for great things, and I'll always be cheering you on, no matter where life takes us."

In that shared understanding, I felt the stirrings of hope amidst the uncertainty. As we sat together in the fading light, I realized that even if our paths diverged, the love we had forged would remain a cherished part of our stories, woven into the very fabric of who we were.

The golden light filtered through the large windows, illuminating the scattered remnants of my creative world. Each design felt like a window into my soul, an exploration of emotions that had bubbled beneath the surface, yearning for expression. As I stood amid a sea of color and texture, I couldn't help but feel that I was crafting something profound—not merely garments, but pieces of art that captured the essence of life itself.

I returned to my sewing machine, the rhythmic hum familiar and comforting. The fabric danced beneath my fingers, a luxurious silk that felt like a gentle whisper against my skin. With every stitch, I poured my hopes and fears into the fabric, each piece evolving into a canvas for my emotions. I had decided that this collection would reflect not just my journey, but also the intricate threads of love and loss that wove through my life.

Carter's presence lingered in my mind, the conversation we shared echoing in the back of my thoughts like a familiar song. I found myself hesitating at times, thinking of the moments we'd spent together—the laughter, the shared dreams, the subtle glances that spoke louder than words. I pushed those thoughts aside, reminding myself that embracing my independence didn't mean forgetting the love that had shaped me.

As the days stretched into weeks, I found a rhythm in my work. The studio became my sanctuary, a vibrant haven where I lost myself in creativity. Friends began to drop by, curious about my progress, their enthusiasm infectious. Jess and Melissa often brought coffee, their laughter filling the space like sunshine breaking through clouds. Their support was unwavering, a reminder that no matter what happened with Carter, I was not alone in this journey.

One afternoon, as I adjusted a hem on a flowing gown, Jess plopped down on a nearby stool, her hair a riot of curls, her eyes sparkling with mischief. "So, spill it! How's it really going with Carter?"

I paused, the fabric in my hands momentarily forgotten. "It's complicated," I replied, the weight of the words lingering between us. "We had a heart-to-heart, and it feels like we're both trying to navigate a maze of our own making."

She nodded, understanding flickering in her gaze. "Love is never straightforward, is it? It's like trying to sew a quilt with mismatched patches. But sometimes those imperfections make it beautiful."

Her analogy struck a chord within me. Perhaps the very act of embracing imperfection, both in my designs and in my relationships, could lead to a more profound understanding of what it meant to love and let go.

That evening, as I closed the door behind Jess, I was struck by an idea for a final piece—something bold and unexpected, a manifestation of my growth. I envisioned a dress that embodied duality: one side light, ethereal, reminiscent of starlit skies; the other side dark, rich, and complex, echoing the depths of emotions I had yet to confront. It would be a celebration of both joy and sorrow, a reminder that life was not simply black and white, but a beautiful tapestry of experiences.

In the following days, I poured myself into this creation. I mixed fabrics, one side shimmering like twilight and the other a deep, velvety black that absorbed the light. As I worked, I found solace in the rhythm of my sewing machine, each stitch resonating with the journey I had undertaken.

Then came the moment that would set everything in motion. As I draped the finished dress on a mannequin, a knock echoed through the studio, startling me from my reverie. I turned to see Carter standing in the doorway, his expression unreadable. The air around us felt charged, crackling with the weight of unspoken words and lingering emotions.

"Wow," he said, stepping closer to admire the dress. "That's incredible. You've really outdone yourself."

I felt a rush of pride at his words but also a flicker of anxiety. "Thanks. It's... a reflection of everything I've been feeling lately."

He nodded, studying the garment with a thoughtful expression. "You've captured a lot in that piece. It's almost like you're weaving your own story into it."

"Exactly," I replied, my heart racing. "I want to embrace the complexities of who I am, the layers of emotion that come with love and independence."

Carter looked at me, and I could see the flicker of understanding in his eyes, as if he was grasping something profound. "I admire that. It's not easy to confront those feelings."

His admission hung in the air, a shared acknowledgment of the challenges we both faced. As the tension ebbed and flowed, I felt a familiar pull toward him, an ache that was difficult to ignore.

"I want you to know," I said, taking a step forward, "that whatever happens between us, I'm grateful for what we've shared. You've helped me discover parts of myself I didn't know existed."

A soft smile spread across his face, but there was an undercurrent of sadness in his eyes. "I feel the same way. I never wanted to be the one to hold you back, but it's hard to let go of something so special."

In that moment, the reality of our situation crashed over me like a wave, both exhilarating and terrifying. The future was uncertain, and the thought of stepping away from the bond we had forged felt insurmountable. Yet, I realized that true love could mean freeing one another to pursue our individual dreams, even if that meant walking separate paths.

"Maybe we can take this one day at a time," I suggested, my voice trembling slightly. "Focus on what we have right now instead of what we might lose."

Carter's expression softened, a hint of relief washing over his features. "I'd like that. We can support each other in our journeys, whatever they may look like."

As we stood in the warmth of the studio, the vibrant colors surrounding us felt like a symbol of our shared understanding. We were both on the precipice of change, poised to take a leap of faith into the unknown, armed with the knowledge that love, in its truest form, was not a destination but a journey.

In the days that followed, I continued to work on my collection, each piece a reflection of the conversations we had shared. Carter remained a steadfast presence, cheering me on while navigating his own aspirations. It was a delicate dance, a balancing act between companionship and individuality, but we approached it with the grace of two artists creating a masterpiece.

As the opening night of my collection drew near, anticipation filled the air. Friends and family gathered, the studio buzzing with excitement as we prepared for the unveiling. I was both nervous and exhilarated, my heart racing at the thought of sharing my work with the world.

When the moment finally arrived, I stood backstage, peeking through the curtains at the vibrant crowd that had gathered. Each face was a reminder of the journey I had taken, the love I had experienced, and the growth I had embraced.

As the first model stepped onto the runway, I took a deep breath, ready to let go of the past and step boldly into the future. The lights shone brightly, illuminating the intricate details of my designs. This was not just a showcase; it was a celebration of resilience, hope, and the beauty that could be found in every choice we made.

And in that moment, I knew that whatever path lay ahead—together or apart—I was ready to embrace it with open arms, weaving the next chapter of my life into the rich tapestry of my existence.

Chapter 29: Stitching Together a Future

The boutique stood like a cherished secret at the edge of downtown, a quaint little space adorned with vibrant awnings that fluttered in the gentle breeze. My fingers brushed against the soft fabric of the delicate lace that hung just inside the door as I pushed it open, the tiny bell tinkling a familiar welcome. The scent of fresh coffee wafted through the air, mingling with the earthy aroma of fabric swatches and the faint notes of lavender from the candles flickering on the counter. The walls were painted a soft, inviting pastel, each hue reflecting the warmth I hoped to encapsulate within this space I called my own. This was more than just a shop; it was an extension of my heart, a canvas for my dreams, where each garment told a story, stitched together with both thread and love.

The first morning light danced through the window, illuminating the eclectic mix of vintage and modern pieces that adorned the racks. I spent countless hours curating each collection, ensuring that every piece spoke to the unique spirit of the woman who might wear it. As I prepared for another day, I couldn't help but feel a twinge of sadness. Carter's absence echoed in the corners of the boutique like a ghost, haunting yet strangely comforting. The decision he had made, so noble in its intent, was a reminder that love, while all-consuming, sometimes required a sacrifice. He had chosen to follow his dreams in the bustling heart of the city, and though I supported him wholeheartedly, it left a void in my life that was hard to ignore.

I took a deep breath, centering myself as I stood before the mirror in the back of the shop, my reflection staring back with an uncharacteristic resolve. My auburn hair fell in soft waves around my shoulders, framing a face that had grown more determined over the past few weeks. My wardrobe had become a tapestry of vibrant colors, each outfit a testament to my creativity. Today, I wore a sunflower-yellow sundress, its flowing fabric twirling around my legs as I moved. I smiled at the reflection, an encouraging nod to the girl who still believed in love and dreams, even when faced with the bittersweet reality of letting go.

As the day unfolded, the boutique buzzed with life. Customers drifted in and out, each one bringing a piece of their story with them. I adored the way their eyes lit up when they discovered something unique, a treasure hidden among the racks. My heart swelled with joy as I helped a young woman choose a dress for her first date, her nervousness palpable as she spun in front of the mirror, giggling at her reflection. In that moment, I felt a renewed sense of purpose. This was my calling—to create a space where women could feel empowered and beautiful, just as I was learning to feel.

Amidst the laughter and chatter, my thoughts often wandered back to Carter. I remembered our late-night talks, sprawled on the couch surrounded by fabric swatches and sketches, dreaming about the future. The plans we had woven together now lay frayed at the edges, like a garment left too long in the sun. The memories were a tapestry in themselves, each thread representing a moment that had brought us closer, binding our lives in a way that felt profound and undeniable. But I also knew that our journeys were diverging, and I needed to honor that.

One evening, as the sun dipped below the horizon, casting a warm glow through the shop windows, I found myself alone, lost in a flurry of fabric and thread. The quiet hum of the sewing machine filled the air, its rhythmic sound a comforting companion. I had thrown myself into my work, stitching away the pain of loss and the weight of uncertainty. Each piece I crafted became a testament to my resilience. I poured my heart into every seam, letting the fabric absorb my feelings—the sadness of saying goodbye, the joy of new beginnings, and the flickering hope that whispered to me from the shadows.

With each completed design, I felt a sense of liberation wash over me. The boutique became a sanctuary, a place where I could channel my emotions into something tangible. I hung the latest creations on the racks, admiring their elegance and the way they seemed to dance in the soft light. My fingers grazed the intricate details of a handmade blouse, a reflection of my journey—the ups and downs, the stitches of laughter and tears that had woven themselves into the fabric of my life.

One particular piece—a deep indigo gown adorned with delicate silver embroidery—caught my eye. It was a dream I had brought to life, the embodiment of my hopes for the future. As I adjusted it on the hanger, I couldn't help but imagine a woman wearing it, feeling radiant and confident, just as I aspired to feel. I closed my eyes, allowing the fabric to wrap around me in a comforting embrace, reminding me that I was not alone in this journey.

As the days turned into weeks, the boutique thrived, becoming a hub of creativity and connection. I welcomed local artisans to showcase their work, transforming the space into a vibrant community where dreams could intertwine. The laughter and camaraderie that filled the air were infectious, reminding me that while I had lost a part of my heart, I had gained so much more in the process. Each woman who walked through the door left a mark on my spirit, and in turn, I hoped to leave a lasting impression on theirs.

Every evening, as the sun set, painting the sky with hues of orange and pink, I would take a moment to reflect on the day. The laughter, the tears, the fabric of stories exchanged—it all reminded me that love, in its myriad forms, was not confined to just one person. It was woven into every connection I made, every life I touched. And as I prepared to close the shop each night, I whispered a promise to myself: to embrace the future, to continue stitching together the tapestry of my life, and to honor the love I had shared with Carter by creating something beautiful in the world.

The boutique had transformed into a sanctuary of creativity, a haven where my dreams and aspirations coalesced into vibrant displays. Each morning, I greeted the day with a sense of purpose, my heart beating in sync with the rhythm of the sewing machine. The sound echoed through the airy space, a gentle reminder that with every stitch, I was forging a new path for myself. The delicate rustle of fabric enveloped me like a warm hug, and I found comfort in the familiarity of my surroundings. My fingers danced over bolts of fabric, each choice a reflection of my mood—playful prints for sunny days and rich, luxurious textures for moments of introspection.

The front window of the boutique became my canvas, where I artfully arranged my latest creations to beckon passersby. A soft green dress, its fabric reminiscent of the leaves rustling in a summer breeze, hung next to a fitted maroon blazer that exuded confidence and sophistication. It was a careful choreography, a testament to my evolving style as I navigated the delicate balance between vulnerability and strength. I often lost myself in this process, daydreaming about the women who would don these pieces and the stories they would carry with them.

Among the throng of customers that poured in each day, one stood out—a charming woman named Amelia with a contagious laugh that echoed through the shop like a favorite song. She had an innate talent for turning even the most mundane moments into something extraordinary, whether it was complimenting a fabric swatch or making a playful quip about a particularly outrageous fashion choice. I welcomed her with open arms, eager to share my vision of the boutique and its potential to become a community hub for creativity.

Together, we brainstormed ideas for local events that would draw in more customers, from craft nights to fashion shows featuring local models. Amelia had a flair for the dramatic, and she proposed an evening event that would showcase not only my designs but also highlight the artistry of local jewelry makers and painters. Her enthusiasm was infectious, and I felt a spark of excitement ignite within me as we envisioned a gathering that would celebrate the creativity pulsing through our town.

The first event, an evening of fashion and art, crept closer with each passing day. I lost myself in preparations, painting canvases to display alongside my clothing and assembling a small team of local artisans eager to showcase their work. As I organized the details, I felt a renewed sense of purpose, a vibrant thread stitching together the disparate parts of my life into a beautiful tapestry. In those moments of frantic creativity, I forgot the heartache of letting Carter go. Instead, I focused on the joys of the present, the laughter shared with friends, and the potential for connection that pulsed through the air.

As the day of the event approached, the excitement in the shop was palpable. I draped dresses on mannequins, painstakingly perfecting each arrangement until they looked as if they were poised to dance off the display. I stayed up late into the night, sewing delicate beaded details onto a gown that I hoped would steal the show. My fingers became calloused, but I welcomed the pain as a reminder of my dedication. With each bead I sewed, I imagined the way the gown would shimmer under the soft glow of the fairy lights strung across the ceiling.

On the night of the event, the boutique transformed into a magical wonderland. Dimmed lights cast a soft glow on the fabric displays, and the air buzzed with excitement and anticipation. Local musicians strummed their guitars, their melodies mingling with the chatter of eager guests. As people began to trickle in, I felt my heart race with both nerves and exhilaration. The first few attendees wandered in, their eyes wide with wonder, and I welcomed them like long-lost friends.

Amelia flitted through the crowd, her laughter ringing like a chime, helping to create an inviting atmosphere that put everyone at ease. The evening unfolded beautifully, filled with laughter and shared stories, each conversation weaving together a sense of community that had long been missing. Guests marveled at the designs I had worked so hard to bring to life, their admiration washing over me like a warm tide. I soaked in their compliments, realizing that I had created not just clothing, but an experience, a moment where everyone felt seen and celebrated.

As the night progressed, I caught sight of Ethan, a fellow artisan whose intricate jewelry adorned many of the models. He was charming and witty, his smile brightening the room as he mingled with the guests. I admired his work from a distance, the way he crafted each piece with meticulous care. We had crossed paths before, often exchanging pleasantries, but tonight felt different. Perhaps it was the electric atmosphere or the camaraderie we shared in our artistic endeavors, but a spark of something more lingered in the air.

Our eyes met, and a flicker of recognition passed between us. In that brief moment, I felt a warmth unfurl in my chest, an understanding that we were both navigating the choppy waters of our respective dreams. As he approached, I felt my nerves stir, the anticipation wrapping around me like a silk ribbon. We exchanged compliments on each other's work, our conversation flowing effortlessly as we discussed our visions for the future. It was refreshing to connect with someone who shared my passion for creativity, and I found myself laughing more freely than I had in a long time.

The evening continued to unfold in a symphony of joy, each moment a note in the melody of the night. I watched as women tried on my designs, spinning in front of mirrors, their laughter mingling with the strumming guitars. As the clock ticked on, I caught sight of a group gathered around a display of handmade necklaces, their eyes alight with wonder. I felt a sense of pride swell within me, a realization that the boutique had become a space for collaboration and inspiration—a place where dreams could take flight.

As the event wound down, I found a moment of stillness amidst the bustle. I leaned against the cool wooden counter, taking a breath as I watched the last of the guests filter out. My heart was full, not just from the success of the night but from the connections made and the laughter shared. For the first time in what felt like ages, I allowed myself to believe that the future could be bright, that love—whether lost or found—could be a source of strength rather than a shackle. The boutique wasn't just a business; it was a testament to resilience, a celebration of dreams woven together like the intricate patterns in my designs.

The air was thick with the scent of freshly brewed coffee and the warmth of laughter as I leaned against the wooden counter, my heart swelling with a sense of belonging that I had never anticipated. The boutique, now a hive of creativity, thrummed with energy, each woman who entered a thread woven into the rich tapestry of our community. I reveled in the little moments—the soft gasp of a customer as she found the perfect dress, the enthusiastic chatter about upcoming events, and the camaraderie that blossomed among strangers who had come together to celebrate art in its many forms.

As the days turned into weeks, I became increasingly aware of the transformations unfolding within me. My mornings were a flurry of activity as I experimented with new designs, letting my creativity flow like water over smooth stones. I began to explore fabrics I had previously shied away from, finding joy in mixing patterns and textures that danced together in unexpected harmony. The thrill of creation became an antidote to the bittersweet ache of Carter's absence. I poured my heart into every piece, letting my imagination roam free as I envisioned garments that could inspire confidence and evoke joy.

Amelia became my right hand in this endeavor, her boundless energy complementing my more introspective nature. We collaborated on new designs, bouncing ideas off one another like two kids in a candy store. Our brainstorming sessions often took place amid a sea of fabric swatches, coffee cups teetering precariously on the edges of the worktable. I cherished those moments of unrestrained creativity, where laughter punctuated our conversations and dreams collided with reality. Together, we stitched a vision of the boutique that exceeded my wildest dreams.

One particularly vibrant afternoon, as the sun streamed through the window in golden rays, we held an impromptu fashion show in the shop. Models from the community—friends, customers, even a few brave souls who had wandered in seeking solace from the outside world—agreed to showcase my latest creations. The atmosphere was electric, each participant bursting with enthusiasm, transforming the boutique into a makeshift runway. I stood behind the scenes, my heart racing with anticipation as I watched my designs come to life, swirling around in a delightful flurry of colors and patterns.

The first model stepped onto the makeshift stage, her confidence radiating as she wore a striking emerald green gown that hugged her figure like a gentle caress. The applause erupted like thunder, echoing in my heart and reminding me of the beauty we were creating together. With each new outfit that graced the runway, my spirit soared higher. The event was a celebration, a reminder that creativity could connect us, binding our diverse stories together through a shared love of art and expression.

After the show, guests mingled, and I found myself cornered by a lively group of women, their laughter like music in the air. They were drawn to the boutique by the vibrant atmosphere and the allure of something unique. I felt a rush of warmth as they praised the designs, their excitement sparking a sense of pride within me. In that moment, I understood that the boutique had become a home—not just for me, but for anyone seeking a space to belong.

In the weeks that followed, the boutique flourished, and with it came a newfound sense of stability. I embraced the ebb and flow of business, learning to navigate the complexities of managing a creative venture while nurturing my vision. Yet, even amidst this success, the absence of Carter lingered like a shadow, a bittersweet reminder of the love we once shared. I found solace in my work, but there were moments when the silence of my heart echoed loudly, a reminder of the connection we had forged.

One evening, as I was closing up the shop, a familiar figure stepped through the door, and my breath caught in my throat. Ethan stood there, his presence like a lighthouse in the fog of my emotions. I felt an undeniable pull towards him, a spark that ignited the air around us. He had come to see how the boutique was evolving, his interest a balm for my lingering insecurities.

"Hey there, stranger," he said, a grin spreading across his face as he surveyed the cozy space. "I thought I'd check in on the queen of fashion."

His playful banter filled the room, momentarily lifting the weight of nostalgia from my heart. We began to talk, our conversation flowing effortlessly as we shared stories about our respective journeys. As he spoke about his recent work—jewelry that shimmered like starlight—I was captivated by his passion. Each piece he crafted was infused with a story, much like the garments I created, and I felt a sense of kinship with him that I hadn't experienced with anyone else since Carter.

Our discussions often turned to dreams and aspirations, a tantalizing dance that hinted at something deeper. I found myself drawn to the spark in his eyes, the way he listened intently as I shared my vision for the boutique. I was surprised at how easily I opened up to him, my thoughts spilling forth like a long-guarded secret. He offered encouragement that felt genuine and sincere, igniting a flicker of hope in my heart.

As the weeks wore on, our bond deepened, the lines between friendship and something more blurring in the soft glow of shared moments. We explored the vibrant streets of our town together, stopping at local cafes and art galleries, reveling in the inspiration that surrounded us. I found myself laughing more freely, my spirit lifting with each passing day. There was something refreshing about Ethan's presence, a reminder that life could still be beautiful after heartache.

One evening, as the sun dipped below the horizon, casting a warm hue across the sky, we ventured to a local park that hosted a small farmers' market. The air was filled with the scent of fresh produce and blooming flowers, and laughter danced in the air like fireflies. We meandered through the stalls, our hands brushing occasionally, igniting sparks that sent shivers down my spine. I felt alive in a way I hadn't thought possible—like a flower unfurling its petals to the sun.

We stopped at a booth selling handmade pottery, and I marveled at the artistry on display. A delicate vase caught my eye, its surface adorned with intricate patterns that reminded me of the designs I stitched into my garments. Ethan noticed my admiration and grinned, his eyes sparkling with mischief. "You should get it. It would look perfect in your boutique."

I chuckled, shaking my head. "And distract customers from the clothes? I can't have that."

"Or inspire them," he countered, his tone light yet earnest. "Art comes in many forms. You know that better than anyone."

His words lingered, and as we stood there amidst the vibrant chaos of the market, I realized how far I had come. The wounds of the past were healing, slowly but surely, replaced by the beauty of new beginnings. I looked at Ethan, his laughter brightening the moment, and felt a wave of gratitude wash over me. He had become a significant part of my journey—a thread woven into my life that I hadn't anticipated.

As we left the market, the sky deepening into indigo, I felt the weight of possibility hanging in the air. Our laughter echoed through the streets, wrapping around us like a cozy blanket. For the first time in a long while, I allowed myself to envision a future unencumbered by the ghosts of my past, one filled with love, friendship, and the unyielding spirit of creativity. I wasn't just stitching together fabric; I was weaving a narrative of resilience and hope, creating a life that honored both the beauty of what had been and the promise of what was yet to come.